GOD'S END

TRAIL OF BLOOD

Michael McBride

snowbooks

Proudly Published by Snowbooks in 2008

Snowbooks Ltd.
120 Pentonville Road
London
N1 9JN
Tel: 0207 837 6482
Fax: 0207 837 6348
email: info@snowbooks.com
www.snowbooks.com

British Library Cataloguing in Publication Data
A catalogue record for this book is available from the British Library.

ISBN 13 978-1-905005-77-2

Printed and Bound by J. H. Haynes & Co. Ltd., Sparkford

To all of my fans, for seeing this journey to its conclusion.
None of this would have been possible without you.

BOOK THREE:

TRAIL OF BLOOD

"The field is the world; the good seed are the children of the kingdom; but the tares are the children of the wicked one."

"The enemy that sowed them is the devil; the harvest is the end of the world; and the reapers are the angels."

"As therefore the tares are gathered and burned in the fire; so shall it be the end of this world."

"The son of man shall send forth his angels, and they shall gather out of his kingdom all things that offend, and them which do iniquity."

"And shall cast them into a furnace of fire; there shall be wailing and gnashing of teeth."

"Then shall the righteous shine forth as the sun in the kingdom of their Father."

"Who hath ears to hear, let him hear."

— Matthew 13: 38–43

CHAPTER 1

I

MORMON TEARS

Time passed on the banks of the Great Salt Lake, though the fear never did. Each setting of the sun brought them one day closer to the final confrontation, but none knew precisely when it would come; each rising of that celestial orb stirred the deep-seated terror that today would be that day. Two days had come and gone since the siege at the hands of War and his reptilian army, the Swarm. Two arduous days of watching the horizon for the first signs of movement, of looking over their shoulders to ensure that no one was sneaking up on them from behind. It was the worst possible way to live, though vastly preferable to the alternative. After the first whole day had ended without event, they had begun the process of trying to establish some semblance of normalcy, though it was merely a play they performed for one another.

Adam stood on the white sand with Phoenix, looking to the east, as it seemed he always did. The sun had finally called an end to the nuclear winter, the blizzard now a memory marked only by the drifts of snow remaining against the stone face of the mountain and the spotted chunks of ice floating out on the lake. It wasn't warm by any stretch, but at least the snowflakes no longer fell and the torrential wind had seen fit to leave them be, if only for a while. The sunshine felt divine on their faces, a sensation all had worried they might never experience again.

"So what comes next?" Adam asked. "We know there are still more of them out there…"

"They're waiting for us to come to them this time."

"And what if we never do? The way I see it, they can wait forever."

"Staying here is suicide. I'm sure of that much."

"So how long do we have, then?"

"I…don't know," Phoenix said, and that was the truth. He hadn't been able to dream since the battle, and the visions had been elusive and incomprehensible. He knew why, of course, but he wasn't willing to admit it yet, as it was still tearing him up inside. His silence troubled Adam, he could tell, but the truth would frighten him worse.

Adam walked to the edge of the water, which had now risen several feet, swelling with the melted snow and ice to the point that the barrier they had constructed on the shoreline was now barely visible over the waves a dozen feet out. The new shore was only ten feet from the mouth of the cave leading to their subterranean dwelling. Small bones rolled in with the tide before being stolen away like seashells, the last reminder of the Swarm, whose corpses had been dragged out into the deep lake by the giant seahorses which dwelled beneath its surface. The very same creatures they were waiting for now.

He could see them out there in the distance, their coarse, spiny necks cresting the surface like the coils of so many sea serpents, growing incrementally closer, stalking them. The time had come to make their journey into Salt Lake City, but the walk was out of the question. Evelyn's truck was useless without the rear wheels, and the gas tank was bone-dry besides. The semi had been consumed by the flames of the barricade they had used to block off the lone point of access from the western side of the mountain and was now buried beneath an enormous pile of charred lumber. They couldn't afford to be gone for several days, not with the future so uncertain, so they had no choice but to count on being able to mount those amphibious steeds. How Phoenix had called to them, summoning them slowly toward the shore, was beyond him, but so little of the world around him made sense anymore that it was simply easier to accept these things and move on.

The beach all around them was still torn asunder from the assault, especially where the ground had opened in widening fissures beneath the red horseman War in his death throes. Sand was only now beginning to slide down into the muddy crevasses that channeled the water during high tide. Originally, they had intended to leave all of the tall spikes that had impaled the invaders leaping down from the top of the cliff, but they had begun to stink to high heaven. They could always replace the poles, as the holes still remained where they had been planted, along with the rent earth the creatures had ravaged while trying to rip through their own flesh to free themselves from the pikes. But it was the sections of mounded sand to the south, one beside another, that Adam couldn't bring himself to look upon. There were six of them in all. Six constant reminders of the debt they now owed and the gravity of the gift they'd been given.

They'd managed to collect Darren's and April's broken and gnawed bones, laying what little remained to rest in the same grave for fear of mixing up the bones. Jill insisted that the young couple would have preferred it that way, regardless. Lindsay was buried beside them, her body mostly intact, as the Swarm had only picked at her on their way to attacking the fresh meat, while Norman was beneath a much smaller mound beside her, his head the only part of him they'd been able to find. Gray's ashes were beneath the ground next to where he had laid his wife Carrie to rest, the tangled vines with their strange red blossoms already beginning to overtake the haphazardly-assembled cross marking her passage. The final grave belonged to the man who had stood up to Richard for them on the island and had been subsequently shot. For his kindness, they had hauled his ashes and burnt bones out of the charcoaled leftovers of the bonfire with Gray's and committed them to what they all now considered to be sacred ground. Here they could be properly mourned, properly thanked. It was a seemingly pathetic gesture, but it was the best they could do for now.

A gentle breeze rose from their right, carrying the smoke from the pit warming the kelp and blowing it over the graves and across the water like a mist. What appeared to be a rocky crag broke the choppy surface, parting the gray cloud and gaining height as it moved inland.

A spiny mane capped its head and neck, spikes crowned with jagged wire-like filaments. Rather than the smooth contours of the equine it had once been, the taut skin stretched between sharp outcroppings along its neck and into its haunches, sloping down its tapered snout. Its eyes were a puzzle of turquoise and black marble, within which Adam found himself lost. As the strange creature stood at the edge of the lake, its spindly legs shin-deep in saltwater, Adam appreciated its unusual beauty, which had been lost during the previous days, when the reclusive herd had slipped out of the lake at sunrise and sunset to feast on the bloated bodies of the Swarm, consuming their fill and dragging the scavenged carcasses back under the landlocked sea.

Phoenix approached the steed, allowing it to sniff his open palm. It shook its head and whinnied, but presented its flank for Phoenix. He stroked the skin that felt like fuzzy flesh drawn snugly over a brittle framework of bone, working his hands toward the tall spines capping its shoulders. He swung up onto the horse's back, gripping the spikes on its neck. It shifted from side to side nervously before adapting to his weight and the gentle touch of the boy's right hand rubbing it behind the erect ears.

"Come on," Phoenix said without looking at Adam. He continued to slide his hand along the side of its neck, tracing the swell of its cheek.

Grabbing one of the bony spines, Adam swung up behind Phoenix, wrapping his arms around the boy and holding on for dear life. The behemoth's wings rose upward like the arms of a praying mantis before extending outward to reach their full length.

As the aura of the dawning sun faded from red to gold, the others emerged from the cave to see them off, shielding their eyes against the blinding glare.

"Be careful!" Evelyn called.

"And then some," Adam said, nearly squeezing Phoenix right through as the horse galloped forward along the tide, its wings billowing. It launched nearly vertically into the air, banking out over the lake. Adam looked back over his shoulder to see the others walk out onto the white sand, too nervous even to wave.

There was a part of him that wished he could have stayed behind where it was warm and somewhat comfortable. While they weren't safe in the cavern, at least there was the element of familiarity, which was far better than flying off into the vast unknown.

They needed to go. It was that or face the possibility of having to defend themselves without the benefit of fortified perimeters. That, and as much as he was thankful for the meals of stewed kelp from Evelyn's flourishing colonies, which had sustained them through the first two days, he needed to find something a little more substantial.

With one last glance at his friends shrinking in front of the shadowed orifice, he turned to look ahead at the rising sun and their destination somewhere beneath, mouthing a silent prayer that he and Phoenix would return, and that the others would still be alive when they did.

II

Jill couldn't shake the last vision she'd been presented by her distant Goshute ancestor. It was there when she fell asleep and again when she awoke, hiding behind her lids every time she so much as blinked. Words couldn't express her gratitude to the tribe that had sacrificed everything to give her a chance at life by offering their souls to the blizzard. She felt guilty accepting the gift of their lives. She was just a young girl after all, barely a stumble-step into womanhood. The fact that they had considered her life to be of such importance that they willingly passed into extinction was a heavy burden to bear. There was nothing special about her, at least not that Jill would admit. There were so many others who were smarter, prettier, of greater consequence to the world as she knew it. She couldn't think of anything she could possibly do moving forward into the unmapped future that would warrant the loss of so many lives, but that wasn't what bothered her most about the images that haunted her. It was the thought of holding her own child in her arms, of the parting words of her spectral ancestor.

Would you sacrifice everything for the child?

The words echoed in her mind, scaring the living hell out of her. What was she supposed to sacrifice for this child who hadn't even been conceived? Her life? That was all she could come up with. She was supposed to give her life for her child as her forefathers had done for her, but would she be strong enough to do so when the time came? It had only been a matter of months since she'd been sitting on her bed in her parents' house debating whether or not to take her stuffed basset hound Snuffles off to college with her. God, she'd even cried over the decision, hadn't she? And in the end she had taken him with her! She was just a kid! She couldn't be a mother, and she definitely couldn't imagine a situation where she would have to offer her life in exchange for a baby whose existence hadn't even begun. Maybe it was selfish, but it was how she felt…and it was killing her.

She wished she had Snuffles now so she could just bury her face in his big, floppy body and cry until everything reverted back to normal.

But nothing would ever be the same again. Her parents were dead. Her classmates were dead. She had seen Tina butchered in the bathroom of a roadside diner and helped bury the scattering of April's remains. There was nothing left to cling to. She was alone, a freak, useful only for her visions of the future. Now that the seed of depression had taken root, it was spreading like crabgrass. She couldn't snap out of it, didn't know if she even wanted to. It was far easier living inside of herself than having to face the day to day rigors of her life without.

"I thought you might be lonely," Mare said from behind her. She'd been so preoccupied with her thoughts that she hadn't heard him drop down through the hole in the roof.

"Leave me alone," she whispered, sniffing back the tears.

"Fat chance of that," he said, plopping down beside her. He tried to drape his arm over her shoulder to bring her closer, but she shrugged out from beneath.

He tried not to let it bother him. There had been so much death, and all of her friends were now in the ground, but it hurt that she was shutting him out. All he wanted to do was make her feel better. Couldn't she see that he loved her?

His eyes widened, and it felt as though his heart stopped. Had he really just thought those words? He could feel his face burning flame-red and prayed she couldn't see him. Not that she was looking anyway. She just stared at that dusty old skeleton she refused to let them bury.

"Who was she?" he asked, content for the moment to simply share her company.

"I don't know how many greats, but she was my grandmother," Jill whispered. She sighed and shook her head. "And I don't even know her name."

"The others are saying that she and her tribe sold their souls to the storm to become those big white birds."

"They gave them willingly. For me. For us. For our…" She let her words trail off.

"For our what?"

"Nothing," she whispered, scooting farther away when their elbows brushed.

"Did I do something?" he asked.

"What do you mean?"

"Did I do something to make you mad? I mean, you've been so distant the last couple of days, while before that we…it felt like there was something between us…"

Jill let the silence speak for her, as she didn't know what to say.

"Was I wrong?" he whispered.

She shook her head.

"Then talk to me, Jill. What's going on behind those beautiful eyes? Let me help you."

"No one can help me."

Mare smiled. "That sounds like a challenge to me."

She looked at him for the first time, through teary eyes, and couldn't help laughing, despite the fact that it sounded more like a sob.

"You're incorrigible, you know that?"

"Is that French for hot?"

Jill laughed again and had to wipe her nose before it drained onto her lip.

"There's a smile," he said. "That's a good place to start."

He offered his hand, and this time she took it, her small fingers ice-cold. She squeezed so hard his knuckles started to ache. They sat in silence, both of them watching the skeleton, the head askew atop the cervical spine, as though waiting for something to happen. The ribcage was filled with spider webs, the bones fading to the color of tobacco spit, but it was nice to just sit in one place and allow the world to speed past without them.

Jill released his hand, brought her knees to her chest and wrapped her arms around them, shivering.

"Do you want me to leave?" he finally asked after a long moment of silence.

"No," she whispered, still looking at anything but him. "Please… just stay with me."

He wanted to wrap his arms around her to assure her that everything was going to be all right and that he was there for her, but he was going to have to be fine with only being close to her…for now. Eventually, she would want to talk about what was plaguing her, and when that time came, he would be there. That was going to have to be enough. He wasn't about to give up on her, on what they had together.

"So, tell me about this grandmother of yours," he said, looking at the bones and imagining Jill's face on the skull.

Jill looked at him at long last, a weary smile crossing her lips.

"All I know is that she loved her family very much, and was willing to do absolutely anything for them."

Would you sacrifice everything for the child?

She started to cry again and leaned against Mare's shoulder, this time allowing him to embrace her and keep her safe. If only for the moment.

III

"Have you gotten your superpowers yet?"

"What?" Ray said, nearly jumping up from the stone floor where he sat by the fire. The voice had startled him. He hadn't heard the footsteps approach over the crackling blaze. He looked toward the source of the voice through hollow sockets as his instincts still demanded.

"When Daredevil lost his sight, that's when his superpowers kicked in," Jake said.

Ray smiled. "Nothing yet, but I promise you'll be the first to know." He had taken to wearing a shirt sleeve tied around his face like a blindfold to keep the others from having to see the gaping black holes and the cauterized flesh around his dead eyes, letting his long bangs fall down over the top, no longer bothering to brush them away with his trademarked sweep.

"I'm sorry," Jake said, a note of sorrow permeating his words. "I was really hoping they would have by now."

Ray heard the scuffing of boots and then jeans scraping rock as Jake sat down beside him.

"Right now I'd even trade superpowers for a big, sloppy burger. One that's so fat you can hardly get it into your mouth and squirts a mess of ketchup and mayonnaise onto your shirt."

"I'd rather have pizza. Pepperoni. The kind with cheese in the crust."

"You're killing me here," Ray said.

"You started it."

"I suppose I did," Ray said with a chuckle. His train of thought derailed and he imagined the last time he had eaten pizza. It had been with Tina, who still occupied nearly every waking thought. They had been at one of those mom and pop joints with the red- and white-checkered, plastic tablecloths. There had been shakers of freshly-ground parmesan cheese and garlic that was still wet with its juices. He had lifted the cheese on her slice and crammed a spoonful of garlic underneath while she had been in the bathroom. He'd never laughed as hard as he did the moment her mouth caught fire from the overload of garlic, her face turning all shades of red as she drained her glass of Pepsi and then her water. When she had finally regained her composure, she had wiped the tears from her eyes and smiled that breathtaking smile, and he had known that he was going to pay. She had savored the prospect of revenge, always taking her time to make sure that he never saw it coming. Only she'd never had the chance to get even for the garlic.

God, he missed her.

"I'm sorry," Jake said.

"Hmm?" Ray said, drawn back to the present.

"I'm sorry you're blind. It's my fault. I know that."

Ray could hear the tears in the boy's voice, the quiver in his exhalations as he tried to hold them back.

"C'mere, kiddo," Ray said, throwing his arm around Jake's shoulder and pulling him closer. "None of this is your fault. Don't ever think that for a minute. I'll admit it freely, though. I'm struggling with this, but you know what? I'm still alive. In that respect, I'm luckier than most. I didn't always see it that way. It's easy to have a pity party for yourself, and I've had more than a few, but at the end of the day, all that matters is that I'm alive. And as long as I still live, I can make sure that you and all of the others stay that way too."

Jake sniffled. "They cut your eyes out because you pretended to be me. You knew they would probably kill you, but you did it anyway. Just so they wouldn't hurt me."

"Anyone would have done the same. We're all in this together, aren't we?"

"No. Richard and the others, they wanted to take me away because of what I can do."

"And what can you do?"

"I can dream."

"Everyone dreams."

"But I see what's going to happen in mine. That's my superpower."

"So tell me what's going to happen now."

"How 'bout I show you instead," Jake said, rising and walking behind Ray. He pressed his small hands to either side of Ray's head, middle fingers on his temples.

"I've got to tell you, little man. There isn't a whole lot you can actually 'show'—"

The darkness peeled back by a degree. He could see the fire in front of him, not as a wavering miasma of oranges and golds, but as a vague gray shape. The core of the blaze was a lighter shade, growing darker as it tapered into the snapping flames.

Ray gasped and turned away, but Jake held tight. He could see two human forms, both of them lighter in the central chest and head areas, becoming darker gray down their arms and legs and into their digits. General contours drew definition against the blackness. There was the pueblo at the back of the cavern, the stalactites riddling the ceiling and the stalagmites rising against them. It was a different sensation entirely from seeing. Sight was an immediate process: he looked at something and there it was. This was more like the heat vision that soldiers used from helicopters. It was nothing nearly as amazing as the ordinary sight he had taken for granted his entire life, but it was more than he imagined he would ever see again.

It was so cold and lonely in the darkness. He felt isolated even in the middle of the group. The cavern created such strange acoustics and random echoes that even when he turned to face whoever was talking to him, their subsequent words sounded as though they originated from a different direction entirely. He was exceedingly self-conscious of his appearance, but worse still were his actions. Walking into walls, tripping over the smallest cracks in the ground, needing help just to get himself pointed in the right direction, worrying that he was relieving himself out in the open for all to see, or heaven forbid, on something of value. He knew it wasn't the case, but he felt as though they merely tolerated his presence. He couldn't carry anything for fear of stumbling and dropping it. He had tried to cook, but had lost more of the kelp to the fire than the pot. All he seemed qualified to do now was sit by the bonfire and throw in more coal when it started to feel like it was dwindling. But now that he could see again, he could pull his own weight, he could—

Jake removed his hands, and the gray tones faded again to black, the all-consuming darkness welcoming him home.

"Please," Ray whispered. "Please do it again…"

"I can't," Jake said. "The rest is up to you."

Ray's sockets burned, as he no longer had the ability to shed tears.

"Please…I want to be able to see…I *need* to…"

"In my dream, I told you something. I've been practicing so I could remember. I said your body remembers how to see. You just need to find a way to teach it again. All I can do is show you that it's possible. Give you hope."

"How am I supposed to do that?" Ray whispered. "I don't have any…I don't have any eyes."

"I know. You gave them so I could be safe," Jake said, sitting again by Ray and holding his hand. "My mom used to say 'Let no good deed go punished.'"

"Unpunished."

"That doesn't make any sense," Jake said with a giggle. "You can't be punished for doing a good deed."

"It happens," Ray said, gesturing to the dirty cloth over his eyes.

"But it isn't supposed to," Jake said, his tone as serious as an eight year-old could make it. "You saved my life. God doesn't forget these things."

Ray tried to forge a smile, but failed. "You're a good kid, Jake, and you're still alive. That's reward enough for me."

"Don't give up. You can do it."

Ray gave Jake's hand a squeeze, and the boy leaned into him. Maybe what he thought he had seen had been an illusion caused by the sudden application of cold hands to the sides of his head. It wasn't possible for him to see and it never would be. He was blind. That was a fact. Those images, the gray shapes…they had been a cruel trick perpetrated by his mind's longing. He didn't blame Jake. He was just a kid, well-intentioned though he may be. He wished the whole thing had never happened, though deep down, he could feel hope take root, which he knew all too well could blossom into roses with thorns sharp enough to cut.

Together they sat quietly by the fire holding hands, both of them facing the flames, though only one could see them.

IV

"They're coming back, aren't they?" Missy asked.

"Of course they are," Evelyn said, though she shared the younger girl's nagging doubts. Neither of them thought for a second that Adam and Phoenix would abandon them, but there were terrible things out there. They had witnessed far too much death recently to think that anywhere was safe. Their domestic act was just that, a measure of normalcy they imposed upon themselves. It was like walking a tightrope. So long as they kept moving and didn't stop to look around, everything appeared to be fine, at least on the surface. The truth of the matter was that nothing was fine.

They stood in silence at the back of the cavern where they'd unraveled one of the Goshute blankets and strung the thick strands between the walls. Kelp stems were twisted into the strings, the leaves dangling toward the ground to dry. They were experimenting with different ways to serve it as all of them were growing weary of kelp salad and boiled kelp, though none admitted it aloud. With such thick leaves, maybe when dried they would take on the texture of jerky. At least it was food though, and it was far better than starving to death.

Whether it worked or not, it occupied their time. Though that's all it felt like they were doing now, killing the time between sunrise and sunset. Hopefully, when Adam and Phoenix returned, they would have something productive into which they could invest their energy. They were defenseless, surrounded by nothing more imposing than a lake on one side and a mountain on the other. Until they were again able to block off the road with more than rubble and shield themselves against an attack from across the now open water, they would continue to wallow in a feeling of helplessness. But if what Phoenix said was true—and they had no reason to doubt him after his visions had proven prophetic—then there wasn't going to be another attack on their fortifications, then they no longer needed to worry, yet still they did. Worse was the fact that Phoenix had said their adversaries were waiting for them to go to wherever it was they were for the battle to end the war. As far as Evelyn was concerned, there was no good cause to leave Mormon Tears. Why on earth would they uproot and strike out through the abandoned cities and feral wilderness?

All thoughts eventually led back to that point, didn't they? None of them would ever know a moment's peace so long as there was the promise of bloodshed hanging over their heads. It lingered in the air, filtering even into their dreams. Awakening in the middle of the night to the sounds of someone sobbing was commonplace. Evelyn herself had been the guilty party on numerous occasions. Night was when true desperation set in, when they were alone inside their heads with no one to talk to, no way of channeling the images of death into useless banter to hold them at bay. Thoughts of loved ones lost were inescapable, the emotions intensified by the exhaustion and frustration at the inability to sleep. It didn't help that the cavern amplified the whimpers and cries, making them sound even more forlorn and filled with gut-wrenching sorrow, like the sad mooning of so many lost ghosts.

She could feel her thoughts spiraling downward into depression and had to change the topic of conversation before it crippled her, even if it was just random prattle.

"So…How are you and Phoenix?" Evelyn asked. "You guys have been getting fairly close, haven't you?"

"I thought so," Missy said, "but lately…lately he's been even more distant than usual."

"How so?"

"Ever since, you know, since that night when whatever happened to him…happened."

"When he went supernova and incinerated that creature?"

"Yeah…That changed him somehow."

"I can only imagine. I think it changed us all to some extent. I know I've never seen anything like it. It was like he was exploding in slow motion, that light growing from him. It felt like it was a thousand degrees in there. It was kind of scary."

"I think it scared him even more than the rest of us. I'm pretty sure he didn't know he could do that."

Missy's eyes had been pinched closed against the pain of having her chest ripped open by that reptilian beast, but had seen the light through her eyelids and felt the heat as though she'd been thrust into an oven. She could only rely on what the others said to know what truly transpired. About the cooked monster that dangled from Phoenix's hands before crumbling into a pile of ash at his feet, about the look of unadulterated rage in his albino eyes. She loved him for his innocence, for the way he always said what was on his mind without filtering it, for the way he treated her, the way he looked at her. She feared that one pivotal event had robbed him of his naïveté and exposed him to emotions he'd never felt before and had been unprepared to deal with. In many ways, he had still been just a kid, a child who had been forced into manhood in the blink of an eye. Missy was afraid. Not of him, but for him.

"Give him time," Evelyn said. "He'll come around."

"I'm sure you're right. I'm just worried about him. He's the first guy that I've actually…you know…loved."

Evelyn smiled and gave her a hug. She knew what the younger girl was going through. She'd been there herself once upon a time. First loves were both the greatest and the worst things in the world. They were completely absorbing. Nothing in the world mattered outside of that one person. Spending every waking moment together, every emotion under a microscope. It was a beautiful and magical time to witness, but living through it was sheer torture.

She didn't know what to call what she and Adam had. When she looked at him, her heart fluttered, and she constantly caught him looking at her. They kissed every now and then and often shared a blanket beside the fire, but nothing had progressed beyond that point. With everything going on around them, she didn't have the time to ponder their relationship—if that was indeed what it was—and she was sure that he didn't either. Maybe under different circumstances they could explore the next logical step, but for now it was enough to know that he was there for her and that he cared. It wasn't the flame that burned inside of Missy, but it was the only thing that was getting her through the tough times when she missed her father or allowed the fear to overwhelm her. Who knew if that was the foundation love was built upon, but for now it was exactly what she needed.

Missy crinkled one of the leaves to make sure it had thoroughly dried, the broken fragments falling into her palm. She held them out to Evelyn, who pinched a small brown triangle and brought it to her lips.

"Here goes nothing," she said, tossing it onto her tongue.

"Well?" Missy asked, still holding her portion in her hand, watching as Evelyn finally started to chew. She tossed hers into her mouth and did the same.

"Not bad," Evelyn said.

"Not good either."

Evelyn laughed. "It is pretty terrible, isn't it?"

Missy joined in, and together they laughed until they had drawn everyone else's attention. Even Mare and Jill poked their heads through hole in the ceiling of the top room of the pueblo.

"Come and get it!" Missy called, unable to stop laughing.

V

Salt Lake City

The low-lying clouds the morning sun had yet to burn off passed to either side as the riders descended. The lake fell away behind them, the briny smell replaced by something far less pleasant. Adam thought at first it must have been a garbage dump, the frozen piles of refuse releasing their foul aroma as the last of the snow melted away and they began to thaw, but from his vantage hundreds of feet above the edge of the city, he could see that it was no such thing. Blocks of enormous warehouses raced along beneath the equine's churning hooves, their roofs collapsed in sections under the amassed weight of the sudden snowfall, still piled in the darkness atop the rubble. It was from these holes that the smell originated, hanging over the entire area like smog.

The stallion set its wings and sliced through the air, right down the center of an industrial parkway, bland gray buildings rising to either side. The straps of flesh stretched between the bony framework of the wings snapped like flags in a gale until the steed's hooves clopped onto the pothole-riddled pavement. It stopped in the middle of a vacant intersection and hopped nervously, pacing and shaking its head.

"It's frightened of something," Phoenix said, tightening his grip with one hand so he could free the other to stroke the horse's neck, calming it ever so slightly.

"Do you know what's scaring it?" Adam asked, trying not to rupture anything vital as he squeezed Phoenix around the gut.

"I don't know…" He looked around, but

everything was silent and still. Several doors and garages stood ajar, housing only shadows. Trash blew down the gutters and wet brown leaves were stuck in the middle of the road. Cars were still parked where their owners had abandoned them, never again to move from those spots. Some had broken windows, while others had bowed hoods from the accumulation, but there were no silhouettes within. The lack of movement was more disturbing than if they had they actually seen anything. It felt as though any minute something black and evil was going to dart out from its hiding place, but there wasn't even the hint of motion. There was only the stench of food rotting in the grocery warehouses and the bloated bodies of the dead decomposing where they were buried beneath the wreckage.

Only the wind whistled along the street, channeled by the buildings. The seahorse stomped its front hooves, their cue to disembark. It acted as though it couldn't stand being there even a second longer. Adam dropped to the ground first and barely moved out of the way before Phoenix leapt off. The strange creature didn't hesitate. It raced back down the street in the direction they had come, spread its wings and took to the sky. It appeared as a blot against the pale blue sky, shrinking steadily until it vanished completely.

"Man, something sure spooked that thing," Adam said, turning in a circle. He felt exposed standing out in the open, surrounded by literally thousands of hiding places.

"Can't you feel it?" Phoenix whispered. "The air is thick with death."

Adam could definitely feel something. It was as though gravity had subtly increased, pulling down on the sky to create a smothering feeling of heaviness and oppression. The entire city, even postmortem, held its breath. The weight of invisible eyes was upon him, though he knew instinctively that nothing living remained. It was easy enough for the combination of festering scents to metamorphose into the smell he remembered all too well from the refugee camp in Iraq: the putrescence that crept into their tents when the wind changed directions, accosting them with the biological taint of the decomposing bodies in their shallow graves. He suddenly felt the same urge as the horse. The compulsion to get the hell out of there was overwhelming. His heart was going crazy, his legs beginning to tremble. He looked back to the sky, hoping to see the flying horse returning for them, but there was nothing but an empty expanse.

"Let's just get what we came for and get out of here," he finally said, starting forward. The first thing they were going to need was a functional truck, preferably a semi. Then they were going to have to load whatever they could find as quickly as they—

Something attracted his attention from the corner of his eye.

He turned and stared down the street to his left. At first, he thought nothing of it; a hotel built to resemble a medieval castle like so many he had seen before. Gray bricks and red shingles on sharp parapets, three stories tall. The first unusual detail to pique his curiosity was that all of the windows had been boarded up, though it had been an ineffective measure against whatever had broken through, loosing jaggedly splintered chunks of wood to clap against the shattered panes on the breeze. The iron fence surrounding the property had been reinforced with coils of barbed wire. A pair of semi-trailers was parked diagonally in front of what he assumed to be the main entrance.

"That's where they fell," Phoenix whispered, following his gaze. "They never stood a chance."

Adam nodded. They had still held out hope that the larger faction might have survived the Swarm as the savage army swept westward, but deep down they had always known the fate the others had unknowingly accepted when they left Mormon Tears with Richard. Now that they had actually seen the aftermath, they would officially have to begin dealing with their feelings and the knowledge that it had been within their power to stop the others from migrating into the city and the dire consequences of that failure.

"I'll bet those trucks work," Adam said. "They would have needed them to move all of that wood and barbed wire."

"You're probably right, but are you sure you want to go there?"

Adam didn't answer, couldn't answer. Fear paralyzed his vocal chords, but unfortunately not his legs, which led him down the street of their own accord. As he approached, the castle grew taller and taller until it loomed over him. Some of the windows were still boarded and intact, while others were completely demolished. Strips of curled black scales adorned the sharp tips of the wire on the fencing, the coils now tangles. A single black arm reached out of the metal mess where its owner had shed it, the claws curled to the sky. The front iron gate hung askew, leaning inward more like a ramp. The swatches of snow remaining on the sidewalk in the building's shadow were slushy with white fluid.

The smell intensified as they neared, but changed slightly. There was no longer the hint of spoiling produce and garbage, the scent now unmistakably that of the dead.

"I don't think I can go in there," Phoenix said when he caught up with him. "There was so much pain, so much...suffering, trapped inside that building with no way to escape. It's still so fresh in there."

"Then just wait here and I'll get the truck."

Phoenix looked around. Neither option held any appeal. At least if he stayed with Adam he wouldn't be alone.

"I'm coming with you," he said, taking Adam by the hand in a gesture more suited to a child half his age.

Sometimes Adam forgot how little experience Phoenix actually had in the outside world. The visions lent him an aura of maturity and confidence, yet he was still so incredibly naïve, though even that faded a little with each passing day.

Adam released the boy's hand when they reached the driveway leading up to the gate. He leaned against it, flattening it just enough to allow Phoenix to climb over and then did the same himself. Black, crusted stains marred the parking lot in starburst patterns that both tried their hardest not to think about. Each represented a life cut short, they knew, but neither could recall the myriad faces that had passed through the gateway to Mormon Tears well enough to mourn them. They were anonymous souls that had touched their lives only briefly, yet they had no choice but to share the responsibility for the ending of their lives.

When they reached the first semi, a white cab and trailer painted brown with dirt and grime, Adam climbed onto the driver's side runner and peered inside. The keys were still in the ignition as he had hoped, the snow on the floorboards still frozen in the shape of the boots that had tracked it within, seemingly impervious to the thaw that affected the world without. On the dashboard was an empty coffee mug, beyond, through the front windshield, what remained of the glass doors leading into the hotel, the plywood sheets they had intended to use to board them still leaning against the wall in the foyer. Shattered glass littered the ground surrounding the metal frames, sparkling atop more of those horrible black stains.

"Go ahead and climb in," Adam said. "I'll be right behind you."

"Don't go in there, Adam…Please."

"I need to know."

"You already do."

"Maybe," Adam said, "but if anyone survived, we can't just leave them here."

"Adam…There are no survivors."

"Then I won't be in there long." He walked around the grille and paused in front of the open mouth of the hotel, the stench of death blowing out into his face on septic breath. Tugging his shirt over his nose and holding it in place with his teeth, he stepped through the hole where the panes had been, his boots crunching on the shards, which fortunately lent traction atop the slick bloodstains. The entire entryway leading to the registration desk was littered with pamphlets advertising local attractions from the overturned rack against the wall, the paper congealed in a crust of crimson on the floor. He walked over the mess, glancing behind the desk before veering to his left into the main lobby.

He gasped at what he saw, the shirt falling down from his face to welcome the odor into his mouth and sinuses.

"Oh, God," he groaned, turning away and clapping his hand over his mouth to keep from vomiting.

VI

MORMON TEARS

The six of them sat around the fire, enjoying a stress-free moment for the first time in a long while, and all thanks to what they agreed to be the worst way to prepare kelp. They had gathered around to try it, smiling and nodding as they chewed, trying to find anything positive to say about it while carefully skirting the glaring negatives. Mare had been the first to crack.

"Mmm. This is good," he had said, smiling even as tears formed in his eyes. "If I'd known sweaty socks tasted this good, I'd have eaten mine long ago."

The laughter had been spontaneous and a welcomed release of tension, allowing them to forget, if only briefly, the horrors around them. As it turned out, re-hydrating the leaves in boiling water made for a consistency like fruit leather, which truly wasn't half bad. With the right seasonings, it could have been quite good.

Mare sat with his back to the pueblo, tossing crusted phosphors he had scraped off the cavern wall into the fire. As soon as they hit the flames, they sparked like miniature firecrackers. Jill sat beside him, though at a distance that was readily apparent to all. She hadn't said much over the last couple of days, so it was truly wonderful to see the sparkle in her eyes as she joined in the revelry. Evelyn and Missy giggled like they'd known each other all their lives, somehow bonding over the meal they had ruined together. Jake sat to Missy's right, sticking his feet into the fire and holding them there until the rubber on the soles of his boots started to melt. He jerked them out only long enough for his toes to cool before shoving them back in again, giggling the whole while. Only Ray seemed distracted, as though only his physical shell was in attendance. He still occasionally chimed into the conversation, but for the better part he just faced the fire, crinkling and un-crinkling his brow, biting his lip and straining, tensing his entire body in an effort to make the fire reappear as it had initially with Jake's help. While he could feel the heat on his face, he could see absolutely nothing.

Eventually, the real world permeated their sanctum and the laughter trickled off, fading into silence.

"Worms," Mare finally said, his voice like an explosion in the quiet. "I'll bet that now that the snow's melted we could dig up some worms."

"Why?" Missy asked. "I'd much rather eat kelp than—"

"No," Mare interrupted. "I could make a fishing pole and bend up an earring or something to make a hook. I was just trying to figure out what to bait it with."

"That sounds wonderful," Ray said. "No offense, Evelyn, but man cannot survive on kelp alone."

"No need to apologize to me. I'd kill for a nice, juicy—"

Their words dissipated as Jill leaned forward, burying her face in her hands. A massive headache was forming at the base of her skull and she was beginning to feel queasy. She was debating whether or not throwing up would help her feel better when the darkness claimed her.

She was standing someplace unfamiliar, sweat draining down her face, through her saturated brow. Her wet hair was slicked back over her scalp, her clothes clinging to her damp body. The air was thick with black smoke, each inhalation bringing it into her lungs despite the cloth she held over her mouth to prevent it. She coughed it out, her lungs dry and brittle, and nearly screamed with the pain that felt like fire burning in her mediastinum and throat.

Flames danced beyond the churning smoke, crackling as they consumed what appeared to be the entire world from where she stood. The ground was scorched black, the soot coming away with her shoes as she walked slowly forward, leaving footprints of brown earth behind. Charcoaled remnants of trees stood all around her, only appearing from the smoke intermittently before being swallowed again. All she could smell were the innumerable scents of forest fire: the acrid aroma of burning wood and sap, the almost sweet smell of pine and various bushes, of ash and soot. It felt different than her other visions at first, as though exhaustion had simply claimed her body and chased her mind into a dream.

Until something moved through the smoke.

Lumbering black shadows took form amidst the clouds of smoke obscuring the landscape. Hulking creations like nothing she had ever seen before. With inordinately broad shoulders and thick appendages, they appeared superhuman, three or four of them darting back into the cover provided by the fire as soon as she saw them.

"Where did they go?" someone shouted, the voice resplendent with panic.

"I can't see them!" another yelled. "They could be anywhere!"

Jill could feel her own terror, her rising blood pressure threatening to erupt as a scream. She wanted to turn and run, but the smoke was all around her. Someone shucked a shell into the chamber of a shotgun behind her.

A thunderous roar filled the air as though an avalanche raced down a steep slope toward them.

Jill screamed in the vision, her cries still echoing in the cavern when she emerged from the forest fire smoke into that from the bonfire, coughing.

Her hands and cheeks were wet with tears, her breathing ragged. She raised her face from her palms to find that all of the others were looking at her expectantly, waiting for her to say something.

Why is she crying?

Was it another vision?

Is she all right?

Though they only asked with their eyes, she could hear their thoughts. She was so tired of having to endure the visions and how they made the others look at her. She just wanted to be free from them, to be normal like the rest of them. Was that too much to ask? Why did it have to be her? She was already struggling to deal with the other vision of having to sacrifice herself for her child. Adding this new one on top was simply too much. She wanted to scream and claw through her skull to remove whatever was wrong with her brain that forced her to see these things. This was no gift. It was a curse, and she just couldn't deal with it anymore.

Her shoulders shook as she started to sob.

"It's okay," Jake said, hugging her from behind. "I have them too."

Jill looked at the boy through watery eyes.

"My mom used to tell me that if you're having a bad dream," he continued, "all you have to do is change it."

"I can't. I have no control over them. Everything I see comes true."

"Then if you can't change the dreams, I guess you'll just have to change real life."

Her tears stopped. Could it possibly be that simple? She'd always seen the visions as an end result, not a beginning point. She knew they would find themselves in the middle of a forest fire with terrible things hiding beyond the smoke, but she also knew that at some other point, she would be holding her own child. If she assumed that the fire came before the birth, then she knew she would survive. And if she could survive, then she could help the others to do so as well. There had been at least two of them there with her. She had heard two distinct voices. All she needed to do was have the vision again. If she could manage to isolate every little detail and scrutinize it, maybe she could figure out how to save them before the event ever came to pass.

There was a weird, paradoxical logic to it that suddenly made sense.

She may still have been cursed with terrifying visions, but somewhere in there, hidden behind the smoke with those creatures, were the pieces of the puzzle to their salvation.

VII

SALT LAKE CITY

Adam could only stand there in shock and revulsion. He wanted to turn away and look at anything else, but for the life of him, he couldn't. He *needed* to see this. He'd never visited a slaughterhouse floor or seen a bear's den, but this was how he imagined the two would look combined. Dried blood was crusted to the vaulted ceiling in brown droplets that would never fall, the walls splashed with the same rust-colored stains and the ribbons of blood that had only been able to drain so far before their momentum petered. The floor was covered with it, so think that in spots it was still wet, his boots slapping it and tossing it into the air, leaving fresh scarlet footprints on the congealed mess as he walked toward the center of the lobby and the most disturbing display of all.

To the right, he could see through the open doorway into a restaurant where tables and chairs were toppled amidst the spoiled remnants of their final meal, now growing a flourishing, furry coat of green and white mold. The dining room wasn't nearly as saturated with blood, allowing reptilian footprints to be showcased on the slate gray tile, save for the strip down the middle where they had obviously flooded into the room. There were even prints on the walls and upturned tables where the wood had been carved away by sharp talons. But there were no bodies in there, only tatters of shredded clothing.

All of the bones had been stripped of their meat and piled in the center of the lobby, the revolting heap easily several feet taller than

Adam. Based on the sheer amount of blood in the room, he was sure that most of them had been dragged, kicking and screaming, into the vestibule to be butchered. The long bones were still capped with the nubs of gnawed tendons like drumsticks, cracked in half to release the trapped marrow. There were splintered ribs and vertebrae singled out from the spinal columns, skulls split along the fissures to grant access to the tender gray matter. A scattering of teeth and the small carpals of the wrists covered the ground like popcorn. Apparently, in the Swarm's hurry to move on and cross the lake, they had left the tougher sections, presumably to tide them over on the return trip. The gristly tendons on the knees and ankles were still attached, though the blood had been sucked clean from them. Adam had no idea what the accumulated bones of ninety-some souls would look like, but based on the sheer enormity of the pile, he guessed they were all accounted for.

He could only imagine the pain to which these poor men and women had been subjected, the torture of having their flesh torn away while they were still alive and conscious enough to experience the excruciating agony. He hoped their deaths had been quick, for he knew there was no chance they'd been painless.

"I told you not to come in," Phoenix said from behind him.

"I needed to see," Adam whispered. When he turned to face the younger man, tears streamed down his cheeks. "I should have been able to prevent this. I should have been able to convince them to stay."

"There was nothing you could have done."

"Do you really believe that?" Adam snapped. "It was within my power to persuade them not to leave and I failed. These people—all of them—died horrible deaths because *I* failed."

"They would have died anyway, Adam. It was their destiny."

"Their destiny? To be torn limb from limb while they were still alive? I refuse to believe that."

"Whether this way or another, they would have still died all the same."

"So what's our destiny then? Are we just going to die, too? What's the point then? Why don't we just do it ourselves on our own terms? Why should we struggle to endure if we're only going to end up like this?"

"Because that's life," Phoenix said with a shrug.

"Tell that to them," Adam said. He walked away from the carnage and past Phoenix without looking back. There were several tables to his left that had been knocked against the wall, the objects that had formerly been atop them piled against the baseboards. Shotguns and rifles, boxes of shells and bullets, hunting jackets. They hadn't even had time to arm themselves.

He pulled out one of the larger jackets and stacked half a dozen shotguns onto it, lifting his cargo by the sleeves. Struggling to balance the awkward weight, he headed through the foyer and out into the fresh air. Inhaling deeply of the oxygen no longer dripping with death, he headed for the semi cab, threw open the passenger door, and slid the guns onto the floorboard. Without pausing, he strode back inside and loaded the coat with as much of the boxed ammunition as he could make fit, and this time just set the whole load, coat and all, atop the steel and polished wood. He was still shaking his head when he climbed up into the driver's seat from the other side and slammed the door.

No matter what Phoenix thought, he should have been able to save them. And that was a burden he would have to bear through the rest of his natural life. Their blood was on his hands.

Phoenix climbed up through the open passenger door, sat down beside him, and gently closed the door. The cuts the birds had inflicted all over his face had healed as though they had never been there at all. Merely noticing that fact caused Adam to ponder the wound in his gut he had received at the hands of War, which had left only the hint of a scar. The boy had special abilities, there was no doubt, but for the first time since Adam had met him, they appeared to be weighing heavily upon him. Phoenix's usual smile and sense of wonder had been conspicuously absent since the night of the siege, but the damage was more than superficial. Something was eating the boy alive from the inside out and he seemed unwilling to open up enough to allow any of them to help.

"I'm fine," Phoenix said.

"So you can read minds now?"

"It was the way you were looking at me."

"You're a terrible liar."

"You aren't the only one with a cross to bear."

"You tried to help me with mine. Surely turnabout's fair."

"There's nothing anyone can do to help me," Phoenix said, still able to feel the darkness inside of him that he had so willingly embraced. The creature that had once been the Man had hurt Missy, but it was far more complicated than that. The Man had been willing to repent, even in his evil reptilian state, but Phoenix had incinerated him in cold blood with a physical power that the rage had awakened inside of him. Not only was that black seed still inside of him, but it was beginning to germinate, sending out roots even into his thoughts. While his visions had never been beautiful, they were now truly dark and insidious.

"I'm here when you need to talk," was all Adam could think to say. He knew that whatever demons Phoenix was battling were far beyond his understanding. He had seen what the boy had done, what he was capable of doing. It terrified Adam, so he could only imagine what it must be doing to Phoenix.

Phoenix placated him with a nod, which Adam took as his cue to drop the subject. He started the engine on the second try and backed the trailer into the bloodstained lot. It took several attempts to make the trailer move behind him like he wanted, but he figured it out and gunned the motor, blowing through the leaning gate and sending it skidding across the road. They turned into the warehouse district, watching the signs of the distribution centers on either side. The detour into the hotel had cost them their buffer and now they were really going to have to hurry. They needed a large stockpile of food and enough wood to replace their demolished defenses. Of course, the main object of their search was already clattering on the floor under Phoenix's feet.

The lot to his left attracted Adam's attention and he slowed the truck to a halt.

They were definitely burning daylight, but this was a necessary stop, he was sure of it. He looked across the console at Phoenix.

"It's the right thing to do," Phoenix said.

Adam started the truck rolling again, turning down the short drive and passing through the open gate into a sea of gray and white granite.

VIII

THE RUINS OF
DENVER,
COLORADO

Death rode Harbinger down the center of the street through the destruction. Rubble was piled high to either side where apartment buildings had collapsed upon themselves, now mountains of fractured concrete and tangles of steel girders, the dust from the mortar blowing across the asphalt like snow. High- and low-end stores shared the same fate, their wares rotting beneath the cold weight of bricks and cinder blocks. Streetlights had toppled from the cracked sidewalks to cross the intersections they had once ruled amidst twinkling shards of melted red, yellow, and green plastic. Crumpled cars had been tossed in every direction by the blast to land on their sides and hoods, some still on their tires, the molten rubber fused to the ground. Overpasses had fallen down, crumpling into Vs of broken concrete with rebar poking out like bones from beneath skin. Sections of the street had collapsed into the sewers and sub-terra, leaving chasms of jagged rock and pavement.

He could smell those trapped beneath, their bodies liquefying where the Swarm had been unable to reach them. Coupled with the feces produced from those that the creatures had been able to scavenge littering the road, the resultant smell was how he supposed a zoo might smell after a plague swept through.

The sound of Harbinger's clopping hooves echoed back at them from the desolate side streets, the skeletal beast leading them to the east under the midday sun. The other steeds trod more softly beneath Famine and

Pestilence, who flanked him to either side, though maintaining their distance behind. The other riders wore their cloaks, their hoods hanging over their faces to obscure all but the shadows beneath. Famine's white fists were curled into Scourge's mane of thorny briars, while Pestilence allowed the serpentine tails rising from Harvester's spine to slither into her sleeves and wrap around her wrists. Death, on the other hand, had grown weary of hiding his visage from the Lord, riding out in the open for even the Divine to see his black scales and broad, adder-like head. The fall of his army, his Swarm, enraged him. They should have easily overwhelmed and crushed the remainder of man. Instead, he was now in a position he had never even contemplated before. He had failed, and he had no choice but to begin anew.

By all rights, the battle should have been over. Each of the horsemen had served their preordained function. Death had created the other three riders and organized his army. Pestilence had released her mosquitoes to separate the souls of the saved from those of the damned and Famine's locusts had laid the genetic seeds of their rebirth. War had led the Swarm, the Lord's armada of vengeance, against the survivors, and even though he had fallen and his troops perished, his designated task had been completed. They had fought the battle for which they'd been created, and whether they won or not, the ordeal should have been over. But Death couldn't allow this to be the end. God had intervened and cheated him. The rules had been changed, so it was only fitting that he make up his own moving forward. He would learn from his mistakes.

The animals were helping the survivors. Thus, all lower forms of life needed to be eliminated entirely from the equation. He knew of the flying stallions that saved the men by the lake from the Swarm and carried them across the countryside. He had seen those giant white falcons through War's eyes as they had descended upon him, had felt the warrior's pain as their beaks and talons had destroyed his armor and shredded his flesh with his counterpart's blood. They had hidden in plain sight under the cover of the snow. Granted the blizzard and the birds were now a memory, but looking forward, he needed to ensure that there could be no recurrence. The time had come to implement his plan to remove that variable, to prevent outside intervention.

To defy the Lord and bar His influence.

The beasts they had spawned in the bowels of their dark tower roared in anticipation as they passed out of the city and into the open prairie to the east, following the path trampled by the Swarm between the torches cast from the inverted skulls of the dead, long since darkened, having burned through their fuel of human glycerol. Where once the amber waves of grain had rippled, there were now brambles and briars with thorns sharp enough to cut flesh through to the bone, as evidenced by the mutated tufts of fur scattered throughout the dense thrush, nourishing the roots of the vicious vegetation with their spilled blood and sloughing carcasses.

Death crested a knoll and trotted Harbinger in a circle. All along the eastern horizon, the bramble had laid claim to the ranches and farmhouses, scaling the wooden siding and burying the roofs, leaving only random patches of shingles and the occasional chimney as testament to their existence. It was an aggressive species of plant with spiraling appendages capped with razor-honed thorns tangling around broad leaves and thick stalks that in a matter of days had grown taller than a man. To the north and south, the suburbs waged a losing war against the encroaching vegetation, which overcame fences and yards to begin consuming the clusters of matchbook homes. To the west, the black skyscraper lorded over the gray rubble of downtown, the edges of the crater surrounding the destruction now invisible beneath the advancing briars. He could only speculate as to the kinds of animals that had adapted to living in the savage underbrush, out of sight, scurrying beneath on the mat of nettles. Soon enough though, every single one of them would be dead.

His minions scurried up the hillside behind Pestilence and Famine, darting from one side of the path to the other, snapping at even the gentle movements of the slithering vines. They were rabid, unflinching creatures, far more animal than man now. Wiry tufts of hair covered their bodies, growing longer atop wide heads lowered to the ground beneath shoulders hunched so dramatically that their arms nearly raked the earth. Their nostrils were upturned, scenting furiously, their round eyes useless black spheres. A mohawk of dense black hair ran the length of their spines, expanding at their shoulder blades and wrapping around their tapered waists. Their ferocious mouths ripped their faces in half when they leaned forward to bellow their hideous growls, their backs flattening and contorting in such a way as to defy skeletal integrity. Hooked teeth lined both jaws, bleeding around the union with their gray gums. A fine layer of pale brown down covered their formerly pink skin to grant the appearance of richly-tanned flesh.

But it was the beast that trailed them that pleased Death the most, a true monster among slavering dogs.

Nothing remained of Richard's humanity within that being, now known as the Leviathan, save for the hatred that burned as brightly inside of that new form as the fire in its eyes. Its skin was heavily scaled, though unlike the smooth serpentine scales that covered Death, its scales were large and abrupt like chain mail, though so black that they were invisible from a distance. They glimmered with the sunshine, but still maintained the sickly ebon of a whole body bruise. Its silhouette crackled with an outline of flames, a living skein of fire flowing over every inch of its form.

The three horsemen sat high atop their steeds and turned to the east toward the never-ending sea of bramble, the creatures of their design gathering in front of them. Death nodded, and the Pack as he had begun to think of them, roared in unison, so loud that even Death's vision trembled. They froze in place, only their heads swiveling as they scoured the impenetrable vegetation, using their sonar-like vision to triangulate the location of their prey. One raised its flat snout to sniff the air to confirm the location of what it "saw," then lowered its head and brayed again. The Leviathan stood beside it, following its line of sight into the thorny tangles. It rose to its full height, its chest swelling, and leaned forward, a stream of magma firing from its extended arms. The tight flume of flame burned straight through the twisted growth, which singed and immediately caught fire.

Something out there, hidden in the overgrown field, screeched, and the bat-like creature that had sighted it bounded through the resultant smoke along the fiery line. When it emerged from the smoke and returned again to the path, it was carrying what looked like a cross between a rabbit and turtle by the heels. The struggling animal had no fur, only a thick, articulated shell covering its entire body, perfectly matching the color of the plants. The beast held it high and roared again, the scorched animal kicking with clawed feet to try to free itself, shredding its captor's skin along its forearm, but it never had a chance. Talons lanced through the joints of the shell. The creature ripped with both hands to expose the unprotected flesh beneath and buried its teeth within. It shook the shrieking rabbit like a dog until it made no more sound and tossed the exoskeleton to either side. When it turned to face its master, it was drenched with blood.

Death nodded his approval and again the Pack started to howl, only this time the Leviathan didn't wait for them to isolate their quarry. Instead, it blasted a column of flames in every direction until it appeared as though the entire planet was ablaze. Shrouded in smoke and surrounded by flames, Death jerked on Harbinger's mane of fire and turned the stallion back to the west, reveling in the almost human-sounding screams of the animals burning out of sight.

Burn it, Death thought as he thundered back down the path toward the ruins of Denver. *Burn it all.*

When he looked back again, the eastern horizon was black with smoke, chased into the heavens by the growing fires like the rising sun.

CHAPTER 2

I

MORMON TEARS

The sun had set close to an hour ago, but Adam had still been able to see the gateway to Mormon Tears on the side of the highway. He turned the semi between the rock formations that looked like praying children facing one another on their knees and drove across the salt flats. Whatever tracks had once been there were now obliterated by the melting snow, but Adam could clearly recognize the mountain they lived inside in the distance. It had taken longer than they had planned to load the supplies into the trailer, now packed full, but it still felt as though they had forgotten half of what they'd intended to grab. Neither looked forward to unloading it all, but at least they would have some help.

Their nerves had been frayed the entire journey and only now that the rocky slope began to rise in front of them did they finally begin to relax. The whole drive along the deserted highway had been tense as shadowed forms darted in and out of their peripheral vision, from behind one tree trunk to the next or ahead on the road at the furthest diffuse range of their headlights. They were silhouettes that neither recognized, unfamiliar shapes only vaguely reminiscent of the animals they had once been. In this new world of mutated livestock and game, none of the creatures they saw were recognizable, causing even the smallest shape to become unnaturally ominous. Lord only knew what these things ate or what they were capable of doing to them.

The truck coasted to a stop in front of the rubble that remained of their barricade. Only the charred hood and shattered windows of the semi were visible beneath the mound of blackened wood. Adam breathed a sigh of relief and killed the headlights.

"Well…" he said, looking across the console at Phoenix. "I guess we'd better start unloading."

He threw open the door and climbed down to the wet sand.

"It's about time," Evelyn called down from the top of the wreckage.

When Adam saw her smile, he wanted to sprint up the hill and embrace her, but he suppressed the urge and waited for her to descend. Missy was right behind her, while her brother and Jill were only beginning to crest the rugged slope.

"What did you bring me?" Evelyn asked. She wrapped her arms around Adam and brought him to her, allowing his arms to fold around her, his chest warm against hers.

"Nothing fancy, I'm afraid."

"I'm just glad you made it back safely," she said, leaning her forehead against his shoulder so he wouldn't see her tears, which had caught her by surprise. She thought she had control over her emotions, that she was content with whatever she and Adam shared, but she couldn't help how she was feeling. She bit her lip and steadied herself. When she released him and stepped out of his arms, the tears were gone. "Did you see anyone or…anything else?"

"Only what was left of the others." He looked away. "They never had a chance."

"You can't keep blaming yourself."

He forced a smile, but it was only for her benefit.

"We'd better get the supplies off the truck," he said, turning and starting toward the rear of the trailer.

Evelyn caught up with him and took his hand. Together they joined the others, who were already climbing up on the tailgate and into the open cargo hold to begin the arduous task ahead. The rear of the unit was packed with mounds of clothing and blankets. Mare stood to one side, Phoenix to the other, both of them tossing the wares out onto the sand. There were coats and snow pants, shirts and jeans, unopened packages of socks and underwear. Behind was a small mountain of wooden dowels like those that had been sharpened and used to repel the Swarm. There were battery-powered lanterns and crates of replacement cells, a pile of rolled sleeping bags, behind which was a wall of cardboard boxes.

"Oh my God," Mare said. "Is this what I think it is?"

He hauled down a large box and tore back the flaps. His eyes lit up when he reached inside and pulled out a small, rectangular blue box. In his hands he held what once was commonplace, but now was one of the greatest treasures in the world.

"Macaroni and cheese," he whispered.

"It gets better," Adam called up to him, laughing as he grabbed a bundle of clothing from the ground and started his trek toward the cave.

"Cheetos!" Mare's voice echoed through the valley.

This was exactly the reaction Adam had been hoping for. All those hours of rummaging through storerooms, the mental and physical strain of the heavy lifting both ahead and behind, the eternity behind the wheel…all worth it. Who knew what the morning would bring, but this was a night to celebrate. Let everyone eat their weight in noodles and junk food and then climb into a padded sleeping bag. Let them remember, if only for this one night, what it felt like to be alive.

Adam set his cargo against the rear wall of the cave and walked back out onto the beach. Above, the stars shined down upon him, granting a momentary glimpse into the heavens. After everything they'd been through, after all of the death and pain, in that one precious moment, all felt right with the world, as though the pall that had hung over them for so long had finally been lifted. He smiled at Orion and followed the North Star along the handle of the Big Dipper. There would undoubtedly be more hard times to come and the penultimate battle that Phoenix promised, but in this one frozen moment in time, it felt as though God was smiling down upon them.

"Mmrmphew doon?" Mare asked, his lips covered with powdered cheese, his mouth full of corn puffs. He refused to relinquish the bag of Cheetos even though his arms overflowed with blankets and clothing.

The others appeared behind him, burdened by even more supplies, their fingertips orange.

"Looking at the stars," Adam said. "I can't remember the last time I actually did so."

"That truck isn't going to unload itself, you know." Mare flashed his cocky grin and deposited his load in the cave by Adam's. They could move it all down into the cavern once it was safely out of the elements.

Adam clapped him on the shoulder and they headed back toward the truck, where they could hear Phoenix still tossing boxes down atop one another.

"Wait for me!" Missy called, jogging to catch up. She fell in stride beside them. "Did you tell Adam about Jill's vision?"

"She had another one?" Adam asked.

"All she said she saw were massive fires and something moving through the smoke."

"Where was this?" Adam asked, reaching the top of the smoldering hill and descending the rubble like a staircase of burned wood.

"She didn't recognize the place. Just lots of what looked like pine trees."

"I suppose we'll just have to find a way to steer clear of every forest we come across then." Adam hadn't meant it as a joke, but Mare laughed.

"We're almost to the heavy stuff," Phoenix said when he heard their voices. The majority of the contents of the trailer now covered the ground in a haphazard jumble of cardboard and cloth as tall as the fender.

"This isn't the heavy stuff?" Missy asked, struggling to lift a large box of canned goods. She looked up at Phoenix to wink at him. Her breath caught and the box slipped from her grasp, ripping when it hit the ground and sending cans rolling in all directions. As soon as her breath returned, she released it as a scream.

Beyond Phoenix, in the shadows at the rear of the trailer, she saw a face. And it was looking right at her.

II

Ray had never realized that his definition of consciousness had been linked to his sense of sight. Awakening from a dream meant opening his eyes, while drifting off to sleep meant closing them. He was now beginning to uncover different levels of consciousness, separate layers of his mental faculties that until now he had never known existed. Before, he was either awake or asleep, while now he was exploring the shades of gray between. What he had once defined as the grogginess of waking, he now knew to be a distinct state of alertness. It was a strange moment where his mind was still tapped into both the rational and irrational parts of his brain at the same time, like streetlights yet to fade though the sun graced the horizon. Where dreams and reality were an indistinguishable conglomeration of consciousness, internal visions indecipherable from external stimuli.

He could tell he was still in the cavern by the droning *plip...plip...* of condensation dripping from the ceiling, the crackling and popping of the fire in front of him and its warmth on his face, and the stale smell of aged earth and stagnant water, but at the same time, he was sitting in the living room of his old house with Tina beside him, silently holding her hand. Had he eyes, he would only have had to open them to dispel one or the other, an abrupt shift in alertness, the toggling of a power switch. Without, he was forced to gently rationalize the distinction between the two, peeling apart layers of sound and smell to settle on the correct location of his body. Though it pained him greatly, he allowed the image of the love of his life to dissociate into the smoke he could smell rising from the bonfire before him, their gray flames wavering from a white-hot core—

Ray snapped to full attention as though he'd been slapped across the face, his vision immediately resuming its smothering blackness.

He had seen the fire as he had when Jake had shown him. He was sure of it. Or had it been part of his dream? He bit his lip, hard, to verify that he was indeed fully awake; with the myriad states of consciousness between, how could he really be sure? The eyes could deceive, but they were also the lenses of truth. Without them, it was up to his mind to separate the real from the unreal. His memories of sight were still so fresh that his imagination seemed more real than the blank images he now created as they lent visual credibility versus a speculative haziness. Had he truly seen the fire, shouldn't he still be able to?

"You fell asleep," Jake said, startling Ray. He hadn't heard the boy's quiet breathing, though now that he tried, he couldn't hear any of the others either.

"Where did everyone go?"

"Adam and Phoenix are back, so they're helping unload the truck."

"Why aren't you out there with them?"

"I wanted to stay with you."

"Why?" Ray asked. Jake had been at his side for the last couple of days, but he'd never thought to question it since it was nice to have the constant companionship.

"I wanted to make sure you were ready."

"For what?"

"We're going to have to leave soon."

"Where are we going?" Ray sensed the tension in the boy's voice and wasn't actually sure that he truly wanted to know.

"I don't know. Not for sure anyway…but this is all going to end soon. One way or another."

"I'm fine, and I'll be ready if and when I need to be. Why don't you go check on the others?"

"They'll be ready, I'm sure. But we won't even get there if you aren't. You're the important one, Ray. Without you, we won't even be able to make it to where we're going."

"I find that hard to believe. The only thing I can do is slow us down."

Jake shook his head, knowing Ray couldn't see the gesture. It was imperative that he make sure that Ray was prepared. He wasn't exactly sure why just yet, but his dreams were insistent. If he couldn't snap Ray out of his self-pitying funk and convince him of his importance, then they were all going to die. That much he understood clearly. Besides, Ray had saved him, and it was only right that he do the same.

"Keep your chin up," he said. "That's what my mom used to say when I was sad."

"Thanks," Ray said, reaching toward the sound of the voice to ruffle Jake's hair. "What do you say we head outside with the others?"

"Okay."

Ray stood and turned away from the fire. He had been trying to keep the world around him at right angles. If he walked straight from the stairs to the fire, then all he would have to do is turn around and he would be pointed in the right direction. Routine was the key. He started walking and felt Jake's hand slide into his, but instead of trying to lead him, the boy simply walked at his side, which Ray genuinely appreciated.

"You don't have to wear the blindfold," Jake said when they reached the stairs. They moved to the right so Ray could feel the stone wall and use it as a guide. "Your eyes don't look as bad as you think they do."

Ray smiled and gave Jake's hand a squeeze. They ascended the rocky stairs until they reached the flat cliff. From there, Ray could feel the air from the tunnel to the outside world, hear its subtle breath, and walked straight toward it. Sixteen steps and they were in the mouth of the walkway, another twenty-one and they reached the bend. Ray traced the wall with his fingertips, learning the imperfections in the stone while counting down the thirty-six paces that would lead them into the cave. He heard the distant voices outside, far enough off to the right that he couldn't clearly understand their words, felt the cool night breeze on his face.

Ray started forward into the cave, but something caught his feet and sent him sprawling. He landed on a pile of something soft and rolled to the side onto his back.

"Dammit!" he cursed, pounding his fists on the ground.

"It's okay," Jake said, trying to help pull him back to his feet.

Ray jerked his hand away. "I can do it!"

Jake flinched and took a step back.

"Jake…" Ray whispered, acutely aware of the quiver in the boy's breathing. He pushed himself back to his feet and resisted the urge to kick the heap of blankets that had tripped him. "I'm sorry. I…I didn't mean to yell at you. I was just…just mad at myself. I shouldn't have taken it out on you. It's just that every time I think I'm finally making progress, I end up doing something stupid."

"It isn't your fault," Jake whispered. The tremor in his voice hurt Ray infinitely worse than any fall could have. "I should have told you to watch out."

"Come here," Ray whispered, kneeling on the blankets. He had to brace himself with both hands to find his balance, but when he did, he extended both arms out to his sides.

Jake threw himself into Ray's embrace, nearly knocking him over.

"I'm so sorry," Ray whispered into his ear. He could feel the child's tears on his cheek, and they burned like acid. "You know how sorry I am, don't you?"

Jake nodded, dragging his damp cheek up and down against Ray's.

"I didn't mean to yell at you."

"I know," Jake sniffled, "but that wasn't what scared me."

"What do you mean?" Ray pulled his face away, puzzled. "What scared you then?"

He felt Jake's arms slide out from beneath his and again when they reached the back of his head. The boy's small fingers fumbled with the knot of the blindfold. Ray lowered his head to allow Jake to pull it off over his hair.

"Here," Jake said, holding the blindfold out to Ray, stretched taut between his hands.

"What am I…?" Ray started, but his words trailed off when he ran his fingers along the length of the fabric. It was warm. Not just the kind of muted damp warmth that was transferred via skin contact, but a dry heat as though it had been baked in a kiln. Sections were tattered and crisp, singed.

Ray brought his hands to his hollow sockets and carefully traced the scarred skin.

"How…?" he gasped.

"Your eyes…" Jake said, taking Ray by the wrists and lowering his hands from his face. "They were on fire."

III

"Phoenix!" Missy screamed, crawling over the tailgate and into the cargo bed. That face was still right behind him. How could he not know there was someone right behind—?

She stopped when she reached him, fists curled into his jacket in preparation of yanking him out of harm's way. The face stared lifelessly at her through smooth marble eyes, the shadows peeling back just enough to reveal the fixed expression of sorrow framed by the cowl of a flowing stone gown. The woman knelt atop a square marble pedestal, hands clasped in front of her breast in prayer. Missy knew right then exactly what it was.

"Are you all right?" Phoenix asked.

She relaxed her hands and released his jacket. "I thought that was someone standing behind you."

"And you were going to save me from them?" Phoenix asked. There was a second question hidden beneath the first, she could see it in his eyes, but she couldn't imagine what it might be.

"Of course," she whispered, wrapping her arms around him and burying her face in his neck. A shiver rippled through him.

He broke their embrace and smiled at her, though she could tell he was humoring her.

"Why won't you talk to me?" she whispered.

Taking her softly by either side of her face, he kissed her forehead. "Another time."

She turned away, shaking her head. His footsteps echoed away from her as he went back to sliding timber off the back of the truck. She stared into the sad marble eyes of the mourning Virgin, amazed that the sculptor had been able to draw such emotion from a block of stone. Beside the ornate headstone were others of differing styles and colors, ranging from a polished white to the sad gray of an overcast sky. There was an angelic, winged cherub standing on one foot with a horn poised to its lips in preparation of heralding the heavens. Another featured the bearded Savior, His gown hanging from Him, several sizes too large, standing with His arms spread wide in a welcoming embrace. He simultaneously stood atop the adjacent grave marker, His twin naked save for a loin cloth and a crown of thorns, arms extended and feet overlapping as though nailed to an invisible cross. She saw the Virgin Mary cradling a swaddled child beside a large gothic cross. There were eight of them in total. She tried not to read anything into the significance of the number, for there were only six graves on the beach.

Footsteps approached from behind.

"Beautiful, aren't they?" Adam said.

"They're very sad."

"They're supposed to be."

"I know," Missy said. "Their sadness is just so…permanent, though."

Missy allowed a wan smile to cross her face and brushed past Adam. Stopping at the tailgate, she looked outside for Phoenix, but he was nowhere to be seen. Jill and Mare were just heading back toward the cave with their arms full of boxes. Marble screeched on the aluminum flooring as Adam began sliding the headstones toward the open rear of the trailer.

"Phoenix?" she called, but there was no answer. She needed to talk to him, needed to know what was going on inside his head. The distance he was creating between them was wearing on her. She loved him and couldn't stand the fact that he was drifting away from her and she felt helpless against it. He was different, she knew, special, saddled with the burden of the entire world, but he didn't have to bear that cross alone. Not when he had her. Maybe there was nothing she could do, but she had to try. If he would just open up to her…

She dropped down from the tailgate and looked around, but there was no one else nearby. There were voices from the other side of the fallen barricade, so she climbed up and stood on the charred planks of the great mound of formerly white sand. Her brother disappeared into the cave off to her left to relieve himself of his burden. The waves rolled in silently along the shoreline, racing up the beach to leave a foamy mark before receding. A haze of smoke from the fire pits lingered over the water. Her eyes followed it toward the southern source. Phoenix sat on the sand beside the lone wooden cross at the head of Carrie's grave, Evelyn right beside him. Missy watched as he plucked a small red blossom from the flowering vines that spiraled around the cross, inspecting it carefully before passing it to Evelyn.

Missy's heart sank into her stomach and a tear rolled from the corner of her eye. She understood now.

Closing her eyes, she wiped the saline from her cheeks and turned away. It felt as though she'd been punched in the gut. The night seemed to close in around her as she descended the rubble again, preparing to wring her like a dishrag. She just needed to put her body to work, and with any luck that would divert her mind. She wanted to crawl out of her flesh, go curl up somewhere in the dark, and cry. She imagined her old bedroom in her old house, the pictures of her mom on the walls and the rows of stuffed animals waiting to cuddle her and absorb her tears. She was tired of being afraid and tired of the emotional pain. Life was now an exercise in tedium. For one fleeting moment, she thought she'd found someone special, someone to bind her world together, but as always, she'd been wrong. Life was as it always was and always would be, and there was only pain to meter its passage.

Missy looked to the sky as she walked, but there was no comfort to be found in the stars, only cold white dots stabbing through the tapestry of night. She had always envisioned her mother somewhere up there, watching over her, but she felt nothing, no celestial kindness or omniscience, only the chilly wind rising from the south.

Gathering an armful of wooden poles yet to be sharpened, she headed back toward the cave, doing everything in her power to keep from looking at the graves and contemplating how utterly alone she felt.

IV

"We should be helping the others unload the truck," Evelyn said, following Phoenix down the beach in the direction of the lone, poorly-assembled cross.

"This will only take a minute," he said without turning to face her. "I want to do this while everyone else is distracted."

He had approached her in the cave after she had piled the bundles of clothing against the rear wall and he was preparing to unload the first of many loads of dowels. There had been something in his eyes, a slight tremor in his voice that added to the insistence of his words. He needed to talk to her—and only her. At first, she thought it must have been something to do with Missy, but as they walked toward the shoreline, she sensed that what troubled him was of a far graver nature.

Carefully treading the flat ground between the mounds of sand, he sat down right beside the cross, still unable to look directly at her. She hovered behind him for a moment, waiting for him to speak, but finally sat down beside him when it became apparent that he wasn't going to say anything until she did so.

"You're very special," he whispered, barely loud enough to be heard over the hiss of the briny foam.

"Phoenix..."

When he looked up at her, there were tears in his eyes, and she knew she needed to allow him to finish.

"What you did with the kelp...You have a gift."

"All I did was warm the water so it could survive."

"It was more than that. You willed those plants to live, and look at them now."

Evelyn glanced back over her shoulder to the point along the beach where the white sand met with the burnt sienna rocks. The kelp had broken the surface of the water like so many bushes on a flood plain and had expanded a dozen feet in all directions. They were now so well acclimated that she was certain they no longer needed the fire pits and the exhaust tubes to maintain the ambient water temperature, but she still felt more confident when she could look from afar and see the four plumes of smoke rising from the pipes.

"It's a resilient species," she said, turning back to Phoenix. "All it needed was a little help."

"You did far more than that."

They sat in silence. While Phoenix looked nervously from her face to his hands in his lap, Evelyn watched the others moving back and forth over the barricade, unloading the truck.

"What's on your mind, Phoenix?" she finally asked.

"I want you to have something." He pulled one of the vines from where it coiled around the vertical post of the cross, laying it carefully across his lap. There were several blood-red blossoms that reminded Evelyn of snapdragons crossed with orchids, long sunset-orange stamens hanging from their open blossoms like a squid's tentacles from a dog's mouth. He touched each of the flowers, the powdery pollen coating his fingertips, before finding the one he desired. Gently pinching off the stem and holding it flat in his palm, he presented it to her. Evelyn studied it for a moment before hesitantly taking it from him.

"Phoenix… You're a very sweet kid, but I…"

Her voice petered off as the tips of the petals started to whiten, spreading downward along the bulb until all the color had drained from the blossom. The stamens released their golden powder with a puff like tiny cigarettes to blow from her palm and along the sand, glittering. She looked at the vines entwined around the makeshift cross. They had faded to white as well. She was just about to ask what was going on when she felt something sting her open palm. All of the color that had seeped from the flower was now a puddle in her hand, though all she felt was warmth. She tried to lift the flower with her free hand, but it wouldn't come away without her skin. The stem had poked through her flesh and felt as though it were embedded with a barbed hook. She could only watch as the collection of fluid contracted, growing smaller by the second like bathwater down a drain. At first, she thought it must have been pouring out through the thin gaps between her fingers, but nothing dripped into her lap. It wasn't until the intense heat began to spread from her hand, through her wrist and into her forearm, that she realized what was happening.

The pale green veins running up her arms swelled and rose to the surface, darkening to the color of palm leaves. She screamed and shook her hand. The dried and shriveled flower finally dropped from her palm. When it hit the beach, it turned to dust. The needle-sized hole in her skin allowed the last of the scarlet fluid to drain beneath and then closed as though it had never been. The veins that had stood out only a heartbeat prior faded back into her flesh, yet the warmth poured unimpeded into her chest, where it resonated before pumping out through the entirety of her body. She felt her face flush and her toes tingle. Her eyes burned—

And then the sensation was gone.

Her skin prickled as the cool breeze relieved her of the lingering heat, and the night closed back in upon her.

"What did you do to me?" she whispered, tears welling in her eyes.

He didn't answer. He was already on his feet and walking back toward the others.

"Phoenix?"

She was sure he could hear her, but he didn't turn around. Rising, her head still spinning, she stumbled after him, unaware that behind her the coiled stems had fallen away from the cross and dissociated on impact. With each step, her equilibrium returned by degree and she began to feel more like herself. The image of the blossom bleeding through her skin vanished like a dream. By the time she reached the crest of the mound, she could barely remember the pain.

Phoenix and Mare were already walking back toward her, carrying what looked like a statue between them. It took her a second to rationalize the polished gray sculpture. It was an ornate headstone.

"Phoenix," she whispered as he passed, but he only stared through her with heartrending eyes and kept walking, using all of his concentration to balance the unwieldy payload while maintaining his tenuous footing on the rubble. His face had noticeably paled, the bags beneath his faded pink eyes more pronounced.

Missy came around the back of the trailer with a bundle of the smooth sticks across her arms, but didn't even look at her when she passed, walking deliberately out of her way to avoid any contact. Her eyelids were puffy and her cheeks glistened with moonlight.

Evelyn climbed down the mess of burnt wood until she reached the flat sand and headed for the rear of the truck. Adam grunted and shoved the final grave marker from the tailgate into the sand, where it rested facedown beside the others, so many fallen angels. He hopped down and was just about to begin standing them up when Evelyn started to cry.

"What's wrong?" he asked as she started around the back of the trailer toward him.

She couldn't hold it back any longer. It was as though suddenly she were alone and trying to find a way to grasp what had just transpired. The tears spilled in waves.

Adam ran to her, taking her by the shoulders and looking deep into her eyes.

"Talk to me, Evelyn. What happened?"

"The flower…it…it…and then Phoenix and Missy…They acted like they didn't even see me."

"Come here," Adam said, pulling her into his arms. "Everything's going to be all right."

She sobbed into his shoulder, trembling against him while he stroked her hair. When she finally calmed enough to speak again, she leaned away from him so she could see his face, but not so far as to vacate his embrace.

"I just don't understand what's happening anymore," she sniffled.

"You and me both. The whole world is changing around us and I…" He paused. "Didn't your eyes used to be hazel?"

"They are hazel."

Adam could only shake his head, his confusion evident by the wrinkle in his brow.

Evelyn pulled away, the tears beginning anew, and ran around the back of the tailgate and to the cab. She hopped up on the runner and

58

twisted the side mirror so that it faced her…and screamed.

Her irises were no longer brown around the pupils, ringed with a pale green like an eclipsed sun, but a blinding shade of shamrock.

V

Ray jerked his hands away from the blindfold and Jake let it fall to the ground.

"There's no way," Ray whispered. He refused to believe it. Jake had to be lying to him, his fingertips conspiring against him. There was absolutely no way that fire had risen from his eye sockets.

"I saw it, Ray."

Ray traced those hollow pits with his fingers again, the warmth now faded to what he assumed to be normal.

"When it happened," Jake asked, "did you see anything?"

"No," Ray said too quickly, scanning the darkness of memory. But he had, hadn't he? He clearly remembered tripping over something. Falling forward. There had been a flash of gray before he hit the ground. Maybe it had simply been the bloom of light that explodes across one's vision with blunt impact to the head, but now that he really tried, he could recall the vague gray outline of the cluttered cave floor before impact. Had there been the faint outline of a mound of clothing? Blankets? The sharp edges of randomly-strewn boxes, the texture of the cave wall?

"You did, didn't you?"

"Maybe," Ray said. "I just can't be sure. I thought…I don't know."

A scream shattered the night, setting a flock of birds sleeping on the lake to screeching flight.

Ray turned toward the sound and stood, this time far more conscious of the piles of blankets beneath him and the maze of cardboard boxes leading to the beach. Scuffing his feet along the stone floor through the transition zone of sand on granite and into the giving sand of the beach, he listened for another scream, any sound to guide him, and followed the direction he had chosen in a straight line. It sounded like the scream had come from the shore to his right, but he couldn't be sure. Wet sand from high tide clapped underfoot and he knew he hadn't veered far enough to the right, so he used the slap of his tread to lead him to the south. Jake caught up and took his hand.

"Evelyn!" Jake called. She stood at the head of Carrie's grave, but she either didn't hear or chose to ignore him. Phoenix was already hurrying away from her in the direction of the fallen barricade. Evelyn stumbled after him, oblivious to the fact that Jake and Ray were heading down the waterline in her direction. "Evelyn!"

She didn't even slow as she ascended the mound.

"What's going on?" Ray asked.

"She didn't hear me," Jake whispered, squeezing Ray's hand.

"Why did she scream? Is everything okay?"

"I…I can't tell." Jake watched Evelyn vanish over the scorched hill. Phoenix and Mare crested it, moving in the opposite direction, carrying what appeared to be a large statue between them. Missy skirted the stone face of the mountain alone, laboring under the weight of an armful of dowels.

Ray peeled apart the layers of sound. Since Jake either wouldn't or couldn't tell him what was happening, he needed to try to figure it out himself. He could hear the advancing waves crashing to shore and hissing as they rolled along the beach. The startled birds circled above with the whistle of wings before dropping back down beyond the breakwaters with so many muffled splashes. Footsteps approached through the shifting sand like the swishing of corduroy, but all he could smell was the smoke from the dwindling fires in the pit, carried downwind into his face by the gentle, silent breeze.

Jake released Ray's hand and knelt at the foot of the thin cross. There were no longer vines spiraling around the upright post; their dried remains crumbled to ash on the sand. How could they have been thriving mere hours ago and now be so far dead? He looked up in time to see that Phoenix and Mare were now nearly upon him with a tombstone between them. Even burdened by such great weight, they tread carefully so as to only walk on the thin strips of level ground between the graves. Jake pulled the cross out of the ground and stepped back to allow them room to set the statue of the weeping Virgin Mary in its stead. After a moment of leveling the pedestal on the soft, shifting ground, they stood back to appraise their work. There was a certain measure of formality and closure provided by the marble, while the crossed sticks had always seemed transient.

"Should we say something?" Mare asked.

"No," Phoenix said. "Everything of importance has already been said. These markers are for those yet to come, so they might know the sacrifices made in their honor, whether they are the children of man or not."

Mare nodded and stretched his arms. "I suppose that means we should head back for another."

Ray was about to ask why Evelyn had screamed when he heard her crying in the distance. He turned toward the sound and started walking. Jake's hand slid into his.

Together they crossed the beach toward what Ray could tell was the charred remains of the barricade by the smell. He heard the swishing of footsteps in the sand as Mare and Phoenix passed them, the clamor of shoes on unsettled planks. The sorrowful, muted sounds of Evelyn—

Ray stopped.

The smell of charcoaled wood was too strong. It had taken him a moment to realize it, though he should have recognized it immediately. The burning wall of pickets had collapsed days ago. Even the last of its ashes had been chased away by the wind, leaving only the blackened remains. What he smelled now wasn't the scent of burnt lumber, but of burning wood.

He turned around to again face the lake, tilting his head directly into the wind that had shifted to blow inland across the waves. The smell was faint, as though carried a great distance, but it was unmistakable.

The wind changed its mind and the aroma was gone, as though in that precious moment it had been brought specifically to him.

"What is it?" Jake asked.

"Look across the lake. What do you see?"

"Just water."

"No smoke?"

"No."

"Not even way off in the distance?"

"No...Why?"

Ray shook his head. "No reason." But there was, and he knew it. Beneath the acrid smell of flaming timber was something else, a scent that had become all too familiar.

Burning flesh.

And it scared the living hell out of him.

VI

The Ruins of Denver, Colorado

Death stood atop the black tower while the world burned around him. Behind, the seamless eastern plains were one enormous blaze that turned night to day, save for the swatches of pure black where everything living had been burned to cinder, the soil hiding beneath a deep layer of soot and ash. With no one remaining to try to douse the flames, only Mother Nature stood a chance of combating the surging fires, and she had yet to shed a single tear. What little remained of the buildings ringing his monolith smoldered, issuing tendrils of smoke into the clogged sky with the wretched ebon smoke that swirled around his head. The fire advanced only as far as the foot of the tower, dying in a circle around it as though even the inferno feared to reach into the wicked fortress, lending the impression from Death's vantage of a lake of molten fire from which only this lone construct of iron and concrete rose. But it wasn't the destruction hundreds of feet below him or its easterly migration that was the focus of his unwavering attention. It was the western horizon, marred by the jagged teeth of the Rocky Mountains that held him enrapt. The foothills glowed with the distant fires, which stretched all the way up the steep slopes to timberline. He had watched the progress of his minions by the wall of flames driven before them, which now spread to the north and south in their wake, fueled by a seemingly limitless supply of evergreens. They had crossed over the Front Range to the west, his children of bedlam, and were now firmly entrenched in the wilderness,

64

incinerating everything in their path. Soon, any creature caught in their advance of hellfire would be slaughtered or driven ahead, no longer to be of any potential help to his ultimate targets on the shores of the Great Salt Lake. He had rolled out a carpet of black death to guide them to him, and come they shall, but not on the backs of their flying steeds. No. Maybe those amphibious equines could escape the Leviathan's fire beneath the refuge of waves, but the time had come to implement his plan to remove them from the equation.

Pestilence and Famine emerged from the stairwell to the roof at his silent summons, assuming their positions at his either hand. Mosquitoes sang in anticipation from beneath Pestilence's parchment skin. They crawled eagerly out from between her lips, from her nostrils, from the corners of her eyes, and formed a writhing skein over her cloaked visage. Wriggling welts rose on Famine's ghostly face, contorting his features as though he were boiling. His sister's spindly, sharp-stingered familiars had drawn blood from every available life form, except one, while his locusts had mutated the genetic patterns of the corpses that remained.

Death turned from the burning mountains as the smoke finally shrouded them from view, and faced his brother and sister of the apocalypse. His glowing reptilian eyes morphed from gold to the color of blood, and a hiss slipped from behind his clenched teeth.

As one, Pestilence and Famine buckled backwards, spines arched inhumanly. Their feet rose from the ground and they began to convulse in midair. Mouths snapping open wide enough to dislocate their mandibles, both issued a screaming sound like steam from twin ruptured valves. Millions of insects fired into the air above them in swirling vortices, the high-pitched humming and buzzing so loud even the girders beneath vibrated. The insect-driven tornadoes spun faster and faster, pushing back the smoke until the chitinous bodies reached up into the stratosphere, their masters snapping like whips.

Death spread his claws and brought his arms out to either side. He craned his neck back to see into the roiling heart of the swarming bugs that appeared to bind his tower to the heavens. He released a hiss from his barrel chest and clapped his hands together in front of him with the sound of thunder. The twin funnels slammed together, and the whirling mass of mosquitoes collided with the locusts. Stingers pierced exoskeletons and brown spew filled the air, raining down onto the three horsemen. The hum and buzz of so many wings crackled like lightning, until the frenetic motion ceased, their diminutive bodies falling from the sky. Carcasses descended as hail, covering the roof and littering the street below.

Death knelt, even that slight movement eliciting the crunching of chitin. He scooped a handful of dead insects from the mat into his palm and stood again to inspect the carnage. The locusts still had their golden wings spread, unable to close with the mosquitoes clamped onto their backs, stingers buried into their thoraces. Neither species moved, their bodies drenched with the brown locus sludge that now dripped from between Death's fingers. He waited patiently, the smoke once again closing in around him now that there were no more wings to stir it. Tiny legs tickled his scales before he saw the first signs of change. The locusts swelled from within as though forming so many chrysalises, and the much smaller mosquitoes popped out and fell to the ground. The formerly brown and gold shells cracked and a pasty mess oozed out, the exoskeletons folding open like baked potatoes. An ochre fluid spilled out, revealing small bluish-green balls, which began to slowly fold open as an armadillo might. Long, slender wings peeled back and the elongated tails that had been wrapped around them unfurled to their full length. Six appendages, three to either side of the abdomen, reached out from where they'd been pinned. The film over their minuscule eyes slid away to reveal reflective black orbs. A subtle buzzing sound rose first from his hand, and then from everywhere around him.

One at a time, they rolled over to right themselves, leaving behind the refuse of their former shells. The wings shivered as though testing the new mechanics, but wasted no time in rising up into the air.

Death cast aside the remainder of the carcasses with a slap of fluids and studied the new breed that hovered right in front of his face, perfectly still and aloft in hummingbird fashion. They looked remarkably like dragonflies, but rather than straight abdominal segments, they were curled under like scorpion stingers in reverse, thrusting and stabbing with small hooked barbs. The night came to life with them, all hovering there with stabbing stingers in a demonic still life of a snowstorm.

His heavily-scaled lips drew wide in a reptilian mockery of a smile. He turned to face Famine and Pestilence, who were both covered from head to toe with a seething skin of these new arthropods as though trying to find their way back into their former homes. His brother and sister knew what he wanted them to do, so they raised their arms up to the black sky. The insects followed, flying upward into a swirling turquoise cyclone that constricted in upon itself before exploding outward. The churning smoke thinned at the behest of so many wings, and the swarming creatures flew away in every direction.

Death trod through the mess of carcasses to the edge of the roof and watched what were now so many dots vanish against the backdrop of the western horizon, blending in with the blue mountaintops. As soon as they were out of sight, the smoke closed in again.

Now all that remained was to wait for his prey to come to him. There were still preparations to be made, but soon…soon the last remaining human blood would soak into the scorched earth.

VII

MORMON TEARS

Mare arched his back to stretch the aching muscles, pressing on the points of pain to either side of his spine between his hips. Catching himself, he dropped his arms and stood straight. It was an exercise he had seen his father perform hundreds of times before, and the last thing in the world he wanted to remember right now was his old man. Even worse was the prospect of becoming like him, if only in such a superficial way. He was simply going to have to allow his weary body to ache.

They had just planted the final grave marker on the shore, but all that accomplished was creating a greater sense of unease. It wasn't the six marble guardians standing sentry over the mounded sand that so unnerved him, but rather the two at the very end that lorded over nothing, evenly spaced like all of the others as though biding their time until their eternal charges were finally entrusted to their care. None of them dared to speak of it. Everything they did seemed to have a secondary motive, so eight tombstones for six graves didn't surprise anyone, though no one wanted to know which of them would be laid to rest beneath the shadows of the open-armed Christ and the Holy Mother with the child cradled in her lap. None chose to ponder the significance of the choice of headstones.

"Where's Jill?" he asked the moment the revelation struck him. She had been out there with them when they had rushed to meet the truck, but now that he stopped to think about it, he hadn't seen her since.

"I...don't know," Adam said. He had dropped to the ground in sheer exhaustion. Evelyn sat beside him, holding his hand on her thigh, leaning her head against his shoulder. He couldn't remember the last time he had seen Jill either. He should have known. He was responsible for each and every one of them, if only to himself.

Mare could see his sister off in the cave, slumped against the rock wall with her face in her hands as though dozing. Ray and his shadow Jake were in there as well, sharing a bag of Cheetos. Phoenix had taken off his shoes and stood barefoot in the shallows, looking glassy-eyed to the east, which he had begun doing more and more frequently.

"Jill!" Mare shouted, drawing all eyes to him. Adam rose and stood beside him, scanning the beach beneath the starlight. "Jill!"

A distant voice, the words so small they blended with the wind, answered from the north.

"Thank God," Mare gasped. He struck off running up the beach, past Phoenix on his right and the cave to his left, shunting the pain in his back and shoulders. Oblivious to everything around him except the invisible spot in the darkness where he imagined Jill's voice had originated.

After what felt like an eternity of sprinting, his legs threatening to betray him and send him sprawling, he saw her shadowed form sitting on the sand. Her arms were wrapped around her legs and her chin rested on her knees. She acknowleded him with a wan smile before turning back to the lake and staring off toward the horizon. Starlight glimmered from the tears on her cheeks.

He wanted to be mad at her, wanted to make sure she knew how badly she had scared him, but instead, he sat down beside her, joining her in staring off toward the point where the black horizon met with the barely indistinguishable blue line of the lake. This was where he had found her that first morning at Mormon Tears, away from the others with April and Darren. He was certain that was of no small significance.

"Hi," he finally whispered.

She wiped her cheeks with the backs of her hands and looked at him, holding his gaze for a moment before leaning against his shoulder and turning back to the inland sea. They sat in silence, only the wind whispering along the stony eaves of the mountain. He had so many questions, but the last thing he needed was to drive the wedge further between them.

The others had gathered down the beach and were watching them to make sure everything was all right. Mare reassured them with a wave, though he was unsure if they could even see the gesture.

"I had another vision," Jill said, breaking the long silence.

Mare nodded and waited for her to continue, not wanting her to feel pressured.

"Everything was black. Burned. Ash filled the sky like snow. I was looking through some kind of doorway. You were there. Shouting words I couldn't hear over some sort of rumbling sound. Behind you there was…there was a black man. Not his skin color, but all of him…just black. And he was on fire. The flames weren't burning him, but growing from him. Does that make sense? Getting taller and taller as he approached. You turned back to face him and I heard myself scream. I…I…" Her words trailed into soft crying.

"It's okay," he whispered, wrapping his arm around her shoulder. "There's no rush."

"I don't…I don't want to lose you."

She turned her face toward him, but couldn't meet his gaze. He reached for her and gently raised her chin.

"I'm not going anywhere," he said. "You couldn't lose me if you tried."

He didn't know he was going to kiss her until their lips had already met. She didn't pull away. His fingers traced the line of her cheek, absorbing her tears. Her arms slid beneath his and wrapped around his back, his skin tingling wherever they touched. Her lips parted and the tip of his tongue grazed hers. The air around them became electric.

After a moment that was simultaneously too short and eternal, she drew away, yet their eyes lingered.

"I love you, Jill," he whispered.

She smiled, though the tears continued to flow.

"You swear?"

"Cross my heart."

"I love you, too," she said, pulling away from him and standing.

He didn't want her to leave, almost cried out for her not to.

She extended her hand toward him. He took it and looked up into her face. Even with her hair tangled by the wind and the dampness glistening on her face, she was breathtaking.

Jill guided him to his feet and turned not in the direction of the cave, but in the opposite direction entirely. There was a part of her that had succumbed to the visions her Goshute ancestor had shared. Maybe it had been her more recent vision of the flaming man coming for Mare and her, the promise of death in the air, which had stirred her emotionally. All she knew was that she loved him. Lord only knew what the future held. Maybe He had allowed her spotted glimpses of it, but the majority still clung to the shadows of uncertainty. Life held no guarantees; living was in the moment. Maybe her lot was to sacrifice her life to bring her unconceived child into the world. Maybe his was to die at the hands of the fiery black figure, but neither had yet come to pass. This was the here. The now. And the only thing that made any semblance of sense was that she loved him, and regardless of how hard she had been trying to push him away, he loved her too. And he would stay by her side until the end. Whatever and whenever that may be.

"Jill," he whispered, slowing and causing her to turn.

"Shhhh." She pulled him along with a soft tug and led him farther along the shoreline beneath the sparkling stars. Away from everyone else, where they could be alone. Where they could be together.

She thought she heard the distant cry of a lone white falcon, but saw nothing in the darkness.

And in the warm glow of the moon and the cool wind that prickled their bare flesh, they took full advantage of the moment as only young lovers could, and in doing so, reached into the vast unknown future.

VIII

All was still on the western coast of the Great Salt Lake. Deep within the mountain, bodies slumbered around a burning pyre of coal in the lone remaining hour before the first hint of the rising sun stained the eastern horizon. It was the sleep of the dead, the utter unconsciousness that only complete exhaustion could bring. The final gift bestowed upon them from above before the tribulations to come. Jill dozed in Mare's arms, her head rising and falling subtly on his chest, their breathing in time. Ray was bedded down in one of the new sleeping bags with Jake in the matching bag beside him, snoring faintly. Phoenix had been victimized by the sleep he was so lacking right there on the stone floor. Adam had draped a blanket over him on his way to bed in the first floor room of the pueblo that he and Evelyn shared, not for the sake of intimacy per se, but because neither were comfortable out in the open where every crackle of flame or drip of condensation from the cavern roof would wake them, yet at the same time, neither could abide the prospect of being alone in the dark. Even through their separate sleeping bags, Adam had curled up against Evelyn from behind, his arm draped over her shoulder. Only Missy slept apart from the others at the furthest reaches of the fire's light. She hadn't thought she would be able to sleep at all with the cacophonous thoughts screaming through her head, so she had chosen a location where she could stare up at the mural gracing the cavern wall in the flickering glow to distract her mind. In the end, it had done just that, but her dreams were haunted by the spectral image of Phoenix floating in the air with his arms out to either side and his feet atop one another, a blazing ball of light threatening to swallow him whole. It was a fitful sleep, but sleep nonetheless.

The hushed sounds of sleep carried from the cavern to the tunnel leading out to the beach and stretched into the darkness until they reached the point where the gentle breathing and snoring mutated into a hardly audible buzzing, which grew louder as the corridor filled with dim light and opened into the cave. The waxing moon shimmered on the cresting waves before what appeared to be a dark cloud eclipsed it. The wind changed directions with a sigh to blow ashore. The buzzing grew incrementally louder and the dark cloud that had absorbed the moon broke apart like television static. A teal-colored insect alighted on the outstretched palm of the marble savior, but it was only alone for a moment before a wall of its brethren rolled across the lake. Long, thin creatures covered the statues, conceding the momentary impression of seething blue life before darting back to the shoreline. They skimmed the water, hovered just out of reach of the waves, and curled their long abdomens under so that only the tips broke the surface. Bulbous knots rose from each thorax and followed the course of the bodies as though being squeezed through a tube. When the engorgements reached the end of the tails and dropped beneath the level of the lake, they swelled even more, causing the bugs to shake and buzz violently. As one, those swellings exploded through their vents, filling the water with wriggling larvae. No sooner had the last offspring dropped from their rears than the metamorphosed insects rose from the water and continued along their western migration.

The larvae swam into deeper water, growing in size until they were nearly an inch long, flagellating with long hooked tails and flat heads with suckers like leeches. Slumbering fowl that had been awakened by the obscene buzzing sat at attention, bobbing atop the waves with stiff legs pointed beneath, necks craned warily in preparation for startled flight, never expecting the assault to come from below. The sharp tails of the insects lanced through the tough skin and injected their toxins before they latched on with hooked teeth to suck out their hosts' poisoned blood. Wings beat the lake as the fowl tried to escape, but only managed to fly a dozen feet before splashing back down to float belly up like so many downy icebergs.

The larvae detached and wiggled away from the corpses, overwhelming schools of shimmering fish. Their scales parted like tissue paper for the stabbing stingers and carcasses surfaced in their wake. Still deeper they advanced, the light from the heavens no longer penetrating the black water. Formations of smooth stone rose from the silt, openings of shadow leading into cavernous dens where the herds of giant seahorses slept, long tails curled into spirals around trapped logs and reeds to tether them. Clear lids covered their eyes. Small transparent fins on their cheeks fanned the water. The submerged caves filled with flagellates before the first stinger pierced hide. All equine eyes snapped open at once, thrashing to get away as the larvae covered their bodies. Flailing with wings and legs, they barreled out of the caves and knifed toward the surface, but their efforts were in vain. By the time their momentum carried them into the waves, their lives were lost, leaving only corpses at the mercy of the currents. Heads hanging limply under the water, legs already beginning to stiffen. Their tails unfurled and crested the choppy water. The living skin of larvae wriggled free and splashed atop the lake like tadpoles in their hurry to fulfill their sole biological imperative before their life spans were complete. They were mayflies birthed to kill rather than reproduce, and soon they would join their victims and settle into the murky depths.

The moon still gazed down with indifference, for it would soon be chased away by the rising sun. It drove the tide toward the shore, its final nightly act of contrition. High tide would bring not the promise of renewal, but the aftermath of the silent siege.

Death.

CHAPTER 3

I

The western slope of the Rocky Mountains had become an inferno, the manifestation of hell on earth. Startled birds took to flight from their fiery nests, flaming feathers only keeping them aloft so long before depositing them atop the detritus, leaving them to hop away too slowly from the advancing flames. Straw-colored stags with golden antlers and tails bounded away from the encroaching wall of fire, darting through the smoke ahead of the does and fawns. They could only run so far before they would have to rest, only then to learn what it felt like to burn. The entire forest echoed with pained bleating and animal cries.

It was music to the ears of the creature that had once been Richard Robinson. Fire roared from its fathomless black form as it launched stream after stream of molten magma into the thickets and underbrush, its reserves inexhaustible. It reveled in the charnel scent of burning flesh, in the snap of boiling sap exploding through the bark, dropping the upper canopies to the ground to incinerate to ash. It forged a trail of fiery death, its flames continuing outward in all directions in an attempt to engulf the entire world.

The hairy beasts scampered ahead, invisible through the smothering smoke. Their roaring was deafening as they triangulated the smoldering ruins around them, making short work of the crying animals pinned beneath blazing branches or in their death throes as feathers and fur burned away to the scorched skin. Blood drained from their sharp teeth down blunted chins, patterning their hairy chests. Their hands were thick with crusted blood and soot, black gloves across which they slathered their tongues in the few moments when nothing screeched to be put out of its misery.

At the crest of a steep slope, the Leviathan paused to survey the great valley of pine forests and skeletal aspens. The sharpened peaks of the Sangre de Cristo Mountains rose ahead, already beginning to seek refuge under a cloud of smoke. Beyond was the home stretch that would guide them toward Utah, the thought spurring it forward with renewed vigor.

Its black arms stretched to its sides and its chest swelled. With a scream, it cocked its head back and sprayed a flume of liquid fire from its mouth out over the nothingness to spatter down upon the forest floor, laying its path before it. Multicolored animals flashed through the sparse meadows, trying to create distance between themselves and the inescapable fiery death stalking them. Flocks of birds erupted from the trees as fire rained into the upper canopy. A choir of tortured mammalian screams filled the valley.

The Leviathan reveled only momentarily in the symphony of death before sprinting down the slope, spraying flames in every direction. The Pack bellowed their awful roars, a sound like thunder in the space between mountains. Boulders broke loose and tumbled down the hillside, avalanches of rock that cracked even the sturdiest of trees in half and tore the remainder from the slanted ground by the roots.

Cleaving a path of destruction through the wilderness, they raced through the night with the hint of the rising sun at their backs staining the smoky world crimson, bearing the gift of their master's namesake for any living being that would stand in their way.

II

MORMON TEARS

Jill stood before the mural on the wall while the pueblo burned to her left. Smoke filled the cave, the churning clouds parting just enough to grant her the occasional glimpse of their chalk doppelgangers in the flickering glow. All of their faces had been replaced by black-eyed skulls. Red and gold flames rose from their bodies. Screams echoed in the closed chamber, but she couldn't bring herself to look for their origins as she knew full well to whom the voices belonged. She reached up to the wall and wiped away her own image. The wall beneath was black, as though scored by fire. There was an inhuman screech and she turned at the sound. A great white falcon perched atop the highest rooftop of the structure. The fire bent away from it as though the bird were contained within a glass bubble. It squalled again and Jill looked back at the wall where two words had been smeared through the soot. She heard herself scream. Flames crawled up her back and ignited her hair, and the words themselves turning to orange fire.

Leave now.

Jill awoke with a cry trapped in her throat. She was hyperventilating, unable to catch her breath. It had been a dream. Not one of her visions, but an actual nightmare. It just felt somehow...different. There wasn't the sense that she was being shown actual events as they would soon unfold, but rather a warning. Whether from her subconscious or something more...spiritual, she couldn't tell, but it shared a sense of urgency with her visions, an imperative she knew needed to be acted upon quickly. Maybe something had changed inside of her, something potentially…what? Hormonal? Was it possible that she had actually conceived? Could there be something, someone else dreaming…inside of her?

She flinched and nearly released her pent-up scream when a cold hand settled upon her shoulder, another closing over her mouth. Eyes wide, she spun to face her assailant, his diminutive form a shadow against the dwindling fire.

"Shh," Jake whispered. "We need to let the others sleep a little longer. They're going to need their strength."

He slowly removed his hand from her mouth and took a step back. The diminished flames reflected in reds on his damp cheeks. Jill looked at Mare, lying on his back on one of the unzipped sleeping bags, the covers they had shared bunched over his waist. He shuffled, dragged the blanket up to his chin, and rolled onto his side.

"Outside," Jake whispered, offering his hand.

Jill stood and took his small hand in hers. His fingers were like ice. They walked away from the fire and carefully up the stone stairs. She studied him from the corner of her eye, but he looked directly ahead, betraying nothing. Once they reached the tunnel and stepped from the weak firelight into the embrace of shadows, he finally spoke.

"I had a dream last night." His voice was so tiny it needed the reinforcement of his echo for Jill to understand. "One of those, you know, real dreams." He paused, the only sound the scuffing of their footfalls on stone. "There was a tall building, a skyscraper, but it was so black, so cold. Everything around it had been burned as far as I could see. And there was still a haze of smoke over everything." He bent with the curve in the tunnel and his voice faded, his tone and mannerisms almost as though he were still sleeping or in a trance. "There was a man clear up on top of the building. I couldn't really see him, but at the same time, I could. He was even blacker than the building, but his eyes were as red as stoplights. I couldn't look away from him. I tried, but I couldn't. He just…held me. Even from so far away I could feel him holding me. I couldn't even move. The ground was hot and hurt my feet, but I couldn't run away."

He stopped when they reached the point where the gray light of dawn stretched through the cave and into the rock corridor. Jill turned to face him. His lower lip quivered and there was snot on his upper. He was terrified.

"Is that when you woke up?" Jill asked, thankful for even this horrible distraction to spare her from thinking about her own nightmare.

"No," he whispered, looking past her into the mouth of the cave. "He said something, but I knew I shouldn't have been able to hear him from so far away. It was like he was standing right behind me and talking down to me, even though I could see him up there on the roof, so small on top of the building."

"What did he say?" Jill asked, rubbing at the hackles that had risen on her arms.

A shiver rippled through Jake's body as though merely trying to conjure the words was a physiological process.

"He said 'And the sea gave up the dead which were in it; and death and hell delivered up the dead which were in them.'"

Jill turned away from the terror in the boy's eyes, his hand falling from hers. Instead, she looked outside to where the sun twinkled on the distant waves. Even its golden light felt somehow cold and tainted by the fleeing night.

"He said that now we must come to him, that we would know the way if we followed the trail of blood."

Jill closed her eyes and willed her pounding heart to slow.

Leave now.

Her own dream was bad enough. She had hoped that as the day chased away the demons that haunted the darkness, so too would the urgency of her nightmare dissipate. Coupled with Jake's dream, however, the message was unmistakable, its insistence undeniable.

His frigid hand slithered into her grasp again, sending a shiver through her body. The tunnel felt suddenly constrictive.

Jill led him into the cave on trembling legs. Even the larger earthen maw felt like a mouth closing with them inside. The sooner they were out on the beach, breathing the fresh air, the better off they would be. Her stare locked on the vastness of the lake to fight the oppressive feeling of being asphyxiated in the mountain. She drew her first deep inhalation of—

Her mouth filled with the taste of death and her mind registered the putrescence. It was a smell she knew intimately, but had been trying desperately to repress. The scent was the same as the stale air that wafted out of the houses within which the dead rotted, that same gut-wrenching reek contained behind the closed windows of the sweltering cars where the black bodies slumped against the dashboard. It was more than death, beyond the simple act of the soul's departure. It was the stench of what remained, the deterioration of flesh at the behest of cellular rot, of liquefying meat dripping from bone.

Jake retched, triggering Jill to do the same.

Leave now.

Her gaze fell to the shoreline and she had to hurriedly look away. The image was already seared into her brain, though, and even as she slapped a hand over her mouth and nose and looked up into the bland sky, she could still see it. Bodies mounded on the foaming scarlet surf. Web-footed fowl pocked the beach, surrounded by fish bones with the gray skin and scales peeling away. Equine flanks stood out of the water like bloated islands. Brightly-colored birds speared long beaks into their festering wounds and draining fluids. More and more bodies tumbled to shore with each wave, carcasses rolling in and out with the tide.

Leave now!

"What's going on out here?" Mare asked through a yawn. He appeared to be having difficulty rubbing the last of the sleep from his eyes.

"It's time to go now," Jake whispered, risking a glance at the carnage.

And the sea gave up the dead which were in it; and death and hell delivered up the dead which were in them.

III

Phoenix sat alone in the darkness. All of the others were awake and outside on the beach, the fire dying to glowing embers in their absence. He just needed to be by himself for a little while, alone in his head with the multitude of thoughts bouncing around like so many rubber balls. None of them would hold still long enough for him to grasp them, offering only fleeting glimpses down the road ahead. He knew the time had come to abandon Mormon Tears and begin their journey eastward, a perilous trek that would lead them into the land of the dead along the Trail of Blood. It was a path that would bring them through the ebon heart of evil, and even should their fate be to succeed, not all of their tracks would be filled on the return trip. It was more than a feeling; it was a certainty. A spectral cloud of death hung over them like a fog and they all knew it. No one had questioned him about the extra pair of headstones they had placed on the beach. They were strong. They were survivors. But the knowledge of their impending demise would rob them of their remaining strength, and perhaps they wouldn't be able to do what needed to be done when the time finally arrived.

He didn't know if *he* would have the strength. There was so much to live for and he was only now beginning to experience it. He had friends and an honest-to-God family for the first time in his life. There was more than just the hope of escaping his darkened surroundings; there was hope for the future. He was in love, an emotion more powerful than any he had ever felt. More powerful than self-preservation, more motivating than fear. More pervasive than the biological urge to breathe. Missy was more important to him than even himself, and it physically pained him to know how much he intended to hurt her.

"Please grant me the strength," he whispered into the shadows, wiping the uncontrollable tears from his cheeks.

Right now, the others would be staring in terror at the masses of dead animals riddling the beach and trying to determine how to dispose of their carcasses. He knew, for he had heard the poor creatures dying during the night, their inhuman cries piercing his brain like nails driven through his cranium. There was nothing he could have done, though. His feeling of helplessness was matched only by the agony of their screams. He imagined Missy mourning each and every one of those dead animals, her raven-black hair shimmering under the fresh dawn. All thoughts inevitably led back to Missy. They always did. She had been his guiding light in the basement prisons he had endured, and even more so now that he was out in the world. He hated himself for the torture he inflicted upon her daily, for the wedge he had no choice but to drive deeper between them every time they spoke. He thought that by hurting her a little more each day it would save her from the awful pain at the end of the Trail of Blood, but she was stronger than he ever imagined. She loved him. Unconditionally. Each silent wound he inflicted was a lashing from a cat-o-nine-tails, yet she persevered, holding out hope that he wouldn't deliberately hurt her the following day, while he went out of his way to do just that.

"I'm so sorry," he sobbed, burying his face in his hands.

"What are you sorry for?" a small voice whispered from the top of the staircase leading down to the fire.

Even without being able to see her, he would have known her voice anywhere. He had been so wrapped up in his own thoughts that he hadn't sensed Missy entering the cavern.

Phoenix sniffed and tried to swipe the damp residue from his face even though he was sure she wouldn't be able to see it. A long moment of silence passed between them before Missy finally spoke.

"I saw you with Evelyn."

He waited for her to continue. He could hear the implication in her words, but the message eluded him.

"Do you love her?"

"Of course," Phoenix said softly. He heard her breath hitch at the confirmation of her fears.

"That's all I needed to know," Missy said, her voice tremulous. She rose from where she sat on the stone outcropping, a rockslide of pebbles cascading to the stone floor far beneath.

This was the perfect opportunity to drive her away, to make her hate him, but he couldn't bear the aura of pain that radiated from her. It was almost as though he could feel her heart breaking, and it made him want to throw himself into the hot coals. How evil was he to hurt her so? Before he knew he was going to say anything, his own voice echoed back at him from the cavern walls.

"Wait."

The sound of her tread stopped, but he could tell she hadn't turned around.

"Please," he whispered. "Don't go…"

"What do you want from me? Haven't you hurt me enough?"

Her words stabbed him like frozen knives. That had been exactly what he had been trying to do, but hearing it from her mouth was the most terrible thing he had ever endured.

He rose and walked toward the stairs, ascending quietly so he could hear her footsteps if she decided to run away, but she stayed where she was. Her breathing grew ragged, a reflection of the sorrow and tears. She was so strong, so amazing. When he reached her, he wanted nothing more than to take her hand and tell her how sorry he was, but he choked back his voice and instead said nothing.

"You should have told me," she said. "That would have been far better than seeing the two of you…together. Watching you give her that flower. I thought…" She caught a sob before it could wrench out of her chest. "I thought you were different. Special. But you aren't, are you? You're just like all the others. You only wanted to be with me until someone…prettier came along. Someone…smarter."

"Prettier?" he whispered. "You're the most beautiful girl I've ever seen."

"A lie. That's just a lie."

"No," he said, taking her by the hand, but she jerked hers away.

"I gave you everything I had. Everything I *am*. But it wasn't enough, was it?"

"It was more than I ever could have hoped for."

"And yet still it wasn't enough. Do you just want more than you can have? You had me. Heart and soul. You had me, and you went after Evelyn. Can't you see that she's in love with Adam?"

"Of course."

"Then what? You just couldn't stand the fact that she wanted him more than you?"

"My heart has no longing for Evelyn. I love her, but not like I love you."

"Don't. I saw you with her. Saw your face when you gave her that flower."

"It was more than just a flower. It was a gift—a very important gift—just for her. I...have a gift for each of you. A part of me. A small part of myself to bestow upon each of you."

"And what do you have for me? Heartache? Is that my gift?" Missy scoffed. "What did you give to Evelyn?"

Phoenix was silent for a moment.

"I...I gave her the gift of life," he finally said. "Your gift is far more special."

She turned to face him in the darkness. "Then why are you treating me like this? Why do you feel the need to push me away when all I've ever wanted is to be with you?"

"I don't want to hurt you."

"Too late for that now. It seems like that's all you want to do."

"It will be easier for you...later. If you hate me."

"Do you think that's how it works? Do you think love can just be turned off? Hurting me may make me sad and it may make me miserable, but love is unconditional. You of all people should know that."

"I've loved you since before we even met, since the only place I could visit you was in my dreams. It was you, the promise of you, that kept me going when all I knew was misery."

"So you think that by pushing me away, by trying to make me hate you, that you're saving me from a greater pain down the road? Are you telling me you're going to die? Well, I've got news for you. We're all going to die. Maybe sooner than later, but it's a fact of life. Wouldn't you rather be happy in whatever amount of time remains?"

"My happiness is nothing if it only brings you sorrow."

"Are you happy now?"

He paused. "No."

"Your unhappiness is bringing me the sorrow you're trying to spare me from. You know that?"

Phoenix was silent.

"Don't push me away when all I want is to be with you for however long it lasts."

This time her hand found his, the union of flesh sending a sensation of warmth through him. He could feel her breath on his face, the heat of her body close to his.

"Tell me the truth," she whispered. "Not what your head tells you, but what's in your heart. Tell me 'no' and I'll make this easy for you. I'll give you as much distance as you want. You'll be completely absolved of your fear of hurting me. All I want is the truth. Just answer this one simple question.

"Do you love me?"

"More than life itself," he whispered.

Their lips met in the darkness, the tears on their cheeks blending where they touched. After a magical moment, their mouths parted, but only by inches as their foreheads leaned against one another's.

"You can't get rid of me, no matter how hard you try," she whispered.

"That's never what I wanted."

He could feel the radiance of her smile.

"What's my gift?" she asked.

"Yours is the most special gift I can possibly give, the only thing I have of any value," he said. "I gave you my heart."

IV

"Jesus," Adam gasped, crouching as close to one of the equine corpses as he could stomach. As the tide had begun to recede, it had left the bloated mound of festering flesh three feet inland from the rolling surf, surrounded by all sorts of dead fish and fowl. From afar, the bodies had still looked intact, but upon closer inspection, they were anything but. The fish had been stripped of their scales, and huge meaty chunks had been stolen away. The mutated ducks still had all of their feathers, though their eyes were conspicuously absent of the orbs. Massive holes had been gouged between their skeletal legs anterior to the tail feathers, everything formerly within now missing, as though they'd been hollowed out in order to be stuffed like so many Thanksgiving turkeys. The seahorses were infinitely worse. Perhaps it was because they were larger and took longer to consume, or maybe the meat was more succulent, but their carcasses were still infested with the creatures that had felled them. At close range, Adam could see the little black holes in the tough hide, deep and circular, as though made by a drill. Blood no longer flowed from the wounds, but the pale flagellates wriggled out of one and burrowed into another, flexible knitting needles guided by unseen hands.

Adam recoiled from the stench. Last night's dinner fought to be free, but he choked it back and covered the lower portion of his face with his shirt. He leaned as close as he could without having to touch it, his eyes finding the horse's, its fluted snout buried in the sand. A large, leech-looking thing squirmed out from under the eyelid and across the eyeball. Sputtering something unintelligible, he stumbled away and fell to his rear. He rolled over and sucked at the relatively fresh air, finally pulling his shirt down.

He felt as though he were covered with those insects, like things were squirming all over his skin.

"Douse it," he finally said, looking at Mare, who stood back with the others, holding a reserve tank of gasoline in either hand. They had siphoned what they could from the semi without draining the tank too much, as it was plainly apparent that unless they wanted to leave on foot, the old truck was now their sole means of exodus.

"This isn't natural," Mare said, starting slowly toward the shoreline. "Nothing should be able to kill so many animals so quickly."

"The mosquitoes did," Ray said. His sense of smell was becoming far more acute in compensation for his loss of sight, forcing him to stand all the way back in the mouth of the cave. "But I don't believe those were natural either, were they?"

"It's a message," Phoenix said, emerging from the tunnel into the cave holding Missy's hand. Her eyes were still somewhat puffy from crying, but she'd managed to wipe away the last of her tears.

"I've got to admit," Mare said, uncapping the twin canisters, "it's got my attention."

"What's the message?" Evelyn asked, finally finding her voice. The entire landscape before her was shocking, terrifying on a truly fundamental level. A Hieronymus Bosch seascape of hell. She knew exactly what the message was. It was written all over each of their faces. She just needed someone else to vocalize it as the implications scared her to death.

"It's time to leave," Jake said. It seemed like all he was capable of saying. He stood apart from the others, arms wrapped around his chest as though he were cold, even with the sun now beginning to shine upon the beach, rising from the lake ahead.

Mare sloshed the gas onto the mess of bodies, drawing thin lines between them. There was no way they would have enough fuel to burn every last one. Not even close. The corpses dotted the shore as far to the north as he could see. To the south, they crashed over and over against the rocks, pounding the jagged stones and being ripped away before hammering them again. Gray flesh floated on the waves. It was more about the ceremony of their incineration than the actual elimination of their physical forms. At least there wouldn't be a rotting mat of corpses in front of their home to fill the cavern with such a delightful aroma. Even the toxic stench of chemical fumes was a vast improvement.

Adam walked to the edge of the fire pit that warmed the kelp. He had thrown the lid back and thrust one of the wooden poles into the dying coals. Pulling it out, he held up the glowing end, small flames rising from the embers, and headed back up the beach to the dead horse. He touched the torch to its haunches and watched the blue flames race across its body. The insects burrowing inside screeched for what seemed like forever before rising out of the burning meat, their little fiery bodies wriggling only so far before shriveling and turning black. Their screams died as the fire raced away to either side, eager to consume the massive amounts of dead creatures. Thick black smoke already hovered over the beach.

Mare tossed the empty containers back toward the cave and sidled up to Adam, who stared through the rising flames toward the distant horizon. Flocks of scavenger birds swirled overhead, an avian tornado, several of the brightly-hued birds crying out before folding their wings to their sides and plummeting to the beach, apparently having gorged themselves on more than just their fill of death, but those wicked leeches as well.

The western shore of the Great Salt Lake, Mormon Tears, their home, no longer felt as comfortable and inviting. Even when they were preparing for the Swarm to attack, it had still felt like this was where they were supposed to be. Now it was tainted, its sanctuary violated. It wasn't just the awful scent of the decomposing animals, slowly changing to the smell of barbecuing spoiled meat, or even the presence of so much death around them. They were magnets too close to a matching pole, the opposite force repelling them away.

"I'm not ready for this," Adam said, unable to mask the tremor in his voice. He needed to be strong, for all of them, but he felt like a lost child.

"Neither am I," Mare said, searching his mind for a quip to pry a smile out of Adam, but he was at a loss for words. "Neither am I."

Evelyn approached Adam and stood at his side, taking him by the hand and leaning her head on his shoulder.

"What do we do now?" she asked.

He sighed and shook his head, unable to tear his gaze from the rising sun.

"We start packing," he said.

Mare had to look away. Now it was official. Jill was still sitting in the mouth of the cave, staring off into space as she had been since he had first found her at the edge of the carnage. Ray sat down beside her and rested his hand on her shoulder, titling his face to the sun.

Ray inhaled the smoke and coughed it back out. He knew it was impossible, but he was certain he smelled pine sap and burning trees for the second time in such a short span.

Mare walked over and sat on the other side of Jill with his back against the stone wall.

"Do you see smoke way off in the distance?" Ray asked.

"The entire beach is on fire," Mare said, taking a moment to enjoy the last bit of rest he would have for quite a while.

"I mean way off on the horizon."

"No," Mare said, closing his eyes so as not to see the burning bodies, but they were still right there at the forefront of his mind, waiting for him in the darkness.

"You will," Ray said, the scent of forest fire slipping away. "Soon enough... You will."

V

Evelyn had migrated to the south, away from everyone else, balancing on a rock above her bed of kelp. The mess of aquatic animals that had washed ashore still burned, the skin and feathers now charcoal, the flames dwindling as they devoured the last of the flesh. Smoke drifted in her direction, the smell of roasting meat that by all means should have set her to salivating instead made her sick to her stomach. Or perhaps that was due to the vile stench of the corpses tangled in the overgrowth of kelp, a briny foam of dissociated flesh floating atop the water, turning the formerly blue lake gray. She could barely see the broad, olive-colored leaves through what now looked like slush. The snout of one of the enormous flying seahorses poked out of the lake like a snorkel, a lone hoof breaking the waves. It took all of her effort to look away from the hollow eye socket that appeared to be winking at her through the wavering plants.

Back to her left, the fire pit that had warmed the plants no longer issued smoke, the coals now exhausted. Out in the breakwaters, the four vents gave up the last of their heat.

The plants would live. Somehow she was sure of it, but she wasn't about to harvest any more of the kelp from water so obviously diseased. No amount of rinsing or boiling could cleanse them of the stain of death. Maybe it was only psychological, but she knew she wouldn't be able to bring any of it close to her mouth without seeing that equine eye winking at her, without smelling the burning meat or the underlying current of rotting black flesh beneath. At least they had harvested recently. There were easily several hundred leaves dried and wrapped back in the cavern, but how long could that possibly last? It didn't matter now. The time had come to make their journey to the east, as they had all known and feared that it would. They would have to abandon everything they had worked so hard to create, the only place where any of them had felt even remotely safe for as long as they could remember.

Why did they really have to leave anyway? She didn't see the logic in striking out to meet death halfway. Couldn't they just stay where they were and let the Reaper come to them? It was contradictory to her very nature. How could giving up the home field advantage possibly benefit them? Here they could rebuild the fortifications that had served them so well when the Swarm had attacked. They could live in that cavern forever, the way she saw it. Heading out into the unknown with nothing more than they could carry was suicide. And who even knew what they were up against? How many traps had been set in their path? She was tired of trusting visions, tired of blindly believing in the power they all ascribed to their dreams. Maybe it would be easier to believe if she were the one having the visions. Why couldn't she be given a sign?

Evelyn chuckled. A beach littered with corpses was probably as good a sign as she could hope for.

What it all boiled down to was fear. She was terrified. Scared of leaving, scared of staying. Scared of a supposedly powerful adversary they couldn't even pin a name or a face on. Phoenix had appeared so confident since the moment he had arrived at Mormon Tears, as though he could see into the future and somehow knew that everything was going to be fine. But now…now he appeared as frightened as any of them. Often more so. Now she prayed that he couldn't see the future, for if his disposition, the ever-present tremble in his eyes, was any indication, they were all going to die.

A chill rippled up her spine and into her arms, which she wrapped around her chest, rubbing her shoulders to chase away the sensation.

Looking upon her kelp, the culmination of her professional aspirations, the proof of her theory that the oceans could be saved by aquatic farming, she had to wonder if this would be the last time she saw the plants. She had invested so much of herself into them that to forsake them would be to leave a portion of herself behind.

Crouching, she reached out and touched a single leaf that stood from the water, a gesture that on some subconscious level was her way of saying goodbye. As soon as her fingertips grazed the kelp, the veins within the leaf began to glow a faint green, infused with life. She gasped and staggered backwards, driving her left leg down into the water and the sand beneath. The glow faded immediately, but she was sure that she had seen the leaf stiffen almost electrically. And had it…grown?

"We need to get going," Adam said from behind her, startling her. She barely caught herself before falling all the way into the lake.

She whirled and looked at him, her face stark white, eyes wide.

"What's wrong?" he asked.

"Nothing," she said, climbing out of the water and finding her balance on another rock, "I just…I don't know."

"Come here," Adam said, offering his hand. He helped her cross a pair of wet rocks and down onto the beach, all the while unable to look away from her shocking green eyes. Bringing her to him, he wrapped his arms around her. She was trembling, or maybe merely shivering. "Talk to me, Evelyn."

"Do we really have to leave?" she whispered into his ear.

"I don't think we have much of a choice."

"We can stay here."

"There's something out there that we have no choice but to face. Can't you feel it…pulling you?"

"Let it come to us then. We survived one attack. We can survive another."

He pulled back so that he could see her face. Her eyes glistened with tears, despite her best efforts to hold them at bay.

"I'm scared too," he whispered. "The prospect of striking out into who knows what terrifies me."

"Then stay here. With me. Just the two of us, if that's how it has to be. Let the others go do what they need to."

"They wouldn't stand a chance."

"What can the two of us do? How could we possibly make a difference?"

"We need to stand together…or fall together, if that's our lot." He offered a weak smile. "That's all we can do."

"I don't know what I'd do if anything happened to you."

"Then I guess you'll have to make sure that nothing does."

She was overwhelmed by a rush of emotions and kissed him. If nothing else, Adam would stay by her side. Through whatever may come, he would stay with her.

"I love you," she whispered, their mouths only just parted.

"I love you, too. And I will protect you with my life if I have to."

Together they turned to the north and held hands, slowly walking back toward the cave, preparing to take their first steps into the unknown.

VI

THE RUINS OF
DENVER,
COLORADO

Everything that could burn had now already done so. Ashes filled the air like the blizzard had not so long ago, choking the sky to the point that the sun was only a vague haze above. The ground appeared to move, a gray carpet at the will of the rising wind. Only charred bricks and warped girders remained, mounded where buildings had once stood. The courtyard in front of his obscene tower was a mockery of its former self. The stagnant water in the fountain had been vaporized, the statuary atop its descending waterfall lying in rubble in the collected ash. Nothing remained of the intricately-maintained shrubbery or the stretches of flowers planted so that something was always in bloom. The iron benches had collapsed in upon themselves, the wooden planks burnt to cinder. Streetlamps designed to look like the old gas lanterns from the eighteenth century were strewn across the plaza where they had fallen, the glass fused to the concrete. Even the asphalt of the streets surrounding the square had been turned to gravel, the boiling tar draining down into the clogged sewers.

Where once his view would have been blocked by office buildings and lofts, he now would be able to see clear to the western slope of the Rocky Mountains when the lingering smoke and ash finally settled. Those structures had crumbled into ruin, monuments of scorched brick and cinderblock to their once mighty existence. One such massive pile of rubble had drawn him from his chamber of bones, where he had been watching the progress of his minions through his mind's eye. This particular heap of devastation had summoned him. All of the other buildings had fallen in the opposite directions, leaving it as the focal point of the world around it.

Death's first thought had been to chuckle at the irony, but he knew there was far more to it than that. It was a message; of that there was no doubt. He had been plotting against the Lord for so long now that the element of danger had worn off, and he had begun to fancy himself untouchable. His apocalyptic duty was complete, yet still he remained, plotting not just the elimination of mankind, but the birth of a new world cast in his image. The deeper he became embroiled in implementing his plan and the longer he went without being struck down from above, the greater his confidence became. Maybe God couldn't smite him, or maybe He just wouldn't, but this message had been sent to let him know that his work hadn't gone unnoticed.

Death smiled, a serpentine grin filled with sharp, interlacing teeth. He would use God's message to send one of his own. And there would be no mistaking his point.

The wind shifted and blew a cloud of ash from the great pile of rubble. A single iron girder stood erect from the top. Eight feet tall and pointing straight to the heavens. Another, six feet long, was still riveted to it horizontally. In that fleeting moment, the sun parted the suffocating clouds and shone directly down upon it. The cross seemed to glow before the clouds closed in again, radiating golden rays as though imbued with celestial fire.

If that was the best the Lord could do, then He had already failed. Death was no more frightened than he was intimidated. His message would be far more direct when the time came.

Oh yes, when the time finally arrived, the golden gates would shake with the screams of the damned.

VII

MORMON TEARS

They all stood on the cliff inside the cavern, wondering why they were being forced to leave and if they would indeed ever see it again. The torches had been extinguished in favor of the battery-powered lanterns arranged beside the cold remains of the fire and along the face of the pueblo. The prospect of killing all of the lights had lent an air of finality that they all sought to avoid, like each had done in their own way before beginning their journey to Mormon Tears. Leaving the lights on may have been of metaphorical comfort, but should they return, it would be the welcomed comfort of home.

Everything deemed necessary had already been loaded into the semi-trailer, leaving enough room for a handful of them to ride beside. Each said their own private prayer that there would be enough gas in the tank to reach Salt Lake City, knowing that with the congestion of stalled cars on the roads, it wouldn't take them any farther anyway. There was no plan from there, though hopefully they would be able to formalize one before they made it that far. Phoenix insisted that the majority of their trek would be off-road, but that they would be able to accomplish a good measure by vehicle. Either way, they all battled through some amount of shock and fear as they said good-bye to their home and prepared to set out toward Lord only knew where to confront some faceless evil that would likely mean their deaths.

"Time to go," Adam said, unable to hide the quiver of doubt in his voice. Without another word, he turned and started down the tunnel to the outside world. One by one they followed, none wanting to speak for fear they would lose their own resolve and threaten the tenuous grip the others maintained on theirs.

Sunlight reached through the mouth of the cave and into the stone corridor, lighting the floor like a yellow carpet leading them onto the beach. The sun was well above the eastern horizon now, the day far too tranquil to even contemplate the dark task ahead. Waves shimmered as far as they could see, though none chose to look at the black carcasses rimming the shore. It was the most beautiful day any of them had seen in a long time, almost like God Himself had created it just for them.

Don't make us go. Please…don't make us go, Jill pleaded silently, but refused to give the words voice and instead squeezed Mare's hand. He offered her a weak smile in return, but was unable to make eye contact. Before, they had been running away from something bad in hopes of finding salvation at the mystical Mormon Tears, but now they were leaving sanctuary to do battle with a foe who promised only suffering. It was a nightmare from which neither could find a way to awaken.

But it wasn't a day for mourning or pity; it was a day of destiny.

They followed Adam over the slope and into the channel between the mountains where the semi waited. Ray tripped and fell but assured them he was okay with a pained smile and wave of his hand.

Mare released Jill's hand and climbed up onto the fender of the trailer, framed by the open doorway, and offered his hand to Jill to help her into the bed. As soon as she was safely aboard, he reached for his sister and assisted her as well. Phoenix climbed up on his own and stood beside Mare, staring through sad eyes over the rubble toward the faint blue glint of the landlocked sea.

Jake climbed through the passenger door and into the cab, clambering behind the seats into the cargo area behind and sat on a fold-out jump-seat. Ray eased up behind him and slid between the seats beside Jake, scooting a beat-up old toolbox out of the way so he could drop to his rear end, tucking his knees to his chest. Evelyn followed, plopping down in the passenger seat and tugging the seatbelt across her chest. She closed the door and looked straight ahead toward the salt flats. Adam was the last in after making a final cursory inspection of the vehicle to ensure that everyone was on board. He settled into the seat and slammed the door, the sound echoing with an air of finality like a gunshot. Latching his seatbelt in place, he cranked the key and the engine grumbled to life. The whole truck shuddered.

He looked at Evelyn with a nervous expression even his best efforts couldn't hide, and clasped the gearshift. Her hand settled atop his and she offered a pained smile.

"You ready to do this?" he asked as she brought her hand back to her lap. He eyed the needle of the gas gauge as it settled at just over a quarter tank.

"As ready as I'll ever be," she said, turning her attention back to the track of smooth stone and the vast expanse of white ahead. "Think we'll ever see this place again?"

Adam didn't immediately answer as he ground the stick forward to the tune of metallic protests. "Yeah," he said as the truck rolled forward, gaining momentum on the packed sand. "I think we will."

A cloud of dust rose from the rear wheels, swirling in the truck's wake. Jill took one last mental snapshot of the lake before it was swallowed by the dirty haze and scooted back away from the open door, looking for anything at all to grasp for leverage, but there was nothing except the scuffed aluminum floor and the smooth walls. Mare took her hand, and allowed her to rest her head on his shoulder. She was going to have to tell him sometime. While it may seem irrational, she was certain that they had conceived. There was nothing logical about the assumption. No palpable swelling of her belly or irrefutable sign from above. Just what? Intuition? Either way, soon enough she was going to have to tell him he was going to be a father. Not now, thought. Not yet. He had enough to worry about. They all did. She couldn't help but think of the words the preacher had said before they lowered her mother into her grave.

Yea, though I walk through the valley of the shadow of death.

That felt like exactly what they were preparing to do.

She closed her eyes and the vision her ancestral grandmother had sent her was right there. The child in her lap stared back up at her, filled with wonderment and life. Her daughter flashed the grin she inherited from her father, and Jill felt a warm, tingling sensation wash over her.

Would you sacrifice everything for the child? a voice whispered in the rush of air behind, as the truck sped away from their home.

"Yes," Jill whispered in response, the hint of a smile crossing her lips.

She was no longer afraid.

VIII

Missy fell asleep against him sometime after they reached the highway. Progress was slow, as it had been on their return trip from the city only the night before. Phoenix watched the stalled cars fall away behind them on the unending strip of asphalt as they wound through the automotive graveyard. He traced his fingertips over her forehead. She was so beautiful, even in sleep. He wished he could be inside her head so he could share her dreams, to make sure that they stayed as perfect as she was. After all, surely he endured enough nightmares for both of them. He knew where they were going. He had seen it clearly in his dreams and had felt the evil emanating from it before they had passed over the mountains on their way to Mormon Tears. The man—if indeed he could still be considered such—who waited for him there was just like him, only not. Phoenix couldn't pin down the idea well enough to even clarify it for himself. The man masquerading under the guise of Death had been chosen, like him, for the battle to come. They were two sides of the same coin; that much he understood, but there was more to it than that. They were the same. They were different. A confusing dichotomy of destiny, as though they both walked blindfolded on separate branches of the same path, the decision at the fork made for them, whether by fate or by God.

Phoenix pitied him, but most of all he feared him. Feared what was going to happen when they arrived. He was terrified that he wasn't going to have the strength to do what was necessary when the time came. His heart was his weakness, and in his heart were his feelings for Missy, feelings so strong that he would have to make the choice between her love and her life. And pain. His body positively trembled in anticipation of the sheer agony that he knew waited over the mountains. Dear God, the pain promised to be more than he could endure.

"What's wrong?" Missy asked, watching the single tear run down his cheek. He hadn't noticed her stirring.

"Nothing," he said, stroking her cheek. "Nothing at all."

She sat up and looked out the back of the trailer at the slalom of stalled cars, some still containing the black bodies of those who had died within. There were housing developments and buildings to the side of the road now, signifying the western edge of town.

"You're an awful liar," she said, looking back at him. He had already wiped the tears from his pink eyes and assumed the unreadable expression he always wore.

He smiled, took her hand, and held it tightly in his lap. "We all have a cross to bear," he said at last, leaning over and kissing her on the top of her head.

Missy knew that was the end of the conversation for now, but she wouldn't forget. She would make him open up sooner or later.

The semi weaved through the snarl of traffic, the unmoving cars growing closer and closer together, and worked its way through the right lane and onto the shoulder. The bed tilted downward as they ascended an off-ramp lined with billboards advertising everything from hotels where you could stay for as little as forty-nine dollars per night to a car dealership that had the largest selection in the west and refused to be undersold. They coasted to a halt at the top of the ramp, the right tires completely off the road to avoid the logjam of vehicles. The engine sputtered the last of the gasoline fumes and died.

"I guess that means we're here," Mare said, scooting to the edge of the trailer and hopping down to the ground. He reached back up and Jill slid down into his arms.

As Missy climbed down, she couldn't help but notice that Jill looked somehow different. Was she coming down with something? Her cheeks were flushed and her were eyes brighter, more radiant.

Adam walked around the side of the truck, stretching his arms over his head and arching the kinks out of his back. The others joined him from the opposite side and they all stood behind the open trailer, looking back to the west where they could only see the faint hint of blue water in the distance.

"So what now?" Missy asked.

"There are a bunch of car dealerships over there," Evelyn said, gesturing to the south. "I'll bet we can find some easier mode of transportation."

"Take only what you can carry," Adam said, climbing up into the trailer. He tossed down blankets stuffed with clothes and food, cinched off with lengths of rope. There was one for each of them, each serving the dual purpose of toting the necessities and providing the nighttime warmth they were sure to need along the way. He wished he had been blessed with the foresight to grab some actual hiking backpacks so they could bring sleeping bags and maybe even a tent, but there had been a part of him that fought the notion that they would indeed have to leave their sanctuary. They were fortunate to have what they did.

When he had tossed down the eighth and final satchel, he passed down the guns.

There were only five of them: four shotguns and a rifle. He hadn't counted them in his hurry to get out of the hotel. With all of the blood and the hideous mound of bones, he considered himself lucky to have even had the presence of mind to grab them at all. It would have to be enough. Jake was too young and small to be struggling with a twelve gauge, and with Ray being blind...That left five weapons for the remaining six, and seeing how, of the girls, only Evelyn and Missy had even fired one before, they would already be more heavily armed than he was truly comfortable with. At least the guns had been equipped with shoulder straps. That was about the only stroke of fate working in their favor.

Adam slung the rifle over his shoulder. He wasn't the world's greatest shot, but with so little experience, the others would want the wide pattern the shotguns provided to minimize the need for accuracy. If they needed it, and he definitely prayed they wouldn't.

He scooted the box with all of the shells and bullets to the edge of the bed and hopped down.

"Each of you stuff your pockets with as many of the red shells as you can fit," he said, filling the side pockets of his camouflaged cargo pants with the remaining half-case. There were only two boxes of shotgun shells, and one of them was already opened. It looked as though each of them maybe took seven or eight total. He didn't want to think about how few shots that gave them in a pinch, but if things truly got bad, they would be extremely lucky to be able to reload after spending the three shots in the chamber anyway.

Adam surveyed them as they stood there, packs slung over one shoulder, guns over the other. Missy had taken one of the shotguns, leaving Jill with only a bundle of goods. Jake struggled a little with his, shifting it from one side to the other, but Ray seemed to have adjusted nicely. They all looked back at him, waiting for him to give the word. It was a measure of power he didn't want, but one he had no choice but to reluctantly accept. He tried to think of something motivating like one of his squad leaders in the army might have said, but came up blank.

"Well…let's get this show on the road," he finally said, and with that turned and headed down the street, listening to their scuffing footsteps on the gravel shoulder as they fell in behind.

CHAPTER 4

I

There had been a Field and Ski shop past a couple car dealerships. With the Jet Skis and watercraft out front, they would have walked past it, were it not for the fact that Jill caught a reflected flash of chrome from behind the showroom. Adam had initially been looking for some sort of all-terrain vehicle small enough to weave through and around the eternal traffic jams, but had been surprised to learn that almost all of them knew how to ride motorcycles. In the enormous lot, past the showcases of speedboats and fishing trawlers, beyond the rows of four-wheeled ATVs, they found a small fleet of used motorcross cycles. They had obviously seen better days, with all of the scrapes and gouges through the paint, but the engines had come to life with a turn of the key, and that was all that really mattered.

Progress was slower than any of them would have liked, even though they were in no hurry to reach their destination, which was still a vague notion at best. Between Jake's dreams and Jill's visions, they were able to establish that what they were searching for was a giant black tower lording over total destruction. All Phoenix had been able to add was that it was on the far side on the mountains and that there would be no mistaking it when they saw it. It was maddening, speeding off toward who knew what in a monolithic structure none of them knew how to find. What were they supposed to do when they arrived? Just storm through the doors and start shooting? That seemed unlikely. They could all tell that Phoenix was holding something back from them, but no amount of coaxing could draw it from him. All would be apparent when the time came, he insisted.

God, Adam hoped that was true.

They traveled in a single file line along the shoulder of Highway 40, heading southeast into the foothills toward the rising blue peaks, mere hours ahead of the slowly setting sun. Adam rode in the lead, on a lime green motorcycle with a big number three on the front, trying to simultaneously navigate the cars and trucks crumpled in the roadway and askew across the shoulders without looking at the decomposing bodies within and constantly glancing over his shoulder to make sure the others were still close. He rode uncomfortably erect, thanks to the plastic gas tank strapped behind him on the seat with a pair of bungee cords, his bundled pack bound on top of it. Evelyn rode twenty feet behind him on a matching cycle, Jake clinging to her from behind. He leaned his head against her back so he could see off the road to the right, where cars spotted the slope leading down to wide, pine-rimmed meadows, his arms so tight around her waist that she thought her bladder might pop. There had barely been enough room behind him to tie down their bags, leaving Evelyn to maneuver with the shotgun across her chest. Mare followed in her wake with Ray holding on behind. Once upon a time, he had been an excellent rider, back when his mother had been alive and his father cared enough to take them into the hills to scream around the dirt tracks. He grinned as he slalomed around the cars, reveling in Ray's instinctive reaction of tightening his arms across his gut, knowing he should take things more carefully, but having too much fun to change his approach. Ray wore Mare's gun over his back, the metal pressing too hard against his spine with their packs roped down behind him. Missy tried to stay right on their tail, but her brother was incorrigible. Phoenix leaned against her from behind, his long dirty hair flagging on the breeze, both of their guns crossed on his back in a great black X, the stocks forming a wooden triangle in front of their bundled goods. Jill brought up the rear, struggling with only the reserve tank of gas and her pack, the weight causing her to fight for balance on the neon orange motorcycle, which wasn't nearly as nice or as easy to handle as the one on which she had crossed out of Oregon, which felt like a million years ago now.

The city proper faded behind them, the clustered buildings of downtown growing smaller and smaller. The homes to either side grew farther apart and fell back away from the road until even the suburbs became a memory as they climbed into the heavily forested hills. They would only be able to go so far before refueling, and even then there were only ten gallons between the two reserve tanks. Lord only knew when they would come across the next gas station with the mountains rising menacingly ahead. Though the thought remained unspoken, they all imagined there would be sections of highway where they could end up pushing the heavy bikes up the asphalt slopes and coasting down the other side.

Adam glanced one final time at the sun descending behind the rising mountains before the shadows swept over them. The road wound to the left, beginning its graceful ascent. The temperature dropped steadily in the darkening shade. The forest closed in on the four-lane highway, the shoulder shrinking as strange trees that once must have been pines and junipers reached toward them with alternately stiff and limp claws, hiding ominous black shadows beneath that moved like mist around the trunks. Creatures scampered through the thorny underbrush, darting from their peripheral vision, never holding still long enough to be clearly seen. Sharp-tipped weeds reminiscent of yuccas grew from the cracks in the road, and in some cases climbed up the sides of the dead cars in preparation of claiming them as their own.

Adam flicked on the single headlight to ward off the coming night, the weak stream barely diffusing into the darkness ahead. They would only be able to drive so much longer. He was exhausted, and his back felt like he'd been folded in half the wrong way. His legs positively ached from the constant vibration of the motor. His stomach cramped, a combination of the stress and hunger, and his bladder felt as swollen as a watermelon pressing against his pelvis. He could only imagine how the others must be feeling. They would need to take a break soon, maybe even set up camp long enough to get what little sleep they could manage before heading back out on the road. His gut told him they were going to need every last ounce of their strength.

The initial, though unspoken, plan had been to drive as far as they could before nightfall, but he hadn't anticipated losing several hours of useful daylight when the sun vanished prematurely behind the peaks.

He glanced back over his shoulder in time to see the string of headlights flash on, noticing that the gaps between riders had lengthened considerably. It looked as though Jill was now a quarter mile behind, forcing him to slow to keep the procession close enough together.

They couldn't afford to be driven past their limits. He had no idea what was in store around each coming bend. They needed to stay sharp, their reflexes honed to a razor edge. If they were sluggish at all, they would be too easily overwhelmed, and he would never be able to forgive himself if he allowed anything to happen to them for the sake of speed. The need to reach their destination had become paramount, but if they didn't heed caution, they might never arrive at all. The next good spot. As soon as they reached the next suitable breaking point, he would pull off the road and allow them a few minutes to recuperate. He knew better though. A bathroom break would turn into a meal break, and the next thing he knew it would be pitch black and they'd be dozing around the fire. But what other option did they have?

The highway wound through the mountains, a valley opening on the far side, the hillside growing steadily steeper directly beside them to the right. Every now and then he caught a glimpse of a river clear down at the bottom, wending through the black pines far below, just the occasional sparkle of the setting sun on racing waves. Higher they climbed, until finally the road leveled off at the summit of the first row of mountains. An off ramp veered to the right, leading to a leveled section of ground where the trees had been cleared away to make room for a large parking lot surrounding a small dark building, beside which an even smaller stone domicile had been erected.

Adam tapped the brakes to make his taillight flash and slowed, performing a quick count of the headlights behind him before riding up the ramp and heading off to the right into the large asphalt circle.

There were several cars in the diagonal parking places along the curb in front of a wide cement path leading up a short slope to the main building. A luxury sedan looked like it had been torn apart from the inside, the leather upholstery shredded, balls of glass covering the ground around it. A single parking space separated it from a white minivan filled with dark silhouettes straining against the seatbelts, wasting away. He couldn't bear to look inside. Some of those shadows were so small, their heads barely higher than the rear seat backs.

Giving the vehicles a wide berth, Adam rode up the handicapped ramp and onto the lawn, heading for the overhang off the side of the building, beneath which were several wooden picnic tables. He coasted up beside one and killed the engine to preserve what little gas remained and straightened the kickstand with his heel. By the time all of the others joined him, he was already off the bike, pacing with both hands to either side of his lumbar spine, trying to stretch out the sore muscles.

The motorcycles were louder than he had hoped they would be. Maybe it was the strange acoustics of the mountaintop, but it almost sounded like thunder. Knitting his brow, he walked away from the others toward the line of trees at the eastern edge of the rest stop. He looked back and saw that several of the cycles were already off. The ground, and even the air around him, vibrated, the thunder growing louder and louder. He heard distant screams beneath the rumble. Slowing, he cocked his head to the sky, his eyes never leaving the wall of mutated evergreens.

"Do you guys hear that?" Adam called without looking back.

The sound grew louder, drowning out any reply that may have been made.

A black cloud rose against the night, swelling over the treetops, which began to sway gently. The cloud swelled far too quickly, faster than any storm Adam had ever seen.

The screams grew shrill, piercing, but they weren't human. They sounded almost—

Dark shapes shredded through the trees, exploding outward, racing toward him.

Adam threw his hands over his head and dove to the ground. The air came to life around him with shrieking, a rush of air bettering him before the assault commenced.

II

"Adam!" Evelyn screamed, but he couldn't hear her. What was he doing out there anyway? It felt as though they were standing in the path of a tornado. "Adam!"

Evelyn ran toward him, but she barely made it several strides before the bank of trees exploded. Needles and branches fired from the thicket like shrapnel from a massive denotation. Tiny black shapes knifed through the greenery. Adam threw himself to the ground a heartbeat before Evelyn did the same, squeezing her eyes shut and screaming down into the grass. In her mind was a snapshot of the last thing she saw, the cloud tearing the forest to shreds, filling the air.

There were screams all around her, horrible shrieking noises that lanced her eardrums like needles. What felt like hands slapped at her body, claws grabbing handfuls of her hair and tugging frantically at the strands to break free. She swatted at one of the bodies, brushing smooth feathers. Something sharp stabbed the back of her hand several times in rapid succession before freeing itself from the tangles.

The rush of wind made her clothing billow and snap, granting something with terribly sharp claws and flapping wings access to her bare back, fighting and flailing until it exited from the bottom of her shirt. She rolled over and covered her face, hoping to keep the remainder of her hair from being torn out and her back from being shredded to ribbons. Daring to open her eyes, she found herself staring up into a massive deluge of birds, downy breasts knifing past right above her. Multicolored shapes, their hues subdued by the darkness, battled for position even within the cloud of their own ranks, beating each other with wings and slashing with claws and talons. Feathers rained down upon her. Evelyn struggled not to scream for fear of what might end up in her mouth.

The roaring wind went on for what seemed like forever while she slapped at the wingtips tapping at her and knocked the frenzied avians off of her. And then as quickly as they had descended upon her, they were gone. The shrill shrieking faded to the west like a freight train thundering through the valley, the dark cloud growing smaller against the night sky until it blended into it. Down fell from the heavens like snow.

It was a moment before Evelyn calmed her heartbeat enough to rise. There were stinging cuts all along her back. A dribble of blood followed the course of her spine. Dabbing at the scratches on her cheeks, she turned to face Adam, who was surveying the lawn around him. Insignificant mounds dotted the field, unmoving amidst the feathers settling on the mat of needles and branches. Several stragglers flew past overhead. Something with inordinately long wings honked like a goose while much smaller red and blue birds darted past.

"What in the name of God was that?" Adam gasped.

"I've never seen anything like it," Evelyn said, turning over dead birds with her toe. "I've never seen so many species flocking together. It's unnatural."

"Something must have really scared them."

"I'd hate to see whatever could do that."

Adam could only nod. He reached for her face and grazed his fingertips across her cheekbone. The scratches were swollen and irritated, but appeared purely superficial.

"I'm fine," she said, brushing away his hands. "I'm more concerned about why so many birds would be in such a hurry to get to the west. It's not a standard migration."

"I suppose we'll find out soon enough," Adam said.

He was right, she knew. Whatever had frightened those birds was undoubtedly positioned directly in their path. She recalled the faint scent of forest fire and thought of Jill's vision. A massive wildfire could certainly stir so many birds to flight, but she had a sinking sensation that it had been more than just an uncontrollable blaze. The true terror lurked beneath the smoke.

She shivered.

"Best rest while we can," Adam said, wrapping his arm around her waist and heading back toward where the others were still climbing out from beneath the picnic tables. "I don't care to speculate as to what we'll come across tomorrow."

Evelyn agreed. They were going to need their rest if they hoped to be sharp enough to face the coming day. Moving that fast, the birds could have been far ahead of the blaze, but she wasn't willing to stake her life on it.

She sidestepped a bird's breast, one long wing pointing up into the sky, its beak askew. The grass rose from the height of her ankles nearly to mid-shin before resuming its normal height. After a couple more steps she looked back and saw the patch of longer grass. It was bereft of the mess of needles and feathers like the rest of the area, as though something had shielded it from the barrage. As they walked farther away, she could tell that the patch had a distinct shape. Long appendages stretched away from a square torso with a single knob for a head.

She nearly gasped aloud.

The grass had grown long precisely where she'd been sprawled only moments prior.

III

A herd of what once had been elk thundered down the slope, slaloming between the tree trunks that grew at angles from the steep incline, roots reaching out from where the ground had eroded away from them like the appendages of so many octopi. The precariously balanced dirt and rocks gave way beneath their mighty hooves, and they slid only long enough to gain a moment's balance before launching themselves toward more solid footing. Golden antlers flashed in the moonlight, rich peach-colored fur leaving tracers against the night, marred by reflections from eyes as bright as stars. There was no time to slow. Behind them the angry ebon cloud of death filtered through the trees. They were going to have to stop at some point. They could only run so far.

There was a loud crack of breaking bone and one of the creatures tumbled headfirst down the hillside, antlers snapping off, shattered leg flopping uselessly. It bleated in pain before pounding a tree trunk with its flank to the tune of fracturing ribs. With a wretched whistle that sounded more like a scream, it called to the others, but they charged past, throwing up dust in their wake. Their instincts told them that the fallen stag was already as good as dead anyway, and it wasn't the first, nor would it be the last, to be abandoned in the panicked stampede.

At the bottom of the slant, they bounded through a wall of pines with needles so sharp they tore out clumps of fur, and into a broad meadow. Chest high grass grabbed at them, trying desperately to loop around their ankles, but they tore through, the fear driving them onward to the point of exhaustion and then beyond. The sky overhead became as bright as day beneath a blood-red sun before molten fire rained from above, spattering all over the field and the terrified creatures charging through it. The weeds caught fire immediately, billowing acrid smoke. An agonized choir of screams filled the night over the rising crackle of the blaze. The smell of burning fur was thick in the field. Flaming haunches bounced through the dense smoke toward the far edge of the meadow as more and more magma poured down from above.

Something roared behind them, a sound like the entire mountain cracking, and was answered by another somewhere in the valley to the right. Atop the crest of the cliff from which they had just fled, a dark human shadow fired rainbows of glowing flame high into the air, expanding before raining down all around them. The wall of smoke rolled down into the valley, a tide of impending asphyxiation washing across the meadow.

The herd crashed through the barrier of trees on the far side of the pasture, shredding underbrush and barreling headlong through thickets that slashed through their hides in bleeding arcs. Rodents squealed and chattered, scampering across the detritus toward holes and warrens that would prove too shallow. The upper canopy caught fire, smoldering needles and leaves dropping to the forest floor like so many lit matches. Liquid fire drained down through the bark, which channeled it to the roots and the kindling scattered around the trunks. The coarse hair that formed their hooves started to burn in peeling strands, the flames lapping up legs that were already ablaze with exertion.

Another bellowing roar…closer.

Flames swept up the rear haunches of the stragglers, churning bodies trailing slipstreams of fire, asteroids barreling through the forest before succumbing to the blistering heat and falling in stride, crumpling into the shrubbery to burn unimpeded. Those in the lead charged even faster, the thunder of their tread echoing from ahead, a sign they knew all too well. The forest peeled back, giving way to a barren slope that terminated abruptly. Beyond were distant hills sharpened by pines and the snow-capped peaks above timberline. The gap between was hazy with smoke. Stiffening their legs and digging into the ground with their hooves, they stopped at the edge of a tall limestone cliff, the ground more than a hundred feet below.

The lead stag snorted and pranced nervously. Its fur had been singed to a crisp black all the way from its right shoulder up its neck and along the side of its face. Its milky eye could only dribble tears into the blistered wound on its cheek. The fire behind glowed in its good eye, the trees becoming an abruption of flame. It took a single stride to the left, its movement answered by a roar like a sonic boom that filled the valley. A quick motion to the right and something large and hairy sprinted into view. The beast lowered its head and roared.

A black shape in the form of a man appeared to grow from the burning forest, passing through the flames unscathed.

The bull elk rose to its full height on its rear legs, kicking at the air in a show of intimidation that had nothing of the desired effect. The creatures stalking the herd only closed the gap.

Whirling, the elk charged away from the burning man, reaching the edge of the cliff and launching itself out over the valley below. The herd followed, shrieking as they hurtled into the nothingness and plummeted toward the ground.

The animal screams echoed from the face of the cliff, followed by the crashing of bodies through the waiting branches of the trees unable to slow their descent. Their bodies pounded the earth. Bones broke, tearing through hide. Organs were pulped, splashing through the rent flesh in explosions of blood. Some still struggled, trying to drag themselves into the thicket with jaggedly fractured limbs, shoving past broken and disemboweled carcasses through mud thickened by blood, their plight permanently terminated as molten fire splashed down upon them. Skin and fur crackled and burned, surrounded by pools of boiling blood.

A triumphant roar tore the night. Joined by another…and another, and another as a shroud of smoke settled over the burning world.

IV

HIGHWAY 40, UTAH

Phoenix stood apart from the others, arms wrapped around his chest for warmth, staring off into the darkness to the west. It wasn't particularly cold, yet his whole body shivered. He could feel his adversary out there, the bitter chill emanating from his dark fortress. Now that he understood what he was feeling, he supposed the sensation had been there all along. Maybe it had been dulled by distance on the shores of the Great Salt Lake, but it had been there nonetheless. He had first noticed it on the back of the motorcycle as they ascended into the mountains, a biting sensation of coldness he could easily blame on the wind and the coming nightfall, heralded by the shadow of the mountain that fell upon them when the sun set behind the peaks, but the feeling intensified with every mile they put behind them. The goose bumps had risen up his arms and into his shoulders, triggering his teeth to begin chattering. Even the buzzing engine beneath him no longer produced sufficient heat. It had been more than the cold, however. He felt somehow magnetized, as though his body were being drawn by some unseen force, urging him faster even than the bikes would go, always guiding him to the east like the needle of an off-kilter compass. He was becoming increasingly polarized, the force attracting his inner magnet growing stronger every minute. That was how it worked. He understood now. He was being drawn to the opposite pole by an irresistible force. Not just a separate, warring pole, but like a magnet, the opposite half of himself.

It was a startling revelation, though he knew he shouldn't have been surprised. It was the cosmic order of balance, not that he was the ultimate good and his doppelganger the epitome of evil. They were both tainted by the original sin of human flesh, by differing measures of love and hate, greed and generosity. Opposite sides of the same coin that together made a whole.

He should have realized from the start that this was never about them as a band of survivors, but about his adversary and him. Theirs was the battle that would determine the fate of mankind. He should never have even allowed the others to come. Maybe he wouldn't have made it to his destination alone, but their lives were worth more to him than his own, and he had willingly jeopardized them. Those who had saved him from his lifetime of imprisonment in so many cold, dark basements, who had welcomed him and given him a family for the first time in his entire life. Those who had loved him. And how did he repay them? By driving them like cattle to their deaths.

Pinching his eyes shut and grinding his teeth, he tried to force the visions to reveal themselves, to show him their destiny, but all that filled his mind was the frigid blackness that had been his whole world for so long. He knew that some of them would fall, but no more than that. He didn't know whether they would prevail in their mission or die along the way. Not knowing was the worst of all. He cocked his head and bit his lip contemplatively. Or maybe that just meant that the outcome had yet to be decided, that they controlled their own destiny. Maybe it wasn't too late to save his friends then. He was certain his own fate was sealed, and that of one more, but beyond that he had no idea if the rest lived or died. Maybe he had it within his power to save them. Maybe, just maybe, he could—

"Come back by the fire," Missy said, wrapping her arm around his waist and leaning her head on his shoulder. She followed his line of sight into the night, but couldn't see what held him enrapt. She had been watching him since he wandered off. He was receding into himself again, and there was nothing she could do about it.

He nodded and turned, allowing her to guide him back to where the others sat at a pair of picnic tables with the barbeque pit between them burning nearly a foot above the grate. As he approached, he looked from one face to the next, wondering which one of their deaths he would be unable to prevent, or if any of them would survive to bury those who didn't.

"Grab something to eat," Adam said between mouthfuls of kelp. "I think we should all try to get a couple hours of sleep before hitting the road again."

"I don't think I'll be able to sleep," Mare said. "Not after those birds. There was just something too creepy about the whole thing. I mean, I haven't seen a single bird since. Not one."

"It's like something scared them all at once," Jill said. "I can't even imagine what could possibly do that."

"Best not to think about it at all," Ray said. "No good can come of it."

"We have to be prepared for whatever is out there," Adam said. "So we *need* to think about it."

"It's the fires," Jill whispered, her eyes glazing over. "They're going to burn the entire world if they have to."

"Who?" Evelyn asked.

Jill could only shake her head.

"It doesn't matter," Ray said. Jake had fallen asleep across his lap while he unconsciously ran his fingers through the boy's hair. "Whatever it is, either we beat it or we die. There's no point in speculating."

"Thank you, Mr. Sunshine," Mare said, but the gravity of his words rang true with all of them, whether they wanted to hear it or not.

Phoenix took a pair of kelp leaves and paced while he ate, thanks to an overabundance of nervous energy. Missy finally had to sit down beside her brother, folding her arms on the table and resting her head on them. With her eyes closed and lips parted, she looked like he imagined an angel might. He wandered over to the side of the visitor's center where a map of the entire state of Utah was framed behind a cracked sheet of Plexiglas. A gold star had been placed beside the words "You Are Here" to mark their current location. It only showed a small sliver of western Colorado, but it still appeared as though they had a long way to go. He traced his finger along the line of the highway they had been traveling to the southeast, the route winding a little farther before straightening out. Several smaller lines intersected with the highway, identified by numbers that meant nothing to him. When his fingertip reached a dotted line, he paused and glanced at the legend at the bottom. A dotted line indicated a trail. When he looked back at the map, the trail was no longer a broken line, but a single rivulet of blood rolling down the glass from where he had sliced his fingertip on the crack.

"The Trail of Blood," he whispered, immediately recoiling and wiping his finger on his pants. That was where they needed to go. Of that, he had no doubt. And it looked as though they would definitely reach it during the coming day.

Everything was happening so fast now that he was scared that even if it was within him to save them all, he might miss the opportunity.

He headed back to the fire. Adam was trying to divvy the gas from the reserve tanks equally between the bikes, while several of the others had begun to doze off. Missy was snoring softly with her head still on the table, and Mare and Jill had climbed atop one of the adjacent tables, side by side beneath the blanket that had been carrying this evening's meal. Ray was now lying on his back on the bench with Jake atop him, running his hand across the boy's back, slower with each pass. Evelyn rested her head on her folded arms like Missy, but Phoenix could see her eyes were still open as she watched Adam.

He walked over to Adam and held the empty tanks in place so they could be strapped back to the seats.

"Our journey begins now," Phoenix said when the work was done.

Adam looked him in the eyes. "What aren't you telling me?"

"We're going to have to abandon the highway."

"Why?"

"There's a trail we're supposed to take. The Trail of Blood."

"I don't like the sound of that."

"Neither do I."

"Why's it called The Trail of Blood?"

"Because Death is at the end."

V

Jill awoke while the moon was still high overhead, the black sky riddled with stars, the sound of Mare's gentle exhalations beside her. He shuffled and rolled onto his side on the picnic table, flopping his arm over her chest. His features were so peaceful, his eyelids resting softly closed, the lines of stress on his forehead and the corners of his lips vanished. His formerly spiked hair no longer stood erect, as it was becoming too long. He was still just a kid. They both were. Surely it had been weeks since he shaved last, but he only had downy growth on his upper lip and chin. And he was going to be a father. They weren't ready to bring a life into the world together. Not even close. The worst part about it was that he didn't even know. Maybe she was waiting for the right place and the right time, but even then, she didn't know what she was supposed to say. How would he react? She imagined the look of horror on his face, his eyes widening and jaw dropping, the metamorphosis to confusion while he struggled to rationalize the life-altering fact. What if he freaked out? Worse still, what if he ran away? What if the shock caused him to no longer love her and their child, the daughter growing inside her?

She felt the heat of the tears on her cheeks and turned away for fear he might open his eyes and see them. What was wrong with her? She rode an emotional roller coaster and was too quick to cry. Sure, there were the wildly surging hormones, but they could only be blamed for so much. She felt as though there were an enormous weight on her chest.

Every so often, there seemed to be a powerful thought, a budding revelation that barged its way to the forefront of her mind, but she could never completely grasp it. It was like the key to some profound cosmic secret, and with it came such intense feelings of dread and fear that she could hardly breathe. The tears would flow and she would find herself on the verge of a panic attack, but she could never truly explain why, even to herself. In these hazy moments following waking, when dreams and the rational world swirled in an indistinguishable miasma, she was sure she could reach right out and grab the key, but she was never quite able. As soon as she was close, her multiple-great grandmother's words always forced their way through, a thought knife slashing through her gray matter.

"Would you sacrifice everything for the child?" she whispered.

The darkness converged from all sides, overwhelming her as though she'd plunged into a sea of oil.

Flames burned through the darkness. At first it felt like the same vision with smoke churning all around her, so dense it hurt her chest and made her cough, but even when it parted on the breeze, she couldn't see the trees around her. The ground beneath her was solid, not the spongy detritus of the last dream. No scent of boiling pine sap or burning wood, but something else altogether, almost the sulfurous reek of rotten eggs. A human shape composed of shadow appeared through the shifting smoke, running toward her through what appeared to be a ragged and uneven doorway.

"It's right behind me!" the shadow shouted, a voice she immediately recognized as Mare's. He pushed her back and grappled with something at the side of the doorway. A black sheet slid partially across the opening with a metallic scream of wrenching metal. He jerked at it, but it appeared to be stuck. "No! No! No!"

Mare turned and looked directly at her in the smoke-clogged darkness. There was a moment of hesitation before he pulled her to him in an embrace.

"Don't do this," she heard herself sob, tightening her fingers into his shirt and holding on with all of her strength.

"I love you," he said into her ear, the crackle of flames like evil laughter. "Make sure she knows how much her daddy loves her, too."

He tried to pull away, but she held him, her fingers knotted so tightly in the fabric of his shirt that they felt as though he would have to break them to free himself from their embrace. She wouldn't let him go. She couldn't. He pushed and struggled against her, but she held on with everything she had. Light flashed from his eyes and she saw the look of sheer terror on his face.

"You have to let me go, Jill!" he shouted. "Let me go!"

Another black figure appeared through the partially closed doorway, only flames rose from this one, long tendrils of fire reaching up into the sky from its shoulders and head.

"Now, Jill! Please!"

She heard her meek voice protest, though the words were jumbled by the fear and tears.

A fiery smile slashed the black face out there before the entire form became a living body of fire, exploding outward. Blinding light filled the doorway. Searing heat blasted her in the face, forcing her to close her eyes. The last thing she saw was Mare's hair catch fire, his mouth stretching into a soundless scream as gold and orange arms of fire wrapped around him. Her skin ignited, every nerve-ending simultaneously experiencing a level of pain like nothing she had ever imagined. She opened her mouth to scream, inviting the flames down her scalded throat and into her lungs, the tissue-like sacs hitching as they—

Jill saw the stars again and Mare's frightened eyes staring down at her. He still had his hair, and his formerly-blistering skin was again intact. She was flopping on her back, gasping for air. Red blossoms of oxygen deficit migrated across her vision, amoebae on the lab slide of the night.

"Give her space!" Adam said, shoving Mare away, but he only allowed himself to be pushed so far. Mare clung to her hand, the pressure binding her to reality. "You have to calm down, Jill. Focus on your breathing. Slow. Even. Deep breath in…blow it all the way out. Another deep breath in…"

The splotches faded from the stars and her breath caught with a gasp. She expelled it as a scream that echoed off into the silence.

"Are you all right?" Mare asked, nuzzling up to her cheek, his breath warm on her ear. She couldn't look at him for fear he would appear as he had in her vision.

"No," she whispered, closing her eyes. All she could see were flames.

Her own screams echoed inside her head. She squeezed his hand and reveled in the damp warmth of his cheek against hers.

Nothing would be all right ever again.

VI

The Ruins of Denver, Colorado

Death could feel him. Even though they were still separated by more than a hundred miles, Death could feel his presence like so many hookworms burrowing beneath his scales. The Lord's chosen, his diametric opposite, was coming to him, precisely as it was meant to be. They would face each other on the field of battle, in the ruins of the once great society that had spawned them both, with nothing less than the future of the world at stake. He would crush the boy and grind his bones to dust, leaving his disciples in a state of disarray, ripe for the slaughter. That was if they even made it this far, anyway. He couldn't overlook the fact that his minions were nearly upon them now, his perfect creatures who would set upon them with fire and savagery. He could almost smell their burning flesh, hear the snapping of powerful jaws tearing meat from bone, the resultant screams and pleas for mercy...

He closed his eyes, the filmy lids snapping shut over his glowing crimson orbs, and savored the moment. An image of his adversary flashed before him, granting a glimpse of what he was surprised and delighted to see was only a child. Long white hair whipping across a face covered with ribbons of blood. Head bucking back, his mouth a rictus of pain. Tears diluting the blood to a shade that matched his pink eyes. The chin finally dropping to his thin, pale chest. Still. Unmoving. The breeze blowing tangles of knotted hair over his face to clot with the blood.

A grin full of wickedly sharp teeth tore Death's face in half, and he finally allowed his eyes to open, spilling scarlet light like blood into the room, washing over the scattered piles of bones covering the floor. He leaned back in his throne of haphazardly assembled skeletons, that hellish monument to the fallen, and peeled apart the layers of shadows for those he knew were there. The tent of stretched skin enclosing the chamber resonated with the red glare. Hollow sockets plead with him from beyond the grave in crushed and battered skulls.

Pestilence and Famine stood to either side of the black doorway, backs against the wall. They were diminished now. With their insect swarms nearly depleted, they were little more than hollow shells, their life forces all but spent. He knew he was still going to need them though. With God conspiring against him, he was going to need every advantage he could get.

They answered his silent summons, crossing the room on bones that cracked and shattered beneath their tread with the sound of glass shards grinding to sand. Both reached the foot of the throne and knelt, one to either side of his legs, slid back the casques of their cloaks and lowered their heads. Famine's alabaster skull shone beneath Death's glare, while Pestilence's leathered flesh appeared far too tight, cracking like a dried pond beneath the desert sun. Only a handful of long black tufts of hair remained, scraggly and disheveled, as though savaged by disease.

Leaning forward again, Death spread his claws and placed his palms on the crowns of their heads. He pressed the sharp tips of his nails into the backs of their skulls, applying just enough pressure to pierce the skin and touch the bare bone beneath. Closing his eyes, he concentrated all of his senses. He felt the blood coursing thorough him and channeled it from his chest outward into his extremities, along his arms and through his wrists, until the power burned in his hands. Neither of them cried out, though smoke rose in tendrils from their scalps, the power building to a crescendo.

Death snapped his hands closed, his fingers breaking through bone and embedding themselves in gray matter. Pestilence and Famine bucked and thrashed against the invasion, eyes bulging outward from the pressure, mouths opening into soundless screams that produced only smoke. Their limbs went limp and they collapsed to the floor, yanking Death's fingers free. He opened his eyes and studied the twin heaps at his feet. Electrical currents flashed through their veins like lightning bolts, striking even across their open eyes. Had he not known better, he would have assumed them dead.

He was fatigued from the transfer of power, but he would recover. Their gifts were but a small fraction of the might he wielded. Rising, he raised his arms out to either side and drew his brother and sister into the air as though marionettes controlled by invisible strings. They hung in midair, limp forms betraying a level of unconsciousness a shade this side of the grave. Death lowered his hands and they started to twirl, slowly at first, then faster and faster until they were blurs of wind, human tornadoes. Their momentum slowly petered until they hovered in place again. Motionless. Though now their eyes were open, blood trailing from them in ochre tears.

Death sat in his throne and lowered them to the ground. They alighted silently on the calcified shards that had fractured beneath their knees and shredded the skin. A shift of Death's gaze dismissed them. They returned to the shadows to either side of the doorway, though now they didn't blend with the darkness, but stood apart from it, pulsating with their new power like beating black hearts. Soon he would send them out into the world to flex their newfound muscle, Pestilence with the ferocious diseases breeding unchecked within her, and Famine with cellular decay at his command.

All was in place now.

Death retreated into himself, wallowing in the anticipated screams of his prey that were soon to come and the ultimate victory they signified. God thundered His rage and assaulted the great black tower with hailstones, but they only added a counterpoint to the chorus of agony Death conducted in his mind.

VII

HIGHWAY 40,
UTAH

◉

None of them had been able to fall back asleep after Jill woke them with her shrill scream. Being roused in such a fashion sent a rush of adrenaline coursing through the body, and as such, all were wide awake. They needed to take advantage of the energy while it lasted. As it was, they were all accustomed to grabbing a few hours of sleep here and there when the opportunity presented itself, for who knew when their next chance might be. Maybe the last few days following the Swarm's siege had spoiled them, but it was easy enough to slip back into their old patterns. Besides, in the time it had taken Jill to recuperate from her vision, Adam had readied the motorcycles.

Ray rode behind Mare on his bike. The feeling of wrapping his arms around another guy and clinging to him from behind was unsettling. Not because of the inherent sexual connotations, for such thoughts had never crossed his mind, but because without his sight, a shift on the seat at the wrong moment, heading into a curve or preparing to skirt a stalled car, could kill them both. He knew it was hard for Mare to try to balance them both. All he could hope to do was stay low and follow Mare's subtle lead when he leaned to the right or left. He felt like an invalid, at the mercy of the generosity of the others, the cross they collectively bore. So long as they stayed on the cycles, the impact would be minimal, but what if they had to walk for any stretch? On a flat level road, he could place one foot in front of the other and keep from falling, but even then he knew he would impede their progress. And if they were forced to travel off-road, or even on a gravel drive, he would quickly become a liability. Repetition had taught him to traverse the paths from the cavern back home to the beach, but he had fallen more times than he cared to admit. Stumbling blindly down an unknown path would be next to impossible without someone at either shoulder to guide the placement of his steps and to keep him from tripping over every small stone and ambitious tree root that broke the surface. None of them would ever say so, but they would be better off without him. Ray wasn't so blind that he couldn't see that undeniable truth.

His sockets burned. They always did when his body wanted to cry, but he was denied the release.

He thought about Tina, and how he should have died with her. He should have been holding her hand when she passed. She shouldn't have been alone on the dirty floor of a truck stop bathroom. It should have been him. It should have been his head that bounded away from his body with an arterial fountain—

Enough. Enough self-pity. These were the cards that he'd been dealt, and he had to play his hand regardless. Mother Nature had a way of thinning the herd, besides. If he straggled or fell, he was certain there would be something waiting to make short work of him. Best not to tempt her though, he thought, a smile spreading his wind-chapped lips.

Spots formed from his darkened vision, not the slowly-migrating amoebae of a blow to the head, but stationary gray dots, almost like—

Ray's heartbeat accelerated and his breath lodged in his chest. He straightened his back and lifted his head so he could see over Mare's shoulder. An ill-defined black line divided his vision like the serrated edge of a buck knife, though not as sharp or evenly spaced. The tops of trees. Holy Mary Mother of God, they were treetops! And above... above were the muted gray pinpricks of stars. He was seeing the stars in the night sky. There was the handle of the Big Dipper. And Orion's belt. A larger one, the waxing moon. He was seeing them! Honest to God, he was actually seeing the—

"No, no, no!' he said, the images beginning to fade as though being swallowed by a black mist. The wind in his face tugged at his cheeks, his long bangs slapping his vacant sockets. The harder he raged against it, the faster the vision faded until again he was alone in the smothering darkness in his head. He wanted to punch something, pound his fists and stomp his feet in frustration. Instead, he settled for screaming at the top of his lungs.

The bike wobbled and he squeezed Mare's gut.

"What's wrong?" Mare shouted over his shoulder. His whole body tensed as he fought to straighten the tires on the gravel shoulder.

"Nothing," Ray said, leaning forward to speak into Mare's ear. "I must have been clipped by a rock from the bike ahead."

It was an improbable lie, he knew. With Mare's body as a shield, he stood little chance of being struck by anything, but Mare seemed pacified, or more likely, content not to press the issue.

Ray relaxed his grasp around Mare, and again lowered his head. There was no denying what he had seen. Perhaps he had been able to rationalize the ambiguous shape of the fire back in the cavern, but this was different. He had seen constellations with unerring clarity. Granted, they were familiar patterns, but not to the extent that he could recreate them in his mind. There was no doubt that he had seen them, but what did that mean? If he had truly envisioned them, then why could he not see them now? Why had they disappeared when he focused on them?

There had to be some logic to it. He had to think about the instances when he had actually seen. Surely there was some sort of pattern. The first time had been when Jake had taken him gently by the head, the second in the hazy moments following waking. He had seen the outline of the boxes and blankets when he fell in the cave, and now he had seen the stars. Tonight, he had been lost in thought and hadn't noticed the sights until they were already there, surprising him as though he had been unconscious and had only awakened with the constellations. Maybe...maybe there was a thread he could grasp. The first night he attributed to Jake, but could it have been the relaxing effect of the small cold hands on his temples? The second instance was in a state just this side of a dream. When he fell, surely all conscious thought had been thrust aside in the weightless moment before impact, and now, tonight, he had been zoned out, perhaps still fuzzy from the short nap and the droning of the motor. He tugged at the thread, unraveling it the slightest bit more. Relaxation. Dream state. Weightlessness. Zoned out. They were four sides of the same square. Each time the vision had faded when his rational mind asserted itself to try to make sense of the impossibility of being able to see without eyes, and focused too intently on what he was seeing.

The motorcycle shivered between his legs and the wind abated. Mare leaned slightly to the right, the ground sloping away beneath them. He sat more erect, noticeably relaxing, as the bike slowed and finally came to a halt. The putter of the engine echoed tinnily, as though from an overhead metal awning, before Mare abruptly silenced it.

Ray climbed off and heard Mare snap down the kickstand.

Someone yawned noisily over the sound of the other motors shutting off. He heard the clatter of metal on metal, a gas nozzle being removed from a car's tank. The cranking of a metal cap being opened. Then another. He walked away to stretch his legs, absorbed by his thoughts, and banged his knee into the fender of the car parked at the pump. The driver, whose stink was unmistakable, must have been overwhelmed by the mosquitoes mid-fill.

"Why don't you see if there's something to drink in there," Adam said.

"Any requests?" Evelyn asked.

"Anything liquid."

Ray needed space. Their voices were distracting. He was sure he was on the cusp of the revelation he sought and needed to follow the progression of his thoughts before they dissipated like the stars. He wandered away in a straight line until their voices remained, but their words were indistinguishable.

Warmth caressed his face, the rising sun chasing away the chill of night and the unseen denizens of the dark. He tilted his face toward the source, breathed out a long sigh, and tried to relax his body and force the deluge of seemingly unanswerable questions from his mind. Just feel the warmth, smell the sappy scent of pines. Ray paid no mind to the subtle scent of burning wood. He existed only in the here and now, where the golden celestial being kissed his face and the wind stood back in awe of its magnificence.

Ray smiled as the ominous darkness peeled back in his mind. The ragged skyline stretched before him, against which the treetops swayed gently. A gray aura diffused into the sky above, in the center of which bloomed a stark white corona above the leading crescent of the rising sun.

He breathed it all in, reveling in every moment. The secret had been unlocked, but he couldn't ponder that now, couldn't stand the prospect of analyzing it away. He simply needed to enjoy it, even if it only lasted for a moment.

Ray savored the sun, in awe of its majesty. No thoughts. No sounds. Only that divine orb rising gracefully over the forest to the east.

"Hey, Ray!" Mare called. "You coming or what?"

"Just a minute," Ray said, taking a mental snapshot that he carried back with him to where the others were already beside their freshly-fueled motorcycles, waiting for him.

VIII

Phoenix didn't know precisely what he was looking for, but he was certain he would know it when he saw it. It wouldn't be clearly marked with a big neon sign, but at the same time, he was sure there would be no mistaking the Trail of Blood. The name lent false expectations. There was no way that there could literally be a path lined with blood. He imagined a dark opening between overgrown trees, shielding it like teeth around a mouth, a cold breath blowing from it, carrying the reek of death. Maybe there would be a marker along the side of the highway announcing it, some scenic detour, possibly with some sort of historical significance, or perhaps it was an unkempt stretch that had once been a railway, the tracks removed, leaving only the occasional rusted spike or rotted railroad tie. He hated to speculate as the Blizzard of Souls had been precisely that and he feared the trail they were looking for would soon be laid not just with blood, but *their* blood.

The thought sent a shiver through his body, forcing him to cling more tightly to Missy, his chest merging with her back.

Asphalt glimmered with the reflected rays of the rising sun, leading them through the mountains. A river had joined them to the left of the highway, wending its way from the Continental Divide to the awaiting Pacific. Its banks were swollen to the point that at times it threatened to spill out onto the road. It ran thick with debris that snarled into impromptu dams against the otherwise hidden boulders. The runoff from the absurd snowstorm had eroded ditches into the hillsides, channeling the water through the dirt and granite at the expense of the uprooted trees. The river flowed so cold it was palpable even from a distance. Shadows from the chiseled cliff to their right alternately hid the road and then revealed it, a cat and mouse game between light and darkness.

He didn't know how far they had come any more than he knew how much farther they had to go, only that he could feel the beating black heart at the core of their destination, the magnetic pull becoming more irresistible with each passing mile. He could feel his adversary's strength swelling like storm clouds on the horizon, already emanating a level of power greater than he had even imagined. And it terrified him. They would be no match for the evil master he was already beginning to think of as omnipotent. They were only children, after all! Jake couldn't even lift one of the shotguns, let alone use it. Besides, he didn't think the weapons would do them much good against an entity that he was sure wielded the power of a god.

Peering over Missy's shoulder, her hair snapping against his face, he watched a bend approaching. Adam disappeared around it first, followed by Mare and Ray. It appeared as though the asphalt simply terminated at the bank of the river, like they could fire through the guardrails and launch out over the racing waves, and then they too were bending to the right and heading into a straightaway. The mountains formed a great valley around the road, the foothills ahead obscured by what at first looked to be fog, but the color was all wrong. It was too dark, too thick. It was then that the wind assaulted him with the myriad scents of forest fire.

"Oh, God," he gasped.

The smoke reached from one side of the sky to the other, filling the entire horizon. The sun had risen above it, casting eerie slanted rays into the back mass, which almost appeared to be another range of mountains atop the first, yet the most unsettling sight of all was the hideous orange–red glow at the base of the clouds. Something stung his eye and he blinked furiously. He opened it again to see the first smattering of ash in the air like snowflakes leading a storm.

Adam slowed in the lead, causing them all to do the same. They crossed a bridge over the river, which now paralleled them to the right where flumes of water cascaded down the eroded rock wall. The forest encroached incrementally from the left now, as though trying to sneak up on them, bringing with it the shadows lurking beneath the lower canopy and slithering around the trunks.

The closer they came to the fire, the larger it appeared, the flames rising above age-old trees that themselves had to be more than fifty feet tall.

They're in there, Phoenix thought. *They're somewhere in the fire.*

The idea frightened him. It had originated in his subconscious and crept to the forefront of his mind as if spoken by someone else entirely. He didn't know who *they* were, but the goose bumps had risen painfully to erection on his shoulders. Closing his eyes, he at first saw only darkness. Flashes of flames. Snapping teeth attached by strands of saliva. Eyes burning with fire. Screams. His eyes snapped open, his heart jack-hammering. He was panting. *Dear God, what kind of monsters are out there?*

An impregnable wall of sharp-coned trees made a play for the road, which bent away and skirted them, rounding a gentle curve out of the sun's reach and into the cool shade. Phoenix saw a flash of red, and then another. Tires screeched on asphalt and it looked for a second like Adam was going to lay the bike down, but he managed to stop just in time. Missy had a heartbeat longer to brake. Phoenix grabbed her far too hard and slammed into her from behind, but managed to relax as they coasted to a halt beside Adam, who squinted as he stared down the road ahead.

The engine rumbled beneath Phoenix. It felt as though the ground were shaking as well.

"What in the hell is that?" Adam gasped.

At first Phoenix didn't see what Adam was talking about. All he saw were rich shadows eclipsing the highway. There was a sedan set askew across the road, the bumper crumpled against the guardrail lining the river.

Something leapt up onto the hood with the sound of crumpling metal, and then was gone, a black shape knifing through the shade. Then another.

Crashing sounds from the forest.

Another black form exploded from the foliage, blowing across the road.

Phoenix looked at the river, which was now down a short incline and had moved away from the road, making room for a thin path.

Nothing.

He was just about to turn back to the forest when an enormous animal thundered up the slope and bounded over the guardrail. Its golden antlers flashed past, sparks rising from its hooves as they struck the pavement. Its flank was scorched black, its hair burned away all the way up to its face. Two more followed its lead, both smaller but no less burned. Movement caught Phoenix's eye and he turned to look down the road.

A stampede of animals thundered their way. Herded together were prey and predator alike. A massive hairy thing like a bear bred to a wolf loped awkwardly on a moving carpet of cream-colored ground squirrels that fell quickly behind. Scarlet canines with glowing eyes darted in and out of waves of maroon creatures that were all ears and hopped like rabbits. What had once been deer bounded through their midst, trampling anything unlucky enough to be under hoof.

They all blew past so fast that Phoenix couldn't get a good look at any of them. Other than their eyes, which all reflected a matching terror. Bodies flew by to either side, banging into them as though none of them even noticed the riders or their mechanical steeds.

Blood seeped from savage burns. Carcasses that looked cooked somehow shambled down the road, losing ground to their brethren. One deer fell mid-stride, dead before it hit the ground. Its hide tore as though made of tissue paper, spilling blood across the road.

And as quickly as it had started, the stampede ceased.

"Jesus," Mare said, the rumble of the animals' panicked flight fading. Silence descended upon them again.

They sat on their bikes, side by side in a row, staring eastward down the interstate. None of them knew what to say. Only the idling motorcycles and the graceful sound of mechanized thunder over the grumbling river provided some meek attachment to reality. Random carcasses littered the roadway, tufts of fur jostling on the breeze to reveal the scorched flesh beneath. Spatters of black blood marred the asphalt, a hellish mockery of the white dashes between lanes.

Without a word, Adam raised his feet and started forward, slowly, weaving in and out of the maze of corpses. The others followed, more out of fear than curiosity. Each felt somehow dissociated from the world around them, advancing by a will other than their own. Adam reached the car first, a Saturn with its hood and roof buckled awkwardly, the front windshield a spider web of glass preparing to shatter onto the dashboard. Each gave it only a cursory glance, unnerved by the thin lines of blood draining through the metal folds and puddling in the dents, before turning to the side of the road and the opening in the forest from which all of the creatures had appeared.

The gravel shoulder had been widened to accommodate parking for a handful of vehicles, cordoned off from the nature preserve beyond by a split-rail fence. There was a gap in the barrier at the mouth of a trail. Fast-food bags and aluminum cans, artifacts of a dead civilization, were scattered around an overturned Dumpster. Adam led them down the gentle decline to the edge of the fence, which upon closer inspection was capped with tufts of hair town away from the fleeing animals. The path led away from the road before veering to the right around a stand of trees.

The dirt trail was muddy with blood. Clumps of fur dotted the passage.

"The Trail of Blood," Phoenix said. "This is where we're supposed to go."

CHAPTER 5

I

THE TRAIL OF
BLOOD

They rode single file, the highway now
a distant memory. Progress was markedly
slower, but they had all known better than
to argue with Phoenix when he insisted that
their destinies were down the bloody trail.
Like everything else that had transpired since
the end of the world as they knew it, the
appearance of the path had defied coincidence,
and they had all felt the undeniable pull of a
force greater than themselves. It was easier
to try not to think about it and acquiesce
to what they had begun to think of as the
inevitable. It may not have been the most
comforting approach, but none could dispute
that it had served them well enough so far.

The trail had led away from the highway to
an overgrown dirt lane. It was wider than the
former railroad line Missy had at first assumed
it to be. Maybe it was some old wagon pass,
something like the Oregon Trail. She wished
she'd paid closer attention in history class.
Perhaps then she'd have some idea where
they were headed. There had been a sign on
its face by the trailhead, but none of them had
wanted to climb off their bikes to exhume it
from the putrid mud. Not that it would have

made much difference anyway, but at least she wouldn't have to keep referring to it as the Trail of Blood in her mind.

Twin tracks of dirt remained to either side of a wide stretch of wild grasses that had to be more than waist-high, separated from the rest of their species by the nearly invisible tracks upon which they rode. Massive trees encroached upon their path, but only the occasional sapling rose from it. Their course followed the topography, bending around the hills. Though they could feel the pressure of their ascent in altitude, the road always seemed level enough, leading them through valleys where small streams wound like serpents through grassy meadows before giving way to steep, pine-laden slopes.

The trail was no longer paved with a continuous sheet of blood, but rather dotted with it here and there, crumpled mats of weeds crusted with it. They still encountered sporadic carcasses, the burns becoming increasingly severe with each body they passed. Some were merely unrecognizable charred skeletons that had somehow managed to remain animate for such a long journey. She could only imagine how much pain they must have been in. It physically hurt her to even ponder it.

Flurries of gray ash rained down upon them when the wind gusted. Her lungs already ached. The air grew warmer the higher they climbed, sweat forming on her belly, where Phoenix's arms crossed. Smoke clung to the tops of the trees at the crest of the mountain ahead, though she couldn't see any flames yet. Clouds of it drifted overhead in dark clumps, bringing with them the acrid scent that overwhelmed even the sweet fragrance of the purple flowers blooming from the thorny weeds peeking out of the tall golden grass. She knew it wouldn't be long before the path climbed up into the wall of smoke, which hung over them like an avalanche poised to break free and crash down.

Missy tried to think of the fires as natural, perhaps started by an errant lightning strike, which without teams of firefighters to contain them, continued to burn unchecked. She knew better, however. Something—and she hesitated to speculate as to what—was setting the blazes intentionally and that something or somethings were working their way to the west even as they headed east, their paths soon to intersect.

She thought of Jill's vision of shadows darting behind the cover of the smoke while flames surrounded them, and almost screamed. It was more than her mind could take.

Force it down, she thought. *Don't think about it. Don't think about anything. Just watch the road. Don't even look at the sky.* But the ashes fluttering around her and the stench of scorched earth refused to allow it.

Phoenix must have felt her body tense. He leaned over her shoulder and spoke into her ear so she could hear him.

"I won't let anyone hurt you." His breath on her ear had an immediate soothing effect.

She tilted her head to the side to feel his cheek against hers as long as she could before again focusing on the path. The layer of smoke above was now so low she thought if she reached up she would be able to touch it. Flickers of light appeared between the tightly-packed trunks atop the mountain, a prelude to the blaze they would soon encounter, stimulating the overwhelming urge to steal her hand from the handlebars to cling to the shotgun hanging by the strap across her chest. What would she do if she had to use it? She hadn't pulled a trigger in at least five years, since the last time her father had taken them out to shoot cans and bottles off the fence posts in the field by the dump. The prospect terrified her.

Every fiber of her being screamed for her to turn around and head back to Mormon Tears, maybe just keep on driving until they reached the Pacific. Running away was fine with her. They could just keep running for the rest of their lives as far as she was concerned. Commandeer a boat and spend some time in the Hawaiian Islands. See Japan. There was an enormous world out there, brimming with places they could hide.

The first genuine flames appeared at the edge of the tree line, racing out into the meadow.

Oh my God. Oh my God. Oh. My. God.

Phoenix adjusted his grip and she nearly shed her skin.

Adam must have seen the flames as well. He flashed his brake light, pulled off into the high weeds beside the path, and waited for them all to circle around him. He looked directly at Phoenix when he finally spoke.

"What now?"

Phoenix's gaze shot up the hill to where another streak of fire spread out from the trees. A tuft of smoke swirled between them.

"We continue forward," Phoenix said. They could now hear the crackle of burning timber. "Into the fire."

A distant grumble that sounded like thunder echoed from the valley ahead.

II

The beast crashed through the underbrush,
slashing through burning branches, filling
the air with a cloud of hot embers. Its wiry
hairs had long since been singed back to its
scorched leather hide, its wild mane now
black nubs of flame. Body covered in a paste
of soot, sweat, and blood, it carved through
everything in its way, its black palms covered
with weeping blisters, but it felt no pain. Only
the paramount urge to quell an insatiable
bloodlust that grew stronger by the second.
No longer were there scampering rodents
or bounding deer as the westerly advance
of The Pack had driven them all ahead, save
the few that disregarded their instincts and
burrowed into the ground, but there was no
time to stop and dig them up. Its muscles
were fueled by a will more powerful than its
own, spurring them to flex and contract at a
full sprint toward its ultimate prey.

It lunged forward, tearing parallel claw
marks through the burning bark of a tree.
The sap spilled out and started to boil.
Landing on all fours, its back arched and its
chest swelled before directing its face to the
thick smoke above. It roared up into the fiery
canopy, stark white teeth glowing against its
ebon face, its mouth unhinging nearly back
to its ears. The world around it came into
momentary focus and its vision filled with
shimmering silver outlines like everything
was covered with a layer of mercury. It saw
the malleable flames crackling all around
it, the glistening outlines of tall tree trunks
and burning shrubs, the slope of the ground
before it. The beast committed it to memory

and hurled itself forward, scampering alternately on two legs and four, leaping up onto boulders that served as launching pads to propel it into the air, soaring with the grace of a puma.

It heard the ruckus of its brethren crashing through the underbrush a quarter mile away to either side, pausing only long enough to erupt with so many roars to find their bearings, the rapid thumping of their heartbeats mirroring its own. One whooshing sound followed another, almost like the beating of helicopter blades, as the black thing trailing them launched geysers of molten fire into the sky to rain down upon the forest, firing streams of superheated death into the thicket in all directions, a ceaseless barrage of destruction.

The cloud of smoke was now so thick it was all the thing could smell or taste, clogging its lungs and making its chest ache mercilessly, yet it heedlessly scampered forward, oblivious to the blood pouring from the lacerations on its cheeks and flanks, to the sharp pangs of hunger, to the—

It skidded to a halt, tearing up lines of dirt and flaming detritus.

Were the beast able to register confusion, that would have been the expression that contorted its face. It lowered its snout to the ground, drawing a deep inhalation across the smoldering earth. After a moment of dissecting the mess of smells, it rose to its hind legs and cocked its head to the burning branches above. It inhaled again, peeling apart the sticky smell of pine needles from the bitter stench of fire-consumed bark, smoke from ash.

There was something else hiding under the now familiar scent of forest fire. It was faint, so weak that it could easily have missed it were it not for the cramping in its gut. The beast had never smelled its like before, but there was no mistaking it. Fresh meat. A variety it had never before encountered, but one that set its mouth to salivating and its stomach to rumbling.

The crashing around it ceased, the whooshing of flame following suit a moment later. The others had smelled it, too. They were close now. So close.

It reared back and roared, and the world again spread out in liquid-silver sight. The rest of the pack answered with so many thunderous bellows, and it lunged forward with renewed vigor.

III

Jill could barely breathe. She was on the verge of hyperventilating; not because of the smoke, which certainly served to exacerbate the problem, but because she knew they were on the cusp of walking right into her vision of the fire and the dark things lurking inside it. Her hands trembled on the handlebars and her grip became so sweaty she had to constantly swipe her palms on her pants to keep them dry enough to maneuver. They were already traveling so slowly that she could barely maintain her balance on the bike, especially with the weight of the supplies and the sloshing gas tank behind her. The headlight diffused into the swirling smoke, staining the world around her a dusty gray. She could barely see the taillight of the motorcycle ahead, which was nearly indistinguishable from the encroaching walls of flame up the forested slope to either side of the valley. A thin stream meandered through the weeds beside them, the only promise of salvation from the fire. If the blaze came too close, they could wade in and lie on their backs. Adam had mentioned something about finding hollow reeds they could breathe through like straws, but her mind had been elsewhere, reliving the vision about to come to pass.

The heat from the fires was intensifying by the second. Her clothes were already sapped to her skin, lines of sweat draining through the folds and creases, her hair wet against her cheeks and neck. A deep breath of smoke burned her lungs, forcing her to cough and retch until she was able to draw her damp shirt up over her mouth and nose, nipping it between her teeth to hold it in place. Her eyes burned, spilling tears that eroded through the black mask of soot. She didn't know how much farther she could go. Eventually, they would have to pass through the leading edge of the fire and into the merely dead, scorched earth behind, wouldn't they? Had there been any way around the inferno, they would have gladly taken it, but from the last meadow, which granted them a clear view of the mountains ahead, it had appeared as though the entire visible horizon had been on fire. Their only option had been to face it head on, with the stream by their side, as much they all detested it.

Jill coughed through her shirt, but managed to keep her teeth ground to hold it in place.

The smoke grew so dense it was as though she had closed her eyes. The images of her vision flooded in from all sides. She could see the burning pines, just as they were no more than twenty yards uphill from her now, the smoke smothering her exactly as it did now. They were close. And those things. Those black shadows darting in and out of the flames, the heart-pounding sound they made when they—

A loud roar interrupted her thoughts. It wasn't the grumble of thunder they assumed they heard from lower in the valley, but sharper, more acute, more...bestial.

Dear Lord. It was the sound from her vision. There was no denying it.

We're all going to die! a voice screamed from somewhere in her subconscious, but she forced it back down.

They weren't going to die. They had come too far to die here in the smoke and flames. They were strong enough to—

Another roar answered the first and this time she screamed aloud.

The red glow of the brake light ahead grew brighter, piercing the smoke like a red laser. Then the one in front of it. They were now side by side, twin scarlet eyes staring at her. She slowed and came to a stop beside them.

"Did you hear that?" she cried, but the others were already talking about it.

"...sounded like it was right on top of us," Mare said.

"I don't think there's any way of doubling back to find a way around—" Adam started, but was interrupted by another roar that shook the earth.

Closer still.

"Jesus," he whispered.

"What are we supposed to do now?" Missy asked, startling Jill, who hadn't heard the motorcycle pull up behind her.

"Maybe we should head back down to the last meadow we passed through," Adam said. "At least we would have some sort of warning when whatever these things are attack. Here, we won't be able to see them until they're—"

"No," Phoenix said. "We can't turn back."

"Just far enough to give us a better chance of defending ourselves. Right here we're sitting ducks."

"This is where it happens," Jill said, so low that at first she worried they hadn't heard. "This is where it happens."

"You saw this in your vision?" Mare asked, pulling his own shirt down from beneath his eyes only long enough to ask.

Jill nodded. "Not here precisely, but right up there." She pointed down the path to a stretch where the stream widened to accommodate what might have been the remainder of an old beaver dam and the hills to either side leveled off.

Another roar. Maybe a hundred yards away.

"There's no outrunning them," Phoenix said. "We'll have to face them."

"Then I suppose we should try to do it on our terms," Adam said, climbing down off the bike. He walked it ahead down the trail without looking back to see if they were following. He passed the crumbled array of sticks and guided the motorcycle through the weeds and into the water just far enough that the lower rims of the tires were underneath. It took him a moment to balance it on the kickstand. When he splashed back out of the stream, he held his rifle across his chest.

A roar rattled the heavens. Then another. They were moving so fast!

The others followed Adam's example, parking their cycles just far enough into the creek that with any luck the fire wouldn't ignite the gas tanks. They sloshed from the shallows and stood together on the path.

"Everyone stand back to back," Adam said, his voice audibly trembling. "If it moves, shoot it."

Jill jumped at the sound of another roar.

Adam slammed the bolt forward with a metallic snap, chambering the first bullet.

A roar.

Another.

Jill screamed when something large and black moved beyond the encroaching flames.

IV

Mare shoved Jake behind him and raised the shotgun, resting the butt against his shoulder. The smaller boy trembled against his back, but no more so than the weapon in his grasp. His left palm was damp with sweat, his fingers opening and closing, seeking the best possible grip on the wooden pump. His right hand shook so badly that it took several attempts to press the safety button and seat his index finger against the trigger. He shucked the first shell into the chamber and nervously licked his lips.

"Three shots," he whispered. He could feel the weight of the shells in his pocket, but feared he wouldn't have time to get at them to reload if he needed to.

His mouth went dry. The only sound he could focus on over the crackling flames was his thumping pulse in his head.

He didn't dare blink as he watched the tree line beyond the stream for fear that was all the opportunity whatever was out there would need. The smoke seared his eyes and burned his lungs, yet he battled the sensations. There would be plenty of time to worry about such things when he was dead.

"There!" Evelyn shouted from behind him, but he knew he couldn't turn. He had to trust her to nail the shot if it presented itself. "No...there!"

There was an explosive roar from behind him, raising the hackles along his spine. The barrel of his gun shook so awfully it was like trying to sight down a flag in a gale.

Another ferocious roar, this time from directly ahead, beyond the wall of smoke clinging to the edge of the forest. Was that...?

He thought he saw movement, a darker shade of gray passing through the smoke, only vaguely humanoid. And then it was gone as though it had never been. His finger tightened on the trigger, nearly discharging a wasted shot.

"I can't see a thing!" Missy shrieked. She was to his right, facing back the way they had come, the smoke creeping down the hillside now obscuring the path of retreat. Panic emanated from her in waves.

"Stay focused," Mare snapped. "If you see anything, shoot it. You can do this."

He tried to sound strong for his sister, but the bottom line was he wasn't even sure he would be able to. If whatever he had seen through the smoke was indeed what was coming for them, it had moved so fast that he wouldn't have been able to draw a bead on it unless it was running right at him. Even then, it would probably be upon him before he could force his finger to squeeze.

Jake whimpered behind him. Ray whispered something to the child, silencing him momentarily. Phoenix, Ray, and Jake were all enclosed in the middle of their pentagon, with Adam facing directly ahead down the path, while Jill and Evelyn covered the opposite slope. Mare couldn't help but think of the old westerns he had loved as a child, watching in his little chaps with a plastic six-shooter in a holster on his hip. What was it the characters always said? *This is the perfect place for an ambush*. And it was. They were boxed into the shallow canyon with an unknown number of assassins hiding all around them.

"They're right on top of us," Phoenix said.

"I can't see a damn thing!" Adam shouted.

"I can feel them. They're all around us."

"Where? Tell me where!"

Jill screamed from behind him. Mare couldn't resist the urge this time and turned to see her barrel pointed up the hill into a thick copse of trees, the bark burning upward into the canopy.

Her cry was answered by a hideous bellow.

Mare whirled back to face ahead, catching a flood of motion. A hazy black shape knifed through the smoke from the cover of one fiery trunk to the next. He aligned his sight on the trunk, waiting for the first sign of movement, his finger tightening on the trigger in preparation of firing.

Bang!

"Where did it go?" Evelyn cried over the ringing in his ears. "It was right there!"

"Did you get it?" Adam shouted.

"I don't know!"

Mare looked back over his shoulder, but all he could see beyond Evelyn's shaking barrel was churning smoke. When he turned again, he didn't even have time to gasp.

A black shadow exploded from the smoke ahead, barreling straight at him.

Bang!

The shotgun bucked against his shoulder before he knew he had pulled the trigger. A cloud of dirt and soot blossomed from the ground where the silhouette had been, the dark from slashing through the smoke overhead like a shooting star. Had it dropped to all fours and launched itself into the air?

Bang! Another shot from behind.

Mare felt warmth on his forehead before the ferocious pain erupted from his scalp. Claws flashed back into the smoke, trailing arcs of his blood. Oh, God, it hurt. It hurt! He shucked the spent casing and chambered another.

"Where did it come from?" Jill screamed.

"I didn't see it!" Missy said. "I can't see anything!"

"Where did they go?" Mare shouted, his voice cracking with panic.

"I can't see them!" Evelyn yelled. "They could be anywhere!"

Ray pulled Jake to him, wrapping his arms around the boy's head while Jake clung to his leg. He turned slowly in a circle, the fear in the voices around him the only thing able to penetrate the ringing in his ears from the gunfire all around him.

Mare pulled a shell from his pocket and fed it into his shotgun.

Ray tensed in preparation of bolting. A horrible roar made even the air around him shiver, curing his body of the instinctual desire for flight.

Jill screamed and he whirled again in her direction, momentarily sure he had heard something scampering across a mat of dead pine needles and broken branches.

He felt so useless. All he could do was stand there and listen to the others in the throes of terror, nearly as ineffectual as he. He couldn't help defend them, though once upon a time he had been a crack shot out on the marshes with his dad in duck season. The best he could hope for was to not shoot them all before whatever made those terrible sounds tore them apart. Even trying to protect Jake with nothing more than his arms was a fool's proposition. Those monsters had to be the size of horses, judging by the sounds they made as they crashed through the forest. He had reached a new pinnacle of helplessness and was starting to feel like he was counting down the heartbeats to his last.

"There!" Missy said, the concussive noise of gunfire right behind.

"Did you get it?" Adam called.

"They're too fast! I didn't even get a good look at it!"

Another wretched howl echoed from the woods, taunting them.

Phoenix bumped into Ray from behind, nearly startling him out of his skin.

"They can't see through the smoke," Phoenix said, his voice unnervingly calm.

Ray could tell the smoke was growing ticker. The heat on his exposed skin intensified steadily, the ash and cinder carried on the smothering clouds thickening on his flesh. Soon the smoke would envelope them and they would be at the mercy of those creatures. They would never see death coming before the darkness claimed them.

But how was it that the shadows stalking them could see through the smoke when they couldn't? How did they—?

A bellowing roar severed his thoughts. It sounded as though it was all around them at once.

"We need to get out of here!" Missy screamed.

"No!" Adam shouted. "We can't give up our position! If we try to fall back, they'll attack! They're toying with us now."

Another roar, from the other side of them as if to prove his theory.

"I can't keep my eyes open!" Jill railed. "The smoke stings too much!"

Ray cocked his head. The serpentine tail of thought slithered through his mental grasp.

"Do your best," Mare said.

"We have to fall back!" Evelyn screamed.

"Then we do so as a unit," Adam said. "Hold this formation! We can't separate even for a second!"

Ray tried to focus his mind through the shouting. If Jill's eyes were burning, then surely those things in the thick smoke would be in much worse shape. Unless they weren't using their eyes...

"Everyone be quiet!" Ray shouted. "They can't see through the smoke either. They have to be using some other means."

If they were being targeted by sound, then they were making themselves easy targets with all of the screaming and wasted gunfire. Maybe if they were all silent they could hide in the smoke like the predators stalking them, but they would have to move. Their current location was already clearly triangulated.

His words must have made sense to the others. The only noise surrounding them now was their harsh breathing and nervous shifting from one foot to the other on the dirt path.

Another roar ripped through the silence, followed by yet another.

Ray had to focus on his thrumming heartbeat, which pounded in his temples and against his ribcage from within, to keep from screaming. Those beasts couldn't have been more than ten yards away! It was too late now. Too late.

Concentrate on your breathing, he told himself. *Don't let them hear anything. One quiet inhalation. Hold it. Exhale slowly. Slowly. Another deep breath—*

A faint gray haze filled his vision, surrounding him. He could see the others around him, their pale silhouettes ghost-like against the smoke. Directly ahead up the mild slope, white tree trunks crackled with flames. Something moved through the haze. It was low to the ground, almost as though it crawled on all fours. Twin ivory cores burned in the center of its head and in its chest, the remainder of its body, formed of various shades of gray darkening outwards from those almost blindingly white—

His sight faded with the revelation. He could see them. While all of the others were blinded by the smoke, *he* could see them.

"Jesus Christ," he gasped. He could see them!

He grabbed Jill and she screamed.

"Give me your gun!" he shouted.

"Ray—"

"Give me the goddamned gun!"

He took it from her and seated it against his shoulder. All he could see was the unwavering sheet of blackness. "Concentrate," he told himself, raging against his frayed nerves. He felt his pulse throbbing in his head. *Count the beats. One. Two. Three. Four. Five. Force everything else out. Eight. Nine. Ten.* The darkness faded away by degree and the forest stretched out before him. The recently-fired barrel glowed white hot, pointing toward the embankment over Jill's shoulder. He raised the sight toward the edge of the thicket, between the burning trees.

There! The shape had moved from where it had been before, and was now on the other side of the tree trunk. He aligned the barrel and held his breath, tightening his finger gently on the trigger—

Bang!

The shape flew backwards, skidding through the soot. The white core where its head had been was no more, and the ground was spotted with whiteness fading to gray. Its legs carved at the earth, shoving it in reverse, spastic movements that slowly stilled.

"I got it," he whispered, then louder. "I got it!"

He shucked out the shell and slammed the pump back and forth, but the chamber was dry. Casting it to the ground, he whirled toward Adam. "Give me your gun!"

There was no time to argue. Adam passed Ray the rifle and ducked as Ray raised it where he had been a heartbeat prior.

Another form dashed across the trail, sprinting toward where the other beast fell, darkening as the light fluids spilled out onto the soft earth. The creature stopped beside the first and spun to face them. Its back arched and the white glare of its head lowered. The start of a roar exploded from it, but was drowned out by the crack of rifle fire. Its chest exploded in a quasar of whites. It staggered backward several feet before losing its balance and falling to the ground, making no effort to try to rise.

The air came to life with roaring from all around them.

"He really got it," Missy said. "Ray, how did you—?"

He cut her off by slamming the bolt back, ejecting a smoldering casing and chambering another.

Another body flashed past the white wall of the burning trees, pausing by the mess of its brethren.

Ray pulled the trigger again, but the creature was already moving. The bullet struck on of the carcasses in its wake with a fountain of gray. It roared as it ran, though it sounded more like a human shout.

"I missed," Ray said, struggling to replace the spent cartridge with trembling hands.

His ears rang, drowning out the sound of everything but his thoughts. He couldn't see where the creature had gone. Only the searing glow of the fire. No movement but the snapping flames. Nothing.

He retched, coughing so hard he nearly doubled over, but he managed to stay erect.

Where did it go? Where did it go?

He spun to his left, sighting around the obstruction of Missy's head. Nothing but the haze of smoke and dots of ash.

"I can't see it!" Ray shouted.

He couldn't hear a thing. Even his own voice sounded like a whisper from down a long hallway. Were it not for the high-pitched ringing, he might have heard the scampering sounds of clawed feet tearing through burning detritus and gouging into the earth. Perhaps even the harsh rasping of heavy breathing or the grunt before something large and angry leapt into the air. The whistle of claws parting the smoke. The scraping of overgrown teeth unhinging like a bear trap.

He could hear the screaming, though.

There was no escaping the screams.

V

The smell of its prey drove it into a frenzy. That divine aroma was all around it now, seeping through its pores to induce a state of euphoria. Whatever small measure of control it once held over its faculties was now a memory. Its instincts assumed full control of its body, and they were tapped into a primal core where only rage and bloodlust resided. The wet scent of human blood caused a descent into madness with the speed of a plummeting elevator. Faster and faster it raced. Branches tore lacerations across its face and chest as it circled its quarry just of sight, clinging to the smoke, becoming a part of it.

The beast leapt onto a boulder, hunched its back, and released a roar that brought the world into focus around it, but even that didn't matter now. With the aroma of its prey in its nostrils and lungs, it no longer felt anything but hunger and desire. It could have sprinted headlong into a tree trunk and broken every rib without the slightest twinge of pain and been back on its feet in a second.

The scent, that wonderful, wonderful scent, intensified when it bellowed. Every sound it made, every crash of detritus underfoot or branch that snapped amplified the smell as though they were swimmers bleeding the shark infested waters red through hundreds of small cuts, opening slowly, tantalizingly. It parted the shroud of smoke and was assaulted by the sweet music of screams, each one thickening the aroma of their fear until it was an oil clinging to its skin, filling it with ecstasy.

It wanted to hurl itself down into their

midst, to carve them to the bone and gorge itself on the meat. The anticipation was maddening, but at the same time, the symphony of fear it conducted was still building to a wet crescendo, and when it reached that point it would throw itself upon them alongside its brethren with savage ferocity and a rush of blood.

The others were feeling the same thing, pausing in their whirlwind torment only long enough to bray into the smoke. One after another—

Bang!

It stopped where it was and flattened to its belly in the cinders. The sound had been peripherally familiar, an echo from a past life. The food corralled between them had made that sound several times, but that one had been different. The explosive noise hadn't culminated with the dry pounding of the earth and a scattering of pellets and gravel, but a damp thud that was followed by the thump of a body hitting the ground amidst a splash of fluids. It could taste the death on the air, the bitter tang of spilled blood, and even though the mess positively reeked, it only added to is fervor.

It arched its back, pushing itself only far enough up from the earth to accommodate its swelling chest, and released a roar.

One of its kin was helpless against the rotten smell of one of their own, unable to resist the bloodlust coursing through its veins. It released a hideous call and tore through the flaming underbrush to scavenge the shuddering carcass. The sound of its advance was too loud, its approach unguarded. No sooner had it reached the bleeding mess than it raised its arms to slash through the bloody flesh—

Bang!

From where it cringed against the ground, the beast heard the bullet *thuck* into flesh and the dull thump of a body striking the dirt behind. The smell of festering blood intensified. The creature's body hit the ground and skidded to a halt in the mud. It registered a sensation that it had never experienced before, a very non-predatory feeling that caused its muscles to tense. Enough toying with them. Enough reveling in the scent of their fear. The time had come to commence with the slaughter.

It roared and propelled itself forward, alighting in a bipedal sprint. The fires lapped its flesh, but it felt no pain. Only longing and an insatiable hunger. It slowed just long enough to witness the stilled bodies of is brothers. In such close proximity, even their foul, meaty scent called out to be feasted upon, but the crack of gunfire cured it of the need. The bullet screamed past behind it and struck the sickly pile of meat.

The world was fading around it, becoming a haze of smoke and flames. It roared to bring its vision into focus, but the proper intonation eluded it. The beast hadn't had the proper inhalation to emit a thunderous roar. Its voice instead sounded similar to the shouts its prey now made.

It shouldered a burning tree, a cloud of cinders raining down upon it, and staggered deeper into the cover of the smoke where it knew it was hidden. Crouching, its chest filled and it roared up into the heavens. A whooshing sound became audible behind it as the bringer of fire finally caught up with them. Or was that black demon deliberately lagging? It snarled at the assumed cowardice and dashed ahead.

The ground sloped away beneath it, lending even more speed as it crossed the path and splashed through the stream.

Bang!

The report echoed all around it, but the pattern of steel had been nowhere close.

"It's back here!" a voice screamed, but it was already up the opposite hillside and concealed behind a burning stand of trunks. It leaned against a tree, the transferred flames covering its thick hide, consuming it.

The beast bellowed and it could see them down there in a circle, the weakest protected between them. Its fingers snapped open, the long claws unfurling. Sharp teeth screeching, it allowed its heartbeat to escalate in anticipation.

It could already taste the blood.

Springing from behind the fiery cover, the flames along its back and head forming a mane of fire, it took two great strides and launched itself into the air above them, already bringing its outstretched arms down, talons whistling through the air in preparation of the killing stroke.

VI

Phoenix heard the creature bellow from behind him at the same time as another roared directly ahead past Jill and Evelyn. The time for playing with them was through. The creatures would now be coming at them with everything they had. He could smell the unbridled rage and aggression seeping from their pores even from the distance, feel the palpable waves of eagerness radiating from them. There were still three of them out there, charging madly through the burning woods. That much was certain. They no longer made any attempt to hide their numbers. Grotesque shadows darted in and out of the smoke, preparing to release their wrath in a flurry of claws and teeth.

And there was something else out there... something lurking in the heart of the blaze. No. Something that was the heart of the blaze, the source of the fire and the evil he could feel spreading down the mountainside. There was something strangely familiar about it too, which caused his stomach to clench and the hackles to rise along his neck. Dear Lord! He knew that creature now. But how—?

A roar erupted from behind him. Not just behind...above.

He spun around, grabbing Jake and dropping to his knees to shield the boy with his body. Gunfire exploded from behind and in front of him at once, the sound chasing him into a world of tinny ringing, masking the sound of claws singing through the sky.

A wash of fluid rained down on him a heartbeat before the body slammed onto his shoulders, driving him down on Jake.

The smaller boy tried to scrabble out from beneath him, his chest fighting to expand to release a scream, but the weight of the creature atop Phoenix pinned them both. It flailed against Phoenix's back as searing pain spread from his shoulders all the way down to his hips. Phoenix screamed and tried to roll out from beneath, but the pain was too great.

He thought for sure he was on fire, his flesh burning away, until he felt a claw snag a rib. The hand controlling it jerked repeatedly to break free.

Mare had seen the black creature falling though the smoke above like a lunar eclipse. It had been too close and moving far too fast to line up a clean shot, leaving him only enough time to raise the shotgun and pull the trigger. The barrel met with resistance, the weight driving it down and shoving the stock so hard into his shoulder that he toppled backward and to the side. From the corner of he eye, a lower leg, severed at the knee by the spray of pellets, hit the ground and bounded into the stream. His breath fled him in a single great expulsion. The gun fell directly on his face.

Instinctively clutching his shoulder, he flopped over onto his side, gasping for air. His fingers probed through the dirt, seeking the weapon. He was unable to open his eyes against the pain. It couldn't have gone very far. Prying his eyelids apart, all he could see through the tears was red. He had broken his nose too many times not to recognize the signs. A watery image of the barrel floated into view with his fingers tracing along the ground beside it until—

He recoiled against the heat of the barrel. It felt as though he had pressed his fingertips onto an iron.

The warm stump kicked at his rear end, the blood soaking right through his clothing.

Mare's breath returned with a choke that led to a throng of coughing as he wrapped his fist around the barrel despite the pain and dragged it onto his chest. He forced himself to sit up and rolled to his knees. The world swam around him as though viewing it from under a lake. He could barely keep his eyes open against the ferocious agony in the bridge of his nose. His face was covered with blood from the wounds on his head and he had to spit the freshets draining from his nostrils away from his mouth in order to breathe. Through his wavering vision, he made out the vague outline of something large, its arms rising and falling like twin serpents striking. Sprays of fluid flew in their wake. Staggering to his feet, he stumbled toward it. Flames burned from the creature's back, a rustic-orange dorsal fin flagging from what remained of the beast's mane.

Reaching into the flames and grabbing hold of the nape of its neck, Mare jerked its head back and pressed the tip of the barrel to its temple. The creature had a moment to register surprise before its consciousness shot out the opposite side of its head to pattern the path with streaming gray matter.

Adam could only stare at Ray as he swiveled with the rifle seated against his shoulder. Flames rose from white hot orbs in Ray's formerly vacant sockets, the molten cores appearing to track the hillside like irises. Fingers of fire covered Ray's forehead, but miraculously didn't burn the skin.

A roar roused him from his stupor and he spun toward the sound, but without his rifle he felt naked and exposed. A dark shape drew his eye up in the smoke, hurtling down toward Mare. The younger man raised his shotgun and fired, a shower of blood exploding from the grotesque ebon form before slamming down atop him.

Another roar pierced the ringing in his ears and he looked to the right in time to see two more of those hideous creatures burst from the tree line ahead of Jill and Evelyn through a cloud of embers, flames streaking behind them like the tails of comets. Ray pulled the trigger from behind Jill with a resounding *bang* that stole the remainder of his hearing. The bullet took a bite out of the leading beast's abdomen, but it hardly slowed. The other passed it from the side as Evelyn fired again.

The steel appeared to pound the ground in front of the charging creature, but when it took the next stride, it stepped down on a severed ankle. It toppled and fell, but was upright in an instant, hobbling straight at her on the ragged end of its tibia. She pulled the trigger again, and nothing happened, the firing pin striking an empty chamber.

Adam's legs moved of their own accord and he lunged at the creature before it was upon her, wrapping his arms around the bloody ankle. The beast slammed to the ground, its face pounding the dirt. It snapped its head around to face him, baring a snarl full of wickedly sharp teeth stretching from ear to ear.

"Shoot it!" he screamed.

Evelyn was on her knees, trying to grab one of the shotgun shells with a trembling hand from where they had fallen in her hurry to pull them from her pocket. Her eyes were startlingly wide, tears leaving trails through the soot on her cheeks. She finally secured one of the red casings in her fist and brought it toward the shotgun—

Adam screamed and looked at his shoulder. Four fingers were embedded in the muscle all the way to the first knuckles. The claws within him scraped against bone, seeking solid purchase. The hand tugged in an effort to drag him closer to that bear trap mouth.

Releasing the ankle against his chest, it pumped a rainbow arc of arterial blood into the air above him. He pawed at the fingers ripping his muscles and saw the monster's empty eyes as it swung its legs around, giving it the leverage it needed to bring its face in line with Adam's, tilting its head and opening its jaws wide.

Something black was thrust into his vision from the left, pressing the creature's head sideways.

Bang!

A cloud of cordite smoke crossed that awful face and then it was gone. Adam felt warmth on his cheeks, chunks of something squishy draining down his neck.

The creature's lower jaw worked up and down, trying to close its teeth against the upper row that were now scattered up the hillside. A flume of scarlet gushed from its exposed throat and it toppled forward.

Adam turned his head before the wave of blood washed over him and started prying the stiff fingers out of his shoulder.

Missy turned to her right and swung the shotgun up the slope, toward the flaming wall of pines. The black things were sprinting down the hill so fast she couldn't keep up with the barrel. One slowed as a spray of fluids erupted from its gut before the other fell beside it, sliding through the dirt.

Jill stood in their path, screaming hysterically and trying to back right through Ray, who strained to maintain his balance against her, unable to steady the sight of the rifle. He fired a shot that soared right up into the treetops, the kick of the rifle knocking it out of his hands. It clattered to the ground beside where one of the creatures was slashing at Phoenix's back, shredding clothing and flesh alike. He reached for it and was rewarded with a slash from four claws that carved his forearm to the bone. Screaming, he recoiled and stumbled backwards into Jill, knocking her to the ground.

Missy stepped up in front of Jill's prone body and leveled the barrel at its chest. It threw itself forward, colliding with her right as she pulled the trigger.

The combined impact from the bucking stock and the creature's momentum separated her shoulder, but she didn't immediately feel it as she was tossed from her feet, her breath knocked from her when she slammed down on Jill with the full weight of the beast on her chest.

Its head hung over Missy's shoulder, its jaws working slowly, its cooked cheek dragging against hers. She smelled the horrible stench of rancid meat on its breath, the contents of her stomach rising in response. It felt as though her sternum had been compressed to her spine, her lungs flattened between. She flopped in panic, but the weight of the thing was too great to knock it off. Its agonal respirations slowed until its jaws finally stilled.

She grunted and shoved, her chest growing hotter by the second, and finally rolled it off her.

Missy was covered with blood from the smears on her cheek all of the way past her waist, the saturated clothing allowing ribbons of heat to slide down the bare skin beneath. Rolling to all fours, she sucked at the air like a bellows, allowing Jill to scurry out from beneath her. She stared down at the monstrous corpse, or more precisely, through it. She could see the mud under it through a hole in its chest large enough to accommodate a melon. Jaggedly fractured ribs stood out like teeth, the singed lips curled back. As she watched, the remaining organs collapsed inward to fill the gaping wound.

Raising her eyes to the burning forest, she thought she saw another shape through the smoke and screamed.

VII

◉

The Leviathan, once the former Congressman Richard Robinson, stood in the flames of its own design. Sap crackled and popped, exploding from knots, the bark providing only momentary resistance. Ash and embers fluttered around it, the deep black smoke swirling and churning, enveloping it in its acrid embrace. Burning branches fell from the sky and trees toppled to the smoldering detritus. It could see them down there, surrounded by the carnage they had wrought, and wanted nothing more than to stride out of the flames and rain fire onto them. The urge was insistent, but this was not the time, the voice of the master whispered in its head. Soon enough it would have its chance, but the master had bigger plans in store for them. Once they reached the master's tower, the Leviathan could have them. All but one, anyway. And then it would set them afire and revel in their dying screams.

The Pack had been foolhardy, savages that they were, victimized by their own insatiable hunger. They had been hardly more than mongrels snapping at heir own tails. Strong though they were, they had rushed too willingly to their deaths. They had served their purpose, though. Not a single living creature remained along the trail leading back to the master. Their prey would be on their own, bereft of any assistance. They would make it to their ultimate destination, but would find only Death waiting.

Its eyelids snapped shut, extinguishing the flames of sentience. When they reopened, something else altogether stared out through the eyes of the Leviathan from a chamber of bones no longer so far away. Death assumed the fire beast's consciousness, inspecting his prey. They appeared more fallible than he had ever envisioned, lying there on the ground, coughing and bleeding. He felt foolish for ever considering them a threat. How they had survived the Swarm's assault or even the Pack was a mystery. No. They had help. Their lives were guided by the hand of the Divine. God could only offer so much help, though. After that they were on their own. Only one of them had the power he possessed, his opposite number, his doppelganger, and once his frail flesh was flayed from his bones, the others would fall with no more effort than blowing the seeds from a dandelion.

He studied his opposition, crawling in the mud, choking on the smoke. Each cough reopened the wounds along the boy's back, refusing to allow the flow of blood to cease. But it would, he knew. The boy's destiny was not to die in the wilderness, but to die at the hands of Death, though only after experiencing tortures beyond his worst nightmares. A part of Death pitied him, but he couldn't allow the feeling to metamorphose into sympathy. His adversary was just a child, a smooth-skinned, naïve little boy with long scraggly hair and a physique about as intimidating as a praying mantis to a lion. How could the Lord have been so misguided as to pour His hope for mankind into such a fragile vessel?

He would pleasure in shattering that chalice, in not only decimating the body, but in breaking the spirit as well.

Let them come.

The Leviathan's eyes closed again, only this time they opened more slowly, the beast's mind resuming control as though in the moments following birth. A breeze rose to chase away the smoke, the flames flapping like flags, and for a second it was sure one of them had seen it.

It whirled and ran, streaking through the untamable fire that reached for it, trying to meld back into the form that had spawned it. Gaining speed with each step, it became a missile, leaving a stream of fire in its wake.

It knew where to go. Where to wait.

The master's instructions were clear in its mind as though written on the insides of its eyelids.

They would come to it.

And they would burn.

CHAPTER 6

I

Phoenix felt a frigid hand slide through the wounds on his back, gripping his spine. Waves of cold emanated through his body. He had felt Death from afar, but this sensation was something else entirely. His adversary was close now, so near that he expected to turn around and see the black beast staring down upon him with predatory eyes, but there was nothing behind him in the smoke and flames. He felt like a sow being sized up for the slaughter, scrutinized by an evil greater than he had ever imagined. And it scared him to death. He had never truly given credence to the doubts before. The larger part of him had always believed that they would triumph, but now he was no longer sure. Death was not watching him from the woods, at least not physically. He was still many, many miles down the Trail of Blood in his black tower. If the mere presence of Death's awareness had caused such a horrible physiological response over such distance, then how would he feel when he faced his opposition in the flesh?

A strange thought struck him. If Death killed him and achieved his ultimate goal, could Death's reign of blood come to an end? Was it possible that by allowing himself to be destroyed, Death in turn would be vanquished?

The icy sensation abruptly ceased.

Phoenix fought to rise to his feet. The ragged edges of the lacerations closed on his back, halting the hot flow of his own blood down his spine. Jake rose from where he had been pinned beneath him and took his hand.

They milled in the same spots where they had taken their stand, as though by breaking the circle, the world would again be thrust into chaos. Mare smeared the blood from his face and nudged what remained of the creature at his feet to ensure that it wouldn't rise again despite the loss of its cranium. Phoenix touched the base of Mare's bleeding skull, stimulating the wound to close.

"Thanks," Mare said, running his fingers through his wet hair.

Phoenix nodded, but said nothing. He turned to Ray and closed his hand around the gashes on Ray's forearm, watching them heal as though they'd never been.

"Is that all of them?" Adam asked, looking to each of them in turn.

"Yes," Phoenix said. "We need to keep moving now. There's no more time to waste."

"Well," Mare said. "That was a nice break. I feel well-rested."

No one so much as chuckled as the smoke swaddled them and the flames encroached from either side down the hillsides.

With the somber silence of a funeral procession, they walked toward the stream, stepping down into the stream. One by one they emerged from the water, rolling the motorcycles up onto the path. Adam climbed astride his bike and took the lead, revving the engine impatiently. He had to hold his shirt over his mouth and nose to filter even a small amount of oxygen from the smoke. The headlights did little more than diffuse into the oppressive clouds in a pale aura. A glance over his shoulder confirmed that the others were ready to fall in behind, so he raised his feet and started forward, pushing the bike only fast enough to keep from toppling. He could barely see the ground in front of him now, navigating instead by the walls of fire to either side, closing steadily in on the trail.

Sweat seeped from every pore, glistening in the firelight before being baked into a salty sheen on his skin.

With the droning buzz of engines behind him, he led them through a landscape he imagined to be hell.

II

They passed through the flames and emerged reborn. The smoke had settled to a low-lying fog, hovering above the black, smoldering earth, clinging to the stands of charred trees in a final embrace. Small fires still burned from deep in the hollows of the wide pine trunks, lapping at the meal already consumed with nowhere left to go but out. Every last bit of detritus had been eliminated. There were no more leaves or needles on the forest floor, let alone any remaining in the skeletal treetops to replenish the formerly thick mat. Only fallen trees marred the ebon perfection, shattered into dozens of thick chunks, from which meek plumes of smoke stretched from dying embers. There was no movement at all except for the rich gray clouds of ash that rose in rooster tails from their tires, settling back to the path hundreds of yards behind. The world around them was dead; an eternal wasteland from which one day new forestation would rise from the enriched soil, but now, nothing remained but the ghosts, trailing away on the wind of their passage as smoke. Even the sun finally managed to reach through the lingering brown haze above in slanted rays that cast spotlights onto the fields of devastation. The stream raced past beside them, flowing thick with ash, damming itself with burnt branches that turned the water black.

No birds flitted from one treetop to the next, vanishing into heavily-needled alcoves. No ground squirrels scampered across carpets of crackling dead leaves from one opening of their burrow to the next. No deer clung to the wilderness in the distance, their curiosity piqued by the rumble of the engines violating their sanctum. An aura of death emanated in their stead, creating a vacuum of life that sapped the strength from the riders speeding through the forests of purgatory.

Phoenix shivered on the motorcycle behind Missy. Not because of the breeze or the weather, for only heat rose in waves from the freshly-baked ground, but because of the narrowing gap between him and his opposite number, the dark half of himself he had begun to think of as some inseparable shadow. With each mile that fell away into the dust, the feeling of dread amplified a thousand-fold. He no longer pretended to know what waited on the far side of the Rocky Mountains. When he closed his eyes, all he could hear were the screams of his friends playing over rapidly changing images of fire and torment. By this time tomorrow, they would be standing at the precipice of their fates.

He was tired. So tired. Exhaustion had passed like a speeding bullet train, leaving him somehow hollowed, his emotions frayed. He wept for the forest and the innocent life forms consumed by the blaze. He cried for the pain and suffering that radiated from the earth in dissipating funnels of smoke. And for the first time in his life, he wept for himself. He was scared. Even locked away in the darkness of the basement that had been his home, he had never been afraid for himself. When the Swarm had dangled over him from the ceiling, waiting for him to rise just a single inch to tear him to bloody ribbons, he hadn't been frightened for himself. He was unaccustomed to such selfishness, the feeling stirring a sense of loathing. His friends needed him, now more than ever, and he was unable to set aside his terror long enough to be strong for them.

Shaking his head, he tried to force his feelings down deep into his well of thought, where maybe he could still hear their echoes, but he wouldn't have to deal with them directly. He tried to focus on anything else, but the eternal forest of scorched nothingness only made the echoes more insistent. He thought of his friends and again heard their agonized cries. Honing in on the buzz of the motorcycles only conjured images of flies circling the corpses of his loved ones.

He experienced a brief moment of lucidity. Those emotions and the pain they summoned, all of the self-doubt and dread, were gifts from his adversary, the first of many battles to come between them.

He had underestimated the power of Death to reach though the ether and wage war against him. What kind of strength did this black monster possess to be able to nearly cripple him from afar? How much greater would that power be when they finally stood face to face?

That line of thinking could only lead him back into the cruel grasp of depression. There was no option but to let the path lead him where it may. He would stand across the field of battle from serpentine Death with the ultimate fate of humanity hanging in the balance…but not today. This was his time to make preparations. His adversary knew it, and thus launched a mental assault to distract him from the task at hand. He needed to not only ready himself, but his newfound family as well. He still had two precious gifts left to bestow, two parts of himself to share in the only way he knew how. Healing Ray's eyes had granted second sight to the blind. In her hands, Evelyn contained the lifeblood of nature. And he had given everything that he was, the promise of love and life, his very heart, to Missy. Jake and Jill had been special without his endowment. They could see not the world as it was, but as it would be, a power that had already served them well, but would be of greatest use should they manage to defeat Death. To begin the world anew, they would need visionaries. That's what they were. Jake was the future of mankind, the child king who would usher in a new era of peace on earth, whose seed would pass on the very best traits and guarantee a future dedicated to humanity's ascension rather than its obliteration. And Jill. Jill was…

"Pregnant?" he whispered. A sense of hope swelled within him, filling his bloodstream and traveling outward to overwhelm his entire body. All thought of bloodshed and screaming death vanished, leaving only a newfound sense of love and understanding. He looked back over his shoulder and saw nothing of the scorched earth or the trees standing as tombstones to mark its demise, only a young girl struggling against a big bike, carrying within her enough hope for the entire world. Within her was another dreamer, whose visions would show nothing of the evils of her species, but the promise of its perpetuation amidst green fields of flowers, of love and laughter…of hope.

They would triumph, Phoenix thought. Not because they were stronger than the evil ahead, but because they must. There was a child who would be king and a queen who must be delivered into safety.

His own life was of no consequence. He would lay it down without a second thought.

The world would endure.

They would survive.

And hope would be birthed into a land that had known none for far too long.

III

The sky clung to its manila hue, but the churning smoke was now well behind them. Adam had been watching the path of the sun, still clearly visible overhead in the unmarred patch between the midnight-blue peaks behind and those still ahead. It had fallen to him to push the others, balancing progress against potential demoralization. They needed a break to refuel themselves and their bikes with the dwindling rations remaining for both. The celestial orb had barely passed its zenith and begun its descent into the waiting arms of the coming night when opportunity finally presented itself. The trail had wound to the south, the forest falling away to the right in the form of a steep slope that led downhill past burnt trees and charred boulders to a lake that could have been a window to heaven. Sunlight had glimmered invitingly from the gentle white caps, small watery hands waving them closer. Never had such a perfect vision called to him. The others had felt it as well, a budding sense of anticipation building as they had woven down through the charred remains and finally driven right out onto the soot-covered shore.

Adam had shed his boots and rolled up his pants, and now stood shin-deep in the crisp water, chewing on leathery kelp and staring toward the center of the lake. Clusters of cattails stood to either side, saved from the fires by the water lapping their stalks. The plants closer to the bank hadn't fared nearly as well, but there was something special about the fact that these had. Every tree as far as he could see, every coarse black trunk outside the water had succumbed to its flaming demise. He couldn't help but draw a measure of symmetry. If these few plants, wavering on the wind and throwing downy seeds from their blossoming brown buds could survive, then maybe, just maybe, they could too.

Swallowing the last of his dubiously satisfying meal, he turned and splashed back toward the shore. The tension had abandoned him through his wrinkled toes, into the relaxing water, and it appeared to have had a similar effect on the others. Jill and Mare held hands on the bank, splashing their feet and giggling like young lovers should. Missy tugged on Phoenix's arm, trying to drag him into deeper water with a sly twinkle in her eyes that promised a good dousing. Jake stood in the shallows, rummaging through the silt for flat stones while Ray counted how many times they skipped by sound. Evelyn sloshed out to meet Adam, wrapping her arms around his waist and turning to head back to shore with him.

"Isn't this beautiful?" she said, gesturing in a wide arc with her free arm. "I can't think of a more perfect spot."

Adam smiled. He loved seeing her happy, if only momentarily.

"You've got something…" she said, pointing to her top front tooth. "Right here."

Adam scraped at his tooth with a fingernail. "Did I get it?" he asked, baring his teeth.

Evelyn laughed. "It looks like a whole plant growing out of your gums."

"Stupid kelp," he said, again chiseling at his tooth with his nail.

"Let me," she said, her mouth closing over his before he could even move his finger. Her tongue teased his teeth, which he allowed to part to welcome it into his mouth. His finger now freed, he wrapped both arms around her and their bodies merged together.

Their lips parted and she leaned her forehead against his. She looked up at him through those fathomless green eyes, and he wished for nothing more than to spend the remainder of his life staring into them.

"Did you get it?" he asked, beaming.

She laughed. "Nope."

He rubbed his upper gums with his index finger and smiled.

"There you go," she said, taking his hand and guiding him toward the shore.

The time had come, he knew. They were burning daylight, though he couldn't understand why they were in such a rush to reach their destination, especially why *he* felt compelled to hurry them along. He was a rancher driving cattle to the slaughter, his herd consisting of his only friends in the world, his family, the love of his life.

He looked at Evelyn, her hair tangled and dirty, her face smudged with mud and a spot of blood by her right ear that she hadn't been able to wipe away, and yet still she was positively radiant, the most beautiful woman he could ever imagine. She was so strong, so brave, and his chest ached at the prospect of having to release her hand when they reached the bank, that union the only thing that felt real in the entire world. Before he knew he was going to do it, he stopped.

"I love you," he said, surprised not by the words, but by the seriousness with which he had spoken them. Making sure she knew that right then and there seemed like the most important thing he had ever done.

She looked into his eyes again, preparing to smile, but the look on his face caught her by surprise.

"Are you all right?" she asked, her brows knitted with concern.

"Yeah…I just…just needed you to know that."

She squeezed his hand. "I love you, too."

A rush of relief passed through him, his strained posture visibly relaxing.

"Are you sure you're okay?"

"Yeah," he said. "I guess maybe my emotions got the better of me for a moment. Let down your guard for a second, right?"

"You don't have to have your guard up with me. You know that."

He smiled and looked toward the others, who had seen his advance back to land, and taken the cue to start preparing themselves to hit the trail again.

"I'm not good at these things," he said.

"You did fine," she said, pulling him closer, wrapping her arm around his waist and leaning her head on his shoulder.

Adam kissed the top of her head and was about to repeat his declaration when his mind was derailed by the revelation of what he saw ahead. The formerly black cattails near the shore were now green and lustrous, thicker than they had been before. As he watched, the thick seed clusters swelled like hotdogs roasting on a stick until they exploded, filling the air with fluttering white seedlings that floated down to the bank, from which long green blades of grass now grew from the charcoal, and alighted on the water.

"You did this," he whispered. "You, Evelyn. You brought them back to life."

She could only shake her head, the color draining from her face as what almost looked like snow surrounded them.

"You're amazing."

Evelyn leaned away and splashed toward the bank, falling to her hands and knees. Thin green lines slithered out from beneath her, curling up between her fanned fingers. They widened into distinct blades and folded almost lovingly over the backs of her hands.

"I can't believe it," she whispered, rising from the ground. Four oblong swatches of grass remained against the soot, patches of fur on a mangy dog.

Everyone had seen, and edged closer to her until she was surrounded. They all crouched and stroked the grass, petting it softly.

Phoenix hung back, for only he was immune to the surprise.

Adam watched the pink-eyed boy, whose white locks were stirred by the rising breeze, cattail blossoms swirling around him, and suddenly it all made sense. Ray's sight. Evelyn's eyes and her miraculous green thumb.

Phoenix caught Adam's stare and looked quickly away.

Until then, Adam hadn't truly noticed how thin Phoenix had become. The bones in his wrists were knobby, his cheekbones more pronounced. He'd become more withdrawn, but not because of the mental preoccupation as Adam had assumed. He was passing his life force into them, sharing the amazing powers that he possessed. And such a thin frame could only hold so much.

He was killing himself for them, Adam knew.

Slowly but surely, he was killing himself for them.

IV

The cold water felt amazing on her feet. Jill hadn't realized just how hot and sweaty they had become inside her shoes. Her head ached and her back felt as though it had been twisted in knots, but for the moment she was able to relax. She leaned forward, cupped a double handful of water, and splashed it into her face. She scrubbed the caked soot and sweat from her cheeks and forehead, thrilling in the sensation of the frigid fingers of water trickling down the back of her head and along her neck.

Jill leaned back, bracing herself on her elbows, and looked up to the heavens, closing her eyes and allowing the sunlight to massage her features. There was a splash beside her, then another as Mare plopped down on the shore to her left. She pretended not to notice, waiting as long as she could bear before kicking her feet and dousing both of them with water. Giggling, she sat up, took his hand, and pulled him closer.

"You'll pay for that," he said, wrapping his arms around her and dragging her toward the lake. She squealed and fought against him all the way until they splashed down into the water.

Jill jumped right back up to her feet, standing there with her arms held away from her body, water draining from her clothing. Mare sat in the silt, looking up at her and laughing. She lunged for him and drove his head back beneath the surface. He emerged a heartbeat later, spitting out the foul taste of the lake, his smile cocked to the side, obviously prepared to go another round, but Jill had already sloshed back to the bank. She sat and patted the ground beside her.

"Uh, uh," Mare said. "You can't start something you aren't prepared to finish."

"I did finish. And in case you didn't notice, I won."

"Then I want a rematch," Mare said, climbing out and plopping down beside her.

"You'll get your chance," she said coyly, taking his hand in hers and setting them on her thigh.

He couldn't take his eyes off her. Even dripping wet, her hair hanging in dirty strands down her cheeks, she was positively radiant. It was almost as though she glowed.

"You smell like wet dog," she said, glancing at him from the corner of her eye before again looking out across the lake.

"I've got news for you, honey. You're a little past ripe yourself."

Jill squeezed Mare's hand and lowered her head to his shoulder. This was how life was supposed to be. And maybe one day soon it could be like this again. She chased away the thoughts of her last vision, of both of them being incinerated by flames. Now was not the time for such things. This was their moment. Their perfect moment. And she wasn't about to spoil it.

She sensed movement to her right and turned to face the reeds. As she watched, those burnt black sticks widened, the black carbon falling away to reveal green stalks straightening and plumping as they grew. Knobs formed atop them, elongating into exaggerated cattails, the soft meat swelling from within until the stems buckled under their weight.

"What in the—?" Mare gasped as the strange blossoms exploded, filling the air with white fuzz like goose down.

Jill smiled and held out her hands, allowing the fluff to land on her open palms. She brought her right hand to her mouth and gently blew the seedlings back into the storm. The entire world, it seemed, was filled with the joyous snow. Jill was mesmerized by it, clumps falling straight down while others swirled on the air currents. It was like being set down in a child's dream where teddy bear stuffing rained from above, and there was nothing more threatening than the accumulation, which invited her to lie down atop it and drift off to sleep. The transition had been so gradual that she hadn't known she had woken into a vision until the white dots coalesced into a great white falcon, wings spread wide and descending toward her with outstretched talons, not from the cloud of seedlings, but from a blizzard of snow. Its claws clamped down on her thigh and its wings folded to its sides. Jill looked for Mare's hand, but it was gone. She sat by herself on the shore, only the snowstorm had closed in so tightly around her that all she could clearly see was the bird, its face inches from her own. She looked into those stark white orbs and was transported.

She was again in the cavern, sitting in one of the earthy rooms of the pueblo. There was a small child swaddled in her arms, her face still bright red, eyes closed. Before Jill, her dark-skinned ancestor sat, looking directly into her eyes, but they were the white eyes of the bird.

"This can't be a vision," Jill said in her mind. "If this were going to happen, you couldn't be here."

The woman nodded. "Yes, child."

"The baby. Does she ever exist?"

"If you are willing to sacrifice everything for her."

"I don't understand. If I lay down my life for her, she can never be born."

Her multiple-great grandmother smiled, but it contained only sadness.

"You must tell him."

"Who? What am I—?"

"Tell him now."

The lake again appeared before her, the last remnants of the cattails settling atop it. She still held handfuls of cotton, and Mare was beside her as he had been all along. She looked at him, at his crooked smile and his crooked nose, at the way he looked at everything through shining eyes full of wonder. She had never loved anyone as much as she loved him at that moment.

"No," she said, her breath freezing in her chest.

He turned to her and smiled, but the expression waned when he saw her consternation.

"What? What's wrong?"

"Mare…"

"Saddle up!" Adam hollered, splashing back to shore.

"Talk to me, Jill."

"That means you two," Evelyn said, placing a hand on Mare's shoulder.

"Give us a minute," he said.

"We're wasting time," Adam said. The others were leisurely working their way back to where they'd parked the motorcycles.

"Jill…"

"It can wait," she said, looking away and grabbing her shoes and socks from the freshly-birthed grass beside her.

"Jill!" he called, but she was already hurrying to her bike.

Mare could only stare after her, confused, wondering what could possibly be troubling her so…fearing that whatever she had to tell him would irrevocably change his world forever.

V

Ray was loving every minute of it. Maybe not every minute, whatever those things had been back in the burning forest had scared the tar out of him, but he reveled in every sight. Every scorched tree trunk that blew past to either side of the road. Every skeletal limb attached to them. Every gap that opened between the upper reaches that revealed the gray sky. The drivers ahead of them, weaving along the path. Even the back of Mare's head: the curvature of his ears was fascinating. Granted, this was a poor substitute for the physical sight he had once known, and he had to be careful not to lean too close to Mare for fear of singing his hair with the flames from his eye sockets, but it was beyond his wildest dreams only days ago. So the sun was merely a luminous nickel in the sky. Big deal. Maybe he only saw the world in shades of gray, but he'd never heard a dog complain, and he certainly wasn't about to start. He'd grown accustomed to seeing the white-hot cores of his friends' hearts and minds, the gray waves of blood flow that defined their appendages. It was wonderful, mind-boggling, and while it wasn't the showcase of colors and hues he had experienced through the first twenty years of his life, it was a miracle he would never take for granted again.

Mere days ago, hours really, he had accepted his uselessness. He had been as blind as a bat and could hardly walk a dozen paces without falling. He was the albatross hanging around the necks of each every one of the others. A burden. He had entertained other notions. Had he been able to find a rope and a tall

"There's a gas station!"

Mare pointed down the hillside through a gap in the deforestation.

"It looks like it's burnt to the ground."

"Yeah, but maybe there's still gas in the pumps. I don't know about you, but my tank's almost dry."

Adam didn't have to glance at his gauge to know he was in the same boat.

"So?" Mare said.

"Worth a try."

Ray stared down the slope, his mind reassembling the fallen structure into what it must have looked like before. Maybe it was his recent thoughts of Tina, but in his head he could only see the truck stop where his girlfriend had been butchered in the bathroom. His newfound sight faded back to black, but this time he was thankful for it.

VI

Missy felt like a passenger on a hijacked flight. She had no idea where they were going, only that very bad things would happen when they arrived. The fact that they were in such a hurry to get there was maddening. She wanted the motorcycles to run out of gas to slow their progress, but at the same time, she certainly didn't relish the idea of having to hoof it through the mountains on foot. That would at least prolong the inevitable, though. Of course, it would also leave them at the mercy of whatever beasts now roamed the forest, while the bikes potentially allowed them to outrun pursuit. The bottom line was she didn't know what she wanted outside of just turning around and heading back to the lake where they had been safe. Perhaps it was because deep down she was certain that if she survived whatever lay ahead, she would be making the return trip alone.

It isn't fair! she screamed in her mind. *What did any of us do to deserve this?*

The sensation of Phoenix's arms around her waist bound her to reality, but exposed her to its dark underbelly as well. She could feel his bones though his skin, the hard knobs where his wrists crossed. They had become even more pronounced since they had first set out. His face had become gaunt, shadows taking to the hollows of his eyes and the sharp cut of his cheekbones, even under the midday sun.

Phoenix was dying. Slowly and visibly, his life force drained steadily from him with each passing mile. She had been able to fool herself for a while. They were all under an enormous amount of stress and sustaining themselves on a staple of seaweed, after all. No one could stave off physical deterioration for long under these conditions, but this was different. Phoenix was fading and there was nothing she could do about it. Nothing. *Nothing!*

He squeezed her from behind, resting his chin on her shoulder so he could speak directly into her ear.

"Don't worry about me. I'll always be with you."

Her chest hitched as she stifled a sob. His courage enraged her. Why couldn't he just turn around and flee with her, start anew someplace far away where none of the bad things would ever be able to reach them? She knew why, of course. This was his destiny, the whole reason he'd been placed on the earth. He was a firefly, his light blazing brighter and brighter until his biological imperative was fulfilled, and only then could he pass on—

Missy shook her head to rattle the thought away. None of this was fair, but she needed to at least act strong, if only for Phoenix's benefit. The last thing he needed was for her to make things any harder for him, any harder for herself.

Adam coasted out of the rut they'd been using as a path down the steep slope and across the highway, the sun reflecting from the pavement as though diamonds had been embedded in the asphalt. The gas station loomed over them past the far shoulder. Or at least what remained of it, anyway. The aluminum canopy over the fuel stations still stood on concrete posts, bowed to the sky and scorched black, but the pumps were now only tangles of metal marking the black pits where the gasoline had once flowed. The underground reservoir to the right was now a crater that had swallowed half of the parking lot, while beyond, gasoline swirled in amoeboid shapes, reflecting the colors of the rainbow on a retaining pond from which the tail end of an Accord stood like a monument. The guardrail at the side of the highway was shredded and rent, marking the vehicle's high-speed passage.

The building itself was in ruins. The half that had once served greasy burgers, eggs, and hash slung by even greasier men who'd never heard of hair nets, had flattened under the weight of the fallen roof. Now only a mound of black bricks topped by a melted air conditioning unit remained in the midst of a sea of melted glass from the windows. The convenience store side had fared little better, the left wall the only part still standing. The front grille of a car poked out of the rubble, upside down where it had been thrown by the explosion.

Adam slowed the bike in front of the remains. His shoulders slumped visibly.

"I was hoping there might still be some gas remaining," he said. "I guess I should have known better."

"It was worth a try," Evelyn said, rolling up beside him. "We could have gotten lucky."

Adam could only shake his head. The prospect of finding luck on their side was comical.

"Hey," Mare said. "I have an idea."

He stopped the bike and kicked down the stand. Climbing down, he walked over behind Jill and untied the bundled satchels behind her, rummaging until he found the supplies they'd had the foresight to bring along with them.

"There isn't a drop left here," Missy said.

He gave his sister a sly wink. "Oh, ye of little faith." He struck off toward the monstrous hole in the earth, skirting the ragged asphalt edges. "Better bring those tanks along."

Mare continued walking, past the crater and across the singed ground to the edge of the small lake, pausing only long enough to hang the tubing over his neck like a snake. He waded into the water, splashing toward the rear end of the Accord. Reaching the handle of the rear door, he opened it beneath the water and used it as a stair to climb up onto the slanted trunk, bracing his feet on the jagged edges of the shattered rear windshield. He leaned around the side and popped open the cover of the gas tank. Unscrewing the cap, he fed the hose in and started to suck on the opposite end. It was only a moment before he was coughing and vomiting petrol into the pond. Gas poured out of the hose, but Missy was right there, waiting with one of the reserve tanks, taking the hose from him and pointing it down into the red plastic drum.

"Who's the man?" Mare asked triumphantly.

Missy smiled and shook her head. As soon as the tank was full, she pulled out the hose and passed it to Adam, who was beside her with another empty vessel.

Mare jumped back down into the water and splashed back to shore with his sister, passing Evelyn, who was just stepping down into the pond.

"Hey, Missy. Remember that time we were almost out of gas and someone used his brilliant powers of deduction to find more?"

"That was two minutes ago, Mare." She rolled her eyes.

"And who was the man who saved us all?"

Missy groaned.

"I said, who's the man?"

"Give me a break."

"Come on, Miss. Who's the—?"

"Mare," Phoenix interrupted.

"Finally," Mare said. "At long last someone acknowledges that…" His words trailed off. He could tell by the grave look on Phoenix's face that he hadn't been playing along.

"I need to talk to you."

"Sure," Mare said hesitantly. Then to Missy, "I'll be right back."

Phoenix took him by the elbow and guided him around the one standing side of the convenience store, glancing back over his shoulder repeatedly until he was sure that they were out of sight. He released Mare's elbow and took him by the hand.

"There's something I need to give you," Phoenix whispered, locking those pink eyes on Mare's.

VII

Mare still wasn't quite sure what had happened behind the remains of the gas station. The whole event was an enigma he tried to unravel as they rode eastward. When Adam had called for them, they had been standing in the rubble, staring into each other's eyes as they had been for several minutes while he waited expectantly for Phoenix to say something. He *had* called him back there, after all. Never once did Phoenix make a move to reach into his pocket for whatever gift he had claimed he was going to give. Instead, Phoenix had simply stood there, looking into his eyes and holding his hand. It hadn't been a comfortable moment. It was as though Phoenix were looking through his eyes to read his soul, if such a thing were possible. He had grown increasingly unsettled, but had been unable to break eye contact. Eternities had seemed to pass, the world standing still around them, before something finally happened, and he still wasn't precisely sure what. All he clearly remembered was Adam shouting for them to get a move on, and now here he was, astride his freshly-fueled motorcycle, speeding down the rugged black soot path with Ray clinging to him from behind.

The sun was setting in the sky, preparing to slink silently behind the rugged peaks, lengthening their shadows ahead of them, the ground to either side marred by dead tree trunks. They would only be able to go so much farther before having to set up camp and calling it a night, for he could only imagine the lack of contrast between the singed earth and the night sky. Even the shade was forcing them to slow.

His thoughts returned again to the mysterious moment he had shared with Phoenix, his mind replaying it for the umpteenth time. He had been drawn into the other boy's eyes, faded pink like an abandoned stretch of asphalt, streaked with crimson, red rays from the black sun of his pupils. The sclera had been bloodshot, the rims of his eyelids irritated to the point it appeared as though blood welled like tears, preparing to spill down his cheeks. Maybe it had been his protective brotherly instincts, but there had always been something about Phoenix, a feeling he couldn't quite pin down, that made him nervous around the other boy, an ant beneath a magnifying glass with the cloud cover preparing to part. Missy loved him, though, and she had seen too much misery in her life for Mare to intervene and deprive her of whatever happiness she could find. Missy was entitled to at least that much, but if Phoenix even thought about hurting her, he would do what brothers did to protect their sisters, whatever that may entail. And perhaps there had been a point where he had thought himself physically able to protect her from heartache, but staring into Phoenix's eyes, he had felt as insignificant as a gnat buzzing around a giant's head. It was as though Phoenix's eyes were windows to vast universes beyond his comprehension.

"Your greatest fear is becoming your father," Phoenix had said after that interminable moment of staring.

Mare hadn't known how to respond. Or if he even could.

"You need not worry. You have more than enough courage to face the demon."

Had he said "the demon" or "that demon"? Mare's memory was hazy, his recollections suspect.

"She will be beautiful and strong. Strong enough to breath life into a dead world," Phoenix had said, his eyes receding into vacuous pits that had made Mare feel like he was falling. A wan smile had crossed Phoenix's lips, but Mare hadn't been able to grasp the emotion behind it. Had it been contentment? And who was "she"? He didn't understand. "You should be very proud."

Mare had felt lost at the time, and now was no better. Had Phoenix been talking to him, or to someone else in one of the vast hidden universes behind his gaze?

Phoenix's eyes had focused upon his then, truly seeing him instead of through him. He had felt Phoenix's right hand squeeze his left, heard Adam calling for them from a million miles away.

"It saddens me to give this gift to you, for it will change nothing. Your power is your courage, while I can only offer you peace. You will do what needs to be done when the time comes, not to prove you aren't your father, but rather because you will know how it feels to be one, however briefly. You will father the future, which, unfortunately, is not a gift I can offer you."

Adam's voice had been joined by others, calling for them, louder, more insistent.

Phoenix had released his hand then and the world had collapsed upon him as though held at bay by a bubble that had finally popped. He remembered gasping for air, fighting the sensation of nausea, and the last thing he had heard, whether real or imagined, were the words Phoenix had whispered as he walked away.

"You will feel no pain."

Even channeling the voice from memory sent a shiver up his spine. What was that supposed to mean? He had a sinking sensation in his stomach, the same feeling he always had walking into his house when his old man was home, not knowing whether he was drunk or not, fearing he would be greeted by raised fists.

Who was "she"? What the hell did any of this mean?

You will feel no pain.

And what in God's name was he supposed to make of that?

He swatted the back of his head. It felt like something was crawling on his scalp beneath his hair. Something warm.

His fingers came away with singed hairs that blew away as soon as he saw them.

"Dammit, Ray!" he snapped, turning around to see the flames rising from Ray's eyes, flagging on the breeze generated by the speeding cycle. He still wasn't accustomed to the sight of his friend's face on fire.

"Sorry," Ray said into his ear. "I didn't mean to hurt you."

Hurt me?

But it hadn't.

Mare turned back to the trail, steering the bike with one hand while he massaged his scalp with the other. The skin was hot to the touch and he could feel the fluid forming beneath a pliable blister, which dimpled under the soft pressure. The hair had been burned away in a section the size of a half dollar, the remaining locks crisp and singed.

He hadn't felt anything more substantial than momentary warmth.

You will feel no pain.

"What did he do to me?" Mare gasped. More importantly…why had he done it?

VIII

◉

Jake could hardly keep his eyes open. The sun had set some time ago, though how long he couldn't be sure. It didn't matter anyway though. His concept of time was skewed beyond repair. Either it was day and they needed to be on the move, or it was night and they needed sleep, but every time his eyelids closed, he was welcomed inside his head by images of monsters racing through rolling clouds of smoke, their nightmarish roars still echoing through his skull. Each time one of those fearsome bat-like faces lunged at him, opening its ferocious jaws, his eyes snapped back open to afford fleeting glimpses of the burned forest flying past beside the path, dead trees standing like zombies over their graves, before slowly beginning to close again. He was terrified either way, wishing for sleep to claim him in the heartbeat before his upper lashes laced with his lower.

Evelyn's warmth soothed him slightly, but she was no substitute for his mother, the very thought of whom never failed to bring tears to his eyes. She needed him to be strong— her memory had told him so many times in his dreams—so strong he would be, but the exhaustion was making it difficult. All he wanted was to curl up in his own bed at home, awaken from this nightmare, and drink warm milk with honey while his mother stroked his forehead, gently tracing circles around his eyes until the sandman whisked him off into dreams of superheroes and cartoon characters. That was never again to be, of course, for before he could ever enjoy a restful night, they would have to storm the gates of hell.

He shifted his head against Evelyn's back, finding a momentary soft spot between her shoulder blades and tightened his grip against her stomach. She lowered her hand from the handlebars only long enough to give his arm a soft, reassuring squeeze. It would have to suffice.

Their speed had slowed dramatically since the onset of night, the headlamps providing little help as they merely cast a glare across the wash of black. They were going to have to stop soon. Try to sleep for a little while. That thought made him even sadder, for he knew tonight would be the last night that all of them would be alive. He didn't know who would join his mother or how, but he had never been more sure of anything in his short life. His dreams where he could see into the future had evaporated, or maybe it was simply because he was getting so little rest that he slept the dreamless sleep of the dead. Regardless, the coming dawn promised only bloodshed and suffering.

Brake lights stained the forest red around him as the bikes coasted to a halt. They had stopped at the base of twin rock formations, which reminded him of tall mushrooms set into the hillside, their flat caps forming a precarious ledge from which a stand of scorched trunks stood like massive yucca plants.

"This looks like as good a place as any," Adam said, killing his engine. He climbed off and leaned it on the kickstand as the remainder of the motors were silenced. They stood there in an eerie quiet, unmarred even by the whisper of the wind, a void of the ordinary sounds of the world.

"It's about time," Missy said. "I was starting to doze off while I was driving."

"You and me both," Jill said, watching Mare climb off his motorcycle. He raised his arms and stretched. She wished she could have been riding behind him, her chest pressed to his back just to feel him near. "I just need to lie down for a little while, and then I ought to be fine to go again."

Jake lowered himself from the seat, and staggered to the side. It still felt as though he was on the moving bike, the way his butt still vibrated. The sensation quickly passed, only to be replaced by a more urgent one. He instinctively grabbed himself and scurried away from the others, heading around the limestone towers to a secluded spot where he was out of sight, but could still hear them close by.

Unzipping his dirty jeans, he hosed down the charred side of a tree trunk, the never-ending stream crackling as the charcoaled wood fell away, a small river racing away from him down the slope. He hadn't realized his body could hold so much fluid. When the flow finally abated, he zipped back up and was preparing to rejoin the others when he noticed something strange from the corner of his eye. There was a gap in the hills against the horizon. That in itself was nothing out of the ordinary. It was the fact that he couldn't see any distant ridges between them. Only the black sky, the stars muffled by a haze of smoke trapped in the atmosphere.

He wandered up toward it, leashing himself to the sound of voices so he couldn't go too far. When he crested the slope, he looked to the east. The scorched land stretched so far out in front of him he wondered if he could see the entire world. The foothills rolled lazily down the eastern slope of the Rockies, leveling into the flat plains, uninterrupted until they reached the distant Mississippi hundreds of miles away. From such a distance, details were vague at best, the black ground at the base of the mountains was rough with debris from burned houses and buildings, piles of rubble and timber that provided only texture to the landscape. It was the same moving onto the plains, the mounds of destruction growing larger and more densely packed as they neared the rim of an enormous crater that looked large enough to cup the moon, the edges leading downward to what must have once been downtown where—

Jake gasped. Had he been able to breathe he would have screamed.

"I was starting to wonder where you might have wandered off—" Ray said from behind him.

Jake whirled around, his heartbeat pounding like a hummingbird's, his shadow snapping behind him on the ground, cast by the flames in Ray's eyes.

"Are you guys having a party up here or something?" Mare asked, joining them at the top of the knoll.

The others slowly joined them and together they stared across the Front Range in silent awe, focusing on the point in the center of the crater, where a single dark skyscraper stood from the ruins, supported from all sides by the buildings that had fallen against it, toppled by the atomic blast. That lone spire lorded over the devastation, radiating pain and suffering in palpable waves, a construct of man, and yet simultaneously not of this earth. A physical manifestation of the evils of humanity that had spawned its near extinction.

"That is where we must go," Phoenix whispered, trying to hide the tremble in his voice.

Nothing more needed to be said, for they had all known it the moment they saw it, precisely as each had imagined it from the uncanny description Jill and Jake had provided from their visions. Even without, it would have been unmistakable.

"They know we're here," Jake said, his hand sliding into Ray's. "I can feel it."

Phoenix couldn't bear to look at it a moment longer and turned away. He knew what needed to be done.

"Death will wait for us," he said, starting back toward their impromptu camp. "Sleep while you can...if you can. Tomorrow we must complete our journey."

The adversary was now so close it felt like a cold hand had clamped over his heart, chilling his blood. He could almost see the specter of their demise hovering over them. He felt so alone. As he must be when he finally faced Death.

Alone.

He headed down the path they had forged through the soot, glancing back to make sure they were all behind him. He needed them distracted, better yet asleep. And soon.

He had a long night ahead of him.

CHAPTER 7

I

The filmy lids over Death's eyes slid back, his waking eyes shining golden into the room only momentarily before turning crimson, giving the bones covering the floor and staked to the walls the impressions of bleeding anew. He hadn't been sleeping, but rather in a state of heightened concentration, his consciousness expanding from the confines of the small throne chamber to study his preparations. He was ready for them now, ready to wage war against the Lord and His pathetic band of survivors. Soon enough the entire earth would be his to do with as he pleased, a smoldering wasteland to rule. He was beyond God's reach and above the consequences. He was Death, harbinger of life eternal and bringer of damnation, and soon to be king of the hell he had spawned on Earth, the fires of which he could now stoke at will.

A sharp-toothed gash ripped his reptilian face. They were here, he could feel them. Close now. Near enough that he could hear the soft thumping of the last blood of mankind coursing through frail bodies soon to release it onto the black ground, christening it in anticipation of his sovereignty.

He rose from the throne and crossed the room, brittle bones cracking and fracturing beneath his heavy tread, talons clicking, making his way to the stairwell leading to the roof, the vantage from which he would reign supreme. Pestilence and Famine stayed where they were, standing sentry beside the front door of the throne room. He had no need for them. Yet. Their time would still come. They would be sent out into the ruins to intercept the stragglers. The boy, however...the boy was all his.

At the top of the stairs, he stepped out into the night. The air was electric. Lighting slashed the black sky, a battery of blue bolts stabbing the ground all around his fortress from the smoke overhead, illuminating the landscape of the damned, the mounds of rubble stretching away to all sides, ringing the towering behemoth nearly to the horizon. He raised his eyes to the west, to where the mountains carved an angry seam across the night, a ragged saw blade. They were up there, barely out of sight. He could feel their stares upon him, certain that they in turn could feel his, their fear radiating from them even across the miles between. His opposite number was among them. Just a child. A weak and pathetic human, growing more so by the second. Once he was eliminated, the others would fall like leaves.

The boy would come to him. Under the cover of night, the boy would ride to face him and beneath the morning sun's first light he would crucify God's chosen warrior and stake claim to the realm of his design.

His heart rate accelerated, cold blood thrumming through his eager form. Where was the Lord now? With His fragile army standing on the brink of eradication, where was He hiding?

Death felt his enemy turn and slink away like the coward that he was and lowered his stare from the high ridge. A flash of light drew his eye from below. With a flick of his eyelids, Death was down on the ground, viewing the remains of the city through the eyes of the source of the sudden flash.

The Leviathan stood in the bottom of a massive hole in the earth to the west where once there had been a large lake in the middle of a beautiful park, before the atomic detonation had vaporized it. Now the formerly luscious grass and bountiful shade trees were gone, replaced by black soot and ash, the banks scattered with the bleached bones of the picnickers who had been witness to its passing.

The creature raised its burning arms out to its sides, directing its palms to the heavens. Its wrists snapped with power before launching geysers of magma into the heavens. The fiery flames rose hundreds of feet into the air before reaching their apex, pausing as though trapped between worlds, and then rained back down. Molten fluid splashed over its body, patterning the divots in the lake bed, beginning to fill the irregularities in the ground where small-mouthed bass had clung to the murky depths in wavering weeds while sunfish and bluegills had darted in schools in the shallows above. The puddles expanded until the creature stood ankle-deep in the widening pools, flames still filling the sky and pouring back down into the deepening melting pot. The Leviathan made no movement, merely generating more and more of the bubbling liquid, the magma reaching the levels of its knees, then its waist. Soon it was shoulder-deep, only the beast's black head above the boiling surface, a stationary buoy. The streams of fire no longer flumed into the sky, instead fueling its depths from beneath, spatters of molten fluids rising from where its hands stayed under the surface until even those twin volcanic eruptions stilled. The level of the magma continued to rise over its head.

Death again retreated into his own skull, watching from high above as the lake of fire finally reached the banks, a glowing beacon visible even to the weak Lord from on high. Bubbles swelled on the flaming surface, issuing tendrils of smoke when they popped. The lake was choppy with waves of fire.

The Leviathan stayed beneath, immersed in its lifeblood of lava, biding its time.

Death could only smile, wicked teeth gnashing.

A distant pinprick of light appeared far ahead from the foothills, and he knew exactly what it was. The end of humanity was nigh, its final hope speeding toward him.

"Come," Death said in a tongue that sounded obscene coming from his mouth.

He couldn't tear his eyes from the light, which faded behind hills and vanished as it dipped into valleys, only to reappear again. Closer. Closer still.

A bellow of triumph burst from his chest, echoing like thunder along the Front Range.

II

THE TRAIL OF
BLOOD

Phoenix stood up from where he'd been
lying beside Missy, on a blanket covering the
scorched earth. There had been no wood to
create a fire or with which to fashion shelter,
so they had all chosen various points along
the limestone cliff out of the rising wind
and the elements. He couldn't bring himself
to look at her. Not yet. Not until it was
finally time to say goodbye, a task that was
tearing him apart inside. He loved her more
than anything else in the entire world and
resented the role he was destined to play, but
everything he did from this moment forward
he would do for her. Despite the broken
heart and the risk that she might hate him
forever, if he succeeded, she would live. And
that was the only thing that mattered to him
now.

The others had fallen asleep more quickly
than he could have even hoped. Maybe some
divine hand had granted a small measure
of assistance, one last chance to recharge
their batteries, to summon every last iota
of strength before the day to come. At least
that would buy him a decent head start. He
wanted to be in the city before any of them
even suspected that he was gone. But first…
first there were several important tasks yet to
complete.

He walked past where Jill and Mare were
sprawled out on a blanket, her hand on his
chest, his arm wrapped around her. Mare
snored softly. Phoenix knelt silently, kissing
his fingertips and placing them gently on
Mare's forehead.

God grant him the strength, he thought, rising and sneaking past. Ray had fallen asleep sitting up with his back against the rock, his chin against his chest, singed bangs covering his hollow sockets. Jake was wrapped in a blanket like a burrito, his head on Ray's lap. It pained Phoenix to sneak past without being able to give them each a hug goodbye. Beyond, he reached Adam and Evelyn. Staring down at them for a moment, watching Evelyn's eyes flick back and forth under her lids in a dream that brought a sad smile to her face while Adam slept flat on his back with his mouth hanging open, he waited for Evelyn to roll away as he knew she would. He eased himself to the ground by Adam's head, and softly placed both hands on the older man's shoulders, closing his eyes to focus his concentration.

Energy coursed though his fingertips, the hair on his forearms standing electrically. The power flowed away from his chest, draining him as it poured into Adam. Phoenix's head sagged, his body acquainting him with its frailties. Exhaustion set in, but it was more than that. He had emptied his vessel of flesh of everything but his blood, reminding him of his nights in The Man's basement confines when the Swarm had descended upon him, stealing his strength to cure their own ills, draining him of everything that he was. Only this time he had done so willingly, sacrificing his very soul in hopes that his friends would live to see the sunset one more time. He was almost done, and soon he would have to abandon them to set off for the terrible tower where Death waited for him with ferociously sharp claws and—

"What are you doing?" Adam asked.

Phoenix's eyes snapped open and he gasped.

"Go back to sleep," he whispered.

Adam tried to sit up, but Phoenix increased the pressure on his shoulders, forcing Adam to crane his neck to look at the younger boy.

"What's going on, Phoenix?"

"You are a healer, Adam. By choice, but more importantly because that's who you are. You were spared because of your compassion, because you cannot accept the inevitability of the things you cannot change." Adam tried to sit up again, surprised by the amount of strength the boy used to hold him down. "My final gift, my gift to you, is little more than you already possess. The power to cure disease and save life is in your hands."

Adam could only stare up into Phoenix's sad, pink eyes, all but obscured by his long, dirty, white locks.

Phoenix released him and stood, turning away without another word and walking back to where Missy slept.

Adam finally sat up, twisting to watch Phoenix go. His shoulders tingled where Phoenix's hands had been, the sensation running all the way down his arms and into his fingers, resonating with pins and needles as though beginning to fall asleep. He hadn't the slightest clue what had just transpired. It wasn't the strangeness of Phoenix's actions that surprised him, for he would have worried more had Phoenix *not* been doing something a little off-kilter, but the finality of it. It had seemed almost ritualistic, like the laying of hands. The words Phoenix had used were almost a summation of his life. Granted, it was the middle of the night, the middle of a very stressful night, but it was still…odd. More odd than usual, anyway. Maybe Phoenix had awakened from some dream or vision that Adam would have had no hope of comprehending and he was still trapped somewhere between the dream and the reality of the coming day. That had to be it.

He watched Phoenix drop to all fours and curl up beside Missy, draping his arm across her stomach. He would ask Phoenix about it. But not until morning. Let the boy have the night with his girlfriend. Besides, everything always looked different under the light of day.

Adam flopped and rolled onto his side so he could feel Evelyn against him and closed his eyes, where sleep waited in ambush.

Phoenix couldn't control the tears streaming from his eyes and down his cheeks. He had been dreading this moment all of his life. Even death would be preferable to the agony he now felt, the twisting in his gut, the pain in his chest that made it hard to even breathe. He had to bite his lip to keep from sobbing aloud and waking her. If he had to look into her eyes again or even hear her voice, he would lose his resolve, what little remained anyway.

"I've loved you all of my life," he whispered, so quietly that he could barely hear it, but loud enough he hoped that on some unconscious level she could. "When I dreamed, I dreamed of you. When I thought of a better life, it was always your image I saw. You loved me when I thought nobody ever could." He had to pause to stifle a sob. "Until I met you, everyone I knew only wanted to take from me, but you... you gave me the world. I never did anything to deserve your love, and yet you gave it willingly, unconditionally." His lips quivered and he closed his hand over his mouth to fight back the growing sounds of sorrow threatening to erupt from his chest. "If I could change this, you know I would. There's nothing I wouldn't do for you, except allow you to suffer. I'm sorry a million times over for...hurting you. For leaving you. I love you, Missy, and no matter where you go, I will always be there with you. As long as you live, you will never be alone. Never."

He leaned forward and pressed his lips to hers, their softness, their heat, were sensations he would treasure beyond the finality of this life. Slowly, and with more regret than he'd ever felt before, he drew his lips away, wanting to wipe the tears from them, but less than he wanted a part of her to come away with him.

She smiled in her sleep, her features softening and taking on an almost angelic glow.

He blinked, taking a mental snapshot of her, his beautiful Missy, to carry with him in his heart.

"I love you," he whispered one last time before rising and walking away from her, fearing that if he looked back she would awaken and he would have to see the look on her face when he broke her heart.

He walked to the closest motorcycle and silently brought the kickstand up with his toe. Holding it by the handles, he guided it back onto the path and quietly pushed it up the hill until he reached the top. He looked out upon the ruins of the formerly magnificent metropolis, the rubble of a once great civilization mourning its passage. There was a small circle of bright orange light. A lake of fire, he knew. He had seen it before in his dreams, the monster that had created it somewhere in its depths. And beyond...the twisted spire of the black tower.

Swinging his right leg up on the seat, he positioned himself exactly as he had seen Missy do so many times. He had learned how to drive it by watching her, but he needed to create distance between them before he risked starting the engine and potentially rousing them for their slumber.

He looked back over his shoulder to where the others slept, oblivious to his intentions, though soon to feel their sting.

"Goodbye, friends," he said. "May the Lord bless you and keep you."

Lifting his feet, he turned back to the path and allowed the bike to coast down the slope, descending into the bowels of hell toward his fate.

III

The wistful moon cast its indifferent gaze down upon the scorched earth, casting invisible shadows from the black skeletons of the dead trees. The wind sighed in exasperation, blowing unimpeded across the bleak landscape, merely turning the upper layers of infertile soil, no longer able to create music with rustling leaves or the clatter of branches, settling instead for the hollow, mourning howl echoing forlornly in the lifeless valleys over the mocking laughter of streams flowing sluggish with the paste of eradication. The stars no longer twinkled but stared, spectators unable to turn away from Mother Earth's deathbed as she struggled to take what they feared were her last breaths.

Where once nocturnal rodents foraged through the mats of brown leaves and yellow needles, moonlight glinting golden from their alert eyes, there were now only swirls of ash blowing around the stunted, burned remains of shrubs. No bats or night hawks slashed through the upper canopies to pick off errant insects; no owls hooted from their invisible enclaves. No sounds of airplanes or helicopters thundering through the sky marred the silence un-customarily bereft of the howl of the hunting coyotes and growls of mountain lions. It was a silence of fearful anticipation. Perhaps it was the thin haze of smoke pinned beneath the atmosphere that obscured the world from God's eye, or maybe, like a physician, He had simply focused His attention on other patients He might have some slim chance of saving. Or perhaps He had no choice now but to allow the disease to run its course.

Only the intermittent droning of a lone motorcycle traveled on the breeze, a fly buzzing over the burnt epidermis.

Below, the black tower stood like a tumor, the source of the symptoms ravaging the earth. Perchance under some great celestial microscope three figures may have been glimpsed from the heavens, moving atop that cancerous lesion, eagerly awaiting the impending triumph over the planet's failing immune system, preparing to metastasize and lay claim to the entire corpse.

Above, humanity's last remaining hope slumbered, oblivious to the fact that even now the enemy was aligning against them. While their bodies recuperated from the ravages of the prior day, the planet trembled.

The sun was still hours away from cresting the eastern horizon, from reflecting upon the spilled blood of humanity.

From bearing witness to the final battle to determine the fate of the world.

Before setting once again. Whether upon the death of the planet or its rebirth, it cared not, for it would callously disregard the bodies destined to fall, and rise yet again.

Only those who survived would determine if the deaths to come mattered, if the lost lives would be mourned or left to rot.

Somewhere in the darkness, the day began before dawn with a whimper, though hopefully the end would not come with the same.

IV

Missy whined in her sleep, her head thrashing side to side on the blanket, eyes darting back and forth beneath her closed lids. Her face tightened into a grimace, her lips curling back as though in pain, her teeth parting to allow another whimper to pass. Tears streamed from the corners of her eyes, trailing over her temples and into her dark hair. Her chest heaved, rising and falling dramatically. Eyes snapping open, she bolted upright, a scream echoing away into the night.

She patted the ground beside her, hoping to feel Phoenix's reassuring warmth, but everywhere she slid her hand she could only feel the blanket, cold from the ground beneath.

"Phoenix?" she whispered, struggling to stave off hyperventilation.

She was panicked. What had she been dreaming about that had upset her so much? She couldn't remember. Not in any kind of detail. There had been darkness and then there had been flames. And what? It felt as though a cold hand had reached through her ribcage and closed around her heart. She couldn't catch her breath, couldn't rationalize her surroundings. Everything was black. The ground. The sky. She looked to her right, hoping Phoenix had heard her terrified scream, hoping he would comfort her, just cradle her to his chest and chase the demons away, make everything all—

He was gone.

The spot on the blanket where he had been sleeping was vacant, barely even wrinkled.

"Phoenix?" she called, louder this time.

She heard someone mumble a sleepy response from a distance, but she was already on her feet.

"Phoenix!" she screamed, her head swiveling, eyes scanning from one tree to the next. She prayed he would come sauntering out from behind one of the trunks, zipping up his fly, but with each moment that passed without him doing so, the less likely it became. She knew better, though. Deep down, she knew better. How could she have been so stupid? So blind? He had all but spelled it out for her. She wanted to hit herself in the head repeatedly for being so dumb, but instead, she ran.

"Phoenix!"

She sprinted to her brother's side, throwing herself to the soot and shaking his shoulders.

"Mare, wake up! Wake up!"

Jill lifted her head form his chest first, looking groggily up at Missy. As soon as she registered the fear in her friend's face, her eyes opened wide and she scrabbled to her feet. Mare leapt up, nearly stumbling into his sister.

"What's going on?" he gasped, whirling to face her. He had never seen her so upset, even when they had committed their mother to the ground or found their father's remains. But she didn't say anything. He had known her all his life, and even had he not, the look in her eyes was unmistakable.

"He's gone," Missy sobbed, collapsing into him only long enough to dampen his shoulder with tears before shoving him away and dashing toward the others.

Mare took Jill by the hand, what felt like a hole opening inside him, a bottomless pit into which his stomach dropped. What were they supposed to do now? Without Phoenix to guide them, he couldn't help but think they didn't stand a chance against what was to come. He couldn't believe Phoenix would just slink off into the night like a coward. They were all scared. Every last one of them wished they could run away, but to actually do so was unthinkable. Now was when they needed him most and he had abandoned them. What about Missy? He had claimed he loved her. To simply leave at her most vulnerable hour was reprehensible. How could he have said he lover her and the just up and—?

"Oh, God," Mare gasped, releasing Jill's hand to run to where they had parked the motorcycles. Phoenix hadn't tucked tail and fled. He had done something far, far worse. *One, two, three, four.* He counted them again to be sure. "Oh, God. Oh, God. Oh, God."

"Adam!" Missy screamed. He was already standing when she reached him. A dire sense of foreboding accosted him, sending a shiver up his spine, pumping acid into his gut. Missy tried to talk, but she was sobbing too hard.

"It's all right," Evelyn said, stroking Missy's back.

"What's wrong?" Adam asked.

"He's gone," Mare said, jogging to join them.

"Who's gone?" Adam's heart beat faster and faster by the second.

"Phoenix." Mare had paled to the point his skin appeared waxy beneath the moon. "He took one of the bikes."

"No," Adam gasped. "He wouldn't leave us." The vague recollection of being awakened during the night flashed from his memory, an elusive specter Adam couldn't quite grasp. Had Phoenix roused him to tell him he was leaving? No…it had been something else entirely, something that was the cause of the tingling in his shoulders.

All of the commotion had woken Ray and Jake as well, who now stood behind them.

"This can't be happening," Jill whispered, repeating it like a mantra.

Missy steeled her lip and a cool calmness settled over her. Her chest no longer shuddered, and though the tears still fell, she no longer sobbed. She curled her hands into fists. "We need to go after him."

"We don't know where he went," Adam said, but that wasn't the truth. They all knew where he had gone.

Missy turned her back on them and stormed up the path to where it crested the hill and she could see down into the city. Where once there had been only darkness, there was now a lake of fire, glowing like a beacon. And there beyond it, standing from the wasteland, a lone tombstone to mark the passage of the world itself, was the hideous black tower. That was where he was going. She felt that truth with as much certainty as anything in her entire life. He was going there for her—

It will be easier for you…later. If you hate me.

To save her.

She screamed in anguish, her voice echoing infinitely to the east.

"He can't have been gone too long," she said, gritting her teeth. She nearly clobbered Mare when she turned. "If we hurry, we might be able to catch him."

"Missy…" Mare said, reaching to place a consolatory hand on her shoulder, but she was already past him and pushing her way though the others, all of whom wore matching expressions of shock.

She reached her motorcycle and climbed onto the seat, already revving the engine before she retracted the kickstand.

"We can't let him face them alone," she said, spearing them with a hard glance. "Try to catch up."

The bike rocketed forward, trying to outrace the headlight she snapped on almost as an afterthought.

"Wait!" Mare shouted, sprinting after her. He leapt onto the seat of another cycle and brought it to life. Jill barely reached him in time to swing up behind him, grabbing him too tightly around the belly and flattening her chest to his back. She lowered her head as the motorcycle launched forward, speeding so fast it felt like the wheels had left the ground.

By the time she dared to open her eyes and risk a glance back, their camp was nearly out of sight. She saw two flashes of light as the remaining motorcycles started forward, and then they were gone. Mare leaned to the left, urging them around the bend at the crest of the hill, the rear tire kicking out sideways and showering the dead forest sloping down the hill with gravel.

Jill pinched her eyes shut and held on for dear life. Mare righted the bike and accelerated downhill, desperately trying to keep his sister's headlight in sight, knowing full well the consequences if he didn't.

V

THE RUINS OF
DENVER,
COLORADO

The devastation was beyond anything he could have ever imagined. Every house he passed had been reduced to charred rubble: mounds of blackened bricks and timber haphazardly heaped atop the fragmented cement of the basements and foundations. How many lives had been lost in each? Every structure was haunted by the melancholy ghosts of its former occupants; a warped swing set nearly melted to the ground, tangles of bikes on the scorched lawns, black ceramic gnomes lording over barren gardens. At least the bodies once rotting within had been incinerated and no longer contributed to the overwhelmingly foul stench of death, which had been replaced by the purified scent of fire. The gutters were clogged with ash-induced slush and debris, the singed fire hydrants standing by uselessly on the street corners. The closer together the houses became, the less distinguishable their remains were, until either side of the road was lined with walls of destruction, giving Phoenix the impression of riding through a trench. Moonlight stretched shadows from the refuse, creating the illusion of movement from the corner of his eye, but he knew better than to suspect an ambush. His adversary would be waiting for him. The conflict was inevitable. Both knew not only that it was coming, but that there would be no escaping it.

Phoenix felt the pull of Death, the attraction undeniable. The closer he came, the harder his heart started to pound, the greater the splitting pain in his head. He had never been so utterly terrified in his life, yet at the same time there was almost a sense of calm that came with the knowledge that soon enough this would all be over. His fate was at the end of the very road he now traveled, the culmination of a journey he had begun at birth.

He tried not to think about Missy, who would wake to find him gone any moment now, but invariably, all thoughts led back to her. She was his greatest weakness, but also the source of his strength. He was willing to kill for her or lay down his life, if need be. Unfortunately, he knew not which option it would be. Not yet.

He focused again on the road, metered by bent or toppled streetlights. Long since abandoned cars filled the highway, folded into each other, but an easily navigable path through the wreckage stretched before him, as though created just for him by dying motorists whose last thoughts had been of clearing a trail for mankind's last hope, its would-be savior. Starlight twinkled from the shattered glass fused to the pavement by the heat of the burning vehicles, guiding him onward toward the horizon, where the black monolith stood apart from the night.

The orange glow he had seen from above appeared ahead and to the right, the heat emanating from it summoning sweat to saturate his clothing. A steel and mortar building had collapsed along the side of the road, the sign designating its name and function now a warped Plexiglas marker hiding shattered bulbs inside a slanting aluminum frame. The building leaned away from the lake of molten fire as though trying to escape, echoes of the screams to come clinging to it in a haze of impending suffering, but he couldn't think about that now. There was nothing he could do to alter the future he saw reflected from the building through time. His destiny was still in front of him, and stopping to try to avert the inevitable would only damn him, and the rest of them at his side.

Tears streamed from his eyes as the building fell behind, the burbling lake yawing wide beyond.

Flames crackled from the turbulent surface in waves. Large bubbles rose from the depths, swelling until they finally popped, turning to parabolic spatters of lava. Smoke gushed from the lake, though not nearly as much as it seemed like there should have been, and somehow through it, in the center of the lake was the white-hot core where the creature lurked beneath. The Leviathan, birthed of the molten lifeblood of the earth and destined to dwell in its infernal depths.

He maketh the deep to boil like a pot, Phoenix thought, though the voice was not his own. *Let those who curse it curse the day, Who are prepared to rouse Leviathan.* It was The Man he heard in his head. He who had shouted the scriptures to the Swarm loud enough overhead to be heard even through the floor above in the basement, whose voice had risen to tumultuous levels when fueled by the fires of Revelations.

Phoenix thought he glimpsed a black head breaching the surface like a crocodile's, but when he turned there were only more bubbles. And had there been a slashed streak of fire like a smile on that face?

The black ground slanted away from the highway, through the maze of incinerated trunks, before leveling off to reach the smoldering banks, which only held back the flaming lake because there was nothing left to burn. While he couldn't be sure that he had seen a face, he could be certain that his passage hadn't gone unnoticed. The beast knew he was there for the same reason that Phoenix was acutely aware of its presence. He feared that the reek of death clung to both of them.

Phoenix turned again to the road, which straightened after rounding the eastern edge of the lake, heading directly toward the black tower, which rose steadily ahead from the leveled downtown region. The heat faded and Phoenix grew cold, though not exclusively from the absence of the flames. The wicked sensation originated from the structure, the coldness of the grave, a suitable home for its lord and master.

Time seemed to stand still and fly by at the same time. He skirted fallen overpasses by riding up the off ramp and then back down the far side, no longer even noticing the snarls of wrecked cars burned black or the incinerated corpses within. His world now solely consisted of the menacing structure and the narrowing gap between. The mounds of rubble grew larger as he approached downtown, burnt wood replaced by buckled and bowed steel girders.

The stars faded overhead and the moon paled with the vague pale pink aura staining the horizon. At long last, the day he had been dreading his entire life had finally arrived.

The asphalt ended in a ragged cliff at the edge of the atomic crater, forcing him to slowly descend the rugged debris, weaving back and forth until the ground flattened again. It was as thought the greater portion of the city proper had simply dropped twenty feet from its former level. While the pavement was cracked into sections that stood askew at severe angles, he was still able to progress. There were giant chasms where entire stretches of the street and guard rails had fallen into the sewers, for which he had to slow to circumnavigate. He finally had to abandon the highway completely when he reached a segment where an overpass had fallen into the river beneath, tentacles of rebar reaching toward him from beneath the surface.

Skirting the river, he came upon a point where a section of one of the smaller streets had fallen down, but was remarkably still flat enough that he could cross without the foot-deep water carrying him away. When he rose up the far slanted side, he emerged onto a four lane road lined with the collapsed concrete and iron skeletons of felled skyscrapers. The hoods and trunks of buried cars pointed out from beneath, nearly obscuring all but the center stripe of the asphalt. At the end of the lane was a great courtyard, in the middle of which was a mound of debris capped by an enormous cross. Behind it, the fortress ascended hundreds of feet into the sky, nearly grasping the heavens.

The air had grown oppressive, as though someone were sitting on his chest. Goose bumps rose over every inch of his flesh. He wiped the tears from his cheeks and managed to steady his trembling jaw.

The street terminated in what had once been a T-intersection, the streetlights cast aside into the devastation. Ash blew along the pavement like miniature tumbleweeds. He rode the motorcycle up the curb and into the wide concrete courtyard, parking the bike and killing the engine at the foot of the mounded debris. He stared up at the ten-foot cross framed against the tower, a confounding juxtaposition. The sun ascended behind, the reddish-orange rays making the skyscraper appear to be on fire.

Taking a deep breath, Phoenix climbed down from the seat and leaned the bike on its kickstand. The air around him stood still, the only sound his harsh breathing. The ground around him was scored black, littered with dots of melted glass shards and the concrete remains of planters and the once elaborate fountain. He looked high up to the top floor expecting to see his enemy glowering down upon him, but he should have known better.

The skin on his back crawled and he closed his eyes, a wave of fear washing over him. He needed to be strong now. Clenching his fists, he turned around, knowing precisely what he would see.

Two figures cloaked in the rotting flesh of the dead closed in upon him from either side, moving in sweeping motions like shadows, hardly appearing to touch the ground. Their faces were hidden in shadow. Another only vaguely human shape stood no more than ten paces directly ahead, eyes glowing scarlet. The creature looked at first to be one of the vanquished Swarm, but he was so much more. Larger, more heavily muscled, his movements less sinewy and more purposeful. An aura of power hung around him. He was the source of the cold, not the building. This was his adversary. There was no doubt.

This was Death.

The Beast smiled at the recognition in his prey's eyes, a horrible gash of sharp teeth. Stretching his arms out to either side, he extended his talons with a flick of his wrists.

Phoenix had to bite his lip to keep from crying out.

Death cocked his head first one way and then the other, his throat swelling in preparation of testing the vocal chords that had remained dormant for so long now.

"Are you prepared to die?" Death said, his voice gravely, though containing the force of an explosion, a concussive wave of sound Phoenix felt in his chest.

Phoenix could only stare at him, summoning his courage to prevent bleating like a lamb when he finally opened his mouth.

"Do what you must," he finally said.

Death's smile stretched impossibly wide.

Rest assured. This time Death's voice was inside his head. *I will.*

Hands fell upon Phoenix, clasping tightly around his biceps.

And you will experience pain beyond the comprehension of the flesh.

Phoenix nipped through his lip to stifle a scream. Blood filled his mouth.

Your suffering shall know no bounds.

He was raised from the ground, but he didn't protest as his arms were stretched painfully out to either side. His back slammed against a metal girder, and he was lifted from the rubble. The emaciated form of Pestilence raised a wiry arm, in her hand a sharply-broken length of rebar. He looked away as she tensed to slam down the spike, only to find the stark white form of Famine doing the same. There was no time to even close his eyes before they struck like angry serpents, biting right through his palms and into the metal frame.

Still, Phoenix didn't cry out.

His shoulders strained when they stepped away, leaving him dangling there. Someone held his feet together and he had to close his eyes, knowing what was coming next.

Thuck!

VI

THE TRAIL OF
BLOOD

Jill screamed, but even with her mouth so close to Mare's ear, he didn't hear it, as her voice was swept away by the wind of their passage and the buzz of engines. Missy's headlight flashed ahead of them, weaving through the maze of the burned trees still left standing, flickering like a reel-to-reel movie projector. They were gaining on her, slowly, but they were pushing the bike too hard. Every turn made them skid a little farther, every stray rock or pothole threatening to catapult them from the path. Any dip launched them into the air, the resulting bounce when they landed again sending them right back into the air. She was horrified they were going to crash, envisioning herself wrapped around a trunk with a broken spine, sharp compound fractures jutting through her bleeding skin. To have come this far, only to die from an accident…

She pressed her face into Mare's back after watching Missy's bike soar from a small knoll, knowing in a matter of second they would do the same. Gritting her teeth and pinching her eyes shut, she whimpered and braced herself. The motorcycle crunched forward, abusing the spring shock on the front tire, and then they were airborne. The sensation of weightlessness was acute. Her gut tingled, but there was something else, that familiar feeling of detachment, of being yanked out of her body and into a realm devoid of her physical bond to the world. Before the tires again met with the earth, her mind was transported somewhere else entirely.

"You have to tell him," a familiar voice said from the darkness.

Jill wasn't sure where she was until she opened her eyes and slowly adapted to the smothering blackness. She was sitting in the top room of the pueblo, which was subtly lit by the wavering glow of a torch somewhere above through the hole in the roof. In front of her sat the skeleton of her ancestor, though the bones appeared softened by the spectral haze of the woman's former physical form, a semi-opaque overlay of life upon death. Her dark eyes blended into the shadows of her hollow sockets, her transparent lips moving over eternally bared teeth. Even from beyond the grave, she exuded a vibrant, golden aura of vitality.

"I can't," Jill said.

"You must."

"How can I even be sure?"

The lips smiled over those awful teeth. There was no light in the expression, just a mixture of patience and sorrow.

"Tell me you can't feel her, already growing inside of you."

Jill said nothing, and was unable to maintain eye contact. After a moment of weighted silence, she nodded.

"Then you must tell him. Now. He needs to know right now, child."

"I don't want to lose him," Jill whimpered. "I love him."

This time the ghost's smile was genuine.

"Of course you do, and he loves you too. That's why you must tell him."

"But if I do…" Jill started, knowing that saying the words would only start her crying. "If I do…he'll die."

"If you don't, you all will."

"You could be wrong."

The smile grew impatient. Lines of worry crossed the skull like gossamer.

"You must tell him now," the voice said as darkness again assaulted Jill, closing her off from the fantasy world around her.

Jill opened her eyes again, and was immediately startled by how loose her grip around Mare's waist had become. His right hand was squeezing her wrist, hard, the bike swaying as he attempted to drive with only his left. He was shouting her name repeatedly, his grip tightening to the point she feared bones might snap. Her head had slid down his back and now rested below this right scapula. Her rear end threatened to drop right off the end of the seat.

She pulled herself back upright, nearly toppling the whole works with the jostling. Mare loosened his grasp when her hands tightened again around him, and glanced back at her every couple of second to make sure she was all right.

The landscape had changed dramatically since her blackout. No longer was she surrounded by burned tree trunks, but by piles of scorched rubble, what little remained of the houses fallen into their basements, warehouses and office building flattened on concrete slabs, half-consumed two-by-fours protruding at odd angles like so many porcupine quills. The dirt path had given way to cracked asphalt, a new growth of weeds rising from the fissures through the ash in small tufts. Missy's taillight glowed red ahead as she slowed and stared from the highway down the embankments to either side at the sad remains.

The sun was finally piercing the horizon, shoving away the night with pink and red arms, though there was still that eerie orange glow hanging over the coming rise.

"I'm pregnant," Jill blurted, though she could tell by Mare's reaction that he hadn't heard. Surely he would have at least acknowledged her in some small way. She leaned closer to his right ear, resting her chin on his shoulder. "Mare!"

He turned his head toward her, startled by her shout, and banged his cheek into her forehead.

"I have to tell you something!" she yelled.

"What?" His eyes flicked back and forth between her face and the road.

Jill hesitated, her courage faltering. What if she told him and he freaked out? What if he got mad? What if—? "I'm pregnant!" she shouted before her nerve abandoned her entirely.

His eyelids snapped back, his orbs appearing close to spilling out. The bike wobbled and nearly capsized. He had to slam the brakes before he lost control. The rear tire locked, leaving a trail of rubber. His feet hit the pavement for balance and he twisted around to see her.

She couldn't read the expression on his face. He was so young, his upper lip and chin covered with downy white fluff. His lips parted, but no sound came out. A confused expression lined his forehead, crinkling his nose and narrowing his eyes. He opened his mouth wider, but the words still eluded him.

"Did you hear me?" she asked, averting her eyes, which had begun to well with tears.

"I'd swear you said..." His voice trailed off as the others caught up from behind. "Did you say...?"

Jill nodded. When she turned back to him, tears were streaming down her cheeks.

"What's wrong?" Adam asked, puttering beside Mare.

"Please," Mare said. "Don't let my sister out of your sight. We'll be right behind you."

Adam gave Mare a questioning look and waited momentarily for him to elaborate, but Missy was already little more than a red dot down the road.

"Don't take too long," Adam said, rocketing forward before Missy disappeared completely, nearly jettisoning Ray from the seat behind him. Evelyn sped to keep up with Jake clinging to her.

"We'd better hurry and catch up," Mare said, his expression still an enigma.

"Don't you have anything to say?" Jill said, struggling to keep her voice firm.

He turned to face the road ahead, his back to her. "My father was an abusive drunk."

Jill waited for him to continue. She finally spoke when it became apparent he wouldn't. There were so many things she wanted to say, but they were nearly out of time. She wanted to reassure him that he wouldn't end up like his father, that everything would work out like it was supposed to. But she couldn't. There would be no future for them.

"I love you," was all she could think to say.

"I love you, too," he said, though he didn't turn around. Jill knew why. She could see the tears trailing down the side of his cheek.

Jill's heart sunk in her chest. She wondered if this was what it felt like when it broke as Mare launched the bike down the road toward the twin red lights vanishing around the bend ahead.

VII

Mare couldn't absorb it all at once. It felt like the world was spinning out of control and there was nothing he could do to stop it. He was scared. Terrified of what awaited them down the road; terrified of the bombshell Jill had just dropped on him. He was still just a kid, for God's sake! Granted, none of the old rules applied. Everything was life or death now, but still, his initiation to adulthood had been as abrupt and painful as his father's overhand right. His father...the last thing he needed right now was to have to remember his old man, the man who had beaten him to the brink of unconsciousness on more than one occasion, whose whiskey-fueled anger had torn his family apart. What if he ended up like his father? They say that while everyone may rage against it, eventually they turn out just like their parents, repeating the same trite adages, the same mannerisms, perpetuating that which they most despise. In his case, violence. He couldn't allow that to happen to him, but what if he had no control over that transformation? What if his temper had been set on a razor-wire trigger like his father's? Would he awaken in the night, frustrated with the baby's incessant crying, and begin beating on him before he knew what he was doing?

All he could see was his father kneeling over him, pinning his arms to the ground with his knees, bludgeoning his face. Over and over. Fists striking like bricks. That image melted away into that of a beaten man sprawled across his bed with the upper half of his cranium dripping back down from the ceiling. Maybe there had been some regret, a small fraction of a conscience after all. Or maybe, after so many poundings, that was the only way his father could think of to hurt him even more.

He couldn't think about that now. He wasn't his father. He would never be like his old man. *Never!*

There was still Jill to think about. And the baby. He had handled the news as poorly as he possibly could have. How must he have looked, standing there slack-jawed with that abject look of horror on his face? He could see how scared she was, but all he could think of was himself. How would this affect him? *Stupid, stupid!* She needed him now more than ever—both of them—and he had reacted like a selfish jerk.

How could she be so sure she was pregnant anyway? It had only been a couple days since their rendezvous on the beach. She couldn't have run down to the convenience store to grab a pregnancy test.

There he went being selfish again. If anyone could know, it was Jill. She could see the future in her visions after all, but why had she needed to tell him at that precise moment? All that could possible do was add more stress to an already—

Stop it! Stop it! He chastened himself. This wasn't just about him. This was about Jill and the baby. This was about his—

"Family," he said aloud, the wind rushing past stealing away the word.

His breath froze in his chest, but a sensation of warmth spread though him. He was going to have a family. He wasn't going to be a father, but a daddy. There was going to be a helpless life depending upon him for everything. A life that was part him and part Jill, a wondrous soul preparing to be birthed into a nightmarish wasteland.

Calmness washed over him. He knew right then and there that he would do absolutely anything to protect that child. Their child.

He felt Jill draped over him from behind, her chest shuddering as she cried, her face pressed into is shoulder to muffle her sobs so he wouldn't hear. What had he done? How could he have hurt her so? Perhaps he hadn't struck her, but he knew that his silence had been an emotional lashing no less painful.

Lowering his right hand to his lap, he gave her clasped hands a gentle squeeze, hoping for now it would be enough.

He couldn't help thinking that somewhere in that belly pressed against the small of his back was a rapidly dividing cluster of cells no larger than the head of a pushpin, defying the odds in its quest for life. Would it have its mother's eyes and his dark hair? He hoped it wouldn't have his nose for sure. In his mind he saw a perfect being, little pink arms and legs, a downy shock of blond hair on her head. Her head? Until that point he'd never imagined it might be a girl. He could do this. He could be strong. Strong enough to face the battle ahead and strong enough to overcome his genetics.

He was going to be a dad.

Tears rolled down his cheeks, streaking back toward his ears.

The motorcycle raced around a bend in the highway, leaving the foothills behind. The city stretched out before them, the horizon marred by haphazardly deconstructed buildings and the scorched remains of hundred year-old trees. There, dead ahead at the end of the road, which now appeared far too short, was the ominous tower. Even in his imagination it hadn't appeared nearly as dark and foreboding, a malignancy rising from a dying land. His heart rate accelerated and he nearly slammed into the back of a pickup before regaining command of the bike and centering himself to the middle of the road.

Half a mile ahead he could see the glow of Evelyn's taillight against the glare of the rising sun, which stained the sky the color of blood. Every nerve in his body screamed at once for him to turn around, but his sister was somewhere ahead. He couldn't abandon her to her fate, but at the same time, he was suddenly torn between responsibilities. He couldn't abide anything happening to Jill and their child either. What was he supposed to do? If he turned back, his actions could potentially damn them all, but if he proceeded he could jeopardize the new life entrusted to him. He wasn't prepared to make such a monumental decision.

He instinctively hit the brakes when he saw the blinding flash of light ahead. It looked like a shooting star had torn through the atmosphere and slammed to the road ahead. No, not a star. The sudden brilliance had left an arched tracer across his vision, a lingering rainbow of orange that originated from the far side of a fallen building and a copse of burned trees, beyond which smoke rose unbidden, imbued with the same fiery hue.

A rush of liquid fire far ahead lifted a car from the road and tossed it onto the far shoulder to bound down the incline.

"Missy!" Mare screamed, pinning the gas and rocketing forward.

"Mare, no!" Jill screamed from behind him. "Please don't! You can't—!"

But her voice was swept away by the buzz of the engines and the wind, which seemed to grow steadily warmer as they raced toward her worst nightmare.

VIII

Phoenix refused to close his eyes, even though the pain was so great that keeping them open strained his failing reserves. Nor did he allow them the satisfaction of his cries. Not so much as a whimper parted his lips. He had passed all of his power to those that needed it most, leaving him a simple, and all-too-human, vessel of flesh and bone. His strength had abandoned him long ago.

All that remained now was to die.

He could feel the blood rolling along his arms and down his legs, patterning his chest where it fell from his chin. Keeping his head raised placed enormous pressure on his neck, but he needed to see the sky. He had spent so many years in the darkness with only spider web-riddled floorboards above, that to lose sight of the sky now would be the fatal injury. Besides, looking down, seeing what they were doing to him, would only break him, absolving him of his vow to not give them the satisfaction of hearing his agony manifested through pain-laced sobs.

The distant mountains stood proudly against the remainder of the night, slowly slinking away with the last of the stars. A cloud of smoke rose from the lake of fire, imbued with a warm glow that at the moment appeared beautiful. Overhead, wispy clouds spanned the perfect blue like stretched cotton balls, their bellies taking on the colors of the sunrise, a muted pink like the rosy blush in Missy's cheeks. His sweet Miss—

He bit his lip to stifle a scream. The rush of pain was so intense that he knew if death didn't claim him soon, they would beat him, body and soul.

Focusing again on the sky through tear-blurred eyes, he wondered how far the atmosphere reached toward the heavens. At what point did the blue give way to the blackness of space? Was it abrupt like dousing a light or was it a gradual transition of grays? He hoped he would find out, that when his soul was separated from his defiled carcass he would be able to soar like a bird over the earth, banking on the gentle currents, exploring a world he had only recently discovered existed at all.

A ripping sound he felt as much as heard forced his eyes shut, a flood of crimson squirting through his bared teeth. He coughed and a cloud of blood exploded into the air.

The muscles in his neck finally gave out, dropping his chin to his chest. He mourned the loss of the precious sky, but soon enough he would be there, unbridled of his torment. With his head down, there was no holding back the tears he had been able to dam thus far. They carved pink trails through the scarlet dots and spatters on his cheeks. His long, bloody bangs peeled away from his face to dangle limply before him, dripping steadily across his vision as he looked from the corner of his right eye. A length of rebar had been driven through his palm and one of the rivet holes in the horizontal iron beam, and bent behind to hold it in place. A crown of jagged bone ringed the pulpy juncture. His fingers had curled inward like a dead spider's legs. He tired to move them, but they were unresponsive, his efforts instead pumping fluid from the wound. All of the tendons and muscles in his arms were stretched taut, his own weight threatening to snap his elbow and dislocate his shoulder. A glance from the corner of his left eye confirmed the other hand to be staked as well, the fingers already beginning to turn blue. His vision swam and his eyes fell again to the ground. Consciousness fled momentarily, but the pain brought it back.

His shirt had been shredded to tatters. The flesh on his chest hadn't fared much better. The skin had been peeled away from the muscles in slow, deliberate fashion, but the meat had been savagely slashed by the same claws that had painstakingly skinned him. Death had wanted him to fight, but Phoenix had faced his foe in silence. In a furor, the beast had finally lashed out against him, giving up on the slow torture meant to draw out his power, and reverting to the animalistic thrashing. Phoenix drew some small measure of satisfaction from the fact that he hadn't caved. He couldn't see Death now, but he could still hear the demon breathing. He no longer had the strength to even move his eyes to look toward the sound.

Phoenix sighed, but the sound it produced was a wet burble.

Darkness closed in upon him, creeping from the periphery. He wanted to close his eyes to welcome it, but his eyelids felt glued in place. Long, thin legs that no longer looked as though they belonged to him dangled below, his knobby knees bowed outward, feet run through atop one another with a single metal spike. Below, the scorched rubble glimmered with the sunlight reflecting from the massive deluge of blood.

The darkness gently accepted him in the form of Missy, her arms spread wide, drawing him to her chest. He could feel himself smiling to match the expression on her face, her eyes full of warmth. Behind them, a light pulled at him, drawing him nearer and nearer, into her and then through—

"Not yet!" Death raged, forcing his head back, claws buried into his cheeks. The wounds barely bled at all.

Phoenix saw a flash of glowering red eyes and a tangle of sharp teeth, and then they were gone.

"No!" Death tore through Phoenix's flimsy flesh, exposing his mandible and teeth. He drew back his arms and slashed over and over, tearing away chunks of muscle until the ribs showed, but Phoenix's body merely sagged further. "You can't do this! The battle has to be ours! I cannot accept…"

The voice faded to a whisper, and then to the sound of wind rushing past. The world fell away beneath him as he ascended, drawn toward a light as bright as the sun on wings made of clouds.

CHAPTER 8

I

Missy fixed her stare to the wretched tower standing against the horizon, despite the stinging glare of the sun rising behind it. There was no doubt in her mind that Phoenix was already there. She screamed in futility, her face drenched with tears. She was too late. Every bone in her body ached. Her chest heaved, barely able to take in the short, choppy breaths preceding hyperventilation and the panic attack threatening to overwhelm her. Only moments prior she had been struck by an intense sorrow, a physical blow akin to slamming the speeding bike into a brick wall, which nearly toppled her from the seat. She had known immediately what had caused the sensation, but she struggled to rationalize it, to deny the feeling of being shattered like a porcelain doll.

I gave you my heart, Phoenix's voice whispered in her mind.

And that was precisely what she had felt breaking.

She screamed again, driving on instinct, slaloming the bike through the vehicular wreckage. Pushing it as fast as she dared, she watched the lone standing skyscraper growing closer too slowly through tear-blurred eyes. There was nothing she could do. Her only remaining option was to accept that the love of her short life was dead, but she would sooner die herself than give up the slim hope to which she clung, no matter how irrational it seemed.

So intently had she been drawn to the tower that she didn't notice the strange orange glow through the dead trees and rubble. Her distracted mind ignored the smell of smoke and the thickening clouds until they drifted across the road, obscuring her vision. There was always smoke. Always fire. Always death. Her subconscious was so well adapted it didn't even trigger her internal alarm until it was too late.

A wash of flaming magma arched over the highway ahead, appearing to hover like a rainbow made of wet paint before splashing back down. It spattered the already cooked cars and covered the asphalt no more than twenty yards ahead.

Missy jammed the brakes. The tires screamed as they bled rubber onto the pavement and the rear wheel skipped side to side. Her thoughts raced. She scanned the road ahead for a way around the stream of lava now crossing all of the lanes. Nothing. She nearly laid the bike down, knowing full well the consequences of skidding down the asphalt on her back, but the bike came to a screeching halt before she reached the fiery crack. The magma was already slowly draining back down the shoulder to the right, returning to a massive lake of flames shrouded beneath a layer of smoke.

Something black breached the surface at the center, fading in and out of the swirling smoke. It emerged from beneath so slowly that she questioned whether or not it was truly moving at all. Details were hazy, but it looked almost like a great black cross.

Until it opened its eyes.

Missy screamed when those blazing embers fixed upon her. A rush of fire raced up the creature's body until it was alive with flames. It raised both arms straight up over its head, and what looked like steel in a smelting pot bubbled from its palms.

Missy spun the motorcycle around so fast she nearly dropped it on its side. She barely kept it level enough to launch it back down the highway in the direction from which she had come.

The Leviathan jerked its arms down to shoulder level and fired a flume of magma at the road directly behind her. It hit with such force that it launched one of the dead cars from the road, sending it flipping through the air to tumble over the median.

She saw the others speeding toward her, the reflection of the fire on their faces. She waved madly at them to turn back, but they either couldn't see or misinterpreted the gesture.

A quick glance to her left. The creature was sprinting across the surface of the lake, nearly paralleling her progress, a cape of fire trailing behind it like the tail of a meteorite.

Missy screamed and waved her arm above her head to ward the others off, but it was too late.

Another arc of fire shot out over the highway behind them, splashing down on the pavement to block their retreat.

To her right, the east- and westbound lanes were divided by a waist-high cement guard rail. There was only one way they could cross over it, and in the time it took all of them to lift the motorcycles over one by one, they would be burned alive. They were going to have to abandon the bikes and try to outrace the beast on foot, but with as far as that thing could shoot those flames, even that seemed like suicide. But it was their only—

The sky directly overhead grew bright. She didn't need to look up to know why; droplets of lava were already patterning the road in front of her. Ducking her head, she prayed and sped straight ahead. The magma spattered the ground behind her. Streaks of the splashing flames lit up the corners of her vision and she screamed, expecting any second to feel the skin on her back burning, but there was no pain.

It was herding them.

With the molten lava still burbling on the road, they couldn't escape the way they had come, and they were cut off from downtown. Crossing the median was out of the question as more and more fire landed on the westbound lanes. They were boxed in. There was nowhere else to go. Soon enough it was going to kill them all. Only one option remained, and even that was a stall tactic at best.

She jerked the handles to the left and sped toward the lake, where the flaming shadow now stood on the fiery waves, the smoke again closing in around it. Gravel flew from her tires as she raced down the shoulder to the front of the demolished warehouse. The entire building leaned away from the lake, the western half by the parking lot collapsed flat. Blackened corrugated aluminum and crushed cinderblocks were piled across what had once been the back door, covering the cement pad where there had been a picnic table for the employees, enclosed by a now absent fence. The steel door had snapped from its hinges and stood crookedly, granting a triangular entrance into the darkness.

Locking up the brakes, she skidded to a halt and leapt from the bike, which clattered to the ground behind her.

The others were already halfway down the shoulder and closing fast.

She looked back to the blazing lake in time to see the creature slowly sinking into it, hip deep, then chest. Finally, its head vanished from sight, no longer betraying its location.

"Hurry!" she screamed, turning back in the direction of the road.

Adam and Evelyn were already off their bikes and squeezing through the gap into the building with Ray and Jake right behind.

"Get in there!" Mare shouted, turning her and shoving her toward the building in one motion. He pushed Jill into the building from behind, and followed her into the darkness.

He turned, grabbed hold of the door, and tried to jerk it back closed, but he lacked the leverage. Groaning and growling, he only managed to tug it a couple of inches before it stopped again.

Shouting in frustration, his eyes were drawn to the shore of the lake thirty feet away, and to the sudden movement of something cresting the surface from beneath.

II

The child had died too easily. He was
supposed to have put up a fight, to have raged
against him in his pain. He was supposed to
have begged for his life, to have bargained
for salvation. With his dying breath he should
have cursed the Lord, who had allowed him
to be killed in such a manner. He should
have been broken, his mind shattered, his soul
tainted by doubt and anger, sent back to God
blackened and ugly, a final message delivered
to the Maker who may have summoned
Death, but who could no longer stand in his
way. Death's time was now, but somehow the
victory felt hollow.

It was more than the fact that the boy had
proven to be of little opposition. There was
something else, a feeling he couldn't quite
rationalize. He hadn't been able to enjoy the
process of torturing him. For every wound
he inflicted on the child, every slash through
the forgiving flesh, one opened within him.
Not physical pain per se, but it was definitely
tangible. Hurting the boy had weakened him
dramatically. Killing him had opened a hole
in his very being, an uncomfortable void that
ate at him like a cancer. No. Not eating at
him, but missing from him.

He stared up at the lifeless body dangling
from the cross. He had watched the last of the
blood drain from the body, which was now so
pale the skin was almost transparent. Bruises
rose where bone met skin in the cheeks and
the rims of the eyes, nearly obscured by the
crusted hair dangling in front of his face. The
boy's hands and feet were now nearly purple.
Yet still Death couldn't tear himself away.

The rising sun behind the tower cast a single beam of light through the shattered windows, spotlighting the boy on the cross, creating a golden aura around his corpse.

It infuriated him. Cocking his head back, he hissed up into the heavens, strands of saliva slapping from his mouth. Even the rubble shivered at the sound.

He had won. He had faced the best the Lord could muster—a child, a weakling child!—and put him down like a mongrel dog, staking claim to the entire world. His world. His realm to rule. So why did he not feel triumphant? Where was the rush of power and accomplishment?

Enraged, he stormed up the heap of refuse to the cross, flicking out his claws and slashing the body across the abdomen. No blood flowed. Nothing. Only four parallel slices through tissue that hardly even parted.

He looked straight through the errant ray of light, directly into the sun. It was as though God was taunting him, tormenting him. His anger boiled over, seizing him in animalistic fury.

The child is dead, a voice from another lifetime spoke in his head, the words laced with an Arabic accent. *Let him be.*

Death lost control and began slashing repeatedly at what was now only a slab of meat.

Thuck!

Scream! I need to hear you scream!

Thuck!

Scream!

Thuck!

SCREAM!

He whirled away from the body, chest heaving, red eyes blazing.

Let him be.

Death rocked back, thrust his arms out to either side and hissed up into the sky. He looked back down, focusing on Pestilence and Famine, both of whom took an unconscious step away. They still flanked the base of the mound, faces shrouded beneath the darkness provided by their cloaks of flesh. If he couldn't make the boy scream, then maybe he could just tear into them, make them feel the pain he had been denied, and through them, he could feel it himself. Even pain would be vastly preferable to the emptiness inside of him. It was almost as though by butchering the child, he had slain a part of himself as well.

That was it, wasn't it? He and the boy: they had been two halves of the same whole, hadn't they? They had both been the children of God. His destiny had been to serve in the capacity of His Wrath, while the boy had been chosen to be His Love. Opposite sides of the same coin. Wrath had triumphed as he had always known it would, but in doing so, he had only beaten himself. Such a bittersweet victory. The wasteland that was the earth was now his, a nuclear-ravaged, fire-scorched planet that would soon know only peace under the reign of one who craved only destruction.

He imagined God laughing at him from on high. There had never truly been any victory to be had. Not for Death. His eradication of mankind only served the Lord's purposes, while if the child would have beaten him, He still would have won. It was a game of chess the Maker played against himself. Death was merely a pawn, but even a pawn could topple a king. He just needed to play the game. He had destroyed humanity's last hope, but that didn't mean there weren't still humans out there. All along he had planned only for their elimination, but the remaining handful could still be useful. With the help of his brother and sister, he could recreate them in his own image. Repopulate his kingdom with denizens who would worship him alone.

Maybe he couldn't beat God, but that didn't mean he couldn't become Him.

He focused on Famine and Pestilence in turn, seeking their eyes through the darkness obscuring them. Both bowed in acknowledgement of his silent command, turned away from one another and struck off down the street. The sound of clopping hooves echoed from the distance, drawing closer by the second.

The survivors would be brought before him.

And they would be remade.

He turned and spared one last glance for the fallen savior nailed to the cross. No longer was his carcass highlighted in a celestial glow. The golden aura was gone, leaving a pathetic, small corpse dangling uselessly, like an autumn leaf. The sun had risen to the top of the building, lending the impression that the entire structure was ablaze, but he didn't care. It was an empty threat.

Striking through the wreckage, he prepared to take his position on the roof, the vantage point from which he would watch his ultimate victory.

III

Mare struggled to pull the metal slab of the door across the gap, but it wouldn't budge. Not from where he stood and with so little leverage. He could hear panicked breathing behind him, screams muffled by hands clasped over mouths so as not to betray their presence in the shadows, but it was too late.

The creature knew exactly where they were.

A black head rose from the burbling magma, followed by a pair of shoulders, maybe ten feet out from the flaming shore.

With renewed vigor, he tugged at the lodged door, his shoulders threatening to dislocate, the skin on his fingers tearing away.

When he looked up again, the thing was out of the lake past its waist, rising straight up as though on a platform, unscathed by the fire.

Mare lowered his shoulder and rammed at the door to free it, if only a little. Rubble and dust rained from above the doorframe, momentarily hiding the monster, which now stood atop the surface, a black figure with flames lapping at its legs. It stretched its arms to either side, palms to the sky.

"You have to close it!" Jill screamed, shoving him to the side and frantically trying to loosen the metal slab, her whole body thrashing with the effort.

A broken metal pipe no more than an inch wide fell from the ceiling, the wires it had formerly housed now hanging exposed from the fractured ceiling.

"Stand back!" Mare shouted, pushing her

away far harder than he had intended, nearly hurling her to the ground.

She looked back at him through teary eyes, wounded.

What have I become? he thought, momentarily frozen. An image of his father catching him in the closet where he had hidden the money he had stolen flashed through his mind. His old man had grabbed him and thrown him to the floor, a maneuver he had nearly duplicated.

"I am not my father," he growled, hurrying through the doorway.

The creature took a swift stride toward him across the molten lake and Mare forced himself to turn his back to it.

"Hand me that pole!" Mare shouted.

Jill grabbed it and thrust it out the door into his waiting palm. He jammed it under the far side of the door, using it like a crowbar to lever the door forward and backward, but it barely moved at all.

He shot a glance back over his shoulder.

The dark man was already to the edge of the lake.

Mare bellowed in frustration as he fought with the stuck door, finally flinging the pole to the ground in frustration.

"Hurry!" Jill screamed. "Please, God. Hurry!"

The others were calling to him, their voices a cacophony of horror. He looked back at them, wide white eyes against dirty faces, clinging to the darkness. Adam tried to shield the rest of them with his body.

The wind shifted, blowing a cloud of smoke toward them.

Mare raced back through the doorway, peeking over his shoulder. The creature still had its arms out at its sides. A streak of fire slashed its face in a smile. Flames rose from its palms and spread up its arms toward its head, the whole body igniting to become a living beast of flames.

"It's right behind me!" Mare shouted, urging Jill out of the doorway. He jerked at the door. It slid only a couple inches and stopped. "No! No! No!"

Jill flinched as though about to be struck.

Mare's mind filled with a million thoughts. The door wouldn't close and that creature would be able to walk right into their midst and torch them all. He had shoved Jill too forcefully. He wasn't his father, but he was going to be a father. Unless he could get the door closed, they were all going to die. But then what? Wait out the beast until their air ran out? They were still dead, regardless of what he did. Unless...

He turned and looked Jill right in the eyes. He knew what he needed to do. Pulling her to him, he hugged her as tightly as he could, knowing it would be the last time he ever did so. He imagined he could feel his daughter through her belly. He was not his father. He was his own man. Damn genetics and his upbringing, there was nothing he wouldn't do for the woman he loved and the child she would bring into the world, regardless of the cost.

"Don't do this," Jill sobbed into his ear, curling her fingers into his shirt and holding tightly.

He heard himself crying as well.

"I love you," he said into her ear. Even though his heart was pounding, he felt a measure of calmness sweep through him. "Make sure she knows how much her daddy loves her, too."

He tried to pull away, but her grip was too strong and he couldn't free himself. Panic set in. He couldn't let anything happen to her and the baby. He looked through the opening and saw the creature striding toward them. They were out of time.

"You have to let me go, Jill!" he wailed, fighting her grasp. "Let me go!"

Screams filled the confines as the others finally saw the demon framed in the opening. Adam forced them to the ground and tried to make himself large enough to take the brunt of the impending fiery assault, knowing there was no way his pathetic flesh would be a good enough barrier.

"Now, Jill! Please!"

She blubbered something unintelligible into his ear as the shadows pealed back around them, the dust- and smoke-clogged chamber filling with the flickering light of flames.

IV

Jill couldn't make herself do it. The pivotal moment was nigh. This was her chance to change the vision of all of them being incinerated, but still she couldn't force herself to do what needed to be done. She loved Mare. There was nothing she had ever been more certain of in her entire life. He was all that mattered. No. There was the baby to think about. And the others…whose lives were now in her hands.

Sacrifice the man she loved and they might all live.

Try to save him and they would all certainly die.

It wasn't fair. No one should have to be placed in the position of making such a choice. Damned if she did, dead if she didn't. All of her former friends and family were now dead. Only pain remained. Lord only knew if by living through this moment that any of them would survive. The creature out there could still kill them all if Mare failed, or maybe some other monster a mile farther down the road. Or maybe they'd be lucky enough to reach their destination, only to be slaughtered on arrival. There were no guarantees. If she had to die, she wanted to do so in the arms of the man she loved.

Would you sacrifice everything for the child? an ancient voice asked in her mind.

"No…" she sobbed. "I can't do it." But the words were garbled by sorrow.

She understood now, though. She understood.

"You have to let me go, Jill!" he shouted into her face, trying to break their embrace.

"Let me go!"

"I can't," she cried, but her voice was drowned out by screams of terror. "I love you too much."

She tightened her grasp on his shirt, watching his face crinkle with fear.

"Now, Jill! Please!"

Why did it have to come to this? It wasn't fair, it wasn't fair, *it wasn't fair!*

The room came to life with the shifting glow of flames, the air crackling with the sound of fire.

Would you sacrifice everything for the child?

"Not him!" she screamed. Her fingers felt like they were going to break.

The smoke grew thicker, clogging the claustrophobic room.

She could see the creature through the gap, the shifting blaze through the smoke. It was nearly upon them.

Would you sacrifice everything for the child?

In her mind she saw both of them locked in an embrace as a wave of molten lava blasted through the doorway and washed over them, skin blistering and then charring, the shrieks of the dying all around her cut short.

Before she realized she had made her decision, her fingers relaxed and Mare turned away.

"Please…" she whimpered. "Please don't take him from me."

Mare ducked through the collapsed doorway and stood between them and the fiery black shadow.

Mare!" she screamed, tearing her throat raw. She fell to her knees, tears spilling down her face. What had she done?

"Mare!"

V

He heard her calling after him as he rushed outside. The flaming creature was no more than fifteen feet from him and closing fast. He couldn't think about that now. Not yet. He turned his back to it and jerked on the door. There was a loud crack and a small landslide of concrete fragments rolled away from it, finally allowing him to drag the door almost all the way across the opening, leaving only a thin gap through which he could see Jill's left eye. She had pressed herself against the steel slab from within, curling her fingers around the edge to try to slide it away.

"I love you," he said, momentarily holding eye contact. He turned away against his will.

All he could see were flames, the black body within no more than a shadow.

"Let's do this," he said, his tremulous voice cracking. Never in his life had he been so terrified, but he couldn't afford to fail. Jill was counting on him. They all were. Especially the little girl he would never know. The thought broke his heart, but even though he would never even see her, he loved her more than life itself. That was what it truly meant to be a father. He had only just learned he was about to become one, yet the revelation had changed his world, the very way he thought. He was now part of something greater than himself. In that moment, as he stared at the fiery creature, he understood how his father must have felt when he shoved the barrel of his handgun into his mouth. His old man had been cruising through life in an alcohol-fueled fugue, wallowing in the self-pity stemming from the loss of his wife, taking out his pain on the only people who could actually understand. But it wasn't until that final beating had awakened him to what he was doing and he made the only noble choice—the only choice he had made as a father in nearly a decade. He had done what it took to save his children from the monster he had become, to save them from himself.

Mare was facing the same decision now. He was about to lose the love of his life and the child he had known so briefly, if only as an abstraction. It hurt him. God, how it hurt! But no harm would come to them. Whatever it took, whatever the price, he would ensure their survival, that they would feel no pain. He would take it all upon himself willingly, if that was the only option. His life meant nothing compared to theirs.

Mare reached down and picked up the metal pole he had used to pry the door loose, the only weapon at his disposal with which to face the demon. He imagined this must have been the same feeling of determination his father felt when he pulled out the gun.

Mare forgave his old man, then and there, for the years of physical and emotional pain, and for his final fateful act, which he had assumed had been designed to hurt his children even more, not knowing until now that it had actually been to save them.

Grasping the pole across his chest in trembling, sweaty fists, he took the first step toward the creature through the rubble. Tears rolled from his eyes, his lips a grim line. He raised his left hand high, using his right to point the sharp, broken end toward the beast's flaming chest.

Its arm shot forward with the speed of a rattlesnake strike and all Mare saw was molten fire.

Screaming, he raced forward, magma washing over him, consuming him.

You will feel no pain, Phoenix's words echoed.

From the corner of his eye, Mare saw his left arm blister, the skin blackening and then finally splitting. He saw exposed muscle and boiling blood, but none of it mattered. His clothes incinerated. His hair vanished. The flesh peeled away from his face and chest as he raised the staff.

Surprise registered on the creature's face. The flames diminished even as it continued to fire the stream at the charging boy. In that heartbeat, its startled eyes appeared almost human, its mouth a ring of fire.

Mare's sight faded, yet still he drove the end of the pole straight through the demon's chest with enough force to stab it all the way through and out the other side.

You will feel no pain.

His dead body crashed into the beast, knocking it backwards and planting the staff in the ground, both of them burning together like blackened logs in an abandoned campfire.

VI

"No!" Jill screamed, yanking on the door, desperately trying to drag it far enough back to squeeze out. Sobbing, she lost control of her faculties, thrashing like a bear trying to free its foot from a trap. Her left hand was burned from a spatter of lava that had struck the door, but she couldn't feel a thing. Her world had just crashed down upon her. It should have been her. She was the one who should have been out there burning on the ground. It had been her visions that had predicted it. She could have changed it. She could have shoved him back and charged out to her death in his stead. They never should have come down this road, never should have tried to hide in this collapsed building. She had known it was coming and had done nothing to prevent it. No...that wasn't true at all. Not only had she not done a thing to stop it, she had willingly sent the man she loved to his gruesome death. All she had needed to do was to hold onto him, refuse to let him go. That had been within her power, and she had simply loosened her grasp and sealed his painful fate. It was her fault that he was dead. Her fault. And now there was nothing she could do to change it.

Would you sacrifice everything for the child?

She screamed as the voice returned unbidden, throwing herself back and forth against the door, which only budged an inch. Through the gap she could see the flames lapping at Mare's smoldering back, issuing thin wisps of deep black smoke.

"Jill," Adam said from behind her.

She whirled and screamed into his face,

pounding her fists against his chest before finally collapsing into his arms.

"It's okay, Jill," he whispered into her ear. "Everything is going to be all right."

Missy slid past them against the wall and peered through the vertical opening. She already knew what she would see, but nothing could have ever prepared her for it. Random patches of fire burned from boiling puddles amidst the rubble, a trail leading to a crisp ebon corpse leaning over another, now little more than a skeleton still grasping the metal pole. Blazing red lava bubbled out of the top of the hollow pole, draining in ribbons down the sides and over the knobby fingers that fortunately had never felt its heat.

She started to sob uncontrollably, wanting to bury her face in her hands, but unable to look away from what had once been her baby brother. It had been her job to protect him, but instead, Mare had always been the one to protect her. From their father. From heartache. And now, from death. She mewled his name over and over, never again to hear his sarcastic and often embarrassing quips. Never again to see his crooked nose or the way the corners of his smile lilted when he was preparing to be mischievous.

Her baby brother was gone. The child who had held her hand when they buried her mother and who had been there every time she needed him, never would be again.

Her baby brother, her best friend in a world that had tried to beat the life out of them both, was dead.

She turned away and found Jill waiting, and together they embraced, both racked with tears, shoulders shuddering.

Adam couldn't bear to watch. It hurt far too much. He felt as though his intestines had been ripped right out. He had loved Mare, too. And his sacrifice, especially the manner in which he had given his life, had been truly beautiful. He had forfeited everything for them. Everything he had and everything he would ever be. He had traded his life for theirs, and there was nothing they could ever do to repay such a gift. No way of satisfactorily honoring him. In the Reserves, he had watched so many people die such horrible deaths, but never with so much dignity or grace. Knowing he would never be able to see Mare again summoned the depths of sadness, but right now he needed to be strong. He had to step up and lead them before they all fell to pieces, himself included.

Sliding past the girls, their combined pain threatening to kill his resolve, he walked through the smoke and grabbed the door, rocking it back and forth until he was able to slide it away.

A gust of the charnel wind blew into his face as he stepped out and walked over to where he had left his motorcycle on its side. Tugging off the cord that restrained the cargo, he pulled out the bundled blanket and emptied its contents onto the ground. He spread the blanket as wide as he could and draped it over the charcoaled remains, smothering the smoke and dwindling flames.

"Thank you, Mare," he said, struggling to hold back his tears. "We will always cherish your memory, and the gift you have given us."

Evelyn's hand slid into his. He turned, buried his face in her neck, and cried, squeezing her tightly until he was able to regain control.

"I love you," he whispered into her ear. "I need you to know that. It can never be said enough."

"I love you, too," she said. "With all of my heart."

Ray could only stand there, balancing precariously on the uneven piles of fractured concrete, holding Jake's hand. He was unable to maintain the kind of concentration required to see, but he didn't need to, didn't want to. There was no denying Mare's fate. He could clearly smell the burnt flesh. It was hard enough holding himself together as it was. Were he able to see the sorrow and pain on the faces of the others, he would surely have lost the façade of control he maintained over his emotions. He needed to be a rock for Jake, though it was tearing him up inside.

It probably would have worried him more to have seen the expression on Jake's face. The boy was markedly detached, wearing a mask of stoicism. Granted, tears swelled from the corners of his eyes, but his affect was bland, his face washed of all but an uneasy understanding, as though the event had come as no surprise, as though he'd seen it before.

"We need to keep moving," Ray said, thankful he couldn't see the reactions to his harsh words. "Phoenix is still somewhere out there."

There was no immediate reply, and he worried he had spoken too soon, but this was by no means the end of their journey. Mare had bought them a temporary stay of execution with his life. They still needed to face their adversary, against whom they might not be so lucky.

"He's right," Adam said, looking to each of the others in turn. "There's nothing more we can do here."

"We can't just leave him," Jill sobbed. "Not like this."

Adam walked over to her and took her by the hands. She nearly jumped out of her skin at the contact. He held her burned hand up where he could see it. The skin was still swelling, ballooning with pus. Her fingertips were black and crusty, the seared nails beginning to peel away.

"Jesus," he whispered. It reminded him of the little girl in Iran, whom Mûwth had been able to cure by touch, but he had ultimately been unable to save. The memory caught him off guard. That little girl was the only reason he was still alive, while his fellow soldiers had never made it out of the Ali Sadr caves. Kotter, Thanh, Keller. Christ, Keller had been transformed into War. What had happened to the others, what had they become? Were they still—?

Smoke rose from his fingers were he touched Jill's hand. He gasped, unable to feel his digits, unable to pry them from her flesh. The blisters popped, the pasty contents spilling down the back of her hand. The thin epidermis peeled back and fell off like the outer layer of an onion. The coarse black skin turned to ash and crumbled away. It was the exact same miracle he had watched Mûwth perform.

Adam could only stare. There were no words for what he was feeling. His thoughts were an incomprehensible jumble.

Jill pulled her hands away and flexed her fingers.

"Please," she whispered. "Please try Mare."

"Jill…"

"Please, Adam. You have to try."

Adam nodded and walked as though in a trance to where the blanket covered the bodies. *What's happening to me?* he thought as he pulled back a corner and closed his hand over the parallel bones in Mare's skeletal forearm. They were still hot.

He waited.

Nothing.

He closed his eyes and tried to concentrate all of his energy into his hand. When he opened them again, nothing had changed.

"I'm sorry, Jill," he whispered. "I am so sorry."

Finally, he removed his hand and covered Mare back up. There was nothing left to heal, if that was even what he was now capable of doing.

Jill turned away, her momentary hopes dashed, and began to sob anew.

VII

They had left him there. Her love. Her life. They had left him lying on the scorched ground beneath a ratty old blanket. No burial. No rites. Only the hard earth to hold him. That and the body of the demon from which he had saved them all. It wasn't fitting. It wasn't fair. He had given them everything, and they had abandoned him.

"This isn't where he should be buried," Adam had said. "I promise you, Jill. I promise. We'll make sure he stays with us. Right there on the beach where he can be remembered and honored."

She trusted Adam, but there were so many variables outside of his control. They still had yet to face evil on its own ground and there were no guarantees they would be making the return trip. The prospect of the first gust of wind tossing the blanket aside and exposing Mare to the elements haunted her. His bones slowly deteriorating to dust and blowing away, his skull sinking into the dirt, his eye sockets packed with mud and insects.

Jill screamed in rage and pain, but no one could hear her over the roar of the engines and the buzz of tires.

Her vision distorted by tears, she watched the black skyscraper rising menacingly ahead. The sun blazed behind and through the shattered windows, making it appear to be on fire. The colors of morning diffused into the sky, staining the sparse clouds in reds and golds that bled into the fading blue of night.

Soon it would all be over. One way or another, at least it would end.

Right now, Jill didn't care how. The guilt was unbearable, the sense of loss crippling. It was she who had sent Mare to his death. It was her fault. She had chosen her life over his. No…She had chosen the life of their unborn child over both, and now she felt dead inside.

Would you sacrifice everything for the child?

And she had. She had sacrificed her whole world. Maybe even that wouldn't be enough.

She was lagging behind, but even that didn't matter. Let them all speed away from her. She had given enough. What more could she possibly do? Everyone she loved died anyway. Her friends. Her family. Mare. She was cursed, and all she could bring them when it mattered was pain and misfortune. Death.

No, she thought. *Not everyone was dead.* There was still the child. Hers and Mare's. And that baby girl needed her mother—dear God, she had never thought of herself in those terms—now more than she ever would in her whole life. Not just in her life, but for her life. She needed to be born, to draw her fist breath, and she needed her mother to survive to do so. That was the best way to honor Mare, to thank him for her life, by bringing his child into the world.

She wiped the tears from her eyes and accelerated. She'd be damned if she was going to allow his sacrifice to be in vain. They had a child on the way, and that was the only thing that mattered. Her feelings were a luxury. There was her daughter to think about, and she would move heaven and earth to see her live.

By the time she caught up with Evelyn, they were nearly downtown, at the juncture of major thoroughfares that had collapsed and fallen to disarray. Even Missy, who still rode in the lead, had to slow to navigate the steeply slanted segments of the demolished overpass.

The city had been more than destroyed, it had been obliterated. Buildings had been converted to mounds of bricks and crumbled concrete several stories high, leaning away form the epicenter of the blast. Twisted girders stood from the jumbled remnants of the professional stadiums; apartment buildings had been all but vaporized. The ground had collapsed beneath, the blast zone a crater, the earth blackened by the atomic detonation indistinguishable from that scored by fire. Dust and ash billowed in rooster tails from their rear tires. The air grew cooler by the minute, the frigid breath of the grave. A fitting place to end their journey.

Adam tried to stay close to Missy, but with Ray on the seat behind him, their amassed weight unwieldy, they were unable to maneuver with the same litheness with which she was able to veer around ruptured segments of asphalt and strewn debris. She was already across the river by the time they reached it, a woman possessed. No matter how hard he pressed, he knew he was fighting a losing battle. He couldn't let her reach the tower alone. It was suicide, and her blood would be on his hands.

"Wait!" he shouted, but she didn't even look back. She hit the level street and rocketing toward the massive dark structure. "Missy! Wait!"

They couldn't afford to race in heedlessly. They needed to be cautious. Carelessness would get them all killed. They would need their combined strength and courage. Together they might be able to stand, but apart they would be butchered. He glanced back before fording the bridge that had buckled down into the river. Evelyn wasn't far behind, Jake's wild hair flapping over her right shoulder. Jill had closed rank behind. He either needed to wait for them or try to catch Missy, and he was running out of time to decide.

Again he looked ahead to the skyscraper, which dominated the land like a nail driven into flesh. A shiver rippled down his spine and it was suddenly hard to breathe.

"Missy!" he screamed as she sped between two enormous mounds that had once been buildings, disappearing from sight.

He pounded the handlebars in frustration, but drove no farther.

"She'll be okay," Ray said into his ear, but his words were only for Adam's benefit. He could have focused and tried to see what he could feel causing Adam to tense, but he didn't want to. The air had chilled and it felt like night to him, though he knew the day was barely passing dawn. He didn't need to see anything to know what was coming.

Adam could only shake his head. She wasn't going to be okay. He had consigned her to her fate.

A fate he now feared they would all share.

VIII

Missy felt smothered, unable to draw a single decent breath. She tried desperately to deny the awful truth she could feel radiating from her marrow. Phoenix was dead. She just couldn't bring herself to believe it, not without seeing it with her own eyes, not after already having to watch her baby brother die. There was no pain like that which she felt right now. She had been stripped of everything that mattered, everything on this earth that had meant anything.

She didn't look back as she opened the throttle and sped down the street, weaving around gaping maws in the pavement and dodging stray bricks, the shadow of the tower now falling over her. The coldness intensified, but she was immune now, her face flushed with anger and despair, every muscle tensed. It didn't matter if she left the others behind. Being with her was a death sentence. The farther she could get from them the better. At least maybe then they would have a slim chance of survival.

Tears dampened her cheeks and her chest heaved with the sobs she could no longer even try to contain. She screamed at random, cursing God, cursing life, cursing herself. Everything she loved. Gone. *Everything*. The only thought in her head was of finding Phoenix, refusing to admit that it would only be his physical remains. She needed to see him, knowing that once she did her journey would be at an end. Let the evil waiting for her do whatever it may from there.

Side streets flashed by, uneven trenches of rubble, without even drawing her eye. The foreboding building directly ahead was her only focus. That was where she would find Phoenix.

The hum of the motor echoed back at her from the ruins. Powdered debris blew across the asphalt. Nothing moved; not even the shadows shifted.

She finally reached a point where she had to slow, the larger toppled structures blocking more and more of the road. The rising sun glinted from the contorted metal and fused glass all around, highlighting the cloud of dust filling the streets.

The tower now dwarfed her, rising angrily into the sky, the road opening up before her. She gunned the bike with a squeal of rubber and raced heedlessly toward it.

Were she not so preoccupied with her pain, and had she not chosen that precise moment to push the engine, she would have heard the clamor of galloping hooves charging toward her, stampeding beneath drapes of human flesh, with shrouded riders clutching the obscene reigns on their backs. But she was oblivious, for atop a mound of ragged cement chunks and cracked bricks, a slant of light shone through the vacant windows of the skyscraper down onto a giant cross, upon which was draped a shadowed human form. Limp hair dangling against its chest. Unmoving body straining against its bonds, trying to slough free to the ground.

"Phoenix!" she cried as the nightmare riders closed off the street behind her, their steeds rising to their hind legs to strike at the sky.

CHAPTER 9

I

The deteriorating road had forced Missy to slow, allowing Adam the briefest of opportunities to gain ground on her, but now that he had reached the same haphazard bottleneck, he was losing what precious little distance he had closed. All he could see of her now was a dark shock of hair appearing and disappearing through the uneven ruins as he wound through the wreckage, praying that he might catch her before she reached the black domicile. They couldn't afford to speed carelessly into what was undoubtedly a trap. They needed to slow down and coordinate their approach. None of them knew what lay in wait for them, only that perhaps they would stand a chance with a measure of preparedness. Racing headlong into the enemy's open arms was surely suicide.

The building's shadow fell over him like a splash of frigid water. Every hair on his body tingled and stood erect. The time for planning was through. They had no choice now but to let the chips fall where they may. The battle was at hand.

Adam veered around a landslide of rubble and the final straightaway opened before

255

him. Missy was now only a hundred yards ahead, hurtling toward the wide courtyard at the foot of the tower where he could see a tall cross staked into a large mound of rubble. If he had any hope of catching her, it was now or never.

The rear tire kicked as he pinned the gas, the scream of the engine echoing all around, the cycle darting forward—

Two shadows closed from either side, appearing as if by magic from the abandoned side streets.

The world around him seemed to simultaneously slow and speed up at the same time. He saw streaks of white, thundering skeletal legs spurring flowing streams of black, but his reflexes were sluggish, the brakes even more so. There was no time to flash the taillight to warn the others. The shapes had appeared from nowhere, blocking off the road and hiding Missy from sight beyond. They were horses, stripped of flesh and yet somehow animated like War's steed had been. One had a long tail like a bridal train of thorny bramble that turned the asphalt to powder, the other a long crocodilian tail, which thrashed side to side before shimmering and turning transparent. Heavily stitched drapes covered everything else but their heads. Twin riders cloaked in the same material that he at first he thought to be leather, clung to the beasts as they pawed wildly at the air between them. One horseman was significantly larger than the other, his hands tangled in a mane of wicked briars originating from the exposed spinous processes of the horse's cervical spine, its bony face snapping back and forth with bared teeth and glowing eyes. The other, smaller rider grasped a living mane composed of hundreds of serpentine tails, writhing things that coiled around her skeletal wrists. Her steed's eyes appeared liquid, unstable.

Adam couldn't see either of their faces in the deep darkness of their cowls.

The bike screeched to a halt, kicking sideways before Adam forced it straight. He looked behind him to see the other bikes skidding on the loose gravel before the rubber finally grabbed pavement.

When he turned back to the hideous beasts, both returned to all fours with a crash of their front legs that shook the ground and echoed like an explosion. The riders trotted them a full circle, the exposed equine skulls still whipping side to side, before coming to rest sideways, their bulk blocking off the debris-clogged street. Adam could feel the weight of inhuman eyes upon him from beneath the hoods, but neither horseman made the slightest movement.

"What are we supposed to do?" Evelyn said.

Adam could only shake his head, fearing his voice might trigger whatever attack was coming, terrified to steal his stare from them in case that was all the opportunity they would need. But they couldn't just sit there all day. Missy was alone somewhere past those creatures, and Lord only knew what prepared to descend upon her.

Sunlight glinted from the swishing crocodile tail and the slithering mane, while the other horse's sickly brambles stirred on a non-existent breeze.

Was this a stand-off, or were these beasts stalling, waiting for them to make the first move?

Adam felt naked without the rifle, which hung over Ray's back behind him. They had one weapon between them, and were otherwise completely unarmed; two men, one blind, two women, and a child. They may have outnumbered their adversaries, but the riders exuded a frightening dark strength.

What were they waiting for?

Adam nudged Ray and they both climbed down. The street around them was silent, save for the occasional impatient stamping of hooves.

"Move back into the rubble," Adam whispered to Ray without taking his eyes off the horsemen for a second. "Train your sights on the big one. First sign of attack, you shoot."

Ray didn't respond, but Adam heard the scuffing of footsteps on the fragments of asphalt and mortar as Ray hurried to the side of the road. Evelyn's cold, trembling hand found his and held it tightly.

"Jill," Adam said, his elevated voice causing the fleshless steeds to shake their heads and stomp impatiently. "I want you and Jake to find a safe place to hide."

"What about you guys?" she whispered.

"Just do it!" he snapped.

The riders spurred their horses to their hind legs again, hooves slicing through the air with a sound like screaming.

Behind a ragged section of broken concrete, fire rose from Ray's eyes, his finger tightening on the trigger, the barrel shaking.

The smaller rider on the right let out a horrible shrieking sound, which trailed off into a low buzzing.

Hooves slammed back to the earth, fissures expanding through the pavement in all directions from where they struck. Skeletal heads snapped around to face them.

Adam clenched Evelyn's hand and then released it.

The horses neighed, a sound like strangling children, and bolted forward.

A resounding *bang* echoed from the crumbling, fallen structures surrounding them as the battle commenced.

II

Missy leapt from the motorcycle before it even stopped, allowing it to skid sideways into the base of the mound of debris. The cement bit into her palms and knees when she fell, but she didn't even feel the abrasions. Stumbling forward, she left bloody handprints on the broken sections of piled cement as she climbed.

She couldn't breathe. Her heart felt like it had stopped beating, though her pulse pounded so hard in her temples that it shook her vision. The world around her fell away as the only thing that mattered was above her in the slanted ray of light.

"Oh, God," she moaned, finally reaching the base of the cross on her hands and knees, coming face to face with a rusted length of rebar dripping with blood from the overlapped feet staked to it. "No, no, no, no, no…"

Her hands trembled as she grasped both heels and gingerly tried to pull them forward. The broken bones within made cracking sounds, but refused to budge.

"Help me!" she screamed back over her shoulder. She stood and grasped Phoenix around the waist, trying to hold him aloft to take the strain off his arms, pressing her shoulder and the side of her face into the exposed muscles on his abdomen, which shimmered with coagulating fluids. "Somebody! Please! Help me!"

He was cold. So cold.

Missy looked up into his face. His long bangs were crusted in crimson clumps, his face stark white. Lacerations crisscrossed his cheeks and forehead, his pale pink eyes staring blankly down at her, the whites now a wet scarlet. His swollen, split lips were parted to reveal his broken front teeth, his entire mouth a crimson wound.

"No!" she screamed, lifting his weight. Droplets of blood pattered her head. "Please, God! Help me!"

She lost whatever semblance of control she maintained, shaking her head and wailing as she lifted and pulled. With a damp sucking sound, his hands slid forward on the rebar stakes. She tugged and his hands sloughed free, dropping his torso onto her shoulder and knocking her backwards to the ground. The sharp rubble gouged her back, but she managed to sit up and pulled on his waist to release his feet with a snapping sound.

"Wake up, Phoenix," she cried, rolling him from atop her. She leaned close to his face and paused, her lips inches from his, praying for the slightest breath to tickle the sensitive skin. His eyes stared through her, the lids fixed halfway open, sealed by blood, the sockets turning into massive bruises. "Please…wake up."

Her words morphed into a moan of sorrow and she collapsed onto him, wrapping her arms around him and holding him to her. *So cold.* Her cheek against his, their hearts aligned. Two hearts that would never again beat in time.

"Don't take him from me," she sobbed, curling her hands to fists beneath him, the rubble cutting her hands. "He's all I have. Please, God…I love him. Please…"

The heavenly spotlight that had illuminated him thorough the building abruptly vanished. A frigid sensation flooded over her. Raising her head, she kissed him softly on his unforgiving lips and looked up along the black face of the tower into the sky. A pair of blood-red eyes met hers, contrasted by a black form, the source of the coldness.

"Come on!" she shrieked, pushing up from the ground and grabbing Phoenix beneath his arms. She pulled him away from the cross and down the treacherous slope, leaving a trail of blood behind. Stumbling, she struggled to balance them both until she reached the bottom and continued dragging him through the courtyard, off the curb, and into the street.

A gunshot pierced the sound of her sobbing from behind her, but she continued pulling Phoenix away from the darkened cross.

The clamor of stampeding hooves was like thunder.

Another *bang!* was punctuated by an inhuman scream.

She hauled Phoenix behind a broken section of the road that stood erect, a black-tarred tombstone. Kneeling over him, she stroked his cheek, unaware of the chaos behind her or the savage red eyes watching her from above. Phoenix's wounds parted for her fingertips, but no fresh blood seeped to the surface. Her tears dripped onto his pallid skin. She finally closed his eyelids and fell on top of him, holding him as tightly as she could, refusing to let go.

Her shoulders shook as she cried.

The entire world around her filled with screams.

III

The first shot whizzed over Evelyn's shoulder, striking the taller rider's steed in the jaw with an explosion of boney shrapnel that sent teeth skittering across the pavement. Its entire snout gone, the beast shook its head violently and turned to face them. Jagged triangular fragments encircled its mouth like a leech's. The second shot shattered its frontal bone above the right eye and demolished the skull. It swung its exposed cervical column back and forth before collapsing to its front hooves. The rear legs still tried to push it back to standing, but instead scooted it forward on the asphalt, propelling the useless snake of vertebrate. The horseman lunged from its back and landed squarely on his feet. The skeletal horse thrashed on the ground behind him in its death throes.

The cloaked figure stood no more than ten feet directly ahead of her, motionless.

Evelyn heard more gunshots and the movement from the corner of her eye became frenetic, but she didn't dare steal her gaze from the man in front of her, his features bathed in darkness.

Slowly, the figure extended a pair of smooth ivory hands from its wide sleeves and reached up to either side of its face, took hold of the hood, and pulled it back.

Evelyn gasped when she saw his face and stumbled unconsciously in reverse. He appeared to be made of pearl, every contour polished and rounded. Even his eyes were white. The only imperfections were the bubbles sliding beneath his porcelain skin, creating the illusion of blood boiling beneath.

Though no expression marred his face, she could feel the coldness of his rage directed at her.

Bang!

Another gunshot from behind and something screamed off to her right.

Famine took a long stride toward her and she heard a *click* from where Ray crouched behind the rubble. *Click. Click. Click.*

Evelyn looked to the ground for any kind of weapon, but there was only a scattering of broken bricks. Grabbing one, she hurled it at the approaching creature, but it only bounced uselessly off his chest.

"Oh, God," she whispered. She started to turn to run, but Famine was too fast.

Twin fists pounded her in the chest, seizing handfuls of her shirt and lifting her from the ground. She kicked repeatedly at him, striking his shins and knees with everything she had. If she was hurting him, he showed no sign as he stared into her eyes. Panicked, she clawed at his face, but his skin was so hard that her nails merely bent backwards. Even the smooth white orbs that served as his eyes were immune to her best efforts.

She looked to her right, hoping Adam was coming to her aid, but the smaller horseman had him pinned on the ground beneath the flaring cloak. All she could see were his raised arms struggling to ward off his assailant.

They were going to die. They had come this far only to fail.

Famine's hands readjusted in the fabric of her shirt, climbing upward toward her neck like spiders. She knew when they reached their target all would be lost.

She grabbed hold of either side of Famine's face, pressing feebly into his temples with her middle fingers and trying to gouge out his eyes with her thumbs, but it was like attempting to break stone with her bare hands. Screaming, his furious grip tightening over the muscle above her clavicle, she squeezed with all her might.

Still dangling above the ground, she felt his hands close around her neck, sealing off any hope of drawing breath. She gasped for air, but nothing reached her lungs. She pulled her hands from his face and curled her fingers under his, her nails tearing ribbons of flesh from her own throat. His hands were made of the same impenetrable skin as the face, beneath which bubbles boiled eagerly, pressing even harder against her neck as they squirmed along his fingers.

Red blotches appeared in the periphery of her vision, moving inward with amoeboid motion, chased by a swelling blackness that constricted her vision like binoculars. Her heart began to pound and her chest heaved. Fingertips and toes tingling, she pinched her eyes shut against the pain, and scraped and clawed at her own neck in a desperate attempt to free herself.

I'm going to die was her last conscious thought before she gave herself over to the animalistic panic.

She gagged in an effort to breathe, but nothing came. Her mouth opened wide, tongue lolling wildly, eyes threatening to bulge out of their sockets. She looked everywhere for any sign of help, but there was nothing. No one. All she could see were her forearms under her chin, the tendons taut as she struggled against the opaline man who still stared directly into her face with that same disimpassioned expression.

The bulging muscles and tendons in her arms visibly relaxed and the darkness closed in upon her. The veins stood out, throbbing in time with her vision, the sickly green growing brighter by the second until the vessels became the color of emeralds.

IV

Adam tried to grab for Evelyn's hand, but something deadly passed between them with a scream and the ensuing *bang* of gunfire. He turned to the right to see the smaller horseman's steed's right eye splash like a rock hurled into a placid pond. A spray of fluid fired out the other side. The skeletal horse staggered from side to side, struggling to maintain its balance, a wash of black tears draining from its popped eyes. It dropped to its belly to the tune of cracking ribs, but still continued to struggle. The cloaked figure climbed easily from its draped back as though immune to its thrashing, stood beside it, and faced him.

The shrouded head snapped back suddenly, throwing off the cowl.

A crack of gunfire echoed through the desolate streets.

The figure appeared struck, standing upright with its head draped back over its shoulders, neck surely broken. Yet the body still stood.

Adam was about to rush to Evelyn's aid, when he saw the smaller rider move. Her head snapped forward into place, brown skin stretched tight over an obviously female framework of bones, strands of long black hair snapping from an otherwise bald pate. She was gaunt and almost looked mummified, her skin torn from her cheek bones in filamentous strings that exposed her maxillae and upper teeth. Even though the shroud made her appear taller, she couldn't have been more than five feet—

"Thanh?" Adam whispered. He glanced

back to his left at the taller white man who he suddenly realized had once been his former Army friend Kotter. What had happened to them in those caves? Jesus Christ! They were his friends. How had they—?

An image flashed across his mind. Four figures standing atop a rocky knoll on the mountainside bordering the Ali Sadr Caves, surveying the land at their feet before a swell of dust from the tires of the transport vehicle obscured them.

Dear God. They had survived, but not in the same incarnation as when they had first splashed down into the sulfurous water. They'd emerged as something else entirely.

When he turned back, Pestilence had closed the gap between them and stood directly before him, studying him through shriveled eyes that hung loosely in her gaping sockets like raisins dried on optic nerve vines.

"Thanh…What happened to you?"

She showed no sign of recognition. Her dried lips peeled back from eternally bared teeth, her parchment skin betraying the manila bone beneath.

"Thanh. Don't you remem—?"

Her hands struck like lightning, tagging his chest with such force that her bony phalanges tore though his shirt and broke the skin, the tips fishing around in his muscles. At first he felt cold, as though she had stabbed him with icicles, but the sensation quickly metamorphosed into fiery pain.

Adam slapped her hands away and clapped his palms over the wounds. He could even feel the heat on his hands, though no blood had been spilled. The punctures puckered and closed beneath. His skin tightened and he got a whiff of what smelled like the rotting meat, a scent he knew all too well. Gangrene. But it was impossible. There was no way the gouges could have begun to fester in such a short amount of time. That kind of infection should have taken at least several days. It couldn't possibly—

Her tiny fingers grabbed handfuls of skin on his hips and her head darted forward, teeth opening to grab a mouthful of the flesh above his navel. He cried out and stumbled away, snagging his feet and slamming down on his back with her still on him, ripping back and forth, until she finally pulled away and sat upright on his legs, a strip of skin dangling from her bloody teeth.

Adam screamed and bucked, but she only clamped down on his thighs, her skeletal fingers easily parting his skin like scalpels to prod the tissue within. Pain beyond anything he had ever imagined blossomed in his gut, forcing him to grab his belly with his hands, his face clenching into a fist of agony. It felt as though his intestines were turning inside out and absolving themselves of their contents, his stomach pouring acid over the inner stew. Sepsis advanced with supernatural speed, the disease eating him alive from the inside out.

Rocking back, he closed his eyes and shouted in agony.

A startlingly cold hand slapped down onto his forehead and sharp bony prominences latched into his skin like fishhooks. The searing pain was immediate, but nothing compared to that which accompanied the swelling of his brain and the intracranial pressure that followed. The blood vessels in his gray matter bulged and swelled, their thin walls weakening to allow the formation of bulbous aneurysms. A single ruptured lumen and he would bleed to death inside his own head.

"Get off me!" he railed, but she was stuck to him like a parasite.

He threw himself from side to side to no avail. Even the slightest movement lit up his nerve tracts.

Death advanced from within, while his body was pinned without.

Click. Click. Click, from behind.

Adam shoved Pestilence's cloaked chest, but the applied pressure only served to make her fingertips feel like they were scalping him.

He was going to die.

In desperation, he raised his hands and grabbed her face, trying to shove it back, to break her jaw, snap her neck, anything. Thin fingers of smoke wafted from the union of their flesh. Pestilence screamed and jerked her head away, extinguishing the diminutive flames that had arisen from her dry flesh. A mouthful of mosquitoes funneled out to form a skin over her face.

Adam felt her claws retract from his skin. This was his opportunity.

He grabbed for her face again, but sudden pain exploded in his calf. Something jerked at the muscle.

Adam screamed.

V

The moment of triumph was at hand.

Death reveled in every second of it. Soon the last of the survivors would be dead, and he would inherit the earth. There was nothing anyone could do to stop him now. Not God. Not the pathetic sack of flesh He had chosen as His champion. Not the frail humans preparing to be slaughtered hundreds of feet below. In a matter of minutes, the final battle would be over, and he would stand above them all, victorious.

And yet something still plagued him.

The boy. His death had come too easily. It was more than the lack of satisfaction in the child's torture and demise. There had been no fight, only a meek acquiescence, as though the boy had given himself over to him. It was all wrong. Everything. The boy had exhibited no signs of power, only the feebleness inherent to his flesh. He was supposed to have been Death's opposite number.

Death needed to be cautious, take nothing for granted. In his black heart, he knew he could best the Lord, but not so easily. There had to be more to come, and he would be ready. He could not allow himself to be caught unaware. So he studied them down there from the distance, scrutinizing their very move.

When the lone girl had slipped through the trap he had laid with Famine and Pestilence, he had thought momentarily that he would be forced to reckon with her, but she had fallen apart when she saw the child's crucified remains. While her anger and sorrow had been venerable, emanating palpable waves of fury, he quickly realized that she posed no threat to him. All she had wanted was to drag the body down off the cross. She had even seen him standing high above, but had averted her eyes in fear.

The others appeared to at least be willing to fight, but his horsemen were overwhelming them handily. Famine had the woman by the throat and would soon cut off her life, while Pestilence was making short work of the man twice her size. There were still three others with them, but they cowered in hiding. One still had a weapon, but no earthly weapon would be able to fell his brethren.

There was another child with them, smaller, younger. Was it possible he'd been wrong about the boy he'd crucified, that this other child was his true adversary? No. He was certain he'd killed the right boy. But why hadn't he battled with everything he had?

Why hadn't he fought?

Death reared back, scaled chest swelling, and hissed up into the heavens with a sound like the electric crackle of lightning. There was some key component that he was missing and it enraged him.

When he looked back down, he could no longer see the girl or the carcass she towed. A momentary sensation of fear assaulted him, a feeling he hadn't felt in his many incarnations, but he shoved it aside when he finally saw the girl's black hair behind a standing section of broken asphalt. The corpse would be with her for sure. The fear was tamed, but the fact that it existed at all unnerved him.

Hide us from the face of Him that sitteth on the throne, a voice from the past whispered inside his mind, more insistent than before.

He stilled. That voice should no longer exist. It belonged to a past life long since ended, a human life, and yet there was no disputing he had heard it.

This needed to end now.

Nothing could threaten his ascension. He would reign on earth. Reign as god. God.

The Lord will be terrible unto them: for He will famish all the gods of the earth, the voice said, stronger, emboldened.

Death hissed again and the sky rumbled in response. He slashed at his chest over and over, his claws parting his scales and carving the flesh beneath. With the pain came focus, silencing the voice, bringing his rage to a boiling crescendo.

Blood pouring from his heaving chest, he turned his attention again to the ground like a Caesar lording over a stadium of gladiators, and thought he heard the voice laughing from far away.

VI

Jill couldn't bear to watch any longer. Whatever those shrouded monsters were, they were killing her friends, and it was only a matter of time before they came after Jake and her as well.

She looked up at the tower, and there atop it was the black beast with the red eyes. She turned to Jake and saw that he was focused on the creature as well, just as his dreams had foretold. Tears streamed down his pale cheeks. His whole body trembled.

A scream summoned her attention back to the fracas in front of her, where Adam was still on his back beneath Pestilence, a cloud of smoke and insects swirling about her desiccated head. He arched his back and screamed again, bloody spittle flying from his mouth to slap back down on his face. Pestilence appeared distracted as she clawed at her own face with bony fingers. Jill saw the source of Adam's torment.

"Stay right here!" she snapped at Jake. "Don't move!"

She grabbed a large section of the broken sidewalk, so big she could hardly lift it with both hands, and hurried out from behind the rubble.

Adam was still bucking and screaming. The skeletal steed, its face now wet with more than its popped eyes, had crawled forward and bitten down on Adam's lower leg. It jerked and tugged in an effort to rip away a mouthful of muscle. The serpentine tails from its neck were wrapped around his ankle

Jill stormed into the fray, heaving the cement as high as she could. Her arms and shoulders burned as she raised it, and cried out with the strain. She stood over the beast and drove the concrete down onto its skull with a resounding crack, the ragged edges tearing the skin on her palms. Fissures expanded along its exposed frontal bone. Jill didn't hesitate to examine the damage. She raised the block and slammed it down again and again until the concrete tumbled out of her bloody hands and she fell backwards, unable even to move her arms to brace herself before hitting the street.

Reaver's entire cranium had caved in and the snout had broken off, though its teeth were still embedded in Adam's leg. The tails of the mane snapped and flagged, reaching for the shattered fragments of bone as though trying to reassemble the head. They shivered and stood erect before finally falling limply back to the spine. Its hind legs kicked at the ground, hooves gouging chunks out of the pavement before eventually stilling with a shudder. Were it possible, the lifeless bones appeared to sag before crumbling to dust.

Jill scrabbled forward again. She grabbed the remainder of the steed's jaws from Adam's leg and flung them away. A rush of blood poured from the wound.

"Oh, my God," she gasped, grabbing his flailing leg and pressing her hands onto the wound to staunch the rapid flow. Warm fluid sluiced through her fingers, bringing with it the vile scent of festering meat.

She looked to her left for help, but Adam was still writhing in agony, his teeth bared and eyes pinched shut. Beyond, Ray charged toward where Famine held Evelyn above the ground by her neck, raising the stock of the rifle high over his head, preparing to strike, the flames in his eyes nearly eclipsing his face.

"Adam!" she screamed, looking back at him, trying frantically to get his attention. "Adam!"

His eyelids parted a slit, issuing streams of tears.

"I can't stop the blood! I can't—"

Jill was cut off mid-sentence by a sharp pain on the vertex of her head. It felt as though someone had driven a spike through her skull. She screamed as her entire upper body was jerked sideways. Something that she imagined to be the hooked tines of a rake had lanced beneath her scalp, and tugged in an attempt to pull out all of her hair and the skin with it. Icy needles of pain spread through her cranium, the pressure building to the point she had to close her eyes.

She toppled over and Pestilence's fingers tore back out. Consciousness abandoned her to the darkness in her mind before her head bounced off the asphalt.

VII

◉

She was on the verge of passing out. Evelyn knew that if she allowed it to happen, she would never wake again. The pearl-skinned creature holding her aloft would simply crush her cartilaginous windpipe, and that would be the end. The green veins in her forearms grew brighter until they were almost fluorescent, pulsing in time with her shrinking field of vision. She looked at Famine's face, hoping to find a momentary flash of mercy. The smooth porcelain shield formed to his face like a death mask had taken on the same emerald glow. Her bright red face reflected in his blank eyes.

Evelyn coughed, the tendons and muscles in her neck beginning to relax.

No! she screamed inside her head. *Not yet! Not like this!*

Jagged green bolts crept across Famine's face like vines growing in fast forward. Not on his face, but beneath it. They crept inward from under the cowl, racing from his cheeks to his eyes, meeting with those stabbing down his forehead and up from his chin.

Sudden movement from behind the cloaked figure drew her attention. She saw a flash of brown and heard what sounded like a baseball bat striking the side of a car.

The pressure was suddenly gone from her neck and there was a momentary sensation of weightlessness before her feet hit the ground. Her legs crumpled beneath her and deposited her in a heap. Sucking at the sudden rush of air, she rolled onto her side, filling her lungs with the oxygen she so desperately needed. The darkness peeled back, though the blotches still swam across her vision. Her extremities tingled and ached as though she had slept on them wrong and her head pounded with a headache beyond any she had ever experienced.

She felt like she was moving in slow motion, her body sluggish. A broken section of polished wood rested on the ground in front of her, surrounded by a scattering of splinters. She looked up to see the creature turn around to face Ray, who stood before it holding the barrel of his rifle like a club. Famine struck with staggering speed, his white hand shooting out of the billowing sleeve of flesh to pound Ray in the center of his face. Ray was lifted from his feet, the fire in his eyes extinguished, and sent hurtling backward through the air. He landed squarely on his shoulders and slid another five feet before his head met an abutment of rubble. The remainder of the gun clattered to the ground and rolled away from his open hand.

Ray didn't even try to get back up.

Famine spun again to face her. The cloak billowed around him, liquid blackness that reeked of death. The green bolts had receded back toward the hood, merely framing his face with emerald etchings.

Evelyn screamed and scrambled away, meeting with the bony remains of the horseman's steed. She toppled over the rib cage draped in human flesh and the sharply-protruding pelvis, landing on the tail of nettles. Thorns prodded her side and then her palms as she struggled to right herself and crouched on the dried train of weeds.

He strode toward her, gliding on feet hidden beneath the vast expanse of blackened flesh, hardly appearing to graze the ground.

Evelyn scanned the earth around her for anything she could use as a weapon. There was only the broken stock of the rifle and piles of rocks she would never be able to reach in time. This was it, she thought, time to die. She looked up into the shrouded face. Shadows washed over the upper half, leaving only the chin and mouth exposed. The formerly stoic features betrayed the hint of a smile. The creature knew her time was up as well.

Something crawled over her fingers where she knelt, scurrying over the backs of her hands. She tried to jerk them away, but they were stuck, the skittering sensation curling around her wrists and up her forearms. She looked down and her breath stilled in her chest. The stiff and lifeless weeds of Scourge's tail had changed from brownish-yellow to green and were now growing up all around her, the tail lengthening and spreading out toward the rubble, climbing up and over.

Evelyn looked at Famine, who was now nearly on top of her, and caught just a momentary falter in his smile.

She looked back down and watched the vines spread out like a mat beneath his feet, racing under his cloak like so many snakes fleeing for the safety of their darkened den. Her arms tingled as she suffused the dead tail with life. The primitive understanding that she was actually doing this dawned on her, though she knew not how. She prayed that she could continue doing so.

The vines grew all the way up her arms to the shoulders, becoming taller all around her, the serpentine weeds reaching for the sun. The world took on a muted green cast, the source of the illumination coming directly from her.

Famine tried to close the remaining yard between them, but he was rooted to the ground. The vines of his own steed's tail spiraled around his ankles and up his legs, constricting around his waist and torso. He clawed through his leathery cloak, tearing it away to reveal that his entire body was wrapped with the overgrowth. Curling his fingers into the stalks, he snapped them away, but they only formed again. Concentrating his power, the weeds began to brown and crumble away, but far too slowly, the more ambitious vines knotting over his knuckles and running up his arms under the cloak. Green veins appeared on his upper chest above the nest of foliage, streaking up his neck and into his face where they glowed like emerald fire, filling his eyes, which shattered as though made of glass, tinkling to the ground at his feet.

Evelyn poured her life force into the thorny bramble, which sapped it up like water, now covering the entire street around her. She was one with them. With a cracking of bone, they broke apart the equine skeleton beside her, grinding it to increasingly smaller chips and calcium dust until the bump beneath them was no longer visible.

The vines tangled around Famine's neck, spiraling around his face. Where they tightened, the thorns cracked his ceramic mask and the bramble constricted like barbed wire. He registered fear a heartbeat before the weeds tore him apart. The cloak ripped away from his shoulders, followed by his arms. The sockets shattered and billowed a cloud of dust from within, fanned by the myriad wings of locusts that sputtered into the air before they stilled and fell back to the earth to be swallowed by the seething foliage. He made a high-pitched screaming sound, but it was cut short by the sawing motion of the vines on his face. His head imploded with a crash that filled the air with glimmering shards, dicing the insect bodies that fired upward from his neck. Yet the body still stood, held upright by the sheer mass of greenery woven around it.

Evelyn was panting, in awe of what was transpiring in front of her. The vines uncoiled from her arms and slithered into the seemingly liquid groundcover, allowing her to stand. She walked atop the plants until she reached Famine's body. She sensed that it was being presented to her.

Every vein in her body glowed through her skin as though they pumped light rather than blood. Slowly the color dimmed, returning her flesh to its normal pink hue.

She turned her back on the creature and heard the clamor of its remains being torn apart, obliterated.

VIII

Adam heard Jill scream, the ear-piercing sound resplendent with palpable waves of pain.

He saw her from the corner of his eye, trying to jerk her head away to no avail. Pestilence's hand was latched onto Jill's skull like a massive spider, the fingertips hooked beneath her scalp. Scarlet striations raced across Jill's forehead in miniature lightning bolts, as though the hand really were a spider injecting its venom. A knot of swelling plumped Jill's forehead. Here eyes closed and her jaw fell slack. When Pestilence snapped her exposed phalanges free from Jill's hair, Jill hovered only momentarily before toppling backwards, the base of her skull bouncing off the road with a crack.

"Get away!" Jake screamed, hurling a rock at the mummified horseman. It struck her across the cheek, ripping away a strip of flesh to expose her entire left cheek bone, but it didn't faze her at all.

Her diseased eyes found Jake's and she extended a single bony finger from the shadow of the cloak's sleeve, beckoning him closer. He froze in place as though incapable of looking away. The rock he had been prepared to hurl dropped from his fingers to the ground.

"Stay…away…" Adam retched, his parched voice barely reaching his own ears. He cleared his throat, tasting blood and the sickly sludge of infection. "Jake…get back!"

He tried to roll toward Pestilence, which only amplified the pain in his leg. Crying out, he reached for it. The flesh felt like a chasm had opened and his first reaction was to close it, his fingers probing through the wetness and dissociating muscle to find anything he could grab—

Warmth poured from his fingers into the sloppy maw. The searing pain faded to a tingling sensation. He felt his skin stretching, the edges of the wound reaching for each other. There was barely time to remove his fingers before they met, sealing off the gash as thought it had never been. It all happened in the span of a blink, but his mind had already wrapped around the implications. When he had clawed at the demon's face, it had dissolved into smoke and mosquitoes. The same power that had healed his leg was a weapon he could turn against her.

He grabbed Pestilence's thin wrist, catching her by surprise. Smoke drifted out from beneath his hand, tendrils of which crept up through his fingers. He held on with all his strength, straining as she tried to yank free. Her forearm flew backwards out of his grasp. He was momentarily confused, until he saw her waving a stump from the end of the cloak. Her hand lay on the ground, fingers curled to the sky, the ashes of her wrist smoldering in a pile.

The pulsating warmth radiated outward from his calf, stretching up his leg and spilling into his pelvis and abdomen. The sickening knots of the septic infection began to resolve. His swelling gut deflated and the pain slowly abated, adding to the clarity breaking through the fog in his mind. He had the element of surprise, but it would only last so long. He needed to take advantage of it right now.

He grabbed her flared sleeve. A sheath of mosquitoes crawled out of the cauterized wound to form a living bandage over the smoking stump. Adam pulled Pestilence toward him until he could grasp her with his other hand, and brought her down on his chest. He wrapped her in an embrace, drawing her cheek to the side of his face and neck. She thrashed against him, issuing a cloud of smoke that made him choke. Her remaining hand found his side and she clawed through his flesh, her fingertips wriggling between his ribs. She screamed into his ear, the sound of a million agitated mosquitoes humming, and snapped at his neck with rotting teeth that latched onto the meat above his clavicle.

Adam cried out and grabbed her by the back of the cloak, clutching the few long strands of hair, wrenching her head away. Her face was covered in blood from the bridge of her nose down, what little skin still remained snapping like bacon in hot grease. She snarled at him, and lunged for his throat again, her scalp tearing off in his hand.

Her heat against his chest was unbearable. The air around them filled with fire, the resultant black smoke swirled by angry insects.

As soon as he felt her teeth sink into his neck, he released her flailing form and closed both hands around her thin throat.

Pestilence gnawed even harder, working into the muscle, but Adam could no longer see her through the smoke. Her body began to spasm, twitching and kicking until she rolled off his chest, falling to the pavement beside him. Flames rose through the seams of her cloak, small at first, but growing larger as they consumed her diminutive form. Adam's hands closed together around nothing but ash and crunchy bits of vertebrae.

Her teeth gnashed one final time and then stopped altogether. He slid his fingers into her mouth, prying the jaws apart. Her head snapped in half. The mandible remained in his right hand, while the upper portion of the skull fell to the asphalt and shattered.

"Are you all right?" Jake asked, hurrying to his side.

"Yeah," Adam said, casting aside the lower jaw. "I think so." The pressure in his skull was gone, but his head still pounded. The tingling sensation was now fading away.

Jake nudged the mandible with his toe and it disintegrated to dust and shards of enamel.

Adam crawled over to where Jill was sprawled on the ground, eyes clenched shut, face a rictus of suffering. He laid his palm on her forehead, felt energy pouring through his fingers, and watched her features slowly soften until she finally opened her eyes and looked up at him. The whites were streaked with red and she appeared disoriented, but at least she would live.

"How are you feeling, kiddo?" he asked, venturing a smile.

"Is she dead?" Jill asked, rubbing at her temples. Adam removed his hand and allowed her to sit up.

He nodded and looked back over his shoulder for Evelyn, who had already helped Ray back to his feet and was leading him in their direction over a carpet of vines that he noticed with a start were slithering across the pavement toward him. He jumped to his feet and ran to her, planted his hands on her cheeks and kissed her.

"I'm so glad you're okay," he gushed, pulling away. "I don't know what I would have done if—"

"Shhh," she whispered, silencing him with a kiss.

The sound of crying drifted to them from down the street.

"There's Missy," Jake called, running toward her. His tiny footfalls echoed in the silence.

"I don't see Phoenix," Evelyn whispered.

"Neither do—"

Adam's words were drowned out by a hissing sound like a stadium filled with an enraged crowd. The ground trembled beneath his feet. He looked skyward at the top of the tower. There was a flash of crimson against an ebon shadow.

CHAPTER 10

I

"Please," Missy sobbed, stroking Phoenix's sallow cheek. "Please don't leave me."

His skin was cool, his mouth expressionless. His open eyes stared right through her.

"Why didn't you just wait for us? We could have faced this together. You didn't have to do this by yourself. You didn't have to die…"

She knew that the others were in trouble behind her, somewhere deep down, but she was lost in her grief. First her brother, and now Phoenix. There was nothing left for her. Nothing at all. Her world had come to an end in the span of an hour. If she could just curl up with Phoenix and die, she would. No more suffering. No more pain. Wherever they were now, she wanted to be there, too.

Her body grew numb. She lowered herself to the ground beside Phoenix's corpse, draping her arm across his chest and looking at his profile through tear-blurred eyes as he stared lifelessly to the heavens.

It will be easier for you later. If you hate me, Phoenix had said. But she couldn't. Not even now. Even were she able to, the pain would have been no less. He had known. He had known all along that this was his fate, to die at the hands of the adversary. What an awful burden it must have been, and still he had tired to spare her from the pain, preferring a destiny of dying alone to causing her the heartache she felt now.

The world around her ceased to exist. The sound of footsteps racing through the devastation toward her, the hissing sound that shook the heavens…none of it filtered through the crippling sorrow. Voices called for her, but she didn't hear them over her unconscious sobs.

If she could have given her life for Phoenix's, she would have gladly done so in a heartbeat. She closed her eyes and tried to will him to live, but when she opened them again, his skin appeared even more waxen. She wished she could hear his voice, if only one last time.

Yours is the most special gift I can possibly give, the only thing I have of any worth, he had said. *I gave you my heart.*

She sobbed anew at the memory, the pain in her chest more than she could bear.

"And I gave you mine," she whispered, her lips grazing his cold ear. Her palm slid down his chest, rising and falling over the ragged edges of the lacerations to settle just to the left of his sternum. "I love you with all my heart. It's yours. My love. My life. Everything."

His chest jumped ever so slightly beneath her hand.

She looked up and saw the others running toward her, their footsteps pounding the ground.

"Oh, God," Evelyn gasped. She knelt beside Missy and placed a hand on the younger girl's shoulder. "Come on, Missy. We have to keep moving."

Missy acknowledged her with a shrug, refusing to relinquish her final embrace with the love of her short life.

His chest twitched again, but this time there was no one running. They all stood still over her. She held her breath and watched his thorax for the slightest hint of movement, scouring his rent flesh—

Was there blood in that gash? A faint glimmer of sunlight on fresh fluid?

"We can't stay here," Jake said, looking up to the top of the tower, where he could no longer see the scarlet-eyed shadow.

"Help me get her to her feet," Adam said, stepping over Phoenix's sprawled legs. He reached beneath Missy's arm—

"No!" she wailed, slapping his hand away.

It wasn't just the one gash. It was all of them. The slowly welling fluid, the moistening lips of the wounds.

"Help him!" Missy shouted up into Adam's face.

"I'll try," was all Adam could muster. He had no idea how this healing power of his worked, but he had been unable to resurrect Mare. From the look of Phoenix, not only had he been bled dry, but he had been dead for a while.

He reached out, placed his hand beside Missy's, and immediately recoiled. Had he felt movement? He set his palm down again. Yes. He was certain of it. There had been little more than a meek contraction of muscle, but he had felt it all the same. He had seen enough corpses in his time to be able to recognize one immediately, and Phoenix had been unmistakably dead.

His fingertips tingled against Phoenix's skin, which began to warm. Was it because of the contact with his flesh, or was it possible that—?

Blood raced to the surface from the deep wounds, overflowing the formerly gaping seams.

"Is he—?" Evelyn gasped, crouching by Phoenix's head and placing her first two fingers on his neck to feel for a pulse. His veins plumped to the surface, a faint blue web that intensified steadily until it was bright green and covered the entirety of his flesh. Then, as quickly as they had risen, the glowing, pulsating veins faded back into his flesh. Had a measure of color returned to his ghastly white skin?

"Please," Jake said, nervously pacing behind them, unable to look away from the skyscraper. The roof was conspicuously empty. The black man must be somewhere in the shadowed floors beneath, working his way down to the ground floor, soon to come for them. His gaze ticked from one darkened window to the next, searching. "I can't see him anymore! We can't stay here any longer!"

Ray gave the boy's shoulder a gentle squeeze before kneeling beside Phoenix as well. He understood what was happening now. He gently rested his palm over the bridge of Phoenix's nose, covering his eyes. As soon as their skin touched, the flames extinguished in Ray's eyes, again leaving only those awful hollow sockets. The heat seared his hand and fire rose through the gaps between his fingers. He jerked his hand away.

Phoenix's eyes snapped open, foot-long flames rising from orbits still rolled back in his head. His pink irises slowly migrated down from inside his skull, dousing the fire.

"Oh, God," Missy moaned. "Thank you. Thank you." She kissed Phoenix on the cheek and repeatedly squeezed him to her.

He looked at each of them in turn, trying to rationalize what had happened. Images flashed through his mind. His head rocking back to look into the heavens as stakes were driven through his hands. Claws like knives slashing his chest. Vision fading, breath escaping him. A hideous black face with eyes of blood hissing in rage as his soul flew from its cage of flesh.

Gasping, he bolted upright, knocking Missy off of him and pawing at his chest. It felt as though ants were crawling all over him, pinching, biting, stinging. The lacerations drew closed under his hands, every nerve ending first tingling and then returning to life with the pain formerly spared him by death.

"He was dead," Adam said, shaking his head. "You were dead."

Phoenix struggled to his feet, swaying. He was dizzy and confused, but one thought cut through the riot of memories and emotions.

"You all need to leave now," he rasped, his throat parched. He turned to face the tower, looking over Missy's shoulder. His bare chest and arms stippled with goose bumps, a shiver rippling through him. "Please…leave now."

II

Death stood back from the window, bathed in the shadows of the throne room, watching them gather down there in the street from the anonymity of darkness. His eyes glowed a deep red just shy of black, his interlaced teeth bared in rage. The memory of watching Pestilence and Famine fall was a fresh wound. He had never even considered the possibility they might fail. They should have been far stronger than their human opposition, but at least now everything made some sort of sense. The boy had succumbed to his torture so easily because he had passed his power into his friends, hidden it inside them. But the child was still dead. That much, at least, had gone according to plan. Now he had but to slaughter those that remained. They had tipped their hand too soon. He was now well aware of what they could do and would be prepared for them.

Babylon the great is fallen, is fallen, and has become a habitation of demons, a prison for every foul spirit, a cage for every unclean and hated bird, the Arabic voice whispered. This time it sounded as though it originated from without, echoing from the hidden corners of the room.

He hissed in anger and kicked the piles of bones, comforted by the sounds of cracking skulls and fracturing ribs. Calcium dust filled the stale air. He forced himself to calm, resuming control of his faculties, breathing in the intoxicating scent of the dried flesh and the rotting meat on the bones, the ripe smell of death.

Death couldn't deny the unmitigated truth

of the voice's words. He was the lord of a wasteland, a master without servants. When he finished off the survivors, the world would indeed be his to rule, but without subjects to reign over, it would be a hollow victory. He had burned most of the animals. How long would it take, how many eons would pass, before those that remained evolved into anything worthy of his rule? The scorched earth was soon to be his, but for what? He felt great pride in beating the Lord, in laying claim to the disorder he had been birthed to cull, but it was all for naught if there was nothing left to worship him, to fear him, to make him into a god.

Rocking back, he opened his jaws to expel another hiss, but stopped.

His thin, clear eyelids snapped down over his blazing irises and then back into his head. A wicked grin split his cheeks, and again, he looked down toward the courtyard below.

He had allowed the rage and bloodlust to cloud his judgment, blinding him from the obvious. So enrapt was he with reaching for the sun that he hadn't contemplated the moon. Killing the remaining humans had been a foregone conclusion in his quest to remake the dominant species in the bowels of the building, but his creations were all now deceased, as well as his means of creating more. His brother and sister could no longer do more than rot into the ground. But that didn't mean that no one remained to rule.

He wouldn't kill all of the humans. Just a few. He would leave breeding pairs to propagate like livestock. They would prosper in oppression, and from their constant terror, he would draw his strength. They would worship him with their dread, pray to him with their screams.

All was not lost, it seemed. Victory was still firmly in his grasp.

The wind arose with a howl, shrieking through the shattered windows in the tongues of the dead.

He reveled in the outrage of the heavens, but there was no longer anything anyone could do to halt his ascension.

All that remained now was a vulgar display of power, a decisive act to put the fear of their new god into those who would deny him his triumph.

A lone figure broke away from the congregation below and sprinted toward his monstrous castle.

His ferocious smile widened even more as he turned from the window and headed back to the stairwell. He climbed upward to the roof, to take his place on the stage for all to see.

Let the foolish attacker come. He would butcher him in front of their eyes, and in doing so, would claim the remainder as his own.

MICHAEL MCBRIDE

III

He couldn't say goodbye. Not again. To even try would be brandishing a blade that could cut deeper than his death could.

Instead, Phoenix shoved through them and ran toward the courtyard where he had sacrificed his life in vain once. This time though, this time the result would be different. He now knew what he must do.

Missy's screams filled the air, drowning out the shouts of the others.

The cross marred by his crusted blood flew past as he weaved around the piles of rubble and dashed through the empty door frame into the darkness. Guided by instinct, he crossed a lobby marked only by the broken and disheveled remains of the former furnishings and into a narrowed section now more tunnel than hallway, past elevator doors hanging askew and opening only to a shadowy fall to the sublevels, and to a steel door that had been thrown away from the threshold it had once barred. He climbed the stairs two at a time, ducking beneath exposed girders and fallen sections of the ceiling, dodging slanted segments where the cement steps had fractured and crumbled away. The stench of fecal matter was a presence around him, the ultimate decay of the remains of humanity processed through the guts of the Swarm. After a moment, he no longer smelled it, no longer tasted the veil of dust hovering over him in the vertical chute untouched by airflow. His sole focus was on maintaining his grasp on the railing and propelling himself higher, rounding the landings and hurtling upward.

The air grew colder by the second, but he no longer cared.

Soon this would all end.

Missy's cries echoed from far below as she finally found the entryway to the stairwell. He wanted to call to her, to tell her to flee this dreary place of death, that everything was finally going to be all right, but he knew his voice would only spur her on, and he needed every step of the head start he had. This all needed to be over before she reached the roof. He couldn't abide the prospect of risking her life.

He lightened his tread, shifting his weight forward to run on his toes so his pounding footfalls wouldn't echo back down to her, though he was certain she already knew where he was and would move heaven and earth to reach him. And he loved her all the more for it. That was why he had to face Death now. For Missy. For all of them.

Higher and higher he climbed, every muscle in his legs burning from the exertion. He couldn't afford to slow, even though his lungs ached and his head swam from dizziness and the vertigo of spiraling into the suffocating darkness. His body was no longer of any consequence. That much he had learned on the other side of mortality, where, for an eternity that passed in the single beat of his heart, he had known such beauty and peace. It had hurt to be summoned back to his frail flesh, but all the while he had known it was his lot, for voices like the tinkling of fluted crystal goblets had told him so from a blinding light that had been both simultaneously warm and frigid. They had promised him that death was only transitory, while resurrection was everlasting. A paradox defined not in terms of blood and tissue, but in words only the soul could understand. He lived again so that he could die again, the act of his penultimate sacrifice in exchange for life eternal. But more than that, his death would bring life to a world on the brink of eradication, to those for whom he would gladly suffer a million torturous bloodlettings if only to offer them the invisible mist of hope.

But time was running out. He could feel Death above him, radiating the cold aura of darkness he had known in the fraction of a second when his pupils had shrunk to pinpricks and his his soul had passed into the light. A hateful, empty sensation he remembered from the horrible nights in the frigid basements where he had bedded down in straw with the leaking pipes and scuttling insects, praying the Swarm would not descend upon him while he tried in vain to sleep. Even back then, Phoenix had known it would come down to the two of them, their undeniable attraction drawing them together, opposite magnetic poles, into the final confrontation that would determine no less than the fate of the world.

Missy screamed his name from a dozen stories below. Her pain echoed all around him in the black confines, summoning his mind back to the moment like an ice pick through his ears. The sound of her suffering cut him worse than Death's claws.

He had no idea how many levels had passed, only that he was nearing the end of his heavenward ascent. The inevitability that spurred him toward the roof was undeniable, growing infinitely stronger now with every labored step.

An open door passed to his right as he rounded another landing, issuing a vile mixture of the organic scents of death. Rotting and tanned flesh. Spilled blood given over to decay. The dust of pulverized bone. Festering remains and aging feces. Such corruption struck him in the gut with enough force to steal his breath, triggering the revelation that he was dealing with an evil beyond his no longer limited comprehension.

He was afraid.

The last stretch of stairs passed in a blur of darkness, in which his thoughts became a convoluted slideshow of images racing past at a million miles an hour, yet he savored the sights and memories. The final mental picture before he slammed into the freezing steel door and thrust his hips into the horizontal release bar was of a raven-haired beauty sitting on the bank of a lake, the sun behind her highlighting her form with a penumbra of fire, her legs dangling into the crystalline water.

The door exploded outward and he stumbled onto the roof, the tarred surface molten beneath his feet. He blinked back the glare of the sun and rubbed his eyes until he could finally see. The blue sky stretched to the horizon and beyond in every direction, a fathomless ocean of air.

Phoenix stopped in the middle of the roof. The wind whistled across bare girders and broken machinery and pipes, whipping his blood-crusted bangs into his face.

Directly ahead, perched at the edge of the world like a gargoyle, looking down, was the ebon figure of his nightmares, its back to him.

"For they have sown the wind," Death rasped, "and they shall reap the whirlwind."Phoenix watched as the creature turned to face him, his eyes locking onto blood-red orbs that at first registered surprise, but quickly metamorphosed into the fires of hell.

The crimson dewlap extended from beneath Death's chin like spurting carotids, trilling as he stretched out his arms and hissed up into the heavens with the sound of thunder.

IV

"Please…leave now," were the last words Phoenix had said to her. No *I love you* or a moment of affection. Maybe then she would have suspected what was coming next, which was probably why he had simply run away, leaving her standing there unable to understand what was transpiring. He had looked so weak, so frail. She had been about to wrap her arms around him to help him stand when he had bolted. It was surreal. She had just seen him return to life. Her only thoughts had been of holding him in her arms and never again letting him go.

And just like that he had been gone, a distant figure dashing away from them with his shadow stretching along the pavement behind. They had stood there—all of them—dumbfounded and in shock, before her body had grasped what her mind couldn't, and she was racing after him, sobbing, watching helplessly as he disappeared into the dark maw of the tower.

The ground had felt as though it had turned to tar, sucking her feet down, causing her to move in slow motion, the distance insurmountable. She had heard footsteps behind her, in time with the tapping of her pulse in her temples, but she'd been unable to look away from the doorway for fear that when she returned her gaze, the opening would have grown farther away or vanished altogether. She hadn't seen the iron cross or the mounds of rubble pass, the courtyard falling away behind as she stepped out of the daylight and into the darkness.

She had screamed for him, but there had

been no answer. Her vision had abandoned her as she passed through the diminishing gray zone and out of the sunlight's reach into the lobby. Debris had been strewn everywhere, grasping for her feet and ankles as she stumbled blindly ahead. She remembered pausing to listen for Phoenix's tread in the cavernous lobby, but had only heard the pounding footsteps behind her, slowing as they passed from cement onto the inner tiles. They had called for her, but she had been too out of breath to answer and wary to make any kind of sound that might have masked a clue as to where Phoenix had gone.

What followed had been a seamless journey though blackness, marred only by the repetitive crunch of broken tile and concrete underfoot, stretching on for what had felt like hours. Trying to run with her arms stretched out in front of her, falling, skinning her hands and knees and fighting back to her feet only to run and fall again until she had finally heard the hollow echo of movement in the stairwell ahead.

Now, here she was, pounding stair after stair, using her arms to tug on the railing to aid her failing legs. Blood streamed down her shins from the wounds on her knees, aggravated by the repeated flexion and extension, her ragged breaths coming in shrieking gasps.

Bang!

She stopped and leaned over the railing, craning her neck to try to see up into the impenetrable darkness. Had that been a gunshot? A faint hint of light diffused through the swirling motes high above. It faded…faded until the shadows reclaimed their realm with the soft click of a closing door.

"Phoenix!" she screamed, climbing again with renewed vigor. The slant of light couldn't have been more than ten floors up, an eternity of stairs, but at least the distance had revealed itself. She had heard him crash through a door, and the light must have been the outside world.

The roof.

Phoenix had gone out onto the roof, where she was sure evil waited for him, surrounded on all four sides by the sheer face of the tower and a bone-shattering fall.

Her footsteps echoed in the concrete chute like a stampede. She was beyond exhausted, tapping into reserves she never knew she had. Yet still progress was maddeningly slow. She attuned her ears to the slightest sound beneath her cumbersome thumping, expecting at any moment to hear agonized screams from above.

A smell like the floor of a slaughterhouse assailed her, a greasy entity that crawled over her skin and burrowed into her sinuses, before she reached the penthouse level and passed the open doorway to hell.

The others shouted for her from several stories down, but she couldn't waste the breath to answer them. Her chest had tightened exponentially, a constrictive band of dyspnea coiling around her throat and chest. Sweat dampened her hair and stung her eyes.

She rounded the final landing and hurtled toward the thin, intermittent line of light reaching beneath the door to the roof. Without a thought as to what might be on the other side, she hit the lever and thrust the door outward.

"No!" Phoenix screamed from where he was sprawled on his back a dozen yards ahead. His eyes widened with fear. He reached for her, his arm marbled with glimmering blood, and struggled to rise.

All she could think was to run to him, oblivious to the shadow that stepped out from behind the stairwell door and the cold breath on the back of her neck. Her shirt snagged on something behind her, tightening across her thorax and neck, impeding her progress.

"Phoen—!" she cried. His name abruptly ended in a whistle.

A black object passed out of sight from the corner of her vision, angled up from beneath her chin. Whatever held her from behind released her and she staggered forward. Icicles prodded her neck. Her chest was suddenly hot and wet.

Missy tried to scream for him again, but no voice came. Instead, the whistling noise faded into a gurgle of fluid.

Phoenix shoved himself up from the ground and threw himself at her.

Missy's eyes fell to the ground, where blood splashed back up at her as though dumped from buckets. Her hands rose to her neck, closing around parallel gouges, her middle finger sinking deep enough to feel cartilage.

Phoenix was still too far away to keep her from falling. A spurt of blood arced across the rooftop between them.

She collapsed into darkness, his anguished scream trailing her into oblivion.

V

Phoenix was certain his heart stopped beating when his stare locked on that of the Beast. Power emanated from the black-scaled Death like radiation from an isotope. Rage. Hatred. And still there was a controlled calmness in his expression and posture that affirmed Death's unfaltering confidence, not doubting that he would butcher Phoenix every bit as easily as he had scant hours before.

"Leave this place," Phoenix said, surprised by the firmness of his voice despite his trembling body. "You have fulfilled your destiny. Now go back from whence you came."

The words startled Phoenix. They had emerged from his mouth, but their origin eluded him. A tingling sensation thrummed through him as though he were a conduit for a power far greater than his.

Death snarled, gnashing his multiple rows of razor-honed teeth.

"This world is mine now," he said, his voice the grumble of a landslide breaking free. He clattered his claws together eagerly in anticipation of what he knew was to come.

Phoenix had to be quick. It was only matter of time before Missy reached the roof and exposed his vulnerability.

"Let me speak to my brother," Phoenix said.

The Beast laughed; the hideous sound of coughing through blood-filled lungs.

"No humanity remains. The vessel fulfilled the prophesy. Its body is now mine alone."

Had there been the hint of an accent in his words?

Phoenix smiled.

Infuriated, Death strode forward, back hunched, the cape of scales beneath his chin shivering. The boy had found his way back from the grave, but that wouldn't stop him from sending the child right back. Phoenix was flesh and blood, the liability of mankind, and was no more frightening than a lamb. Only this time, Death was going to relish every second of the kill. No one would rob him of the satisfaction. Not now. Not when the moment to seize his reign had finally arrived. His ascension was at hand.

Phoenix closed his eyes and lowered his head, summoning every ounce of his strength. He raised his arms to his sides, electricity coursing through his arteries like power lines.

Death crouched, legs bent, muscles flexed, hands pressed to the tarred roof, waiting for the boy to lift his chin and expose his throat, waiting to hurl himself at his adversary. A coiled spring preparing to launch.

"Your time on earth is over," Phoenix said, his voice filled with the hollow resonance of cannon fire. His eyelids snapped open and his pink irises glowed against a murky white background before vanishing within, as though his eyes were glass orbs filled with clouds.

Death hissed and sprung at the boy, arms reaching striking position, lining up with those emerging eyes he knew all too well. He would not abide His interference. This was Death's realm now. And no one, not even the Lord himself, would abolish him from it. His blood boiled, his rage driving him to frenzy. His eyes focused on the boy's, on the Presence staring through them. He wanted to see the look of pain, the silent flash of fear and celestial indignation that would register before the opened neck poured out his life.

Slashing with his right arm first and then his left, he felt the forgiving flesh open for his nails, felt the warmth and wetness, but not where he had intended. Without a flinch to betray his intentions, the boy had glided to the side just enough to offer his shoulder rather than his neck. Claws met with bone, angering Death beyond comprehension. His right hand passed through the meat, showering the rooftop with a violent spray of blood, but by the time his left hand hit its mark, he knew exactly what to do. Curling his fingers into the socket, latching around the girdle of bones inside, Death held on and used his momentum to yank the boy from his feet. Landing again in a crouch, the child hanging from his grasp like a rag doll, Death spun in a circle and hurled Phoenix away toward the other side of the roof, loosening his grip just enough to allow his claws to tear straight down through the fleshy biceps as he released him.

Phoenix cried out before the air exploded from his abruptly compressed lungs, silencing him, sending him skidding backwards along the rugged tarred surface. The base of his skull bounced several times before he abandoned his inertia, gasping for breath and staring up into the sky. His back was skinned nearly to the bone and he could barely make his fingers twitch through the ferocious pain in his arm. He tried to sit up, but the agony pinned him to the ground.

"Phoenix!" Missy called from far way, muffled by the steel door.

Her voice lent Phoenix the strength to raise his head. Death looked him directly in the eyes and read the expression on Phoenix's face.

Death's wide mouth spread into an evil grin.

No! Phoenix screamed inside his head, unable to fill his lungs. *Please, God. Not Missy!*

Death walked in reverse, slinking back into the shadows cast by the steel-girdered cube housing the stairwell until he stood just beside the door.

"No!" Phoenix croaked with what little oxygen finally reached his chest. He raised his shoulders from the ground, fighting through the pain, head throbbing, but too slowly…too slowly. He heard the sound of footsteps pounding up the cement stairs, the clatter of the release bar. "Please…"

His stare sought out Death's. Those frightening scarlet teardrops had narrowed to triangular slits, his claws hanging at his sides.

"Please," he whispered. "Not her…you can have me."

Death bared his gnarled fangs in response. Phoenix searched his eyes for any sign of mercy until the steel slab was flung open to reveal the darkened stairwell, the door hiding Death behind.

"No!" Phoenix screamed with everything he had. Missy's shadow formed from the darkness. The light passed over her feet and up her body until he could see her face. In that split-second her features ran the gamut of emotions from happiness to surprise to terror.

He pushed himself up and reached for her, screaming inside his head.

MICHAEL MCBRIDE

Death slipped out from behind the door and stood behind her as Missy ran toward him. Death grabbed her by the back of her shirt.

"Phoen—!" she cried before Death's black hand reached over her shoulder and glided across her throat. Her neck yawned around parallel mouths of flesh from which streaks of red arched, glistening in the sun's rays.

She stumbled forward, clutching her throat, blood spurting from between her fingers and pouring down her chest. Her eyes grew wide, latching onto his as the pain finally reached her brain and the grim understanding of what had just happened hit her.

"No!" Phoenix screamed, forcing himself to his knees. He crawled toward her despite the pain and the overwhelming grief that exploded from him in incoherent sobs.

Missy staggered another couple of steps before falling to her knees. She wavered for what felt like an eternity to Phoenix before collapsing forward onto the roof in front of him. Her hands fell from her neck, but didn't even try to brace her body for impact. Her chin and nose pounded the roof with a crack.

Blood spread from the wound into an expanding puddle.

Phoenix screamed and crawled to her, but before he could reach out to close his hands over the pumping slashes on her neck, what felt like spikes pounded into his back, hooking around his ribs, yanking him away. He raged and fought against the pain, trying desperately to reach Missy. Death's claws snapped his ribs and tore back out through the flesh, slamming him again onto his back. He stared up into Death's reptilian mouth, lined with the teeth of a great white shark, as it opened wide enough to take off half of his head.

VI

Adam sprinted up the stairs in the lead, leaving Evelyn and Jill more than a flight behind. All he heard was pounding footsteps above and below, throbbing inside his skull. The aftereffects of Pestilence's assault still plagued him.

He prayed that Ray had listened to him and that he and Jake had found someplace safe to hide. At least if the rest of them died in this awful monolith, maybe Ray and Jake would still have some slim hope for survival.

There was a bang like a gunshot from two stories above and sunlight fogged the dusty air above.

"Phoen—" he heard Missy shout over the drum roll of footsteps. Phoenix cried out, his pained voice silenced by the door slamming closed again.

"Wait," Adam gasped, rounding another landing. His eyes focused through the pitch black on the spot where he had seen the light and he listened for any noise from outside on the roof.

"Missy!" Evelyn screamed from below.

Adam charged up the stairs to the next landing and was smacked in the face by the wretched aroma of a morgue weeks after the coolers failed, so intense he could no longer hold back the revolt in his stomach and patterned the wall with a splatter.

Two more sections of stairs, one more landing, and he would be at the door to the roof. He still couldn't hear any voices or sounds of struggle to know if the others were still alive up there or if he was sprinting to his demise. He swung around the final platform and the world around him flowed with the sluggishness of a dream. His feet moved of their own accord, his arms faintly highlighted by the line of light beneath the door as they reached ahead of him in preparation of thrusting the release bar. The cold metal brushed his palms, and with the sound of metal slamming against metal, he burst out into the blazing sunlight.

Missy was sprawled out on the ground in front of him in a puddle of blood that shimmered like a ruby against the black tar, her face flattened in an unnatural way. Her arms were crumpled beneath her, elbows bowed outward, the pool of fluids widening even in the short time he watched.

Adam sprinted to her and rolled her onto her back, the openings in her neck parting like so many trout's gills. Her skin was stark white, splotchy bruises filling the sparse gaps between spatters of blood. Eyes fixed into a wide, startled expression of horror, she stared blankly past him.

Blood trickled from her nostrils and the corners of her mouth, but with so much everywhere around her, Adam was surprised there was any left in her at all.

He wrapped his hands around her neck and willed it to heal, forcing all of his energy into his fingers. There was no tingling, no crackle of energy rippling through his flesh. The power that had been within him was gone, as he had known it would be. His hands were now useless clamps merely holding together the gaping lacerations.

Missy was dead.

Adam raised his head from her face, tears streaming down his cheeks. His eyes met Phoenix's from where the boy struggled to rise to his feet ahead. A black monster towered over him from behind, scales glittering.

Phoenix read Adam's expression. His lips quivered and his mouth contorted around a gut-wrenching cry that broke Adam's heart.

Death fanned his claws and raised them high, slashing so fast that Adam had no time to warn Phoenix before streaks of blood pattered the ground from his back.

Phoenix crawled forward, mewling, seemingly oblivious to Death, who raked his claws across Phoenix's back over and over, filling the air with crimson droplets. And yet still Phoenix crawled toward Missy, reaching for her with trembling hands. He was nearly to her, fresh blood trembling on his fingertips, struggling to touch her, when Death struck.

Adam saw claws latch into the top of Phoenix's eye sockets from behind, piercing the upper lids and grabbing bony leverage, a dark hand palming his head from behind. Blood poured across the surface of Phoenix's eyes, yet still he battled the awful pain, hoping to reach just…a little…farther.

Death cleaved him from the ground by his head, holding him in the air, his other hand reaching for Phoenix's exposed throat.

Flames erupted from the boy's eyes, rising over the scaled fingers. Phoenix's spine buckled backwards and his arms shot out to his sides.

The beast ripped his hand away, tearing seams though Phoenix's scalp, the long, dirty hair falling away from so many bloody parts.

Phoenix still hovered in mid-air, toes pointing at the earth, palms to the heavens.

A blinding light enveloped him, brighter even than the rising sun, forcing Adam to shield his eyes as a rush of heat washed over him.

VII

Phoenix succumbed to the pain and sadness, the rage. Everything around him became golden, shimmering. He saw Adam shield his eyes and realized that he himself was the source of the light.

Death's claws ripped through his eyelids, tearing deep lacerations into his forehead, over the top of his head, and down his neck. But there was no pain. Not even as blood poured over his ears and along his neck. Spreading his arms to either side, he felt himself rise higher, attached neither to the earth nor the heavens. He twirled in the sky until he faced the reptilian creature crouching on the roof. The creature's scarlet eyes filled with fear, though only for a heartbeat before Death flashed his wicked claws and bared a nasty snarl of teeth.

Phoenix could only think of Missy. Each second lost was one she could never have back. With that realization, the fury took hold of him, launching him toward Death. He grabbed his adversary by either side of the ruggedly scaled face, smoke billowing from their union.

Death hissed and slashed Phoenix across the face, opening wounds that split his cheeks and the bridge of his nose. Phoenix didn't even cringe. He drew his thumbs inward and plunged them into Death's blazing eyes, summoning a rush of pustulates and a hiss that made the sky shiver.

Death's claws sought Phoenix's throat, closing around it and squeezing until the nails punctured the skin and slid into the muscle and tissue, but the boy's grip didn't falter, his thumbs pressing harder still until they met with bone, which cracked with the pressure and sent electric bolts of agony into Death's brain.

In that moment, Death smelled failure on the breeze, resplendent with the aroma of his cooking flesh and boiling blood.

He tore his talons out of Phoenix's neck, slashing at whatever he could reach. Blood flew from the boy's face and chest, but the grip on his head only tightened. The pain magnified as Death felt himself being lifted upward, his feet leaving the ground. He kicked and flailed, pressure mounting in his spine as he hung by his head. He snapped his jaws but found nothing within range. His sight was gone, the remainder of his squashed orbs dribbling over his scaled lips.

Phoenix screamed, an anguished sound of loss and torment, rage and longing, and ripped his hands apart.

Death heard the crack inside his head. A fissure raced across the crown of his skull.

For Phoenix, there were no words, only a jumble of thoughts and images. Missy lying in a pool of her own blood. Mare scorched to black bones, leaning over the incinerated creature of fire. Headstones along the beach guarding the bodies of the dead. The silhouette of a girl framed by the sun, dangling her feet into a shimmering lake.

Hatred filled him, scalding him from within like boiling oil. He didn't just want to kill Death, he wanted to tear him limb from limb, to rip out his beating heart, unfurl his coiled guts, make him experience the pain he had caused so many, to drag his death out infinitely as punishment for all of the suffering he had caused. He squeezed and twisted Death's skull, his fingers delving deeper, fragmenting bone, conducting a symphony of hissing. His nostrils filled with the addictive stench of burning scales.

He looked at his hands, the tendons straining in his blood-soaked wrists. His teeth ached from baring them, every muscle knotted by rage. The Beast no longer snapped at him. Its claws no longer thrashed, but hung limply where they were latched into his chest.

"Blessed are the merciful; for they shall obtain mercy," he whispered, lowering his body again to the ground.

He released Death's head and the black creature crumpled to his knees at Phoenix's feet, chin lolling to his chest.

Phoenix looked back over his shoulder at Adam. The golden glow faded from around him, and saw the fear in Adam's eyes. Adam was looking right at him. Afraid of him. Beyond Adam, standing in the open doorway, he could see the same expression on Evelyn's pallid face. He felt blood on his cheeks and flames crackling from his eyes. Gore dripped from his hands, which he raised in front of him. He studied the implements that had caused such carnage as though they belonged to someone else entirely.

What had he become?

His stare fell to Death as he raised his ruined face. Nothing remained of his eyes but sludge, the savage mouth hanging slack and pouring blood to the ground. The dewlap flattened to his neck. The sun no longer glimmered on his scales.

Phoenix listened to the agonal breathing, the gasping through lungs full of blood as the creature drowned inside itself.

He looked again at his hands, dripping with the signs of torture and impending death.

"End…this…" Death rasped in the weak voice of a man with an Arabic accent.

Phoenix titled his face to the heavens, though the rays of the sun didn't warm his tear-drenched cheeks. This wasn't how things were supposed to be.

He turned away from Death and walked to where Missy had fallen, kneeling behind her head. Leaning across her face, his chin touching her nose, he kissed her gently on the lips. Tears of grief shivered loose from his jaw and patterned her cheeks. He withdrew his mouth and whispered, "I love you with all of my heart and soul."

His eyes rose to meet Adam's.

"Please," Phoenix implored. "Take her from this place."

"Phoenix…"

"Please, Adam."

Adam nodded. He reached one arm beneath Missy's legs and the other under her shoulders. By the time he lifted her from the ground, Phoenix had turned and walked back to where Death knelt.

"There is…" Death gurgled, "hope…even in…death."

Phoenix glanced back over his shoulder, meeting Adam's and Evelyn's eyes. They hesitated momentarily, and then descended into the darkness.

"I'm sorry," Phoenix whispered, turning back to Death and sliding his arms beneath the creature's armpits to help him to his feet. He stared into the bludgeoned face of the brother he had never known.

Closing his eyes, Phoenix drew the creature into an embrace.

He felt the heat first, then a radiant glow so bright it hurt his eyes even through the lids. It swelled until it fully enveloped both of them.

VIII

Jake held Ray's hand, his grip tightening as he stared up at the roof of the foreboding tower. What had at first appeared to be a small fire had grown exponentially until it now looked like a second sun perched atop the building. Its heat chased away the coldness that clung to him, and though it hurt his eyes, he knew he needed to watch, that it was imperative that he didn't look away even for a second. The ball of light slowly expanded into a great celestial dome. Time passed and yet stood still in the same instant.

"Tell me what you see," Ray said, the radiance caressing his face.

"It looks like the sun is rising from the top of the building."

"Dawn," Ray whispered. "It feels like dawn."

He pulled Jake to his hip at the sound of approaching footsteps, the scuffing of asphalt.

Jake had to shield his eyes against the glare to see the shadows walking toward them.

He recognized Adam's shape first, laboring beneath the weight of the body draped across his chest, stumbling as though about to collapse. Evelyn clung to his left arm, offering what little support she could, while Jill trailed, looking back over her shoulder every few steps at the blossom of illumination swelling behind.

Jake released Ray's hand and raced toward them. The limp form in Adam's arms finally came into focus. Shoulder-length black hair. Thin legs. Missy.

He pulled up short, his heart rate slowing. "Where's Phoenix?"

Evelyn let go of Adam's arm and lifted Jake to her chest. He wrapped his arms around her neck, his chin settling in the nook. "He's still up there," she whispered into his ear.

His gaze rose again to the high roof. The golden energy expanded in a bubble that appeared strained and ready to pop. He thought he saw a single shadow in its center, a bird of fire rising to the heavens, and then it was gone.

Adam lowered Missy to the ground at Ray's feet, carefully resting her head on the asphalt. He dropped to his knees, exhausted, and placed his index and middle fingers against her carotid, breathing a sigh of relief as he felt the weak tapping of blood flow. The gaping wounds in her neck had closed, leaving puffy pink scars. The entire upper half of her body was sticky with blood, her face a mask of drying crimson. Her irises twitched beneath her lids, the lashes shivering before parting to reveal bloodshot crescents and icy blue half-moons.

"Phoenix?" she whispered, sounding like her throat was full of stringy phlegm.

Adam glanced at Evelyn, then back to Missy. He didn't know what to say.

Missy nodded meekly and allowed her eyes to close again, forcing a single large tear from the outside corners to drain through the blood on her cheeks.

Jill sat on the pavement above Missy's head and stroked Missy's bangs from her forehead, the horizontal creases of pain softening. Wiping her own tears away, she stared up at the brilliant expanding glow.

"Is it over?" Ray asked.

"I don't know," Adam said, tracing his fingers along the seams on Missy's throat. The glare behind him intensified, stretching his shadow across Missy and up Ray's legs. He turned and had to shield his eyes.

The outer rim of the ball of light shivered and retracted suddenly to half its size, focusing the light into an even brighter sphere before exploding outward. They all turned away as a hot wind buffeted them, screaming past them, baking the moisture from their skin. Even through their closed eyes they could see the light strobe, washing over them in waves, a warm embrace that passed through them.

Jill thought she smelled Phoenix in the gale and looked down at Missy, whose lips stretched into a smile.

The glow faded and the breeze tapered to a soft caress.

Jake opened his eyes and relaxed his stranglehold on Evelyn's neck. The light was no longer perched atop the roof of the tower. There was now nothing but endless blue sky. The edges of the roof were lined with something green, which cascaded over the top floor like a frozen waterfall.

"Vines," Jake said. They lengthened as he watched, reaching down for the earth. He looked at the piles of rubble surrounding them. Small shoots of emerald rose from the cracks and poked through the fissures in the broken pavement in stark contrast to the scorched earth.

"Now it's over," Adam said, rising and walking over to Evelyn. He wrapped his arms around her and leaned his cheek against the side of Jake's head. "Time to go home."

A small bud bloomed from a swatch of green growing from the rubble at the base of the bloodstained cross, blossoming into a crimson flower beneath the azure sky.

EPILGUE

I

MORMON TEARS

With the spring had come renewal. Pine saplings had poked their bristled necks out of the crevices in the stone all around the cave, lengthening to foot-long miniature representations of what they would someday become. Beds of kelp lined the white sand as far as the eye could see, save for the gap of open water they tried to maintain to launch the rowboat beached ten feet inland. The minnows had appeared in early May, clinging to the cover of the kelp until they had grown venturous enough to strike out for the deeper water, where they enticed Adam with ripples.

There had been much work to be done, but it was nearly complete. And now, with the late September sun shortening the day, promising that the snow would again fall, they would be ready for the winter.

Adam stood in the middle of the beach, the setting sun reflecting in oranges and reds on the cresting waves of the Great Salt Lake. He was thankful every day for this opportunity, grateful for all of the loving sacrifices made to afford him this luxury. Never had he appreciated life as much as he did now. Multicolored fish rose to steal the insects from the surface of the lake with quiet *splooshes* at the edge of sight and an infant's cries echoed out of the cave.

To his left was the windmill he had built with his own two hands, spinning lazily in the cool evening breeze; to his right the white picket fence enclosing the graveyard.

A hand slid under his arm and Evelyn leaned her head on his shoulder.

"It's beautiful, isn't it?" she said.

He kissed her on the top of her head. "You're beautiful."

She smiled and stared across the glimmering sea.

"How are you feeling?" he asked.

"Momentarily heartburn free, but it feels like there's a bowling ball on my bladder." She rubbed her free hand over her bulbous belly. The small knob of a heel pushed against her palm from within. "And I think he's going to be a soccer player."

Adam laughed and drew her closer, imagining children running barefoot through the sand chasing a ball.

"You're sure it's a boy?"

"Yeah," she said coyly. "And he'll have his father's eyes."

"And his mother's heart."

"He'll be perfect."

II

Ray stirred the stew over the fire while Jake stoked the flames. They made a good team. Without his sight, Ray's sense of smell had developed to the point that he could tell precisely when the pot of fish chunks, potatoes, and kelp was ready, and Jake was always eager to take the first slurp to confirm it. They boy's appetite had grown voracious and he must have shot up at least two inches since the start of summer.

"Go check on Jill while I serve this up," Ray said. "See if she's ready to eat."

Jake scampered through the cavern, scaled the series of ladders to reach the uppermost room of the pueblo, and lowered his head through the hole in the roof. He was about to call down to her when he noticed she was sleeping. Good, he thought, she needed her rest. For as long as she had been in labor, he figured she'd probably need to sleep for a month straight. The swaddled infant suckled at her breast.

They were all thankful for the reprieve from the crying.

Silently, Jake retreated from the hole in the ceiling and descended to the stone floor. He jogged over to Ray.

"She's asleep," he said.

"Good." He offered Jake a steaming ladle of the white stew.

Jake blew on it, then pressed his lips to it and slurped loudly.

"Best batch yet," Jake said.

"You say that every night."

"And it's always true."

"You're just sucking up because you haven't found where I've stashed the chocolate yet, aren't you?"

Jake struggled to keep his grin from betraying him.

"That's what I thought," Ray said, ruffling the younger boy's shaggy hair. "I can see right through you by now."

III

Jill had never truly known exhaustion until today. The pain prodded her relentlessly with each step, but this was something she needed to do. The others had been great through the whole pregnancy, right up until the very end when she had squeezed Evelyn's hand on one side and Missy's on the other to deliver her baby girl into Adam's waiting hands. They had all taken such good care of her, but there had been one face conspicuously absent.

She walked along the beach with her daughter in her arms, which cradled her perfectly as though designed solely for that purpose. Sand sluiced between her toes as she passed Adam and Evelyn where they stared out toward the distant island, now fuzzy and green with the signs of forestation.

Jill followed the white line of the wooden fence to the gate, opened it, and stepped inside. The mounds of sand had been leveled by time, though the paths between them were choppy and well-worn. She walked nearly to the end on the left as she did every night, and lowered herself uneasily to the ground, her child snug against her chest. Her eyes rose to the marble headstone of the Virgin cradling her infant son, which sat atop the marker nearly exactly as they were now.

A wan smile traced her lips and her lower lashes welled with tears.

"Hi, Mare. There's someone I want you to meet," she said, tilting her daughter to face the tombstone. The red-faced girl, her head still misshapen from the birthing canal, parted her lids and revealed eyes just like her mother's. She smiled as her lids fell closed again. Her father's smile. "This is Mary."

IV

Missy sat on a rock at the edge of the lake, dangling her feet into the cold water, the setting sun sparkling on the water like so many jewels. She'd aged by lifetimes in the year since the world ended, a shock of white scarring her raven-black hair, which now hung to the middle of her back. The first three months following that fateful day at the evil tower had been the worst. She had slept all day and stared up into the sky all night, furious with God for taking the two people she had loved most in the world. She wished she could have just stayed dead, where there was no pain. Why couldn't she have just been allowed to remain with those who mattered most? She remembered nothing of the minutes she had spent in the afterlife, though when she focused on the distant stars and lost herself in their beauty, she felt like she could almost grasp the memories, but she never did. Sometimes she imagined her brother and the love of her short life looking down at her, winking through the twinkling of the stars, and she didn't feel quite so alone.

There hadn't been a single cathartic event that had roused her from her fugue, but a gradual understanding of the magnitude of the gift she'd been given. Her brother had given his life in exchange for theirs, for the amazing child now sitting on her mother's lap by his grave. Phoenix had sacrificed himself to eliminate the threat of Death, and had given his life force to her so that she would live. To not take full advantage of her life would be to dishonor their memories and tarnish their final act of love. She often wondered if the amount of himself that he poured into her to resurrect her would have given Phoenix the strength to vanquish Death without having to die in the process. Had he just left her for dead, would he still be alive? She had blamed herself for the longest time, but eventually she had realized that Phoenix's destiny had always been to give his life as he had. He had been groomed for it since his birth. Now she understood that she had been fortunate to have had what little time she had with him. She had known and loved the most wonderful exotic bird, but she had never been meant to keep him. His destiny had always been to rise from the ashes and ascend to the heavens in a ball of fire.

Yet a part of him would always remain in her heart, his fleeting beauty commemorated by the lives yet to come. Lives that would know nothing of the suffering they had endured.

She stared ahead at the future on the gentle, glowing waves, not toward the end, but toward a new beginning.

The time had come to live again.

ABOUT THE AUTHOR

Michael McBride lives with his wife and four children in the shadow of the Rocky Mountains, where he shoots people for money. He thanks you for seeing this journey to its conclusion, and hopes you'll join him in the hunt for the Reaper in Spectral Crossings. To explore the author's other novels and short fiction or to contact him directly, please visit:

www.mcbridehorror.com.

SPECIAL THANKS

Anna Torborg, Emma Barnes, and Snowbooks; Shane Staley; Dennis Duncan; Greg Gifune; Leigh Haig; Brian Keene; Troy Knutson; Don Koish; David Marty; Dallas Mayr; Elizabeth and Tom Monteleone, and the BBC grunts; Matt Schwartz; Tom Tessier; and my wife and family.